S0-AKI-805

Mama
Told Me
Not To Come

A comedy novel of travel and friendship

by

M.J. Brett

Blue Harmony 🎵 *Press*

To Breanna
Enjoy a laugh on me
Margaret Brettschneider

Blue Harmony  **Press**

528 Southern Cross Drive
Colorado Springs, CO 80906

First Printing, June 2009

Copyright by M.J. Brett
EbrettMBour@aol.com
Website at www.mjbrett.com

Printed in the United States of America

Without limiting the rights under copyright reserved above, no part of this novel may be reproduced, stored in or introduced into a retrieval system, or transmitted in any form or by any means, (electronic, technological, mechanical, photocopying, recording, or otherwise), without the prior written permission of the copyright owner.

Though based loosely on the lives of both real and fictional persons and events in a real place, this is a work of fiction. Names, characters, and incidents are either the product of the author's imagination or are used fictitiously, condensed, or expanded. Except for public figures of the era, any other resemblance is purely coincidental

Dedication

This book is dedicated to the Department of Defense Dependents School (DoDDS) teachers of the world, with whom I was privileged to spend twenty-one years of my life.

Overseas teachers are a special breed: adventurous enough to leave their home, *and* sometimes a steady paycheck, to travel to a foreign land, adapt to a foreign culture, live on a different economy, and adjust to a military lifestyle. They must learn a new language, do without the normal Stateside classrooms, books, or supplies, operate under military rule, and yet still remain effective and loving with each new class of students. Certainly the DoDDS teachers who led the children of the Vietnam and Cold War eras, and those now dealing with Iraq and Afghanistan, must be ever mindful of military secrecy, and more supportive and sensitive with children whose parents are constantly in harm's way.

I've never known more dedicated people, who dote on their students while building a strong educational model, often under harrowing conditions. The wonderful successes of our "overseas brats" in transferring back to schools and colleges in the States with exceeded standards, and their success in going on to live responsible, productive lives, attests to the dedication of these teachers.

But let it not be said that on weekends and vacations, these dedicated souls aren't also adventurous enough to set off for foreign shores or try parties or sports where many of their Stateside colleagues would throw up their hands and stay home.

DeeDee and Megan are composites of many of our overseas teachers who may arrive in a naïve state, but who quickly become acclimated to military requirements, to a classroom that may be a renovated slaughterhouse or Quonset hut as easily as a normal-looking brick school, and to the many travel opportunities.

In overcoming their naiveté and learning the balance necessary to be successful, often the friendships formed become the most important ones of a lifetime. Yea, teachers!

Foreward

In the seventies, when the Cold War was at some of its most "tightened" levels, a new, naïve, fearful, and sheltered teacher enters the overseas DoDDS program, for a stated purpose.

She is sponsored, or "greeted" by an accident-prone, reluctant, more experienced overseas teacher, not long out of her own naïve state. The two seem oceans apart.

But through sharing their travels and troubles, even the most unlikely people can become buddies.

This book is NOT serious like my other four. Feel free to laugh at my characters.

In fact, the closest idea of what this book might be about is probably "Lucy and Ethel set Europe and the Mid East on Edge."

The cartoon drawings are collected from a few DoDDS travel diaries, and certainly are *not* works of art, but I hope including them just as they are will add to the reader's sense of fun.

If we need a theme for this comedy, it might be that trust and love may be formed in adventure and adversity, but those kinds of friendships will last a lifetime.

Though all of the events actually happened to someone in DoDDS, poor DeeDee and Megan must carry the weight of them all.

Two more unlikely comrades probably never existed.

Chapter 1 - First Impressions - August 1977

From my first glimpse of D.D. Otero, I realized why the old axiom "never volunteer" was a good one. The idea of being a "meeter-greeter" for a newly arriving overseas teacher had seemed reasonable back in June when I was heading for summer vacation Stateside. But now I understood why the other teachers had slunk out of the room when the principal asked for volunteers.

I must have been certifiably insane, but I never dreamed that this particular person arriving to be my temporarily assigned responsibility would change my life forever.

It had been a bad day.

I'd slammed my finger in the car door trying to hurry, and tripped over a curb that ruined my nylons. I ran through the Frankfurt International Airport to the concourse where military transport planes arrived, and stood in the crowd with my hand-lettered sign held high. None of the arriving passengers showed any sign of recognition. Maybe the school office had the name wrong. They hadn't said if D.D. Otero was a man or a woman. While watching all the people go by, I sucked on my smashed finger to cool the pain, and speculated on what this D.D. might be like. If D.D. was male, I certainly hoped he'd be more honest than those I'd seen of late.

As the last passengers cleared customs, only one person remained at the entry door. She *had* to be D.D. I bumped against a pole while hurrying to help her, and reached up to rub my head. I pasted on my best smile, and swept by the customs counter with a wave, hoping this was *not* the new teacher for whom I'd be responsible. *She was unusual, to say the least.* Again I waved my sign, but the woman staggered forward so bogged down that she didn't even notice.

She stood about five foot four, rather thin, probably

dangling between thirty-six and forty, certainly older than me. In addition to hand luggage criss-crossed over both shoulders, which pinned down a large purse, she lugged one bulging suitcase and dragged another. Her purple flowered jersey dress hit at her calves in the front and hiked up alarmingly in the rear, pulled up no doubt by the straps of luggage weighing down her front side.

Hair of a faded light brown straggled from what must have started out as a demure bun, under a mousy little hat perched precariously on her forehead. No lipstick remained, if there ever had been any, but she kept running her tongue over her lips as though she expected to find some. She clutched her handbag in a death grip.

For this assignment I left a sunlit California beach early and bumped my way back to Germany on a rainy flight? How in God's green world can I introduce this woman to my friends at the Officers' Club?

"You must be D.D, " I said aloud, trying to sound encouraging.

"Oh, my," said the woman, struggling with her luggage, "Mama told me not to come."

She wore what my mom would have called "sensible" shoes, low heeled and boxy, yet they had a leather bow on the front like a ten year old pushed by a stage-door mother. *She won't last long here.*

But, I had to recant that thought, since I'd probably looked a little disheveled and bewildered when I'd first arrived in Germany, too. And besides, it was Department of Defense Dependent Schools, or DoDDs, tradition that *someone* had to be the greeter to help each new teacher get settled, find an apartment, a car, and learn the ropes socially and militarily. Teachers willing to leave their homes behind to teach children of overseas personnel in far-flung places are a special breed. And they welcome their own. Pay it forward, right? Reminding myself why I'd come brightened my spirits a bit.

"I'm Megan James from Bamberg. I'm here to officially welcome you to Germany. Here, let me help you with that suitcase you're dragging. Didn't you see the luggage carts when you got off the plane?"

The woman turned toward me with a guarded look, and we sort of tugged back and forth several times with the heavy suitcase. I won the struggle when she dropped it on my foot.

I limped backward from the pain.

"Are you *sure* you're from Bamberg?" she challenged in a high-pitched, screechy voice, as though she thought I might try to steal her suitcase. Her stare was pointed enough to pick out my tousled head and freckly face from *any* police line-up. I could see uncertainty in her eyes as she surveyed my daily collection of cuts and bruises. The glancing blow of that pole was now an angry red bump erupting from my forehead, my finger still throbbed, and I could feel my foot swelling from the suitcase crush. I lifted the offending foot gingerly. *What is she carrying in there, anyway?*

"Of course, I am," I groaned. "How else would I have your name on my little sign here?" I held up the sign, but she was still staring at my protruding forehead. "Don't mind me. I just had a couple of little accidents. It's nothing new."

D.D. shook her head. "How do I know where to go? I don't know anyone here, and I don't speak the language." She sighed, the lines in her face deepened, and her shoulders slumped forward, reminding me that she must be exhausted. "Mama told me not to come," she repeated.

"That's why I'm here, and I'll help you with all that." I ignored the Mama thing coming from a grown woman. I reached out to remove one of the bags from her shoulder, but she grabbed it tightly, throwing her free arm across her breast as though fearful of mayhem.

"I'll carry it," she insisted, pushing her purse more pointedly under the straps.

After *that* little performance, I was ready to walk off and leave the woman. I was only trying to help. But to meet and greet, one must *actually* meet and greet, so I stifled my urge to throttle her and forced one more smile. *This is your last chance, Missy.*

D.D. trundled beside me with her load, watching me suspiciously as I dragged her bag forward to the customs officer. She had enough luggage for a six-week safari.

"One just can't be too careful," D.D. said. "Mama told me to watch my pocketbook at all times, and I can see she was right. There were so many people on that plane, and they all jostled me. I was so scared that I waited until everyone else got off the plane."

Now, everyone knows *I'm* scared of flying, but since I'm always convinced the other passengers and I will be sharing a fiery death at any moment, it sure never occurs to me to be scared of the *passengers!* I couldn't believe D.D. seemed afraid of *everyone*.

"I was too scared to check my bags." She shook her head with wide eyes and looked around to see if anyone was listening. We were quite alone. "The stewardess said I had too much for carry-on, and I rode with my feet up on one suitcase, and my shoulder bags in my lap the whole way. It was uncomfortable, but I couldn't trust my suitcases with my iron and sewing machine to those baggage handlers." She cupped her hand around her mouth and whispered, "I hear these airlines will steal you blind."

Well, now at least I knew what had crushed my foot.

"D.D. It's a military aircraft. These are all military people. They're assigned to bases here in Germany, just like you. They aren't going to steal anything of yours." I tried hard not to sound irritated, but my finger, head, foot, *and* my patience, still felt battered. I helped D.D. peel off her straps for the customs agent who drummed his fingers on the counter, waiting. Another agent strained to lift her suitcases atop the belt.

"Where are they going with my bags?" It was a shriek.

"Shh! They're German customs agents. They just want to see if there's any contraband."

Customs agents from the now-vacated belts gathered around us, barely concealing their amusement as Ms Otero got into another tug-of-war with an agent for one of her shoulder bags.

Pulling back and forth with the man, D.D. squealed, "Don't let them open that bag. My unmentionables are in it!"

Well, they're hardly unmentionable any more!

Her wild reaction convinced the customs man that she was carrying an atomic bomb in that bag. *Everything* came out into a growing pile. D.D. grabbed items out of the agent's hands as fast as he picked them up, trying to stuff them into her purse.

"Miss!" the beleaguered man shouted at her, and two more guards rushed over.

I squelched my embarrassment long enough to pull her hands away before she single-handedly started World War III.

"Look at me, D.D. This is important. They have the right to open whatever bags they want, and your struggling only makes it look like you're trying to hide something. Back off." I tried to say it kindly, but there were tears running from her eyes as the agent popped the lock on every single bag and poked around inside. Several items dropped to the floor behind the belt.

"He shouldn't be looking at my unmentionables," she cried. "He could be any kind of pervert. I want to go home."

I sighed. "D.D., everyone wants to go home when they first arrive in a foreign country. You'll get over it. Think of this as a great adventure, and you'll love it here in Germany." She still looked scared. "I'll help you. I promise. You'll get through this."

As soon as I got the words out of my mouth, I regretted them. D.D. suddenly became pathetically eager, clinging to my hand and practically massaging it.

I winced and tried to pull away when she squeezed my swollen finger.

"Oh, thank you so much for helping me. I'll try hard to get through all this, if you'll just stay with me," she gushed.

"Great!" I tried to sound enthusiastic, but all I could think of was how much time and effort it would take to make D.D. even *marginally* normal. *No hope for independent!* But, then, I'd be hard-pressed to say what *normal* was, anyway, given my background. I shrugged it off.

As the agents closed up her bags and moved them down the glass cubicle, D.D. ran to grab her handbag. What was it she called it? Her pocketbook? I hadn't heard that term since my great-grandma died. But, there was D.D., clutching it to her breast and again loading up with luggage over that terrible dress. *That dress will have to go. Maybe I can manage to spill ink on it.*

I jerked my thoughts back to the present, asking carefully, "Is it okay if I help you with one of the shoulder bags to lighten your load?"

A small, mincing smirk apparently was the best she could do for a smile. She nodded, so I guess I passed the test of trustworthiness. I threw the sign in the nearest trash basket, shouldered one bag and dragged another as we struggled through the myriad of underground passages to the trains and parking lots of Frankfurt Airport. The challenge to find my car was probably intensified as my mind frantically scrambled to figure how to avoid my new charge becoming my shadow for life. On the other hand, I grappled with my own mixed reactions. She really did need help, *lots of it*, and I had this empathy thing for puppies, babies, and the helpless.

Finally, I spotted my nasty-tempered, yellow Fiat and managed to squeeze all D.D.'s bags in and still get the hatchback shut. "This is Bosco," I said, by way of introduction to my car. "You'll get used to him. He has a mind of his own."

Bosco started right away, which was a great relief. "Of course, that just means he's lying in wait to shut off at some more crucial moment," I said, trying to make D.D. laugh.

She didn't.

"The farmer down the street from my apartment has become a first-name friend, since he often has to bring his tractor to push me over the crest of the hill to start the car rolling."

D.D. said nothing. She seemed not to notice Bosco's putrid

lemon color. *Oh well, nothing else has gone right today, either.*

Soon we were out into the sunlight and onto the Autobahn, heading toward Nürnberg and eventually, 505 Highway north to Bamberg and the Border. I was on familiar ground now, and figured I'd try to draw this woman out on our two-hour trip, if only to make time go faster. "What does D.D. stand for?" I asked for openers.

She looked up from digging in her purse. "Mama named me Dolly Dozie after my grandmother, and she always called me that. Daddy hated it, so he called me D.D. for short.

"Is that D-e-e-D-e-e or D.D.?"

"D-e-e-D-e-e. I have four older brothers and no other girls, so Dolly Dozie didn't fit. The boys always made fun of it. I put D.D. on my DoDDS application because I didn't want them to know I was a girl."

That's odd. "Why not?"

"Well, in upstate New York, they don't hire girls as fast as they do boys. My brother said the Federal Government might be the same way, so I left the 'm' and 'f' spots blank and hoped."

I took another look at DeeDee and felt a little uncomfortable with someone her age putting herself in the category of "girls and boys." From her dress and mannerisms, I guessed her at several years older than my thirty-five years.

"I went to Catholic school," DeeDee said. "The nuns said I was lucky my parents owned an Italian restaurant so I'd always have food. Mama cooks and Daddy's the host, and my brothers wait tables—you know, a family business. They sent me to Catholic college, too, because Daddy said teaching was the *only* honorable place for a good girl, so I got my certificate. I taught five years in Ithaca, and we all lived at home, one big pasta-eating family."

DeeDee flashed a rare smile. "I make really good pasta, you know." Then she sobered again. "My brothers looked out for me to be sure no one took advantage. They escorted me whenever I went out." She looked earnestly in my direction and said, "But it was the strangest thing. Even if I liked the boys who asked me out, they never came back after the first date, so I guess they didn't like me. I must've done something wrong." She shook her head slowly. *She's gotta be kidding?* I avoided her pensive look. *No, she was dead serious!* Didn't she realize no one would come back if they had to deal with her brothers? Was she really that stupid, or had she just been sheltered too long? I heard no clue in her voice, so I changed the subject.

"Didn't you ever want an apartment of your own, or didn't your brothers?"

DeeDee's hands flew to her mouth. "Oh, heavens no." Whenever one of us wanted to move out or take a job in another city, poor Mama would have one of her sinking spells, so we always stayed together, don't you see? We couldn't let Mama get sick again."

"What's a 'sinking spell'?"

"Oh, you know, she would clutch her heart and fall to the floor."

"Wow!" My head buzzed with the revelation in that statement. *No wonder this woman is so unusual. I'll be charitable and not think weird.* "Did your mother have a heart condition?"

"I don't know. She would never tell, but she had sinking spells pretty often."

"Did you ever take her to the hospital?"

DeeDee cheered up. "No, we didn't. As soon as the problem was resolved, she felt all better again, and was just fine. Weren't we lucky?"

I'd better ignore that can of worms. "What happened to finally make you leave?"

"I had my twenty-ninth birthday this year."

Twenty-nine! Boy, did I guess wrong. She's younger than me? Yikes!

"My brothers had a council meeting and said I was going to be an old maid like my friends if I stayed there. They said I had to escape before that happened. Andy wrote off for the application to DoDDS and Tony helped me fill out the forms. They said I mustn't tell Mama until it was time to go. By then it would be all right because I would have signed a contract and couldn't renege. Daddy would never have tolerated any of us reneging on our obligations, so Tony said Daddy would let me go. But I was terrified for keeping a secret from Mama." She shook her head slowly. "I always tell Mama everything, but Tony said I couldn't tell her about leaving, and he made me double dare, pinkie swear, so I didn't."

Double dare, pinkie swear? Whew! She was breathless in her rapid-fire tale by this time, and I was breathless listening to her. Were there still families like this in the mid 1970's? Was it just Italian families, or families in upstate New York, or those with only one girl? It was like she'd sprung from another planet. Her monologue revealed undercurrents of being almost imprisoned by overprotective, maybe even selfish, people. But, she obviously didn't see that for herself.

"I'm a virgin," she announced, glancing out the car window as we passed Würzberg.

Startled, I jerked the steering wheel back into my own lane with a BMW's horn blaring behind me. *Way too much information,* I thought. This announcement was not what I'd expected for a first meeting. I hardly thought her sex life, or lack thereof was any of my business.

"That's nice," I muttered. *Well, what was I supposed to say to something like that?*

Desperate for a safer topic, I asked, "How did it go when you left?"

Tears again ran over her long lashes. "It was just terrible! The boys brought down my bags, and Mama followed me down the stairs crying and grabbing her heart. She almost fainted against the railing, and she said it would kill her if I left. She kept screaming, 'Do you want to kill your own Mama?' I felt so bad, I didn't know what to do."

I handed DeeDee a tissue from the box I always carried between Bosco's bucket seats.

She honked noisily into it and mopped her eyes. "It was so

awful, and I didn't want to go, but Tony said he and Daddy would take care of Mama. Andy and Florio just picked me up by the elbows and dragged me out the door while Mario grabbed my bags. I could still hear Mama's voice as they drove me away. Her last words were, "Keep your pants on." I couldn't imagine why she said that because I was wearing my best dress and she never approved of pants."

Don't say anything, Megan, I told myself. *You don't want to touch that one!*

"I cried all the way to the airport," DeeDee continued. "The boys walked me clear up to the gangway of the airplane. I was still crying about leaving Mama when she was having a sinking spell, and they kept saying I had to go *now*, because I would never get another chance." She sniffled and wiped her eyes again. "I don't even know if Mama is all right. I'll need to find a place I can call home when we get to Bamberg."

Suddenly, I felt sorry for this twenty-nine year-old, who was still attached to Mama's umbilical cord. Her Mama apparently had blackmailing ways of keeping her baby girl at home.

"I have a feeling your brothers and your Dad know your Mom will be okay. She'll be proud of you for taking steps to have an independent career for yourself, once she gets used to the idea."

"Oh, do you really think so? I'd like to make her proud of me." She brightened, hugging her handbag to her chest. "I'd like her to be proud and not have any more sinking spells."

Her pathetic eagerness gave me paroxysms of guilt for telling such a whopper. Her mother would probably make her feel guilty for leaving for the rest of her natural life.

DeeDee seemed to gather her thoughts for a while as my Fiat raced by several small, farming towns and fields of golden flax. I didn't want to intrude in order to point out the beauty of Southern Germany.

But then she asked, "Why did *you* come into DoDDS?"

I laughed and told her of my dream to see the world. "I was in junior high school when I read this book about two young women who toured Europe in the 1920's. I guess it was considered like finishing school for young women to go abroad before they settled down. These two had adventure after adventure, while I'd never traveled further than our mulberry tree in the back yard. I dreamed of following in their footsteps and seeing the world.

"Who were they?" DeeDee looked mildly interested.

"The book was _Our Hearts Were Young and Gay_. I thought the two girls, Cornelia Otis Skinner and Emily Kimbrough, were everything I wanted to be one day: wealthy, adventurous, witty. Since I was a long way from the wealthy and witty part, I figured this opportunity to work overseas with DoDDS would let me be adventurous on all the weekends and holidays, and earn my living at the same time--a win-win situation, don't you think?"

DeeDee had stifled her tears, so I figured I had distracted her a bit.

"It sounds wonderful for you to have a plan. I could never plan anything alone. But aren't you afraid to go off wandering in this strange country? Mama says one could get lost or kidnapped or raped or robbed or…or…just anything could happen."

"Good grief, no. You learn a bit of the language, you have a map, and you pick a destination. What more would you need? I've had a wonderful time traveling. I'm looking forward to another year of teaching great kids during the week and exploring Europe on the weekends. You're going to love our DoDDS kids. They call themselves 'overseas brats' and they're so much fun."

"You sound confident. I wish I could feel that way."

Her voice breathed awe, in a way that made me feel distinctly uncomfortable. Confidence wasn't exactly my forte. It had escaped me ever since I'd fallen down the stairs during my grand entrance to the Nativity play in grammar school. I was in no way deserving of awe from anyone.

My sleeve caught on Bosco's shift lever, and I had to make a quick correction. "You'll feel confident, as soon as you get settled and can find your way around." I hesitated, wondering if I should actually tell her my own issue, but maybe it would make her feel better to know that everyone had difficulties. "I do have one little problem. I'm notoriously accident-prone, as you may have noticed." I pointed to my now bulging forehead with my throbbing finger. "I'd really like to be like Cornelia and Emily and just breeze through every adventure with poise and aplomb, but I seem to be addicted to Murphy's Law--everything that *can* go wrong, will. As you can see, I'm hardly graceful at anything, unless there's music playing. I'm pretty good with music." I waved at the car radio I kept on while driving, for safety reasons.

"Oh, but you seem wonderfully confident to me, and you found your way around that big airport so easily. I would have been so lost. I'll bet you're a super-duper traveler."

Super-duper? Oh my! "Well, I never get lost. That part's easy. It's trying to keep from breaking something that's the problem. Friends tell me I'm probably the only person in the world who can get herself so deeply into problems. Things just seem to happen everywhere I go. I don't know why."

"Hey, what did you say your name was again? I was too scared earlier to remember."

"Megan James."

"I've got this wonderful idea, Megan. Whenever you travel, you can take me along, because nothing unusual *ever* happens to me. My good luck will rub off on you, so you don't have any more accidents. You can be 'Cornelia' and I'll be 'Emily,' and we can have simply marvy adventures together. What do you say?" DeeDee had become positively bubbly.

I've always thought it pretty dumb when cartoon characters gulp loudly when in a tight fix, but right then, my voice couldn't even emit a squeak. *Simply marvy?* What could I say to back-pedal my way out of spending the rest of my life traveling with this stereotypical old maid, without hurting her feelings? *What about my dates? What about my weekend getaways? I sure didn't want to be stuck with this woman all the time, and yet--something about her was so pathetically in need of attention.*

Eagerness beamed in DeeDee's face. "Well, what do you say 'Cornelia?'"

"Oh, um…I guess we can try one trip…um…'Emily.'" *What was that advice about never volunteering?*

Chapter 2 - Reconnoitering

"What are we doing for the rest of the week, after we get to Bamberg?" DeeDee asked, as we sped down the Autobahn. If you could get him started, Bosco loved having no speed limit.

"Hmm...." I wracked my brain for a dental appointment or something, but I couldn't think of anything believable. *We?* I'd envisioned spending the first week introducing DeeDee to other teachers and military officers as they returned, and then my greeter mission would be over. It never entered my mind that she might need what my students call a "do-over" before meeting anyone. She'd been so sheltered, I feared trying to make her understand our mission on the Cold War Border, too, and I felt at a loss to know where to take her or what to do with her.

But while my mind whirred, her big brown eyes watched me for an answer. I feared my negative thoughts curled around a frown on my face, because her question hung in the air too long. I was at least stuck with her until school started and, as her greeter, I'd have to get her integrated into the system, *somehow*. I pointed out the beautiful medieval buildings and carved doorways of Poppenweiler, as we drove by, while I stalled, trying to think.

"We'll find some things to do," I said aloud. "Don't worry." She smiled and laid her head back on the seat rest.

The forested part of our journey closed around us as we headed up the 505 to its dead end. Nobody went to the Border unless they were ordered there, yet I always loved this quiet drive, even though it really didn't go anyplace. It simply stopped at the Soviet guard towers, barbed wire, and mine fields beyond Bamberg and Hof. The Border and its denizens had become "home" to me. Maybe they would to DeeDee, too, if we could get past these first awkward days.

I broke the silence with an encouraging thought. "I'll be showing you around this week and helping you get settled. Then, you'll meet lots of people you'll want to travel with and go out with." I'd have to break her in *slowly*, so I added, "This is a fun place to be. Just put the proximity of the Border and the communists out of your mind, and you'll do fine."

"What communists?" DeeDee immediately squirmed around and looked over her shoulder as though communists hid in the back seat. "Are you talking about Red ones?"

Oops! Another blooper on my part. That wasn't slowly enough, Megan! "Why, the communists near the Border where we'll be living." I tried to make it sound light. "Didn't anyone tell you Bamberg and Hof are a line base on the East/West Communist Border?"

With eyes wide as Frisbees, DeeDee slunk lower in her seat. "I thought it was a school? Are Reds nearby? Will spies see us?" she whispered. "I shouldn't have come. Mama was right."

"It's okay, DeeDee. Honestly. Our soldiers are here to protect us, and they're out on the Border in any Alert. It's nothing to worry about. There'll be NEO briefings later to tell you what to do in an emergency."

"What kind of emergency? What's NEO?"

Her shaky voice tells me I just opened another can of worms. Stupid, stupid, stupid, Megan! But I flashed my most cheerful, toothy grin and said, "NEO is an acronym for Non-combatant Evacuation Orders. It's about what our jobs would be if the Soviets decided to cross the Border and take all of Europe instead of the half they control now. Actually the NEO plan won't work for us, because we are too close, but it works for the rest of families stationed in Germany." *I'd better tell her about Alerts later. I've already stuck my foot in my mouth enough for now.*

I tried to sound casual. I hadn't realized the Border caused so many secrets or was so close when I came, either. "It's nothing to worry about, DeeDee. We're all used to it, and you'll get used to it, too. The Soviets will stay on their own side, because they don't want to tangle with our soldiers unless they think they can win. And our guys are always there whenever the Soviets try anything." *Big grin, Megan!*

"But if they did come…?"

Again, I felt the necessity to avoid an answer while looking outside the car and reminding myself why I loved this place. The road to my apartment in Wernsdorf flashed by with its graceful arches and its cozy little beer garden. Several old German farmers were already gathering under the trees for their lunchtime meal and stein of beer. They waved, and I waved back. Some of them I knew, and they recognized my ugly yellow Bosco. The others were near enough to the Border that they were waving at me *just because* I was an American. My green license plates gave that away.

"There's no way we Americans could hide in the German population," I told DeeDee. "But the closer one gets to the Border, the more the natives appreciate Americans for being here to protect them from communist incursion. West Germany has recovered completely from World War II--prosperous, colorful, and confident--while the East side, under communism, is about as desolate and un-recovered as possible." *Was she listening? I couldn't tell.*

We passed a convoy of dusty tanks on the road. DeeDee's alarmed gaze followed them silently. *How could I make this woman feel safe enough to fit into our Border lifestyle?*

"There are contingency plans, DeeDee. Nothing for you to worry about." I chalked up another thing I'd probably have to explain later. The list was getting pretty long. I can't let her go through all this change alone. She's unbelievably helpless and scared.

DeeDee was silent a long while, and just as I began congratulating myself on having diverted her fear, *and* her enthusiasm for being my best buddy for life, she asked again, "So, 'Cornelia,' where shall we go on our first adventure? That's assuming it's safe to go anywhere."

Rats, I hadn't diverted anything! "We can go north, south and west. Europe is pretty big and there's a lot to see. But, you need to get acclimated to Bamberg first, the city and the military Kaserne, so I think a few days closer to home will be a good thing." *She's not ready to go far.*

As we arrived at the *Drei Kronen*, a German Pension in Memmelsdorf, I got out. She hung back.

"It's okay, DeeDee. This is where you'll stay until we find you a German apartment." It crossed my mind that it'll be hard to find an apartment where she'll feel secure with all her foibles and fears. "Look, DeeDee. It's almost lunchtime." As I pulled her bags out of Bosco's hatchback onto the curb, I said, "Why don't we have a bowl of soup here at the *Drei Kronen*. Then you can shower and rest awhile, and I'll come back later to take you to dinner. Tomorrow, we can take the bus downtown, so you can find your way on your own." The plan sounded reasonable to me, and would give me a few minutes alone to pick up groceries and visit the laundromat. I still had a suitcase full of dirty clothes from my vacation in the states.

"The bus? Oh, no! We can't go on the bus. Somebody might rob us."

I desperately need an aspirin, or three. "We'll talk about it later, DeeDee. Right now, let's get you settled, have lunch, and make plans, so you can get some sleep. Come on and get out, now!" *I couldn't help it. The 'now' came out stronger than I intended.*

"I'm not sleepy at all," she insisted. "Don't leave me here!" Her lower lip trembled like a kindergartner, but at least she got out of the car.

"Okay, Okay, DeeDee." *Laundry will have to wait.* "Let's just please have lunch. I'm hungry, and you must be too, because I'll bet you didn't eat much on the plane."

"I never like to eat except in Mama's kitchen where I know it's clean. Mama said only hard boiled eggs and tea were safe to eat in a foreign land. We don't know if this restaurant is clean."

I slammed my door shut. "SHH! The owners know English. They'll be insulted if you say such a thing. You can practically eat off the sidewalk in Germany. Stop worrying about everything!" I tried hard to contain myself, but really! I'll bet DeeDee's Mama heard an old travelogue someplace from the turn of the century. I think I read of someone who followed that old wives' tale. Was it in something of Mitchner's? "Besides, DeeDee, if you only eat eggs and tea, you won't get much of the flavor of seeing and smelling and trying everything in a new land. That's a big part of the joy of traveling. Now, please be quiet. Here comes the owner."

DeeDee sighed, but she allowed Herr Bauer to help us get the luggage upstairs without repeating her tug-of-war act. I washed my hands at the little sink in her room, and I could see she was looking for the bathroom. I pointed down the hall. *Drei Kronen* was a charming *Gasthaus* three or four hundred years old but, like most charming European places, the plumbing had been added as an afterthought, probably a hundred years ago. She'll get used to pull-chains.

DeeDee slumped her shoulders. I muttered, "Get over it" and headed downstairs. I didn't care whether she followed me or not. I was already fed up with nurse-maiding.

I needn't have worried. DeeDee wasn't about to let me out of her sight. She rushed after me down the stairs and into the restaurant. I asked the maitre'd for seating for two, and he directed us to a table where three other people were already seated. DeeDee froze in her tracks, apparently assuming we'd have an American-style table all to ourselves. Germans don't bother with that. I politely asked, and was granted permission. I sat. DeeDee stood behind me awkwardly, so I pulled out the chair next to mine and ordered, "Sit!"

She did. But she was silent as I introduced myself to our three tablemates and made small talk. "I don't know these people," DeeDee whispered through clenched teeth.

"You don't have to. It's the custom here to welcome people to your table whether you know them or not. Lighten up and smile, *please*."

She grimaced in a straight-lipped attempt, and suddenly I couldn't do anything except laugh at our ludicrous situation. My laughter spilled over to the other three guests who, of course, had no idea why I was laughing. But I could see DeeDee was offended.

"I'm sorry, DeeDee," I said quickly, "but you look so pained, and these folks are trying to be nice to us. It shouldn't hurt to smile at people."

"Mama said not to talk to strangers."

"That was when you were five years old! DeeDee. You're twenty-nine. Mama's not here! I'm in charge for now, and I give you complete permission to smile at any stranger you want. In fact, I *command* you to smile at everyone you see. Otherwise, everybody on God's green earth will remain strangers until the day you die!" I tried to control my rising tone. It was a lost cause.

She looked startled, and stared at her shaking hands hugging the menu she couldn't read. I *had* to soften the blow. I could see her tears forming again. I guess I'd sounded too forceful. "Look, DeeDee. Since I've been in DoDDS, I have a method that works for me, and I'll share it with you. Whenever I enter a room full of people I don't know, I approach the person that looks more scared than me, and I talk to him or her. Because they feel out of place, too, they're grateful somebody came, and soon we both feel better. All the friends I've made that way have turned into lifelong friends. Nobody wants to be alone in a room of strangers. Your job from now on is not to be a stranger to others. Get it? You have to just wade right in."

She nodded, but she still clutched the menu to her breast and shook.

"Okay then, let me see you smile genuinely to these people, like you mean it."

She glanced frantically around the room. "But I can't speak German."

"DeeDee, Honey-bun, a smile is not in any particular language. It's the same in *all* languages. Now get to it!"

DeeDee slowly stuck her neck out a little from where she'd been hiding behind me, and even more slowly her lips turned up a little.

"That's it, a little more."

She approached her limit of a curved smile. The others smiled back.

"Great. Now, did that hurt you any?"

"I guess not," she said.

"Then I want you to smile at them at least three or four times during lunch."

"Why?"

"No reason, except to advance German-American relations and to humor me. You don't want to see me when I'm in a bad mood."

I thought she would laugh at my silly comment, but instead, she cried out, "Oh, Megan, I'm so sorry!" Her voice raised two octaves, only one decibel below a wail. "Please, I didn't mean to make you mad. You're all I've got, and I don't want you to be mad at me." These words were accompanied by yet more tears.

Earth to Meg—don't try to be funny with this girl. She takes every joke for real.

"Oh, shoot! DeeDee. I'm *not* mad. I'm just trying desperately to make you to loosen up and laugh a little. Don't take everything so seriously." Motioning over my head, I added, "Just let things go over like water off a duck's back."

"That's cute. I've never heard that before." She waved her own hand over her head and smiled--a real smile. I didn't want to tell her the cliché was older than dirt, or that I wondered where she'd been hiding twenty-nine years in order to stay so doggone sheltered. I was just glad to see a real smile, and I returned it right away. *Now, maybe we can make some progress.*

I ordered *Gulasche Zuppe* and *Spezi*, pointing to the soup on the menu so she could find it later by herself. It was a sure thing that the *Zuppe* would be hot, and the *Spezi* would be cold. But she wanted a darned hard-boiled egg. I ordered her *Ei* and showed it to her on the menu as well. She wanted a Coke, but I told her it would be served at room temperature, and there'd be no ice. *Spezi* was half cola and half *Limonade* and would at least be served chilled.

"Why? She asked, furrowing her expressive brows.

"Darned if I know. That's just the way it is. When in Rome...."

"Oh, are we near Rome?"

I rested my face in my hands and took a deep breath. "No,

DeeDee, we're *not* near Rome. It's just another old cliché that means you do things in a foreign country the way the natives do."

"Oh. There's so much to learn." She hung her head in such a dispirited way.

My feelings softened immediately. She needed reassurance. "Don't worry, DeeDee. We all feel a little overwhelmed when we come here. I was too. You'll be fine, I promise."

"Maybe we can make Rome our first adventure and pretend we're 'Cornelia and Emily,'" she countered. "What do you think?"

"Eat your Ei, DeeDee."

The other guests wished us *"Guten Appetit,"* and she smiled at them. "Good girl," I whispered.

After lunch, we returned to her room. She claimed not to be tired, though I knew her jet lag must catch up with her sooner or later. "If you don't want to lie down now, you'll have to stay awake until about 2200 hours, and then in the morning, your jet lag will be controllable. Otherwise, it'll last for days."

After asking what 2200 was, she opted to stay up, though I think it was so I wouldn't leave her alone at the hotel. I suggested we hang up her clothing together. I wanted to see what she'd brought that might be more appropriate than those malignant purple flowers.

As hanger after hanger filled up with 1930 - 1950's style suits and dresses, and hats lined up on the shelf, I tried to ask tactfully where she bought her clothing.

"Oh, Daddy gave me some of Mama's dress-up suits to bring. He said she always looked pretty in them, and that I looked just like her." She smiled and held up a dress to her body.

I changed gears and asked if she had any slacks, or sweaters, or blouses, or shoes for walking, or volleyball, or teaching.

"Oh, I've never played volleyball. I played softball once in junior high and my best friends were on the team, too. They bumped into each other trying to catch a fly ball, and it was so funny." DeeDee giggled like that junior high school girl.

I couldn't help smiling as she continued.

"Then the next ball came on the ground, and when I tried to get it, it went right through my glove, up my front and hit me in the chin. Knocked me out. I haven't tried sports since then."

"Well what about slacks for school and traveling?"

Her face froze in a disapproving stare. "Mama never lets me wear slacks."

"Doggone it, DeeDee. Do you always do what your Mama says? Wasn't it the idea of your brothers for you to get away by yourself and be your own person?" My exasperation was showing. "We'll go shopping tomorrow." I didn't allow any argument. Just gathered up my jacket and purse and keys and said, "If you want to see downtown Bamberg, come now. You can finish this later." I'd seen what I needed to know.

DeeDee wheeled toward the mirror, and darned if she wasn't putting that hat back on her head and trying to upsweep her hair, bobby pins in her mouth as she worked.

I intervened. "Look, please, lose the hat and gloves. No one has worn those for years."

She looked bewildered, so I grabbed her brush, pulled out the hairpins and brushed her hair down to a normal length, loosely around her face. "Not bad," I muttered under my breath as she tried to pull back the hairpins. "Forget those," I said, grabbing them. "Let your hair down. Dang it, DeeDee, this is the last time I'm going to wrestle you for anything. Let go!"

She did, whipping her hands behind her back like a kid caught in the cookie jar. But still, those cow brown eyes followed my every move.

I threw her a jacket. *I guess there's nothing we can do about that purple dress...yet.*

As I trotted down the stairs, I missed the bottom step and stumbled over the carpet. I righted myself with only a minor bump to my knee, but I didn't look back. I knew DeeDee would be shadowing me. I found the idea disconcerting.

I got into my Fiat, and stuck in the key. DeeDee jumped in so fast I knew she didn't want to be left behind. Of course, Bosco wouldn't start—up to his dirty tricks again. DeeDee wailed, "Oh, my goodness. What will we do?"

"We don't cry, DeeDee. Bosco hates tears." A quick rocking motion on the backside and a brief push got Bosco's attention, and when I trounced angrily on the starter and gas pedal the next time, he responded. *He darned well better. I'd had enough today, already!*

I explained to DeeDee in my best evenly controlled voice, "The other teachers aren't back yet, and the men are all out on the Border right now. We usually go as a group, but I'll give you a quickie tour of downtown Bamberg--cobblestones, old courtyards, *Schlenkerla, Rauch Bier, Bratwurst, and Spatsle.* Just tag along, keep up, and ask questions whenever you need to. I'll tell you later about teaching on a military line base, and keeping military secrets."

"Oh, my goodness, I hope nobody ever tells me any of those...."

I raised my eyes to the heavens and prayed for patience, patience, patience, as I backed into a tiny parking place downtown and dented the door on the curb getting out. "I'll see to it that they don't, DeeDee." *Believe me! I'll see to it!*

"I still think Rome should be our first trip as 'Cornelia and Emily,'" suggested DeeDee. You wouldn't skin up your car door, or fall down again, because nothing ever happens to me."

"Right!"

When I arrived at *Drei Kronen* the next morning to pick up DeeDee, we made some progress. We got rid of the hats!

"But what should I do with all Mama's nice hats, if I don't wear them?" she asked.

"Burn 'em," I suggested, with only a hint of malice.

"Oh, I couldn't do that. Mama would have a sinking spell."

"I've got a great idea. Send them back to Mama." I'd brought along a box in case we could arrive at this moment, so I started packing up Mama's hats.

DeeDee watched for a moment with eyes wide, then she put the last hat in herself, after lovingly coaxing the little veil back into shape over the brimless cloche. "Mama can wear them to church."

"Right. You can suggest that when you write her. No one has worn hats since the early 60's except as part of a costume. Now the fad is mini skirts and disco boots."

"Oh, I could never…."

"I know. I know. Mama wouldn't like it. Since phone calls are so expensive here on the German economy, and none of us has a phone anyway, I'll take you to the Mars station this morning, so you can call your family to rest your mind about your Mama."

Eager to make the call, DeeDee let me talk her into leaving her hair down.

"It does take less time this way, doesn't it?" she observed. "Mama is never wrong, though." She twirled in front of the mirror. "Maybe it'll be okay down, just for today."

I smiled. *There's hope for her yet.* "Come on, DeeDee. As soon as we finish the call, we'll go shopping to find you some functional teaching clothes, some normal, comfortable shoes, and a gown that looks nice for parties." After that bulky purple-flowered dress, I wasn't sure she even *had* a figure, but she would at least need something for traveling and climbing around her classroom, if for nothing else.

The Mars shack was just that—a run-down lean-to way out on Muna Annex, propped up against an old German building from some war or other. A laconic staff sergeant snoozing over his morning coffee roused himself to brief DeeDee on the protocol then went back to his nap. One of DeeDee's brothers put her mother on the phone, but it quickly became a jumbled mess of transmissions, with neither Mama nor DeeDee remembering to say, "Over," when they finished each sentence.

In desperation, I finally grabbed the headset and said to her mother, "DeeDee will write you often while she's here, Mama. Over and Out." That ended the call.

"Won't Mama be mad," DeeDee asked, with hands again

atwitch.

"Not if you write her often like I promised. And she must be perfectly fine, health wise, or she couldn't have talked on the radio. You need to quit worrying about her."

But DeeDee's conversation was worry-filled all the way into downtown Bamberg to Hertie's, a German department store on the main square. I diverted attention from her continuing list of Mama's ailments by steering her into the lady's slacks department.

"Why do I need new clothes?" DeeDee asked. "I have all Mama's suits for school."

"They won't work for school, DeeDee." I launched into the DoDDS mantra. "We overseas teachers have to get used to skinning our own skunks. If something needs fixing, we often do it ourselves rather than go up the chain of command. That means you'll be cleaning up the paint spills, or climbing on your desk to fix a fan. You wouldn't want to get your mama's pretty suits dirty, would you? Often, our classrooms are former Quonset huts, German barracks, or slaughterhouses, so we climb around a lot to set up bulletin boards or displays. Slacks are much more modest than a dress, here, don't you see. Get it?"

"Oh." DeeDee ground on that thought awhile.

"Besides, you aren't going to be at school all the time, and everyone wears more casual clothes for evenings at the Club and traveling. You at least need a pair or two."

"Mama wouldn't…."

"Never mind Mama. She wouldn't want you to get cold in Germany, now, would she?"

"Well…I don't…."

"Good, it's settled. We'll tell her how cold it is here," I said, as I peeled off my cardigan in the August heat. I handed DeeDee a pair of black slacks and a soft pink sweater. "Go try these on." When she stood still holding the garments, I herded her toward the dressing room.

She asked, "Are you sure? Is there anything else I should try?"

"Use your own judgment," I answered, but that was a

mistake. Either she didn't have any, or she didn't trust it. I felt a little silly picking out clothes for a grown woman, but I brought her things to try on. That worked pretty well, except the German saleslady kept handing DeeDee weird outfits to try, as well. As the saleslady put them over the top of the dressing room door, I collected them from under the door. It soon became a bit obvious.

"What's happening?" DeeDee said, as I removed some things she had already prepared to try on. "Things are flying in and out and I don't know…."

"You don't want that, DeeDee," I said quickly. "The color is bilious."

"Die Fraulein muss haben ein anderes Hemt mit…" said the saleslady.

"No shoulder pads, danke," I said firmly, as I removed the offending blouse. It looked as though it had sprouted wings, German style. Eventually, we got out of the store with two pair of nice slacks and a couple of sweaters, "…because German winters are so cold," I kept reminding DeeDee. Even the gown we found would be fine once we removed the stiff fake corsage that came attached to the center of the bosom. Germans are prone to sticking things to the front of every garment, while we Americans keep cutting them off for more simplicity.

DeeDee was actually pleased with her treasures. "I'll write Mama right away and tell her all about them."

"Hmm. Let's wait awhile to tell her about the slacks, DeeDee, until it's winter," I said, "for the cold, remember?"

I was exhausted.

Chapter 3 - Facts of Life, DoDDS Style

Within a week, school started, our fellow teachers arrived safely from the States, and our male officers returned from the Border raring to party and get ready for ski season. We teachers eagerly greeted our thirty new little kidlets in each classroom. The first day of school is still as exciting for me as it is for the kids. I could tell DeeDee was as pleased with her new Kindergartners as I was with my new fifth graders. We talked of nothing else.

DeeDee was as frustrated with the lack of materials and books in an overseas school as I had been on my arrival. My hints to "wing it" fell on deaf ears as she frantically searched in every old storage closet for non-existent textbooks or bulletin board supplies. Her classroom was out in Muna Annex, which was short for Ammunition Dump, but I didn't tell her that yet. There would be time for her to figure that out for herself.

"There *must* be more supplies hidden someplace," she insisted, digging through at least the fiftieth old, dusty box in the Annex attic.

"You won't find any, DeeDee. Mostly, we make our own things, or we bring them in our luggage when we return from summer break in the States. Not much is available over here. If I get desperate, I write my mom to send me something from California." I couldn't resist a smile at the dust all over her face from her one-woman archeology dig. I dabbed at it with a tissue until we both were laughing.

"I could write to my two best friends in Ithaca. They're both teachers, and they'll know exactly what I need. I'm hoping they'll come visit later. Will you help me show them around?"

I nodded, noncommittally, hoping she'd forget about it by then. "It's expensive to ship things. You can borrow what you need from me, and our supply man can often find the 'impossible' somewhere on base. If you're really desperate, you can ask the combat engineers. They know where everything in the world is buried—even the bombs under the road."

Again, I quickly regretted my statement because we got into "What bombs?" "Are they really under the road?" "Which road?" "How do we know where it's safe to drive?" "What if they blow up?" and the phrase I now detested, "Mama told me not to come."

I explained that the bombs weren't armed, and wouldn't be, unless attack by the Soviets was imminent. "The detonators are stored nearby, but they're only in the three gaps that would have to be defended first, Hof, Coberg, and Fulda."

"Will I see them?"

"Even if you see one marked, you're to forget you saw it— do you understand that?"

"Why?"

"Just take my word for it, DeeDee. There are secrets around a Border base…around any military base, but especially a Border base. One of those secrets leaked out last year and friends of mine were hurt. Don't talk to *anyone* about anything you see."

Her eyes shot left and right. "Do you mean there are spies around?"

"Let's just say that you shouldn't be blabbing to anyone. If you have questions, ask one of us—the guys, the more experienced teachers, or Marco."

"Marco? The maitre'd at the O'Club?"

"Yes. Marco takes good care of us, and he knows everything. Enough of that, let's get back to our classrooms." *I shouldn't have mentioned Marco.*

I had to admit DeeDee was great with kids. They loved her immediately, though I was afraid she might unwittingly pass along some of her irrational fears to them. The best I could do was to encourage her to "Be brave, so your kids will be brave." I knew from experience that the overseas military kids were the most adaptable in the world. They knew not to ask questions--just to follow orders in any emergency. I'd had a crisis a year earlier. My kids had responded like champs when an act of espionage released thousands of gallons of aviation fuel around our classrooms. I wanted DeeDee to develop trust in what a good thing it was to be with military people in Bamberg. The proximity of the Border made friends tight as family, and we all depended on each other. She didn't understand yet, but I wouldn't give up.

After school each day, I took DeeDee to look at apartments, or out to nearby villages to learn a little of their history and to orient her to the area. She still feared being alone, but didn't feel comfortable with others, either. However, she was beginning to notice some of the scenery she had missed entirely on her way in, and she asked good questions.

Gert and Cathie, fellow teachers from the junior high, had suggested we four go to Rome over the Labor Day weekend. It sounded great to me. I enjoyed traveling with beautiful, blonde, show-me-where-the-cute-guys-are Cathie and practical, call-it-as-you-see-it Gert, and it was nice of them to include DeeDee.

Immediately, DeeDee said, "Oh, could we, 'Cornelia?' It's Rome!" wrapping her hands together under her chin. *Those darn eager eyes again. I can't say no to those eyes.*

Gert said, "You'll have to explain this 'Cornelia business' to us, unless you've hidden some secret middle name." I shriveled, and DeeDee put her hand over her mouth when I gave her a look.

"It's just a private joke," I said, "sort of a traveling thing."

We found an apartment off base that DeeDee could move into right away. It was only a short distance from mine--a mile by car around the roads, but only about half a mile on foot, if we cut through the farmer's fields. Technically, my apartment was in Wernsdorf and hers was in Amlingstadt, but the two ancient villages had almost merged. I wasn't thrilled at first, that it was that close to mine, but apartments were hard to find, and she was delighted to be so close.

The Housing Office on post lent her appliances and enough furniture to start out. We found her a used Ford, and after coaching from Cathie, Gert, and Ruthie, another primary teacher, during recesses in the lounge, DeeDee even passed her German driver's license on the second try. Things were looking up for achieving some degree of independence. Her curly hair, now that we had gotten rid of the bobby pins, was brushed and gleaming. With soft eyes and long lashes that dominated her face, she was actually pretty, underneath her Mama's camouflage. *If she just wasn't so fearful.*

But Rome didn't turn out to be our first trip. That week someone told DeeDee about ITT, International Tours and Travel—an agency that arranged inexpensive trips for military people. She appeared after school with tickets in her hand.

"Barbara, the other Kindergarten teacher, said we should see Rothenburg am Tauber, so I went over to ITT and thought I'd surprise you with a day-trip, since you've been so nice to me."

"How thoughtful of you, DeeDee, but when is it? I may have something else going."

"This Saturday. You said you hadn't planned anything for the weekend, and the ITT agent said it was a fine shopping trip for ladies, so I thought…."

Her eyes got to me again. I sighed and nodded. "Sure, DeeDee. Rothenburg is one of my favorite towns. A day trip will be nice. Thank you."

DeeDee was bubbly the rest of the week until I picked her up to go meet the bus.

About twenty other ladies, all German, were on the bus with us, as we headed down the road to the old medieval city--one of only three in Europe with its original defensive wall still encircling the town. We settled down with books on the bus ride, and I napped a little. Suddenly, DeeDee was shaking me.

"The two ladies in front of us got sleepy, too, Megan," she whispered. "But one put her head on her friend's shoulder and the friend put her arm around her. Look."

I tried to pry my eyes open, but I was too tired. "In Germany, ladies even dance together, DeeDee," I mumbled. "It doesn't mean anything."

"Well, it seemed strange and got my attention, so I was watching," DeeDee whispered.

"You're imagining things, Dee. Go to sleep. We'll be there

in another hour."

I could hear DeeDee shifting around, and out of the corner of one half-open eye, I noticed she'd put her book over her face.

When we arrived at my favorite old print shop on Rothenburg's main square, DeeDee excused herself to go to the restroom, as did most of the other ladies.

She came flying right back out, screaming at me. "My God, you won't believe what those women are doing." DeeDee was breathless. "I tried to tell you they were acting strange. You said they were just very European."

"Well, I was half asleep and, if I was wrong. I'm sorry. What did I miss?"

Two women walked out of the restroom still kissing. *Whoo-boy...now what?*

"You had me thinking I was over-reacting. But I wasn't."

"No, I guess not. But we have no other way of getting home besides the bus. We'll just stay to ourselves and not look."

DeeDee started to cry. "I'm sorry for getting us into this predicament, 'Cornelia,'" she blubbered. "The ITT lady said it was just a nice group of ladies going shopping, and I...."

"It's okay, DeeDee," I said, putting my arm around her shoulders to comfort her.

A pair of the other women walked by arm in arm and giggled as they looked at us. We both jumped back like cats on a griddle.

After walking around the old city for hours, going in opposite directions from our bus mates, we had to re-board the bus for the trip home. We sat as far apart as we could get on our seat and became terribly absorbed in our books.

"When that woman across the aisle kissed her seatmate, my stomach started to roll," whispered DeeDee. "I've never seen anything like that before. Have you?"

I scanned the bus quickly and saw a lot of couples were *quite* cozy, doing things rather overtly. I shook my head. "Never."

We both tried hard to avoid eye contact with these other women who were holding hands and kissing all over the place.

"I thought it would be okay," DeeDee whispered again, obviously still distraught. "The ITT lady never said…. You aren't going to hold this against me, are you? It was the first time I tried to plan a trip for us all by myself, and I never thought…."

"Of course not, 'Emily.'" I tried to make her laugh. "We'll just chalk this up to our first adventure together, our lesson in the facts of life. Embarrassing, yes, but we'll survive."

"Thank you for not being mad, 'Cornelia.'" We studiously avoided looking at any of the other women until we got safely back to downtown Bamberg to pick up Bosco.

"Well, Dee, if you came to Europe to get a husband, you sure didn't get one on that trip.

"Boy am I glad to be back," said DeeDee, and we both broke out laughing.

How the others heard about our fiasco day-trip, I never found out, but it was the topic of the teacher's lounge when we entered on Monday.

Cathie held her stomach, almost wheezing with laughter. "Didn't you guys realize it was a Lesbian tour? That's probably why ITT emphasized it being so 'special.'"

"I didn't know," said DeeDee. "I thought she meant it was special because it was all ladies going shopping, like the poster said, "…on a beautiful medieval city tour."

"What happened?" asked petite little Ruthie. She'd just bounced in from playground duty with her wind-blown red hair framing her freckled face.

So the story was told all over again until everyone was laughing at our expense. I could see DeeDee's red face and knew it mirrored my own. It wasn't exactly the way I'd intended for DeeDee to get integrated with the faculty.

Cathie turned to the whole group and said loudly, "Something like that could *only* happen with Megan along. Unusual things happen wherever she goes. Also, you two are the probably the most naive people in the world. You're lucky you emerged unscathed, DeeDee."

DeeDee glanced at me, somewhat chagrined.

Gee, and here she thought I was confident. "You can guess we spent the rest of the day trying not to stare at anyone," I said.

"Meg explained to me what they were on the way home, but I couldn't look any of them in the face after that. They kept talking as though we were like them," said DeeDee. "I was so embarrassed. My Mama would be so embarrassed, too."

"Well, we can all thank God that your Mama wasn't there," said Ruthie, patting DeeDee on the shoulder. "And I don't think you'd better tell her about this, either."

DeeDee was really pretty with her relaxed hair and new slacks and sweaters that fit her, but I still practically had to drag her into the Officers' Club once the guys got back from Alert.

Our Officers' Club was a late 18th century building that had probably served German officers through at least a half dozen wars, but it had marvelous old world charm. I could imagine Bismarck visiting its ornate halls. With graceful friezes over the hand-carved doors, a marvelous rock fireplace in the "Red Room" used for special dinners or serious dates, lovely chandeliers, and a large dining room where we met for meals and planning activities, it was the center of our expatriate universe. The Club had a huge ballroom for everything from disco dancing to ski club meetings, and a patio with tree-shaded lawn we often used for picnics. The Maitre'd, Marco, knew us all and catered to our needs and kept a wary eye out for everyone's safety and comfort.

And then there was the O'Club Bar.

I'd been reluctant to enter a "bar" when I first arrived, but I soon found it wasn't the den of iniquity I had imagined. Actually, it was everyone's "living room." None of the single teachers or military officers living either in Bachelor Officers' Quarters, BOQ on post, or in off post apartments had televisions or telephones, and few had kitchens, so the Bar served for meals, message center, card playing, book swapping, debate headquarters, and one could always get into a contest of beer deckle-flipping with so-called experts at flipping over twenty cardboard drink coasters at once.

All were welcome and comfortable in the bar…except DeeDee.

I told her to meet me there a couple of weeks after school started, so I could introduce her to everyone. She knew some of the female teachers and seemed okay with them. But she began hiccoughing and hiding her face when I tried to introduce her to my friends, Jimmy, Fred, Don, and some of the other male members of our group.

Jimmy is a top-notch Border pilot, a pilot's pilot, as the guys call him, and he's my best friend for debating and good talk. We solve all the problems of the world each time we meet. He's a big guy with big shoulders, a big smile, and a big heart. We go out together a lot, but he sort of understands that I've had a bad time somewhere along the line, and I'm a bit afraid to get serious about anyone. He doesn't press me for details, and I appreciate that.

Jimmy came over and sat down while DeeDee was in the ladies' room. "We don't seem to be alone much, since your new friend arrived." His eyes were vibrant, and his long lashes matched the unruly shock of dark hair over his forehead.

It seemed almost a habit that I brushed his hair back with my fingers. "I know, Jimmy, and I'm sorry. I'm trying to get her to lighten up, but I need to keep her under my wing for a little longer. She really isn't confident enough to walk into social situations alone just yet."

"I get it," he said and smiled. "But this'll cause you a few problems in *your* social life, Megan, since you don't seem to be able to go anywhere without her being right behind you."

I rested my chin on one hand and enjoyed looking in his eyes. "You're right. Another friend who came here when I did told me that, too. But, I can't desert DeeDee when she's not ready. I think she's attached herself to me as a substitute for her Mama, while I'm trying to ditch Mama for good. Mama has too much influence on someone her age, don't you think?"

"Definitely, but here she comes now, so shh."

I turned around too quickly to greet DeeDee and dumped my Tab into my lap. Nothing new. Jimmy grabbed his big napkin and dabbed, but DeeDee laughed at me.

"You weren't kidding about being accident-prone, were you, Megan?" I've seen you fall, walk into open doors, or run them over your big toe. You need to watch better?"

"I told you that was my biggest cross to bear. I think it has something to do with trying to do several things at once, or maybe my depth perception is off kilter, or maybe I move too fast. I always bounce back, though."

Jimmy put his hand over mine as we blotted up my diet soda together.

"Maybe you can learn to look where you're going more, or take fewer risks, and I can learn to laugh and meet people better, if we spend more time watching out for each other," she said.

Jimmy met my eyes over the Tab stains, and he smiled that crooked grin of his. I think he saw me that moment as one of the non-identical Bobbsey Twins, or Me and My Shadow.

DeeDee did affect my social life. A few of the other teachers, since they seemed to think I had DeeDee's ear from our meeter-greeter stint, took me aside to complain.

Barbara, an old hand in DoDDS, having taught from Bermuda to Iceland, started first. "Can you tactfully mention to that gal that we don't want to play 'Mama says' every time we have a date?" She tossed her chestnut hair and grimaced at the other teachers standing around.

"I've tried, you guys, and I'll try again." I had to admit DeeDee sort of bothered me, too, since every time I wanted to go out with some other friend, she was right there, Johnny-on-the-spot, to give me advice for the evening, until someone invited her along. "It's hard to find a way to tactfully tell her 'no.'" She'd gone along with Jesse and me to the Ski Club Party, with Amy and me Volksmarching, and with Jimmy and me to the movies. I didn't mind too much, except I would have liked to have a little more time alone with Jimmy. He and I enjoyed talking about a lot of issues that others weren't interested in at all, like world politics, and archeology, and just about everything. I missed that one-on-one time with him. "I'll keep trying, you guys. I promise."

So, I was sitting at a table in the O'Club with Jimmy one evening when DeeDee arrived, and we tried to tactfully explain to her that she shouldn't invite herself along with others--that she should wait for an invitation. "You could excuse yourself with a headache or something, and go back to your new apartment," I suggested. "Most couples would like a little romantic time alone."

Her hands flew to her face. "But those men might get fresh with our teachers, if no one is along to chaperone. Mama always said…."

"DeeDee, that's exactly what I mean. Your Mama isn't here, and whatever you've learned from Mama may be fine for *you*, if you choose, but it's not necessarily right for everyone else. These ladies are in their late twenties and thirties. They can manage just fine, alone."

DeeDee shook her head vigorously from left to right. "Oh, Mama's never wrong. Mama's rules work for *every* young girl, not just me. Maybe the other girls just weren't lucky enough to have a Mama like mine, don't you think?"

Oh, good heavens! I bet they're glad of that! "No, DeeDee. I don't think so. These are adults, not teen-agers, and you really need to learn to mind your own business." I smiled when I said it.

I didn't get through to her, though, because immediately after our little talk, DeeDee crossed the room toward the polished mahogany table my friend Marsha shared with Mike, a pilot she'd hoped would invite her out for the last six months. I could see Marsha's attraction. Mike was definitely a handsome devil. The two sat with shiny dark heads together speaking softly, as he held her hand. This might be the night.

When DeeDee approached, they looked up. DeeDee said, ever so sincerely and eagerly, "I'd be happy to chaperone for you, if you two plan to go out later tonight."

Marsha held out a hand toward me across the room, with a beaten cocker spaniel look, and I frantically motioned to DeeDee to come back to our table. She ignored the gesture.

"Your virginity is a marvelous gift to give your future husband," DeeDee said, "and…."

Mike coughed hard and looked around the room, desperately searching for someone to save him. Finally he said, "Marsha, maybe this was a mistake. We'll take a rain check for sometime you don't have business with your new friend." He got up and left.

Marsha stormed to the table I was sharing with Jimmy and said, quite loudly, "Will you please have another talk with that friend of yours? I finally get an invitation from Mike, and she ruins it all." I could feel every dart from her steely blue eyes.

DeeDee hurried back, wringing her hands. "I was just trying to help, Marsha. Honest, I didn't mean to make you mad." Marsha just glared at her, threw her hands in the air, and left, striding past everyone on the way out with not even a wave.

I gritted my teeth and pointed out that all these people were adults and could do as they pleased. "So can you," I hastened to add. "There might be a time when someone asks you out, and you're certainly old enough not to need a chaperone. Trust me."

DeeDee stood unconvinced, until she finally left to go home in her new, used car.

Jimmy was almost exploding trying to maintain a straight face. I swear there was steam coming from his ears and even his traditional cavalry mustache twitched. Finally, he couldn't hold his laughter in any longer and sputtered with mirth.

"Why didn't you help me explain?" I asked him.

"You got yourself into this one, Sweetie, and I'm sure you can get yourself out." He snickered, lifting his beer mug in salute.

Chapter 4 - When in Rome

Before we knew it, Labor Day was upon us. As planned, we four gals packed our stuff in the back of Bosco after school on Friday for the airport drive and our flight to Italy. Gert, organized and business-like, had made reservations at a Pension, in the words of the travel folder, "conveniently located." In a city the size of Rome, that could be anywhere at all.

DeeDee dragged two suitcases over from her car. "Mama said I should look good when traveling?"

Dear God, was Mama going to be with us forever? I want to kill the woman, and I'm a benevolent, non-violent person. "Mama will think you to look just fine with only one suitcase."

"But…."

"No buts. Take it back, DeeDee. There's only room in Bosco, and the rental car, for one backpack each."

Cathie sat in the back seat, nodding, and Gert snickering.

"How can you take only one carry-on for a whole weekend? It's such a teensy space."

Gert said, "I don't bother with excess weight."

"And all you really need for a weekend is a couple of outfits, underwear, a toothbrush, hairbrush, PJ.s, and walking shoes," added Cathie, a little less harshly. "You'll learn to pack."

I was glad to have Cathie and Gert along to help keep DeeDee on track, and this trip would get her comfortable traveling with someone besides me. *Break her in easy.*

DeeDee took one suitcase back to her car while I wedged the other one into Bosco's hatchback. When she came back, she sat in the front seat. But in only a few minutes, I noticed her squirming like a worm on a stick.

"What are you doing?" I asked. "You're fidgeting all over the front seat." As we headed down 505 toward the *Autobahn*, I tried to keep my mind on the narrow, winding highway because it was known for some terrible accidents, but DeeDee's gyrations were distracting. "You haven't sat still since we started."

"I know," she said with a grimace. "I bought something secret to carry my money in, so no one could see it or steal it. I heard that in Italy, lots of things get stolen."

Now, I was curious. "What on earth did you buy?"

"It's a leather pouch I have on, but itches and rides up."

"Where do you have it?" *I was getting that funny feeling....*

DeeDee leaned across the car's console and whispered, "It's under my unmentionables."

I exploded. "In your panties? You gotta be kidding! Those money belts go around your waist, DeeDee. How will you get into it if you need something in a shop or at the airport?"

"Uh Oh."

I don't like the sound of that. "Don't tell me--let me guess. Your passport and plane tickets are inside your panties, inside the money belt, aren't they?"

She put her hands over her face and started to cry. Those in the back stifled giggles.

"Oh, crumb, DeeDee. Turn off the waterworks! We'll find a restroom at the airport, and you can get the money belt around your waist where it belongs. You'wouldn't be comfortable flying clear to Rome with that monstrosity in your drawers, anyway."

"I'm sorry," DeeDee said meekly. "I thought it would be safe there."

I'm sure it's safe all right! I'd learned not to expect logic. "Don't worry about it. The real Emily and Cornelia had a money pocket, too, back in 1920. Theirs dangled between their legs under their skirts. Their pockets hit the knees of their boyfriends when they tried to dance together, causing quite an embarrassing time."

"Really?"

DeeDee had the widest eyes I'd ever seen. It was a temptation to tease, but I felt guilty if I did, since she took it all so seriously, often crying over silly stuff. *She's gonna be okay, but will it be soon enough not to alienate every friend I have?*

The plane's takeoff was uneventful. "Lucky for you, Megan," teased Gert from her seat across the aisle.

DeeDee looked at me and asked the dreaded question? "Why are you so frightened of flying? I've been on a plane now about"…she counted up…"two times, and I like it."

Cathie picked up a magazine from the seat pocket and said, "Megan is so frightened on planes that if there's a way to drive, she'll drive every time. I bet you'd drive across the Atlantic, if you could, yes?" She raised her eyebrows at me and grinned.

"I think it's because every time I have a good flight and think, 'that wasn't so bad,' the very next flight is a disaster. I've been on planes when an engine went out, when lightning hit, and when turbulence was so wild that the stewardess slid down the aisle on her stomach holding the coffee pot in front of her. Pilots for Texas International, really 'Tinker Toy Airline,' are Confederate Air Force stunt pilots on weekends. I think they practice on their passenger flights during the week. I'm *entitled* to be scared of planes." *Why do I feel the need to defend myself?*

DeeDee patted my hand and whispered, "It's okay. I'm scared of some things, too." I hoped my *one* fear of flying wasn't equivalent to her *multiple* fears of living, but then again, who knows? It was nice to have someone on my side, at least.

Gert leaned forward with her elbow on the seat in front of her and said, "You know, of course, that the statistics for air fatalities are much lower than that of cars?"

"Oh, don't get mathematical on me. I know what I know, and airplanes don't like me much. Your statistics mean nothing."

Cathie laughed raucously. "Here we are flying in smooth weather over the lovely green continent of Europe, and you won't even look down. Tell me your worst experience, and I'll explain how it couldn't have been that bad. You're fearless otherwise."

I swallowed hard. "My worst?" *So many to choose from.* "My first ever flight stopped in Shannon, Ireland. Taxiing out, there was this loud sound under me, like the bouncing of a basketball, so I asked the people around me to listen. Soon everyone was screaming at the stewardess that something was wrong. She bent over my seat and hissed at me, 'It's nothing, just Leprechauns in the gas tank.' Then, she *ran* up the aisle to the pilot's deck, yelled through the doorway, and the plane came to a whiplash halt. After mechanics swarmed over the plane, we taxied out again an hour later. The noise was gone. The stewardess came to my seat, flashed her saccharine smile, and cooed, 'See, I told you it was nothing at all.' I've never trusted a flight crew since. They can smile and lie at the same time. Most of us can do only one or the other."

"Well, said Gert, "I can see why she wouldn't tell *you* the truth because you panicked all the people sitting around you. They're trained not to rile up the passengers. Was that the worst?"

"Probably not. In a small, charter plane, a strong wind forced the pilot to abort three landings. The plane kept blowing across the tarmac sidewise almost dragging one wing. I asked him if we could go someplace else to land, and he said, 'I don't have enough gas, so this next pass will make us or break us.' I wanted to get out and walk, but he didn't offer me that choice."

Even DeeDee was laughing by this time, as all three tried to talk me out of what I already *knew* to be true. Gert nudged me and said, "I'm not convinced. Go on." She actually snickered. I could see they were playing, but maybe I could really *convince* them.

"You've never been on a flight when you *knew* there was trouble," I said, by way of justification. "A Delta pilot did a normal touch down in Atlanta, then he yelled, 'Oh Shit!' and gunned the engines to shiver us back up into the sky again. His mike was on! The plane shook with the effort to get up, and this lady next to me broke out her holy water, threw it over her seatmates, and announced in stentorian tones, 'It's time we all begin to pray.'

"I told her, 'Lady, you're late! The time for prayer was back there when the pilot said 'Oh, Shit.' I have enough pilot buddies to know those are always the last two words on any black box flight recorder after a crash." She thought I was crazy, but I was too busy holding up the plane by the armrests to worry about what she thought.

"The pilot, once he had us back around in the emergency

traffic pattern, still shaking like the fuselage would fall apart, announced, 'Ladies and gentlemen, I'm so sorry for my language back there. But another airliner crossed our runway right after we touched down, and we narrowly missed a collision. I had to get us up in the air over the top of the other plane. Now we're going back around and give this airport *one more try*, and if they don't do it right, we're going someplace else!' He was greeted with cheers from frightened passengers. We made the six-o-clock news with that landing, takeoff, and landing again."

"Well," admitted Gert, "maybe you *do* have a right to worry." But then she choked up giggling and had to wipe the tears of laughter away.

I didn't think my airplane mishaps were funny. I thought they proved my point.

But DeeDee saw them as funny, too. She said between fits of laughter, "I've never had anything like that happen on *my* flights. You need me around to be your good luck charm."

"You've only flown twice," said Cathie. "It might be just as likely that Megan's bad luck with airplanes, and everything else, could rub off on you."

DeeDee raised her eyebrows. "Oh, no! It couldn't! Nothing *ever* happens to me!"

"Look," I said, trying to be calm, since they just didn't *know* how planes *really* were, "because of my history of flight, I know if this flight to Rome goes smoothly, it's because there's some other catastrophe waiting for me on the next trip. Airplanes are just like my car, Bosco—they have a mind of their own."

Cathie and Gert were hooting in derision, but by that time, the flight was practically over, and I could see they still didn't take me seriously. They thought planes were safe. *Poor fools.*

"I don't like the reality, but there it is. I can hide my fear by sitting next to someone who's even more frightened than me. It always works better if someone *else* needs me to be calm."

"That's true," DeeDee said, nodding. "Megan is good at calming *other* people, even if I see her knees shaking now that we're getting ready to land." Again, she patted my hand and said,

"You always keep me calm when I'm scared."

"Thank you--I guess." I sighed with resignation.

"And thank you," said Cathie, "for entertaining us on our flight to Rome. Let's enjoy."

Upon our arrival, we picked up a rental car. "If it were any smaller, it would be a Mo-ped," I noted.

"I'm scared of wild Italian drivers I've heard about, so I'm not driving," Cathie said.

Gert gave me a wicked smirk. "You *only* have disasters in the air, Megan, so you'll be fine on the ground, won't you?"

Threading our way through downtown Rome, I noticed gazillions of confusing traffic circles where drivers honked in a continuous din. They made five lanes of traffic where only two lanes existed by going up and over medians and curbs to get ahead of other cars. It was a free-for-all. Such mundane things as speed limits seemed to be completely ignored.

DeeDee crouched on the floorboards of the back seat and squealed, "I can't look." Every time she heard the screech of brakes, she crossed herself and vowed in a squeaky voice, "Mother Mary, I'll never go anywhere in Europe again."

A taxi jumped in front of another car and hooked fenders in front of us. Both screeched to a halt in the middle of the street, blocking our way. The drivers jumped to the hoods of their cars in and shouted Italian obscenities, shaking their fists at each other.

DeeDee raised her head to peer over the front seat and started crying. "They're going to kill each other. What if we're caught here when there's a murder? We'll have to be witnesses and then the Mafia would be after us? I can't even understand what they're saying to each other."

"That's *why* we couldn't be witnesses," said Cathie dryly, patting DeeDee's hand.

Thank you Cathie.

Miraculously, when the two actually wound up on one car hood and traded blows, surrounding cars backed and wheeled to go around. Apparently Italians didn't want to be witnesses to murder, either. We reached our Pension unscathed. I parked the car and swore we would walk everywhere from that point on. No one disagreed.

The Pension where Gert made reservations turned out to be a convent on St. Peters Square—conveniently located for most famous sites. Only statues in niches along the high, street-side walls broke its imposing, square shape. We entered the courtyard, noticing a graceful fountain in its center with no running water. But when we saw the Mother Superior hurrying down the hall toward us to answer our pull of the bell cord, Cathie whispered out of the corner of her mouth, "I bet she won't even let us inside. Gert, where did you find this place?"

"Well, it was cheap, but I didn't know it was religiously-run," Gert responded. "We'll probably set these nuns back a hundred years. Should we curtsey or what?"

We were close to hysterical giggles as the Mother Superior approached. She was taller than all of us by at least a foot, and she drew herself up to her full haughty grandeur.

"Are you ladies *sure* you have the right address?" she asked, with flashes from her dark eyes shooting right through us.

"I think so, Ma'am," said Gert. "We have reservations for the weekend."

"Who gave you this number?" the woman demanded. A thin wisp of facial hair over her upper lip quivered as she raised her nose, undoubtedly to consult with Heaven.

"International Tours and Travel made the reservation for us, Ma'am—ITT."

In a swirling flash of black, she turned, leaving the door open, and we followed her down the dark hallway. She opened a side door and said, looking down from above as though she were finding our whole group exceedingly distasteful, "You'll all have to share this room. We serve hard rolls and coffee only in the morning between six and eight--nothing else. The doors close at nine at night, and you'll have to pay now, because we'll be at mass when you leave on Sunday."

It was not exactly a welcome, and three of us exchanged

uncomfortable glances.

But DeeDee was oblivious. She stared wide-eyed and genuflected. She was bowled over that the Mother Superior, *herself*, had come to greet us, however unhappy the woman had obviously been to do so. "Such a great lady," DeeDee whispered.

The rest of us remained silent.

Cathie crept into the room, and we all followed. It was large, cold, Spartan, and probably left over from either from hundreds of years of nuns with impressions of their knee prints on the bare concrete floor, judging from its unevenness.

"These beds are more like folding camp cots," said Gert. "They'll probably be better for our souls, than for our spines."

One light bulb dangled from a frayed cord in the middle of a high ceiling.

"Should we ask Mother Superior where the bathrooms and showers are?" asked DeeDee.

"I'd rather not confront her again so soon," said Gert. "We'll find 'em somehow."

I ventured down the hall until I found an open door with the necessary, though ancient, plumbing, and informed the others.

We went out for a taste of Rome before it got dark. We didn't venture far. We were tired, it was getting late, and we were unsure about finding our convent again. So, we concentrated on the main plaza of Vatican City. Cathie told us how centuries of intrigue surrounded the Vatican, while DeeDee was entranced. "Just think," she said breathlessly. "The Holy Father, himself, will be on that balcony up there on Sunday. Wait 'til I tell Mama."

Gert looked at me and winked. "I'd hoped we'd left Mama behind on this trip."

St. Peter's Square, reveling in its historic, shadowy buildings, was larger than we had anticipated. But when we returned to our convent, we found Mother Superior waiting for us. She didn't look happy.

"I'll bet she has a cat-o-nine-tails for us coming in close to curfew," muttered Gert with a giggle. We tiptoed past the frowning and formidable lady while DeeDee was busy genuflecting. The woman only nodded her head in grudging acknowledgement, and disappeared in a swish of her full-skirted habit.

"I wonder if she ever smiles?" asked Cathie.

"She's probably one of those conspirators left over from the Inquisition," quipped Gert.

We took turns padding down the hall to the shower. It was green around the edges, so we wore our shower shoes--a necessary item on every trip, for it could hardly be said that we traveled first class on teachers' salaries.

On the hard cots, we giggled and told jokes until, one by one, we slept. But, the overhead light suddenly went on, and we all sat bolt upright in bed. There was DeeDee correcting a four-inch stack of student papers.

"What the blazes are you doing?" yelled Gert. "We're trying to get some sleep."

DeeDee sheepishly held up the papers she'd lugged in her suitcase. "I thought I could grade papers in our spare time."

"DeeDee," I said, as patiently as I could, "One does not *have* spare time when one has only three days to see Rome! One finishes one's papers before or after the trip."

She clutched the stack to her bosom. "I have to get them done," she said.

"But DeeDee," said Cathie, who taught ninth graders, "the rest of us need sleep. You needn't have brought them along. You can't possibly have that much work for little Kindergartners. That looks more like term papers for high-schoolers."

"But, I have to give every paper back to them when I get back to school."

Gert leaned up on her elbow and asked, "Why? What do

those little kids do with the papers once you give them back all corrected? They throw 'em away. They're just coloring papers."

DeeDee's eyes were clabbering up to churn again. I could see it coming. She silently stared from one of us to the others.

Three of us tried to go back to sleep with the big overhead light on. It was impossible. Cathie got up, stretching, yawning, and patting her tangled blonde curls. She walked over to DeeDee's cot, grabbed the whole stack of papers, dropped them in the wastebasket, and turned out the overhead light.

DeeDee was taken too unawares to do her usual tug-of-war. "But what will I tell them when we go back to school?" she wailed.

"Tell them the papers got stolen by Vatican spies, and let them tell stories about how they imagine it happened," said Gert. "Next trip, *if* there is one, plan better."

DeeDee cried herself to sleep, and we let her--no matter how much I wanted to run over and tell her everything would be all right. But the next morning, her mood was light, she was ready to go see Rome, and she didn't even look at the wastebasket.

"Maybe Mama was wrong about slacks," she admitted, as she slipped into a brown corduroy pair. "These *are* more comfortable for some things than a dress, aren't they?"

I looked to heaven with thanksgiving for this teensy disobedience to Mama. *Yes, DeeDee is coming along.*

We found the Coliseum draped in scaffolding for one of its many renovations, so we couldn't go in. I was disappointed not to be able to wander among its galleries imagining all the gallant gladiators who fought there for their very lives.

We visited the ruins of the Roman Senate, instead. Statues lined the ruins of what must have been wide corridors. Many heads were missing, or toes or noses broken off, but my imagination has always been a bit too vivid. I could almost hear those old Roman senators pronouncing great ideas into laws Western Civilization has internalized for centuries, and I envisioned their serenity in togas and crowns of olive or myrtle leaves. Why Caesar, Nero, all the famous Romans must have spoken here.

However, I got so tangled up in my reveries of times gone by, that the current time slipped away from me. Cicero had just warmed up his audience when I ignominiously tripped over a low wall of stone and tumbled into the ruins.

It was DeeDee who scrambled down to help me, calling, "Are you hurt?"

Gert and Cathie laughed. Cathie said, "There you go again, Megan. You need to look down before you roam around pontificating like a senator." Gert wiped tears from her eyes.

"Never you mind, 'Cornelia,'" whispered DeeDee. "They just don't understand. I could tell you weren't even *here*. You were way back in the old Roman Senate, weren't you?"

"Yeah, uh, I guess so. But, thank you for coming to my rescue...'Emily.'"

She grinned. I was beginning to like this woman, in spite of my initial misgivings. What she lacked in knowledge and fearlessness in the world, I lacked in grace and attention to detail. *Besides, did I mention that she makes killer lasagna?*

I climbed out of the old foundation ruin with only a skinned knee and elbow, and Gert stopped laughing long enough to get out band-aids she carried in her purse. "Whenever we travel with you, Megan, we know to bring along extra first-aid supplies."

I nodded, grateful for the aid, and wishing I could soak the offending knee in hot water.

"I'll carry band-aids, too, 'Cornelia,'" whispered 'Emily.'

All day we were on the run, not wanting to miss any of the grand sights--San Angelo's Castle with its angel gleaming in the sun atop its dome, museums with the marvelous works of DaVinci and Michelangelo, gigantic Roman arches and statues on every corner. Cathie often had her nose in the guidebook as we walked, calling out historic facts for each place we visited. Though the antiquities of Rome kept us enthralled, picking up trash seemed not to be a high priority with modern-day Italians, since garbage was scattered literally everywhere—on streets, in gutters, lying on ledges even right by the lovely old palace and museum buildings.

"We'll just have to enjoy the old Rome and ignore the

new," said Cathie, trying to be charitable about the smelly trash washing against the shore under centuries-old stone bridges.

We struggled with street crossings, narrowly missing getting hit, even when we had the green light in our favor. As the evening rush hour came, cars streaked every which way and crossed each other's path with dizzying speeds.

"Demolition Derby," said Gert. "Did the guide book say how a pedestrian should cross a boulevard among maniacs?"

Cathie shook her head.

"This is scarier than riding in that rental car," said DeeDee, after I yanked her out of the path of a truck by the back of her new sweater. *Good thing we'd trashed the purple dress, she'd have been a goner for sure!* Brakes screeched, narrowly missing Cathie and two taxis skidded sideways to avoid both each other and Gert. We clambered back to the safety of our curb. But a silver gray sports car whizzed up over the curb to pass a truck, and we jumped out of the way. I clung to the lamppost, looking back frantically to see if the others had escaped, too.

"Let's try to get over there," said Cathie, pointing. "I think I see a restaurant." However, when we waited for a green light in our direction and ventured across the boulevard, people shook their fists at us from their car windows, and we again ran back. "What do you think we're doing wrong?" Cathie asked. "Not one car stopped for us."

"Obviously there's no safety in numbers, either" said Gert. "Maybe we can squeak through one at a time. That way, one of us *might* survive to bury the others."

DeeDee was crying again. "What shall we do?"

"We don't cry about it, DeeDee. That's one thing we *don't* do. Now hush," I told her.

A young man in a uniform of some kind approached us confidently and asked in near perfect English, "My name is Carlo. May I show you how to cross?"

I caught Cathie taking his measurements with her eyes. "Thank you," she said. "We've been trying, but these people don't seem to pay attention to red lights."

"Red lights don't mean to stop--only to be cautious—a suggestion, not a law. Let me show you," he said. His smile revealed sparkling white teeth, and Cathie moved in closer. "I can show you the secret to getting across."

"Are you a policeman?" Gert was always straightforward, though not always tactful.

The young man chuckled. "Yes, all men must perform two years of government service, some of us assigned to the Italian military, and some to the constabulary."

"Where did you learn English?" Cathie asked. She was actually batting her eyes at him.

"The university in Milano. I hope to go to the United States one day to see New York."

"Try Los Angeles too, while you're at it," I told him.

"Could I be a movie star in Hollywood?"

"I don't know, but if you can rescue us, now, I'd return the favor and introduce you around. But in L.A. the traffic lights *do* mean something. A car *must* stop for a pedestrian."

The young man grinned revealing dimples in his cheeks and chin. "That would take all the fun out of it, now wouldn't it? This is a game both the drivers and the pedestrians share."

"You're shamefully forward," DeeDee whispered. "We don't even know this man."

"DeeDee, honestly! He's Carlo. Would you rather stand on this corner all night?"

"But...."

"But nothing! Shh!"

"Here, let me show you how it's done." Carlo walked across the street without looking left or right or waiting for a green light. Cars zipped in front or behind him, as I held my breath. But nothing touched him. At the other side of the broad boulevard, he waved and motioned for us to follow. I tried for about six feet and had to jump back up on the curb. Gert caught my sleeve to keep me from falling. "No time to have accidents," she admonished.

Carlo returned, again looking neither left nor right, and on a red light, too. "You walk straight ahead at an even pace. You must not vary your pace, or someone will hit you."

"But about the light…."

"Forget the light…and whatever you do, don't look at cars coming from any side. That's the worst thing you can do."

"I don't see why. That doesn't make any sense," I said.

The young man smiled again. "You Amis, you Americans, always need a reason. Just join in the fun. If you look at the traffic, you'll either stop, or speed up, and you'll get hit. The drivers are good at gauging distances. They will miss you either in the front or in the back, but they *won't* stop."

We tried, but the temptation to look was too great. Americans are indoctrinated from toddler-hood to look both ways, and it was impossible not to peek. The young man laughed at our efforts. "You must trust me. Come, one of you." I stepped up beside him and set my pace to his. He kept repeating "don't look, don't look" as we walked. He did the same with each of the four of us until we were all safely on the other side. I was congratulating myself on arriving unscathed when our young friend said, "Now you must each go back alone."

I gasped, and DeeDee yelled out, "Oh, no!"

"Oh, yes!" Carlo said emphatically, shaking his finger at us. "You must look purposeful and confident to be able to play the game by yourself in Italy. Never show fear." He stood up tall and ballooned out his chest. "You must be the winner in the game."

He made us cross again and again until even DeeDee could do it, though her "confidence and purpose" took several trips longer with Carlo at her side saying, "Don't look. Stop peeking."

Finally, we all felt quite proud of ourselves, and Carlo felt like an old friend.

"Where can we find some good Italian pizza?" asked Gert. He searched our faces and lit up another of those sexy smiles. "I *could* take you where the pizza is exceptional. Follow me."

Three of us fell into step with Carlo, while DeeDee hung back until I reached out and grabbed her arm. "Come on, DeeDee."

"You don't know him, Megan. He might be a kidnapper."

"A kidnapper wouldn't have bothered teaching us how to

cross streets. He seems like a nice guy. And he promises pizza."

"Mama always said kidnappers promise candy." Her feet were still planted firmly.

"DeeDee" I said in exasperation. "That's for children. Mama isn't here! I'm hungry! Not one more word!"

She followed silently, digging one hand deeply in her coat pocket and hugging her purse to her chest with the other.

We followed Carlo down a quaint alley and entered the back door of an antique building into a warm and homey kitchen. Wonderful smells rose from the oven, and even DeeDee smiled.

"This is my Mama's kitchen, ladies. Mama makes the best pizza in the whole world, and she makes it for my friends in the fire department and constabulary almost every night when we get off work. You'll not find pizza like *this* anywhere but here." His friends, six young men in various stages of uniform lounged around a table. "Everyone, these nice Ami ladies needing someone to rescue them crossing the streets, so I brought them here to share pizza with us." He leaned over to kiss his Mama on the forehead. She tweaked his cheek, saying something in Italian.

Surprisingly, it was DeeDee who returned the greeting and immediately bent over the pot of sauce simmering on the burner. Mama and DeeDee seemed to have some infinite intimacy at first sight. Soon Mama tied an apron around DeeDee's waist and had her ladling sauce on the dough while she placed pepperoni and sprinkled cheese on top. The rest of us met the young men, most of whom spoke no English, so we struggled with sign language.

Black pots hung from the ceiling of the dark, old-fashioned kitchen, along with strings of garlic and peppers. A hanging copper lamp spread its glow over a huge wooden table covered with red oilcloth. The young men brought folding chairs for us, while an old man by the chimney--we assumed he was Carlo's father--tamped his pipe and smiled and nodded in our direction. The old man caused a roar of laughter when he said something in Italian.

When Carlo translated his words, I'm afraid we all blushed. "He said, 'Carlo's Mama taught him to help little old ladies across the road, like a Boy Scout, but Carlo keeps helping pretty young ladies and bringing them home, too.'"

Though we didn't think of ourselves as "young or pretty" ladies, we had a wonderful evening eating pizza until we couldn't manage another bite, even with Mama coaxing "just one more slice" onto our plates. One young man, Antonio, played the accordion, and Papa pulled Cathie's hand to dance. We all wound up dancing, though what the dance was, I couldn't tell, but we were whisked into it anyway. DeeDee didn't dance, but she caught on to the Italian words and sang along, as though she had known them in some other life.

After a well-fed evening, thanks, and goodbyes, Papa leaned over to kiss Cathie on the cheek..."Molta buena," he said.

Mama smacked him playfully with the corner of her dishtowel and laughed until she shook. "Molto vieho," she said, jerking her thumb in Papa's direction.

Carlo rose to walk us back to our hotel, and the whole crew fell in beside us. DeeDee ran back to say something to Mama in Italian, and Mama hugged her. In the street, DeeDee mopped her eyes with her tissue, as the rest of us sang our way down the street.

"Mother Superior will be mad at us again," said Cathie. "It's past nine o'clock curfew.

"I don't care," said Gert. "This is a great evening to remember Rome, plus we now know how to properly cross an Italian boulevard."

I hung back a moment to ask DeeDee, "What did you say to Carlo's Mama?"

"I told her that she reminded me of my Italian Mama in Ithaca, and I missed my Mama."

I couldn't help it. I took DeeDee's arm tightly and pulled her up into the middle of this singing group as we approached the convent. We couldn't shush the young men serenading us as we entered, even though we'd hoped we could sneak in quietly.

No such luck! Mother Superior stood in the doorway with arms akimbo, her eyes again searching the heavens for guidance.

"It's past curfew, and you shall have no breakfast in the morning," she scolded. Her face twitched, reminding me suddenly of a rat with whiskers. She strode toward the young men and shooed them away as one would a gaggle of geese. Carlo gave her a slow salute, but we could hear them all singing more softly as they headed back to Mama and Papa's.

We tried to think of some excuse to give Mother Superior for our being late, but her stern countenance made us sure she saw us as nothing but "loose women" somehow "invading" her convent. Even DeeDee broke into giggles as we ran down the hall under Mother's stony glare.

"I love Rome," said DeeDee, spreading her arms to embrace the entire city as she lay on her cot. "Rome reminds me of home, yet it shows me all I've missed in the whole wide world."

She kept jabbering away until finally Cathie said, "Pipe down, DeeDee. Go to sleep."

DeeDee woke us in time to go wait for the Pope to appear on his balcony. Gert went with her, while Cathie and I tried to make our way to the Sistine Chapel. We felt like salmon swimming upstream. We must have been the only two Protestants in the city, since absolutely everyone else, millions of them it seemed, was making his or her way to Vatican Square for the blessing of the Pope. We quickly lost each other edging through the crowd, but found each other again in the chapel, which we had almost to ourselves at that hour.

What a joy to see this beautiful ceiling of Michelangelo's. It was a once in a lifetime moment, and we were awed with his sensitivity, his warmth of color, and his dedication in lying on his back for months on scaffolding to create this monumental work.

"I read Irving Stone's book, Cathie. You have to appreciate Michelangelo's philosophy of 'finding and freeing the soul *within* the stone, rather than shaping it to fit his perception.'"

"It looks like he's done the same with the Sistine Chapel's great open ceiling," said Cathie. "Like he found this work somewhere within himself. It's magnificent."

We were glad to have time to stand, breathing it all in and feeling the awe of centuries.

When we returned to the convent, we found DeeDee awed by seeing the Pope, as well.

"She took two rolls of film of his Holiness," Gert said, "but we were too far away, DeeDee. All you'll see of him is a pinpoint in a sea of humanity."

"I don't care," DeeDee said, with tears of joy in her eyes. "Wait until I tell Mama I saw the Pope. She'll be so pleased to have all these photos of him, no matter how far away."

After that exhilarating experience, it was almost anti-climatic that Mother Superior wasn't present to bid us "scarlet women" goodbye, the rental car started just fine, and the flight home was uneventful. I was so relieved that my dire predictions about flying home hadn't come true, that I decided maybe I'd been wrong. This flight to and from Rome hadn't been half bad. Or did that just mean that it was the *next* one waiting for me that would be catastrophic?

The really good news was how DeeDee had adapted to a real Italian family, had a good time in Rome, and had traveled with little problem with two other people. *There's hope for her, yet, I decided with relief.*

Chapter 5 - A Christmas to Remember

Both school and social activities went well for the next month. DeeDee wrote to her Mama every day, but Mama didn't invade her conversations quite so often.

We gathered in the teacher's lounge one afternoon after Thanksgiving. Our so-called "lounge" was tucked into an unused closet on the ground floor. It was, like everything else for Americans overseas, furnished with the 1950's overstuffed sofas and chairs recently re-upholstered in what someone in the Housing Office considered modern 70's--orange and avocado. Teachers defeated the room's depressing location and furnishings by adding colorful posters from Spain or Britain on its sad, ecru walls, last painted when Bismarck was in power. A pint-sized German refrigerator held our lunches and soft drinks.

About ten teachers relaxed over a Coke or Tab at recess and discussed the ski trip just completed over the four-day weekend. DeeDee was far too quiet. She had refused to "risk her life skiing," so I'd gone without her—a whole busload of laughing skiers—it doesn't get better than that. But her demeanor made me feel guilty for having left her. *Well, heck, she has her car, her apartment; she's a big girl and can go wherever she wants. It's not my fault if she sits home for the entire weekend, is it?* But I found myself promising that next time, I'd insist she go. *So much for my goal of getting her go with somebody--anybody, else--I still feel responsible.*

I broke into the recess chatter with a question. "Hey, as long as we're discussing trips, who's up for going to Jordan and Israel over Christmas vacation? I found this really neat tour."

Dead silence, but everyone stopped in their tracks.

"Good grief," erupted Sharon, a third grade teacher from Chicago. "There's a war going on down there. Aren't you following the headlines in *Stars and Stripes*? The Israelis and Arabs barely have a cease-fire, and fighting could erupt again at any moment." She took a sip of Coke and absently turned pages in her math textbook. In her mind, the subject was closed.

"But it's not a *declared* war," I countered. "ITT wouldn't offer a tour to a war zone."

"I don't think the great International Tours and Travel knows what it's doing anyway," said Sharon. "Remember when DeeDee planned that day trip to Rothenburg with ITT?"

DeeDee cringed. "Can't we forget about that one, please?" Grins erupted around the room, but no one said anything further about her most embarrassing fiasco.

"Why is Israel so important that you'd go with a war almost on?" Cathie asked.

"I've dreamed from when I was a little girl of being in Bethlehem on Christmas Eve," I said. "It's simply one of those things I want to do before I die."

Barbara laughed. "You've got a long time before you die, Megan. Why don't you at least wait until their war is over?"

"It might never be over, the way they see different sides of the same coin. And I really want to be at the manger in the Church of the Nativity on Christmas Eve."

"But Megan," chimed in Ruthie, "you'll miss the dance at the O'Club and the annual Christmas party at Seehof Palace. The guys are supposed to be in, unless the Soviets try something stupid at the last minute just to ruin our holidays." Ruthie grinned wickedly.

We all knew Ruthie had a handsome, combat engineering captain, Don, who was crazy about her, and she would not have missed a dance with him just to travel the world.

DeeDee was quiet still, and she didn't offer any advice.

"Okay, guys, who'll go with me?"

There was silence in the room, many shaking their heads at my "folly," until finally DeeDee lifted her hand. "I guess I could go with you, 'Cornelia,'…if you *really* want to go that much. I couldn't let you go to a place like that all alone."

Good old loyal DeeDee. I was beginning to appreciate her steadfastness, at least, or maybe she just didn't want me to go anywhere without her. I felt sorry about the ski trip.

"Great, I'll order the tickets after school today. Does anyone else want to go?"

All shook their heads as Barbara said, "Okay, so you're *both* crazy. But, you two haven't explained this 'Cornelia and Emily' business, you know. Can you let us in on the joke?"

I looked quickly at DeeDee, and she smiled, realizing she had slipped up again, while I almost had not noticed, it was getting so "normal."

"It's just old names we borrowed from a book about travel," I said. "We both like to travel."

DeeDee's smile crinkled.

During the weeks before our trip, one person after another tried to talk us out of going. Jimmy, asked me not to go, saying it was too big a risk. I asked him to go along, instead. He couldn't leave his unit, since the Soviets had a penchant for trying to find our troops asleep at the switch, usually over holidays.

"Megan, you know with my security clearance, I can't travel to either Soviet or Middle Eastern countries." I knew that, but I thought maybe he could get some special dispensation. He couldn't.

I 'd resisted any permanent commitments from any of the nice officers that were part of our group of singles. It had taken me a long time to start dating again after what happened. I guess it was a trust issue. I'd had some bumps in the romantic road and had little desire to try again. Men were great to go out with, play volleyball with, ski with, debate with, or entertain for dinner, but I was still skittish about the dating game. It had changed a lot during the late 1960's and early 70's. That's all it seemed to be now...a game...for a lot of people, anyway.

But Jimmy was a nice guy, and I liked him a lot. If I could trust anyone, it might eventually be him, but I was in no hurry to trust *anyone* again. It could turn excruciatingly painful in just one heartbeat--or one gunshot—or one lie.

At my urging, Jimmy had arranged a couple of blind double dates with his friends for DeeDee. I really thought it would do her good to have male friends besides her over-protective brothers. But he whispered to me one night at dinner that DeeDee made the guys nervous.

"Holy cow! She's so serious it's enough to scare *any* of the guys," he said. "When they come in to base, they want to dance and play and meet girlfriends. But weddings and baby talk doesn't cut it. They break and run like rabbits."

"I know you're right," I said. "But I haven't found a tactful way to clue in DeeDee in that you all have enough to worry about without being afraid some girl's going to take you too seriously."

"You know I don't mean you, Megan."

I ignored his hint. "You can't persuade DeeDee much. She scares so easily. After all, she's come a long way since I picked her up at Frankfurt in August."

"She relies too much on you for everything."

"I know. Sometimes I feel tempted to tell her something really weird, just to see if she'll say, 'Yes, Megan.' You know, something like the moon having green men and green cheese."

"But you stifle those inclinations, don't you?" Jimmy had me figured out.

"I'd hate to force her into anything too soon. I just hope I can get around to the subject naturally, before anything happens to make her take some guy too seriously and get hurt."

Jimmy took my hand in his. "Like you were?"

I nodded. It was a sore subject. "But heck, I bounce, remember?"

He smiled, and squeezed my hand. "That's my girl."

So, Jimmy drove DeeDee and me to the airport to catch our flight to Amman, Jordan, and refrained from kissing me goodbye in front of DeeDee. "We can't set her a bad example, now, can we?" he whispered while getting my bag. "Mama might be watching." We both grinned.

Soon we were aloft with no problems? I had, as always, assumed something drastic would happen. But I didn't want to worry DeeDee beforehand. When we could see the runway lights of Amman, Jordan, I was amazed that the airport and the city were actually on a high plateau, surrounded by desert down on the plains. *How does the pilot land on such a tiny spot of land?* But we circled in for a perfect landing. *Disaster is just waiting for next time; I know it.*

"Inshallah" was the first word we learned. It means more or less "when Allah wills" or "whenever." Nothing was ever on time, and no one seemed to worry about it. Of sixteen flights listed for departure, fifteen were "delayed." Though our plane had arrived late, the bus ordered for our tour group had not materialized. Even when it finally arrived, and we had been carefully searched right down to our paperwork before getting on, the porters hired to load all the luggage underneath just stopped working mid task, while we sat on the bus with the motor running. After two hours of waiting, a couple of the guys from our tour of about forty, thought they could speed up the process by loading the rest of the luggage themselves. They got off and loaded perhaps three bags, when the guards appeared, fuming.

"Now, everyone's luggage must be inspected again," one said. We had to get off the bus, reclaim our bags, and repeat the whole search process. The guys who thought they could make things go faster, actually cost us another two hours. Finally, over five hours late, we arrived at Amman's ritziest hotel, The Grande Palace. On second thought, maybe it was the *only* hotel.

In spite of our late arrival, champagne greeted us in the western-style hotel. The lobby's high ceiling was gilded, and its walls exposed exotic paintings of ladies in unusual poses, draped in a myriad of silk scarves, and little else—certainly not a burka. We were in an Islamic country, yet the staff had tried hard to welcome us for the Christian holiday. They had no fir trees, but they created a Christmas "tree" of swooping upside-down gladiolas with a tinfoil star on top, and little bags of almonds as presents. It was quite festive, and we genuinely appreciated their kind gesture. The hotel's host said he considered our trip as our "pilgrimage" to a holy place, much as they each dreamed of going to their own holy places in Mecca and Medina.

We soon found out two things of importance. First, they had somehow lost our luggage and we must "be patient." How they managed that when they were loaded on the *same* bus was a mystery. Second, on our busy itinerary for the next eight days, I realized we would be leaving for the "lost" city of Petra early the very next morning.

"DeeDee, let's go downtown to look around this evening."

"You heard the tour guide's dire predictions of exotic diseases waiting outside the hotel."

"But this will be our only night in Amman. Come on, 'Emily.' I want to see at least some of the city. Let's eat downtown and do a little exploring. We'll be back here before it's late."

She shook her head vehemently. "Please don't go. Stay here in the hotel where it's safe, and drink tea and eat hard-boiled eggs with me, like Mama says. You take too many risks, and you'll get raped or kidnapped or get sick eating down there."

It was the "...like Mama says," that convinced me to leave in spite of DeeDee's protests.

I wasn't about to miss Amman, so I bid DeeDee a rather cool good night and tripped across the street--literally of course, falling off the curb--toward the gate of King Hussein's Palace. Every house had what looked like a fifty-gallon tank on the roof filled with water. Apparently sun on the roof brought the residents warm water by gravity. I thought it a clever idea, though the houses themselves were certainly primitive. Some were little more than caves, and the occupants sat out front in the evening. These homes marched up and down the hilly city, and were practically invisible, melding into the rock piles of mud brown, from any distance at all. Though much building was taking place, leftover building materials were not carted away, so things still looked cluttered, with no landscaping to soften the dinginess.

In front of the palace fence was a large sign in English that said, "Bus Stop." A solitary camel was tied to the bus stop pole. I fervently hoped he--*no* doubt it was a he--wasn't the "bus." He didn't bother me, and I didn't bother him. I waited, but though several Jordanians joined me under the sign, no bus appeared.

Finally, a rusty, bedraggled auto slowed, and all these people climbed in, hanging out doors and windows like a bunch of Keystone Cops. Bewildered, I stood still under the sign. Then, a portly man in the front seat with a very black, curly beard, said to me in broken English, "You wait for bus?" When I nodded, he said, "This it. Come."

With some trepidation, I approached the overcrowded vehicle and said, "There isn't room. I'll wait for the next one, thank you."

"No be next one. Get in." With that, the bearded man opened the front door and motioned me into his lap.

I gasped, not sure what I should do, but he kept patting his lap and saying, "Last bus." I held my breath, hoping I was not too heavy, and climbed in. The ride was hair-raising. Jordanians drive with their horns, as though everyone should "…get out of my way, beep beep." The driver simultaneously ground gears and gunned the motor, until I wasn't sure how the rust bucket held together. I quickly realized it wasn't held together by any suspension system, because my hipbones collided with the gentleman's thighbones underneath me with every bounce. The wide boulevards near the King's Palace and Western-style hotel soon gave way to narrow alleys with cobblestones, and then to packed dirt. The houses went from mansions of international ambassadors to the squalid, smelly huts of the market place.

When we reached the souk area, I climbed out the door as others climbed out windows. The gentleman who had kindly lent me his lap said, "Our buses out of condition. Never run on time. So when car passes heading downtown, everybody gets in for ride."

"What do I pay him?"

"A small coin, about fifteen cents' worth, he'll be happy."

I offered the coin to the driver. He smiled and drove away. I turned to see that we were in the middle of a huge vendor area, a souk, or Middle Eastern market place, with myriads of richly colored silks and cottons drying overhead in the limited space between second story buildings. The smells of exotic spices almost covered the stench of open sewers. One street corner held at least five gold merchants, and I wondered why they would all be bunched together. In America, they would each want to have an exclusive shopping area to themselves.

As though he had read my mind, my exotic benefactor said, "Silks together, all gold merchants, all banks, et cetera. You find what you want easy this way." He smiled. "I'm Mamoud, pharmacist at university hospital, night shift. On lunch hour." He pointed at a corner opposite. When you ready go back hotel, stand on corner. Some will stop. Give him coin, and be hotel safe again. In meantime," he said, "would like me show you how to buy?"

I was so overwhelmed by the melodic sounds of bargaining in the narrow, congested streets, that I just nodded. Mamoud led me into the first open air stand where I wanted to buy one of those loosely wrapped-around headpieces the Arabs wear, a red and white military Kaffeyah with a black Ainue band holding it in place. I thought a military man like Jimmy would like a military headpiece from another country, and these were really quite dashing, like Lawrence of Arabia. Mamoud wore a black and white Kaffeyeh, so I knew he was a civilian.

"Don't pay price on ticket," said Mamoud. "It's part of game for to bargain over cup of tea until everybody happy." He took my arm and escorted me up to the counter full of woven, red-checked Kaffeyahs.

The proprietor gave a price, but Mamoud shook his head. The man offered us tea and gave a new price. Fifteen minutes, many prices, and a cup of tea later, I left the shop with my Kaffeyeh for what I thought was a good price, and the proprietor was bowing and smiling me to the door, so I guess he thought he'd gotten a fair price as well. Now, I'd seen games in both Rome and Amman. I wondered if we Americans played any games with foreigners.

"That's how it's done, lady." Mamoud said. "I used up time, so must go back to night job at hospital. I wish you splendid stay in my country." Mamoud bowed. I bowed, and he went to stand on the opposite corner. I felt bad that he had missed dinner.

I walked around the souk enjoying the singsong of another

language, and the exotic colors and smells. The scene needed to be a painting, and I hungered for a photo, but I hadn't brought my camera. The little caves were apparently storage, so the vendors displayed their wares out in the narrow street. Nothing was refrigerated or covered. A side of beef hung from hooks covered with rainbow colors and flies. Live chickens were tethered underfoot.

One man advertised "Genuine Sheepskin Jackets While You Wait." He cut up the sheepskins from drying racks and stitched them up on an old treadle sewing machine right in the street. Huge open burlap sacks sat in the spice vendor's booth bursting with pungent aromas of cinnamon and cloves and the harsher scent of curry. Young boys shouted everywhere in the marketplace balancing huge copper trays of cakes or breads on their heads. They sold these for pennies.

My hunger awoke with the scent of roasting lamb, and I followed my nose to an open rack on a spit. The vender was making Cherma, shaving the lamb off into an open Pita bread. My stomach wouldn't wait longer. I pointed at the lamb and held out my hand with coins. The vender smiled, fixed me a really large helping, and chose a Jordanian coin.

I looked around and suddenly realized two things. First, *no one* on the street was eating outside like we would a hot dog on 3rd Avenue at home. There had to be someplace people took their food to eat it, and I felt a little embarrassed to realize I had this big Pita and lamb roll in my hands and was standing out on the street. The second thing I noticed was that there were *no* other women anywhere. It was *all* men. I was an outsider, stared at, and not particularly approved of, judging from the eyes of men on the street. I pulled my silk scarf up to cover my hair, so I wouldn't offend anyone, though I feared I already had done so, just by being a woman.

I glanced at the vender and motioned to my Cherma with a question in my eyes. He sensed my predicament and pointed down a long dark hall to a room at the end with a makeshift light bulb dangling on its cord from the ceiling.

I was reluctant to go down that dark hallway, yet I was hungry and even more reluctant to stand on the street trying to cram this delicacy into my mouth with no napkin or place to sit, and no other females, so I followed his gesture down the hallway toward the light.

In the wider room at the end of the hall, I saw walls cracked for so long that plants forced their tendrils through, and ceiling beams that must have leaked, had it been raining. Mold, body odor, and cooking smells blended together until they were no longer individually significant. Men wearing the traditional black checked Kafeyehs filled four of the five wobbly wooden tables, drinking, gambling, and eating. They all stopped and stared as I entered. I wasn't sure what to do. Should I flee? Should I sit?

The choice was made for me, as the proprietor came in from the kitchen smiling and bowing me to the empty table. He flipped out a red embroidered tablecloth and settled it on my table. I sat, gratefully, not sure what I should do next.

While I was thinking, I became acutely aware that all the men in the room were still staring at me. *Am I that much of an oddity?* I wished I'd dragged DeeDee along with me, whether she wanted to come or not. *I wondered if I'd blundered into a bad situation, again?*

When in doubt, smile. So I smiled and nodded. They returned the nod, but not the smile. In the meantime, my host held up his hands with fingers spread stiffly to punctuate his words. "Wait, wait." I froze in place. He ran to the kitchen and came back with a plate and knife and fork, obviously not used often, since all the others ate with their hands, dipping their right hand into a common bowl of what appeared to be rice and lamb bones. I had read somewhere about what they did with their left hands, and the prospect didn't intrigue me, so I just smiled and nodded my thanks to the proprietor.

But he was again saying, "Wait, Wait," so I hung in mid air with half a bite of my Cherma and waited. He returned with a glass of lukewarm tap water. "America, drink water," he said, smiling and bowing again.

How does he know I'm American?

What could I do? I knew I wasn't supposed to drink the water in a place like this, but I felt the weight of American Presbyterian and Jordanian Islamic friendship on trial. If I refused to drink the water, would they hate me for somehow insulting their country and their heritage?

It was risking all the nasty diseases available in underdeveloped countries on a weak Westerner's tummy, but it simply was not the time to single-handedly sever American-Jordanian relations by being the Ugly American in response to their kind hospitality.

I drank the water!

I smiled as though it was really good, and nodded to the men who leaned forward for my reaction. As I drained the glass, they smiled and nodded. I ate my lamb, nodding and smiling like an idiotic bobble-headed doll. *Oh well, whatever damage could be done to my insides, it was done by now, all in the name of international relations. Kissenger should be proud of me.*

I had paid for my feast outside, but I felt guilty for not ordering something in here, too. This man might be a different vender, and I sensed they all earned very little. I asked for a salad.

The man brought me a plate of thinly sliced, red radishes at least three to four inches in diameter. I think my eyes were the size of DeeDee's. I feared hot radishes, but I realized I'd have to eat them. I'd need more water, for sure, so I held up my glass.

To my surprise, the radishes were sweet, not hot at all, crisp and crunchy, quite delicious, in fact. I ate the plateful even though my jaws were pained from all the nodding and smiling. When I tried to pay for the salad, the proprietor pushed away my money and continued to bow. I stood and bowed, He bowed, and I bowed, wondering how this could ever end, as I shuffled my way toward the door. But once again he held up his hands. "Wait, Wait!" and he disappeared.

He returned carrying at least a peck-sized glassine bag of more sliced radishes as a present. I couldn't refuse without seeming as though I hadn't liked my "salad," so I accepted with my thanks, which I hoped he understood. All the men in the room nodded their approval and we were back to the nodding and bowing routine until I could finally work my way to the door and retreat back down that long hallway to the street.

It was dark outside. Had I really been in the little cafe that long? I felt a shiver of anxiety, being on the street with only men, and all alone. But I smiled the fear away, crossed the street, and stood on the corner Mamoud had indicated. Within fifteen minutes, five more people joined me. Again, I was the only female, but after their immediate scowl of disapproval, they ignored me. I pulled my scarf over my hair more firmly. A car stopped, we all crowded in, and the driver took us up the hill to our original bus stop for the small coin, beeping all the way. One could almost imagine that the horn was the power source for the vehicle.

It was almost ten, and I felt a bit guilty for leaving DeeDee that long. I thought she might be frightened, alone in a strange country with people she didn't know yet. But when I entered the hotel lobby, there was quite a hubbub. I couldn't find either DeeDee or our tour leader to inquire what was going on. I snagged one of the women from our tour group and asked where everyone was. In the confusion, management, maids, and clerks all were running from place to place.

"They're all sick," she said, in a heavy French accent. "Me, too."

"Sick? Everybody?"

She nodded. "The doctor is making rounds of all the rooms now. I need to lie down again." She scurried across the polished granite floor, holding her stomach with one hand and gagging into a handkerchief with the other.

I was determined to find DeeDee in case she was among those stricken. I didn't mess with the gilded old birdcage elevator but raced up the stairs. I found her moaning in bed in our darkened room. She had an ice pack on her head, and a bedpan conveniently by her side.

"The nurse put it there in case I puke again," she wailed. "I wish Mama was here."

The tears, of course, followed. I took her shaking hand and said, "It's okay, DeeDee, I'm here with you, instead. You'll be all right by morning."

Her face was chalky white, and her movements were jerky as she covered her eyes to the nightlight I turned on.

"But, you stayed behind so you could have your nice, safe, hard-boiled eggs and tea," I said. "What happened? Did everybody get sick from the food in the hotel?"

She rolled over slightly and groaned at the effort. "I don't know. I did have a little wine, but it came from a bottle, so I thought it safe--you know, to wash down the hard-boiled eggs."

At the mere mention of food, I had to hold the bedpan while she upchucked again. I cleaned up her face and the sheet with a damp washcloth.

"You'll get sick from going out to eat, too. Are you all right? I was afraid you'd be raped or kidnapped out there all alone. You take too many risks." Then she shook her finger at me in accusation. "You didn't drink the water, did you?"

"Yes, I drank the water, but I'm not sick. *You're* the one who's tossing your cookies."

DeeDee struggled up on her elbow, looking me over as though I should suddenly turn green. She finally sighed, and said, "Maybe this hard boiled eggs and tea business is the *only* thing Mama is wrong about. Do you think?"

I couldn't help my grin, and I couldn't wipe it off my face even as I had to hold the bedpan for her again.

It was pretty ironic. I, the trouble-prone, drank the water, yet all the careful ones got sick.

Chapter 6 - The Mystery of Petra

I was so anxious to go see the fabled city of Petra the next day that I woke DeeDee early to be sure she would be navigable. She had been up much of the night with multiple trips to the WC. She groaned and rolled over. "How can you get so excited about a pile of pink rock?"

"But DeeDee, this city was lost to the outside world for centuries and only recently discovered again. Don't you want to see a lost city?"

"Not necessarily. If you say it's been found, that's good enough for me." She put her pillow over her head. I could tell she was not fully awake, because usually she was amiable.

"Come on. I know you feel bad, but you'll feel much better once you're up and fed."

"No food!"

"Oh, come on 'Emily.' We're to be on the bus by 0700."

She sighed and responded by swinging her legs over the side of the luxurious hotel bed, accidentally shoving the bedpan out on the floor with a clatter. "Oh, Megan, I didn't mean that to happen." She covered her face as I picked up the offending vessel and cleaned it in the bathroom.

We were on the bus by 0700, with DeeDee holding her barf bag nervously in her lap. "I still feel a little shaky," she explained.

Three people were too sick to move, so the tour guide had decided they would stay over another day, skip Petra, and catch up with us again in Jerusalem.

The hotel packed box lunches with juice, since there would be no facilities available once we left the Aqaba Road.

Getting into the seat, I somehow managed to klunk my head on the overhead shelf normally used for coats and bags. I could have sworn I'd ducked enough to miss it, but apparently I hadn't, as the klunk was loud, and people turned my way from all over the bus. I ducked further from embarrassment and slid into the seat, followed by DeeDee.

"Did you hurt your head, again?" She lifted my bangs to examine my forehead. "I think your depth perception is off, Megan. You always think things are further away than they are."

I pushed away her hand and rubbed the offending spot. "I'm fine. This isn't anything new. Don't make a fuss with all these people looking."

"I figured you'd feel nauseous from last night, too,"

"Nope, no nausea--nothing at all. I guess my little international escapade with the food and water of Amman did nothing to my tummy," I answered, hoping she would laugh.

It was a feeble laugh. "Thanks for not saying, 'I told you so,' about the eggs and tea."

I just smiled. We'd grown relatively comfortable together, so we both settled back for the ride out of Amman on narrow, bumpy, dirt roads passing through almost deserted regions of desert. Nomads moved alongside our route on camels. We passed numerous Bedouin camps, with tents made of black woven blankets. They lived much the same as they had 3000 years ago, as herders. They made a greasewood brush enclosure, put their sheep, goats, camels or donkeys inside, set up their tent near a water source, and they were "at home." It fell to the children to take the animals out to graze. I thought of the child-shepherds who had "watched their flocks by night" in the time of Christ, and I was even more excited to see the manger at Bethlehem.

"Many Palestinians live in primitive camps along the desert road, fed and tended medically by the U.N," our guide said. "Though it was hoped they would assimilate into the general Jordanian population, most chose not to. They want to keep their refugee status, hoping to go 'home' someday, though that home no longer exists."

We'd heard that it was from these refugee camps that terrorist gangs were recruited, like the Black September and PLO groups.

"Have some radishes, DeeDee," I offered. I'd brought along my big bag, not knowing what else to do with them since I couldn't eat any more, and they were too good to throw away. I passed them around to everyone on the bus, and several declared them helpful for calming their stomachs a bit. But, I still had well over half a bag left, and we were all about "radished out."

I'm sure the trip was unpleasant for the queasy passengers on the bus on rough roads with many twists and turns. The smell of barf bags wasn't exactly my favorite eau de cologne, either. The bus driver stopped frequently for the sick ones, though most "facilities" were "squatty potties," (a hole in the ground) dirty, seatless western toilets, or merely board fences, which the desperate passengers had to go behind in the wilderness.

DeeDee said forcefully, "I won't get *that* desperate!"

We also stopped twice at police stations, where our passports and papers were scrutinized before the bus was allowed to continue on.

"What does that mean, Megan? Do they think we might get lost and never return?"

"I think they're more worried about whether or not we might be Western reporters or spies." I said this jokingly, but DeeDee was apprehensive of almost everything. *We'll need some more work on that.* However, I kept reminding myself she was the only one willing to come at all, so she had already shown some spunk. I was beginning to have more confidence that the rest of her transformation to independence would come. *Besides, I had to laugh as I rubbed my swelling forehead; I certainly wasn't such a good catch for a friend, either.*

The tour guide approached our seats halfway down the aisle. He was Palestinian, and said proudly that he was a refugee in Jordan and had left his home in what was now Israel.

"I see that you are the only two people on this trip who work with the American military. All the rest are civilians from the United States or foreign nationals of European countries. We do not often get American military people in the Middle East as unprotected tourists."

DeeDee and I looked at each other, puzzled that he had singled us out.

"Does it matter?" I asked. *What does he mean by "unprotected"?*

He smiled, not exactly in a friendly manner, and said, "Perhaps not. We'll see."

"What does that mean?" asked DeeDee.

"Probably nothing," he said. He tapped his watch, and turned away to pick up his microphone and talk to the tourists.

"What do you think that was all about?" DeeDee asked.

"Darned if I know. Could be he just likes to make people uncomfortable or something."

We forgot about the incident quickly, though, listening to him give us the history of the area. We were surprised that a Palestinian Muslim should know so much Biblical history. But after all, Christians, Jews, and Muslims had all sprung from the loins of Abraham, so perhaps it was not so surprising. DeeDee mentioned that the guide kept looking at us more than the others as he spoke. There was nothing we could do about that, so I dismissed it from my mind.

"The present country of Jordan was one of the major Biblical lands," the guide announced over the microphone. People straightened up from hovering over their barf bags to listen. "Many old ruins connect to Biblical characters. East Jordan was part of Moab, Gilead, and Edom. Many of the wadis, or streams, feed the Jordan River. Petra's Biblical name is Sellah. Jordan contained many Biblical petty kingdoms, and Amman, our capital, is one of the highest points at over 4,000 feet above the Dead Sea and River Jordan that separates us from our enemy, Israel."

I was startled at the word "enemy," but I tried to keep an open mind.

DeeDee took notes, writing down everything the guide said. "Shorthand," she explained. "Mama made me learn it. She said it would come in handy some day, and now it has."

I wasn't surprised. I'd seen DeeDee take shorthand notes during a church sermon. The woman was addicted to note taking.

After Mt. Nemo and Moab, an area divided between Lot's sons, we passed a lush area of banana trees. But the homes were brush shelters, so the people still seemed poor and nomadic.

We entered an area like an endless gravel pit with large round humps and valleys, but something seemed wrong about the landscape. I watched out the window as the guide droned on.

"Jordan's first semi-benevolent ruler, Amir Abdullah, who became king after WWII," continued the guide, "brought Jordan new status as a country. He also started steps toward modernization. But the succession of young King Hussein brought more roads, tourist hotels, new buildings, and new crops to diversify this pastoral and semi-nomadic land."

Some of the electric or phone wires along the road disappeared into the tops of the mounds. A small stovepipe might stick up from a mound only about four inches. I suddenly realized these mounds were bunkers. At one point, a couple of tanks were visible in a pit just behind white rock piles and tunnels, and a few soldiers walked between them. We were out in the most barren section of the desert, yet here were their border fortifications. I kept up my vigil, trying to sort out how their fortified army worked. I figured Jimmy would be interested.

"We've seen these efforts to bring Jordan into the twentieth century," droned the guide. "Our people idolize the handsome King Hussein. New industries for export, like phosphate, have shored up our economy, since we have no oil. Excavations of ancient archeological sites are key to bringing tourists, which also increases the nation's prosperity. Petra is such an attraction."

As we drew closer to the border, I watched miles and miles of nothing, apparently a deserted desert—no cars, no people, no buildings, nothing. And then, suddenly on a little plateau were about twenty soldiers playing soccer. Where had they come from? They could only have come from underground, and I pointed out to DeeDee the incongruity of a soccer game, as though the players had drifted down from outer space. We both thought it odd, and sort of funny.

DeeDee finished her notes with a flourish, and we looked up to see our guide standing right beside our seat again.

"What are you writing?" he demanded, as though she were

doing something wrong.

"Just notes on what you were telling us about the history," she answered, beginning to shiver a bit, probably at his tone.

"Isn't taking notes all right in Jordan?" I asked. I'll admit my tone matched his.

He leaned over the seat and peered at DeeDee's notes. She held up the tablet.

"What code is that written in?" the guide demanded. His face grew red and bulbous.

This was beginning to get me mad. "What difference does it make?"

"You will not write in code here," he said, with a snarl. "We are hosting you in our country and you are not to spy on our defenses or…."

"It's only shorthand," said DeeDee. "If I read it back, you'd see that it is only what you…you….yourself, told us."

I could tell she was about to cry. When she stumbled over words, it was a bad sign. Guides did not usually accost travelers with such accusations, and DeeDee was shivering. It made me angry that he should intimidate her so.

"We don't care anything about your defenses," I said, "and we're hardly spies. If you worry that much about tourists taking notes, maybe you should not invite them to your country with all that advertising your tour company sends out."

With one more glare at DeeDee's tablet, he stalked back to the front of the bus.

She looked at me for an explanation, but I had none that made sense. "The guy's just paranoid. Stay calm," I said, making a face to make her laugh about the episode.

It worked. Soon she was pointing out the sites eagerly. We passed the looming ruins of Biblical towns like Jerash, more nomadic Beduoin camps, and Crusader castles. These settlements had occupied old trading routes and sheep-herding grounds over many centuries.

Something about the fortifications bothered me. Many were set up right among the Bedouin camps. If someone tried to bomb the fortifications, they would undoubtedly rain bombs down on the innocent Bedouins, as well. *Is this part of their strategy, so they can accuse Israel of atrocities*. I wondered if the Bedouins *chose* to be human shields, or were forced.

"Our excavations have found the deserts were home to many settlers back in the Stone Age," continued the guide over his microphone. "This proves that water must have been present for the people and animals in what is now arid desert."

DeeDee folded her hands in the air with glee, shaking them like a boxer acknowledging a TKO. "Wow! That reinforces the truth of the meandering of Moses and his people after their captivity in Egypt. All those years it had to be a true story, because now we know they would have had water sources," said DeeDee. "It's lovely to see confirmation of our Biblical stories when some nonbelievers try to say they couldn't possibly have happened."

When we saw Shobak and then Ain Musa, which we were told was actually the "spring of Moses," DeeDee's face shone in awe, and I wondered if my face showed the same excitement. It had become nice to share such moments.

"I know so little of the world," I said. "I thought I knew more from reading so much, but when we travel, I constantly see there's so much of it I haven't seen and haven't known."

"I've never been able to get away from my family to travel," lamented DeeDee. "And now, I'm here!" She hugged her arms to her body in glee.

"Perhaps your family was just being a little over-protective. As for my part, I've never had money to make it possible before I took this overseas job."

"Then we're overcoming obstacles even better than 'Cornelia and Emily,' aren't we?"

"I guess so. They never got out of Europe, either, and here we are in the Holy Land. So, we're on our own here…no 'Cornelia and Emily' to guide us."

"Then *we'll* be the real adventurers, won't we?" DeeDee's grin was wide.

"Yep…but we'll live up to their standards. Nothing can get

in the way of our having a fine time." I was aware that DeeDee's bubbling enthusiasm somehow lifted my spirits.

"We'll spend some time catching up in the post library when we get back to Bamberg," said DeeDee, and I was right there with her, already thinking what I'd like to research first.

When we approached the Wadi Sik near Petra, we stopped for an additional local guide to board our bus. The police arranged local guides to take over for our normal trip guide, and we were required to pay them extra.

"That's strange, isn't it?" I said. "Maybe that's the only job available in this remote spot."

"Or maybe that's the way the local police get their money, too." DeeDee sounded as though she thought it might be a bribe.

The new guide said something over the intercom, but his accent, plus his thick mustache and beard, made him almost impossible to understand. I caught the part about having to leave our bus at the entrance to the gorge of Es Sik and hire horses or pack mules.

"Did he say something about horses?" asked DeeDee.

"I think so, but I'm not sure."

"I can't ride a horse. Can you?"

"I haven't ridden since I was eight, but I liked it then. Don't worry." I tried to sound confident. "They probably have such gentle old nags that go so slow we'll be bored stiff. *I hope I remember how to ride. I won't be able to help DeeDee, if I can't stay on board myself.*

"Not me!" DeeDee squealed. "They can't be slow enough for me. I'd rather walk. I've never been on a horse in my life, and I don't intend to start now."

Her shoulders and lips were set stolidly in straight lines, with arms folded in defiance. I'd learned to spot that streak of stubbornness, so I kept silent awhile to let it wear down a little.

"Maybe the horses will be calm if I give them some of our radishes." I held up the remnants in their bag.

When we descended from the bus, glad for a little fresh air, we found the trail was between steep, almost overhanging, rock walls, much too rocky for DeeDee to walk to Petra. The slanted ground going down between the sheer walls was jumbled with rocks of the little pointy kind; nothing except what a horse or camel could navigate, single file. DeeDee gasped at the narrow, steeply descending trail. I could see her shaking increase while the guide briefed us.

"The trail is slick, steep, and no more than twelve feet at its widest point," he said. "In the old trading days, it needed only two men to guard the whole valley, since it's far too narrow for invaders to use without becoming trapped inside, single file, so they could be picked off one by one. We must watch the weather, as flash floods are common in this area. We lost four tourists a few years ago who did not leave in time and were caught in the canyon. Of course, you can see there is no way you could climb up the steep, straight walls. You'll notice we've added a little berm here at the entrance, hopefully, to protect against flooding, but you must follow the directions of your guide at all times." The guide added that DeeDee's only "non-horsy" option would be to wait at the bus for our return from the narrow canyon, as some elders chose to do.

"That's what I'll do, too, Megan. You go. I'll just wait here until you get back."

"DeeDee," I insisted. "This is supposed to be the most romantic experience in the world. The guidebook said so. It says this canyon is '...entering a dream-like, unreal world of soft, sand stone cliffs of varied and unusual colors and fantastic shapes, a gorge straight out of fairyland.' Doesn't that sound like fun?" *Maybe I looked too eager.*

She just stared at me. She had that "...you brought me here to die" look in her eyes, with her straight-lined mouth in a stubborn pout.

"DeeDee, please, this is just like the eggs and tea, something you must overcome. If you don't get on that horse and go with us, you'll have missed the mysterious city of Petra, and you'll never get another chance to see it again. This is a once in a lifetime event. Please just get on the horse. Think of what Emily would do?"

"Megan," she said with a quavering voice and those little jerky movements of her hands, "Mama said horses were dirty animals, and I'm really scared...."

"I don't want to hear about Mama again! Just get on the damned horse! We came this far to see one of the oldest trails in the whole world. Traders came through here with silks and spices over 10,000 years before Christ. Even the Queen of Sheba was here. If a queen could ride the damned horses, I'm sure you can." I didn't mention that the Queen of Sheba had probably ridden in a bejeweled palanquin carried by several of her slaves.

"But even if I *tried* to get on the horse, look at those steep rock walls. The guide said it's miles long, with the walls probably two hundred feet up, and they're so steep like they almost touch at the top. What if they should fall on us?"

"If they haven't fallen enough to stop trade in 12,000 years, they aren't gonna pick today to start falling."

She was near tears. "But you said everything always happens to you, and you haven't bumped into anything except on the bus today, so the rocks *could* fall, or the horse *might* slip, or I *might* fall off, just because *you're* along."

Good point, but I didn't want to admit that out loud. "Hey, 'Emily,' you're the one who wanted to travel with me, remember? Look at it this way. You always say nothing *ever* happens to you, so your good luck will be enough to keep us *both* safe, right?"

DeeDee smiled a little then, and said, "Oh, that's right, 'Cornelia.' I can help *you* this time."

Okay, so I lied. But I wasn't about to miss my chance to see Petra. Besides, I knew I could get her to do almost anything to keep from being left behind.

I asked our local guide if one of the Bedouins could lead DeeDee's horse, a mangy old animal that looked like he was long overdue to fall down and die. His gasps and heaves were alarming, especially since he didn't even have anyone on his back yet. The local guide motioned with more of an outward, upward swing of his dirty hand, than a "come here" inward motion westerners would use. One of the men came over. I held out the reins and pulled a little, hoping he would understand. Together, and tediously, we tried hoisting DeeDee up onto the horse.

"I can't, I can't," she kept repeating.

"You can too…'Emily,'" I insisted while pushing her up. I was already sweating.

"My feet don't have anyplace to go…and he's moving …help! Let me down."

We kept pushing and finally got her feet into the badly worn, nomad-style stirrups. I mounted my steed, one perhaps two weeks younger than hers, and I was careful to stay right beside her. She sat bolt upright, with those flying saucer eyes, holding the reins so tightly that the horse couldn't have gone forward had his life depended on it. Perhaps his life did, judging from the rolling of his eyes that matched DeeDee's, and his laid back ears. He sensed her terror.

I called to her to loosen up, but it was no use. She had a death grip on the reins, and the poor horse had no choice but to go backward. The handler grabbed the bridal to halt the horse, and snatched the reins out of DeeDee's hands, glaring at her forcefully enough that silence replaced her tears. From her terrorized expression, you'd have thought the man had a Bedouin knife between his teeth--and I admit he looked the part. Who knew what he carried under the sash that tied together his long robes? He wore the red Kaffeyeh of the warrior. But finally, a toothless grin parted his heavy beard and mustache, indicating he and DeeDee were ready. By this time, we were the last in a line of about twenty tourists who had decided to brave the ride.

"DeeDee," I said, as I slowed my horse next to hers.
"Relax, and let the poor animal breathe. Just hold on to the saddle
and this man will lead you. She didn't resist further, and our
Bedouin bandit look-alike motioned me to go in front of them as
the trail narrowed. I could see that the slippery, rocky path was
difficult for my horse, as he occasionally double clutched in a skid
to keep from falling. Perhaps that's why the Bedouins gave the old,
experienced horses to tourists. A young or skittish animal would
probably spook as the high, smooth mountain walls closed in on
us. We moved toward the dark cleft of the Siq with odd small
lurches of an unidentifiable gait.

The sliver of blue sky at the top was framed by towering
rock walls as the passage narrowed and slanted downward. A
primitive water delivery system was built into the wall, a channel
about twelve feet up, utilizing the natural gravity to flow water
down to the city of Petra. I could hear the water sloshing in the
channel, and marveled at the early builders who had thought of
everything. But, it soon became claustrophobic in the canyon. I
could imagine evil mythological centaurs and goblins hiding in
every little indentation along the walls. *Too much imagination
again, Megan.* The dark, narrow trail turned and twisted like a
maze, and it seemed a very long way through. I couldn't see the
road ahead more than a few feet or, as the Bedu said, any further
than the nether end of the next horse. At least that was the
translation I got. I have a hunch he was really more colorful than
that. My horse stumbled and caught himself on the slippery rocks
several times, and each time I braced myself for a fall, but he
apparently knew what he was doing, and I was just along for the
ride. I let him have his head, and hummed to his syncopated
rhythm. I turned as often as I could to see if DeeDee was all right.

Her horse, however, was definitely aware of her fear. In
spite of the handler pulling on his halter and DeeDee clinging
precariously to his saddle, awkwardly leaning first to one side and
then the other, the horse would periodically stop dead. No amount
of kicks by the handler would get him moving again.

I untied the bag of radishes I had on my belt, and reached

them back to the handler behind me. He tasted a few, then offered some to the horse, and this action was repeated all the way through the narrow walls. I began to wonder if feeding the animal so many of the radishes was a good idea, but the handler seemed in a hurry to get the horse to eat them all.

Soon the poor animal was sending those radishes right out his other end, to DeeDee's acute embarrassment. The Bedu kept feeding him, as that seemed to be the only way the horse would keep going—sort of primitive jet-propulsion. The acoustic walls echoed every burst.

Finally, the canyon leveled, opened out, and revealed the first of the fabled rose red monuments of Petra, the "lost" city. Everything was pure pink or blood red sandstone. While we blinked in the sudden bright sunlight, I caught my breath in awe, turning my head in a slow arc with hands shading my eyes. It was as beautiful as what I had read, and then some.

We had come upon the most perfectly preserved building-- the Khaznat Far'on, an ancient tomb of two stories, carved out of the rock wall with elaborate doorways. It had graceful pillars, gryphons in bas-relief, and classical artistic touches worthy of the ancient Greeks or Romans. Though it was thought to have been built by the Nabataeans, the guide said there was a period around 63 B.C. when Jordan had been more or less dependent upon Rome.

The trail continued past this marvelous carving and on to the cul-de-sac housing the high pink walls of the famous treasury building.

"Petra was inhabited back as far as 10,000 BC by several groups-- Nabataeans, Greeks, Romans, and Nomads," the guide said. "The buildings were carved into the face of sandstone cliffs, hidden in this desert cul-de-sac, a secret from the rest of the world." I was entranced by the mystery of it all.

"Can't you just imagine the camel caravans passing through this gorge with cargos of salt and spices and coming upon this beautiful city?" I called out to DeeDee. "I'll bet the highwaymen made quite a living by ambushing and plundering the traders in that canyon. There were so many good places to hide and...."

DeeDee just glared back at me.

A small group of Bedouins were resting in the open area, lying or sitting about campfires, with several dirty children running and playing among the mufti tents. DeeDee's horse handler acknowledged the men with a touch to his forehead. The caravan of horses stopped and folks dismounted, somewhat stiffly, all except DeeDee. She sat paralyzed in the saddle, braced as though she thought the old horse would bolt and run.

Both the handler and I tried to get her down off that horse. He was "too high,' he was "moving," he was "angry at her," though I think poor old nag was simply tired. DeeDee was afraid to let go, and in spite of our best efforts, she wound up sort of "hanging" from the small Bedouin saddle horn--which I knew was only meant to carry the nomadic rolled-up rug and the wooden "pillow" that stuck into the sand for sleeping in the desert— certainly not the full weight of a shell-shocked woman.

"You've got to let go to reach the ground, DeeDee," I begged, but it was no use. She was draped on her back over the side of the horse, neither up nor down, and quite paralyzed to either stay or let go. Finally, we persuaded her to roll over onto her stomach with both the handler and I trying to slide her down the horses flank to where her toes could touch the ground.

I was glad the rest of the tour group was ahead of us. The ever-present Bedu, in business as photographers, took pictures of the tourists for a quick dollar once they came back out. I figured DeeDee would not like the photo one Bedu took of her backside over the top of the horse. It was best not to mention it, I thought, so when he became persistent, I handed him a coin and shooed him away. He shuffled off grinning, so in my haste to get rid of him, and with no time to haggle, I had probably paid him way too much.

I ran to catch up with the tour guide, as I didn't want to miss a minute of the history of this magical place. DeeDee followed slowly, at a stiff gait, her legs far apart. I promised myself I wouldn't laugh, since she hadn't laughed at my altercation with the bus's overhead bin.

Looking up at the facades of these ornate buildings carved out of sheer walls, we marveled at the monumental task of building such structures.

"How do you think they did this?" asked DeeDee. "Wouldn't they have had to swing on ropes from the plateau above to reach the house fronts? It seems impossible to build, much less that anyone could ever find this place to do any trading, anyway."

"You're right. It was 'lost' for three centuries, though I read it was lost only to the outsiders. The natives apparently knew where it was. Jordan was considered "insignificant" for eleven or twelve centuries. They rediscovered these lands only recently."

The facades of the buildings were all that showed. Rooms carved back into caves in the rock behind were meticulously square, like real rooms. We tramped through all that could be reached. Some were in ruins. Most were thought to be tombs of the Nabateans, but the guide said some were shrines, and some were perhaps bathhouses, the newest over 2000 years old.

Narrow stairways a foot wide led up the rock walls to the plateau high atop the canyon. "How would anyone have the nerve to climb those without railings?" asked DeeDee. "You couldn't."

I had no answer for that one. I wouldn't have wanted to try it with my penchant for falls and injuries. "Maybe none of the Nabateans were accident-prone." I gritted my teeth at her.

Large storage rooms and eerie chambers were carved into the red cliffs behind the most famous building, the Treasury. We entered slowly into the dim caves, with only a pair of hanging lanterns to light the way. In the coolness, the local guide regaled us with tales of the traders, merchants, royalty and rogues who had traversed the narrow trail we had just come through. "During some eras," he said, "the robbers hid in the narrow crevices that split the sheer walls. The traders were helpless with no room to fight back."

"That gives me goose bumps," said DeeDee. "I thought about being ambushed all through that tunnel…at least, when I could concentrate on anything besides that stupid horse."

"That must have been a short thought." I snickered.

DeeDee *almost* laughed with me, then caught herself and

glared instead.

The sun only reached into the city when it was straight overhead, so it was now obvious why we'd started so early. Soon shadows were falling across the face of the Treasury, bathing it in a mysterious golden glow we would have liked to enjoy longer. However, it began to rain. Our guide told us to remount our horses, rather forcefully, I thought, but rain could mean flooding.

It was difficult to convince DeeDee she could not walk back, but a pile of horse manure at the entrance of the cavern made her realize why it was better to be on top than on bottom. Also, the rain was beginning to influence her not to dilly-dally. But the handler and I had the same difficulty getting her up on top. After several aborted tries, we succeeded, and set off, again at the tail end of the caravan. This was probably a good thing, considering DeeDee's horse maintained his digestive aura from the radishes.

It was so dark one could barely see the rocky trail for the shadows, as we toiled up steeply. I imagined the old caravans on their camels, with precious gems, silks, teas, and spices going through these walls to trade. In reverie, I could almost smell the incense and myrrh--I always wondered about myrrh—about what it really was, anyway. I was lost in thought, distracted enough that I didn't even see the rocks fall from the top of the canyon.

Screams tore through my reverie as people up front shouted warnings. Their echoed shouts didn't help, since there was no place to get away from the shower of stones descending on us. One hit the right shoulder of my horse, narrowly missing his head. He reared, while I struggled to stay on. His backing and whinnying spooked DeeDee's horse and the one in front of me. I turned to find DeeDee. But I had my hands full with my own frantic steed.

I could see DeeDee's handler hauling his weight on the reins to keep her horse from rearing along with mine, or from trying to run ahead when there was no room to pass. DeeDee was lying way forward with her arms wrapped around her horse's neck. What her full weight on his neck did to his equilibrium, I couldn't imagine, but it seemed disaster couldn't be averted. The frightened animal danced sideways and brushed DeeDee's leg against the wall. My horse also was trying to get to the wall, which was not a comfortable fit for my leg on the right side, but I lifted my foot and shoved away from the wall, while DeeDee wasn't confident enough to defend herself. She was too busy hugging her horse's neck for all she was worth. Shouting drowned out her screams. I couldn't tell what she was saying, and I couldn't quite reach her.

One could still hear the people ahead screaming, and horses hooves on the canyon floor writhing in panic. Mine, as did the others, tried to run ahead. The canyon was too narrow and convoluted for the frantic horses to pass each other, and the echoes just magnified the chaos. Instead, the horses ran up against each other, which panicked both them and their riders even more. The front people were like a row of dominoes as trouble worked its way back to us. Handlers and guides shouted in Arabic that none of us could understand. I could only quiet my own horse and reach out a hand to steady DeeDee as her horse tried to squeeze up next to mine in the confusion. I really think he was trying to rub her off his neck, but she was wrapped around him like glue. To add to the confusion, the way underfoot was already deep with fast running rainwater. The gravity that helped Petra's ancient water supply was now working against us in the mud and water under us.

Finally, those who knew how to ride got their horses quieted, and handlers managed to get control of those who didn't. Only one man actually fell, and his horse went down with him on the slippery rocks, which cut and drenched them both. No life-threatening harm was done, and eventually, though a bit shaken by all the yells and confusion, we were on our way back through the tunnel of rock, in more or less single file again, but in a bit of a hurry because of the fear of flash flood. When I looked behind at DeeDee to see if she was okay, she looked away and didn't answer my call. She said nothing the rest of the way back to the clearing.

Then, once we were down from our horses and heading back to the bus in the increasing rain, she surprised me completely.

"I *knew* you would cause something to happen," DeeDee yelled at me. "I just knew it!"

She limped a bit where she had scraped her leg on the wall

of the canyon. I tried to look at the wound to see if she needed attention, but she pushed me away and marched ahead to the bus. When I sat down next to her, she turned to look out the window. And thus we traveled, in stiff silence, almost to the border.

Finally, as we passed the Moabite Mountains, and zigzagged our way down to the Dead Sea, I could stand her silence no longer and tried to reason with her. "It wasn't anyone's fault, DeeDee. The horses were just reacting to some rocks falling. I'm sorry you bumped your leg on the side of the canyon, but it wasn't really anyone's fault. It just happened."

"Yeah, but you said things like this 'just happen' everywhere you go, and I'm not sure traveling with you is a safe thing to do. We could have been crushed or drowned or God knows what. Mama said to watch the company I keep."

I couldn't stop laughing. "Didn't I tell you that from the first day we met? You're the one who said nothing ever happened to you, so you could keep *me* safe." My laughter grew when I looked at her elaborate pout, until she couldn't keep a straight face, either.

"You really looked funny when your horse reared on his hind legs," she said, choking as her pout exploded into giggles. "I was sure any moment you'd fall off backward."

"Not half as funny as you hanging around your poor horse's neck for dear life."

"Well, the handler had my reins, and there was nothing else except his neck to hang on to." Finally, she said, "I'm sorry. I guess it wasn't your fault that I couldn't ride and was so scared. And my good luck didn't help a bit to keep you safe, either. Sorry about that. Do you think we should still travel together 'Cornelia'?"

"Sure, 'Emily.' Maybe this was all the excitement destined for this trip, so nothing more can possibly happen."

She nodded, "I sure hope so. I could use some peace and quiet."

We hadn't counted on Christmas Eve in Bethlehem.

Chapter 7 - Nights in Jerusalem

A checkpoint near Jericho, a lovely oasis with shade trees and bougainvillea, seemed out of place in this disputed territory. Each side claimed the west bank of the Jordan, as though each was waiting for the next conflict to settle the matter--at any moment.

The Dead Sea area was heavily fortified, but while the Jordanians went to great lengths to conceal their soldiers and tanks underground, and most of our tour group had not even noticed them, the Israelis had them right out front. Armed Israeli soldiers stood on every corner, walked every ditch, and stood in every street. I felt sure that was considered a deterrent in itself. If so, it certainly made folks in our tour group sit up and take notice.

Going through the checkpoint took three slow hours as every package was checked. We had a meager tent for shelter from the sun. But the Bedouins, who never had recognized any country or any dividing line, and who wandered wherever their herds of animals took them, had a more difficult crossing. Passing through from the Jordanian side, they were subjected to a three days' wait. Inshallah again. Holding pens, much like those for cattle, held the leather-skinned Nomads working their way through the process. I cringed watching an old Bedu woman with her possessions wrapped in an ancient prayer rug. The rug was rolled out, and her three-day supply of hard rolls fell on the ground. The Israeli soldier picked up each and broke it in half to check for explosives, then handed back the contents.

When he noticed DeeDee and I were staring, and our faces must have given away our horror, he turned and said, "Do you Americans have any idea how many of these people are caught smuggling bomb materials into the West Bank to use against our people? Yes, inside bread, too. We regret having to check the nomads so thoroughly, but we must protect everyone, Muslim, Christian, and Jew, from constant acts of terrorism." He sighed and wiped the sweat from his forehead. "Investigating everyone may seem cruel to you, but so does the fact that some Muslims are willing to blow themselves up to kill Israelis. Don't believe they wouldn't blow up you tourists, too. If we do a good job, hopefully you'll be safe, and so will our people." The soldier went back to sorting through this mass of humanity.

The whole Mid-East situation was a tough dilemma, and we certainly had no answers.

The bright lights of the King David Hotel of Jerusalem greeted us, its façade a glowing sanctuary in the night. We delighted in the ancient architecture, interior gardens and fountains the guide pointed out, but it didn't take anyone long after dinner to go up to shower and get some sleep. Many groaned over sore muscles from their horse ride. I poured a little antiseptic I always carried on DeeDee's calf and ace-bandaged it.

"Ouch," she yelped from the momentary sting.

"It's no more than a bad scrape," I reassured her.

"Thanks, 'Cornelia.'"

"Good night, 'Emily.'"

The rest of the week, we couldn't get enough of Jerusalem. We walked in the footsteps of Jesus up the Via Doloroso, tiring as we climbed, yet aware that His journey was much more difficult. The way snaked through Christian, Jewish, and Islamic areas, with some type of church built on every station of the cross.

At the Garden of Gethsemane, we sat quietly for an hour, surveying desert-style flowers coaxing their way up through harsh boulders and considering what had taken place here.

"What do you suppose He was thinking during those last hours?" asked DeeDee.

"Like anyone else, I think He would have been asking God, 'Why me?' He must have received the answer and the courage He needed to weather the pain of the Crucifixion."

"Yes, I think of Him as being much like us, too, which makes it all the more of a miracle that He could *know* about the suffering, and still go back to face it."

We sat in silence awhile, appreciating the contemplation of that long ago time. She was now fond of exploring, as long as it didn't involve horses, what Mama wouldn't like, or anything scary. *Even Mama would like this place.*

"We don't really know where these events took place. The Catholics think the Church of the Sepulcher houses the tomb, but the Protestants feel the Garden Tomb is the right one."

"I'm Catholic, but the Garden Tomb sort of 'feels' right to me," said DeeDee.

"With the way the early Christians and Byzantines covered up each site with church on top of church, I guess we're lucky to find anything at all of the original sites of His life."

Exploring Jerusalem was a treasure hunt, where we found exciting little pieces of history at almost every turn. Mostly, we explored on our own, but on the occasions when the guide took us on the bus with the group, we found there were differences among our tour mates. One delightful elderly couple from Berlin, the Schwartz's, had come on the trip for much the same reason I had-- a childhood vow to visit Bethlehem on Christmas Eve. They were in their eighties, wrinkly and jovial, and they had many stories to tell. They invited us to come visit when this tour was over. We promised we would do so, as Berlin was still on "Cornelia and Emily's to-do list." They were genuinely good people, we enjoyed them, and they practically adopted us. Soon, they were referring to us as "their girls," since their children had not survived World War II. They had us calling them "Oma and Opa," grandma and grandpa, and we spent pleasant Jerusalem evenings with them.

But one middle-aged woman from Cincinnati, Earlene, was new to traveling. At our first stop, she raced up the aisle, crying, "Let me out, let me out," knocking others out of her way, so she could be first off the bus. Then she knelt to pray at the little shrine of Jerash, an ancient town of Roman forums and Byzantine churches, while her quiet husband, Joe, took pictures of her.

She soon became the brunt of every jokester on the bus. She claimed to be deeply religious, Catholic, like DeeDee, but everywhere we stopped, her little routine caused others to call out,

"Stand back, everybody, here comes Earlene. Get your praying over with," or "Don't forget your holy water, Earlene."

"It's so phony when repeated for the fiftieth time," remarked Opa.

"But, perhaps she's a *sincere* phony," said Oma with a tolerant smile.

At one stop, our guide said in bored tones, "Over here on is Mary's Well. Immediately Earlene was off that bus, on her knees, her face molded into a beatific expression that would have made Michelangelo's cherubs proud. Joe, of course, took pictures.

Then the guide continued, "On the other hand, some sources claim that this is *really* Mary's well over on the left."

All stood back to let Earlene rush through so she could kneel at the alternate site.

"I'm ready to throw *her* in the well, whichever one it is," said one man up front.

I said quietly to DeeDee, "Can you imagine what their scrapbook will look like when they get home, with only photos of Earlene praying here and praying there, all over Israel?"

The first time this happened, DeeDee said that Earlene seemed "sainted" to pray at each shrine. By the time Earlene had prayed at every pit stop, detour sign, and flock of sheep, DeeDee said, "I don't think it's religious fealty that drives her. She wants to be *seen* praying, rather than actually *doing* it. She's a Pharisee."

DeeDee was becoming more discerning about people. It wasn't that she was getting more courageous, but at least she was beginning to notice that some people were phony. I liked it when she figured out something for herself.

On one of our forays into the souk of Jerusalem, we found a man selling necklaces on leather thongs that he guaranteed were "...silver nails from the original cross." I bought one for each of us, fully aware that ours were only one among at least 500 necklaces. While he guaranteed the necklace nails to be genuine, he dumped out another whole box containing hundreds more.

"If there were *that* many nails in the cross, it couldn't have been lifted," I told DeeDee.

But the necklace entranced her. "Do you think wearing one would mean you wanted the nails that bore Christ's blood close to your heart, so it's a holy relic, or is having the very nails that hurt Him actually sacrilegious and one shouldn't have them at all?" She couldn't resolve that problem. We decided to enjoy the necklaces just for their artistic twists of metal.

"They couldn't be real, anyway," I told her.

"But the man said...."

"I know, but look how many there are, and think a bit. Interpret as you choose, 'Emily.'"

She mouthed the word of her discovery, "Oh!"

We were aware of the commercialization of the Holy Land. In Rome, too, we'd been shocked by the millions of little plastic crucifixes on sale at every street corner. Here, the Arabs had also discovered the mighty dollar and were out to get all they could from visiting Christians and Jews.

I was merely disappointed, but DeeDee was troubled by the crass commercialism we'd found in both countries. "I'd like so much for everything to be real," she said.

Though Israeli soldiers were everywhere, we got used to them as they blended into their surroundings. However, one morning, as I stood on our hotel's balcony, a loud roar shattered the bustle of the street scene. Soldiers from every street ran out, merging into formation to clomp down the street toward the noise.

"What was that?" said DeeDee, joining me on the balcony.

"It sounds like an explosion. See, there's smoke over there. It looks like it's only a block or so away. I wonder what got hit?"

"Why aren't the people in the street reacting, like running away or something? They just go on with whatever they're doing."

"I'm sure if they were at the scene, they'd be wading in to help survivors." I leaned as far over as I could to watch the fire trucks and ambulances threading their way through the crowds. "This must be sort of an everyday occurrence to them, since the regular guy in the street takes no notice."

"But the army guys sure reacted quickly."

"That's their mission."

These events were not discussed, but we later found out the explosion was only a block away from our hotel in a bus station.

Our hotel clerk was Israeli, and he told us that all Israelis were in the Army Reserve. "They're called up for thirty-three days per year. Every Israeli is thus trained and responds as a citizen Army. We must be very alert since Israel is surrounded by hostile nations who vow openly and publicly to drive us into the sea."

"I didn't realize that," said DeeDee. She didn't say much for quite awhile as she let things soak in.

The soldiers were, indeed, plentiful. We were even checked going into department stores, so it was impossible not to be aware this was a war zone--a constant terrorist war for which conventional soldiers were ill equipped.

"They must be weary of having to be on the defensive all the time," said DeeDee, as we walked by a group of soldiers. "I hope we never have to feel so threatened. It would be so hard."

"I imagine it's hard for normal, civilized people to make sense of the mentality of someone blowing themselves up just in order to kill others, and then claim such acts of terror are for religious reasons. We Americans take religious freedom for granted. Israelis have to fight for it, and be aware of threats from their neighbors *all* the time."

We drove through Haifa in the rain, on roads flooded from gutter to gutter, on our way to see the Golan Heights, at least to gaze up to them, because they were no longer a part of Israel. That trip accented our understanding of the strange conflict even further.

A young Israeli soldier in battle dress was our local guide, and he explained while we stood in the rain. "We Israelis gave up the Golan Heights to Syria, in response to international and U.N. demands for a ceasefire. But the Syrians now use the Heights they were given to rain shells down on Israel. It was a mistake to trust their word enough to give up our high ground." He removed his cap, ran fingers through his hair, and replaced the cap smartly.

"Someday we may have to take the high ground back to protect our citizens from the constant Arab shelling. We'd like to live in peace, but our neighbors all want to drive us out." He stood up straighter when he said, "We have vowed that never again will another ideology exterminate us *silently*, as they did in Nazi Germany. 'Never again' is our motto, and we will fight to defend our homeland to the last man, woman and child."

I could feel the tension in his stance and his strong jaw jutting toward the hillside trenches and corrugated iron gun emplacements, pockmarked by shell damage.

"Do they shell this spot often?" DeeDee asked. Her eyes darted back and forth across the defensive positions.

The young man laughed. "Don't worry. Though the Syrians keep up a bombardment most times, they *never* fire when they see a tour bus. They'd rather let you go back to your homes believing that they're abiding by the U.N. ceasefire. If they killed a few tourists, it would be bad press, and the U.N. might give us another hearing to settle this matter. They sure don't want that."

"I believe him," said DeeDee. "He was certainly sincere."

"So did I, and I'm glad the Israelis are on our side."

Though the Arab/Israeli political situation was stressful, there were many good things in the Holy Land, too. We found we liked Mid-Eastern cuisine. Breakfasts always had grated carrots on the buffet. No sugar was added, but they, like the radishes, were crisp and sweet. We discovered kumquat Jell-O.

"Whoever heard of kumquat Jell-O?" asked DeeDee.

A local delicacy of ground-up chickpeas was one of many discoveries. "It looks like gray sand with oil floating on it," said DeeDee, squinching her face into wrinkles and turning away.

"It's called hummus. Maybe if we can get past how it looks, it might be tasty." When I tried it and pronounced it good, DeeDee tweaked a little taste onto a cracker. I rejoiced that she was beginning to sample new foods. We found we liked the unfamiliar bright orange lentils, unusual seed grains, fresh fruit, marvelous Arab breads, and the amazing honey pastries.

Israel had *forced* the desert to bloom, irrigating and constantly turning the rocky soil. They were totally self-sufficient. Even the cats in Israel were sleek, well fed, and contented, always a sign of prosperity. However, the Jordanian side didn't sustain themselves at all. They were fed by the U.N. It was a mystery.

We found the merchant tunnels in Jerusalem fascinating, and tried to explore a little further each day. We watched each merchant make his way downtown to his cave-like stall with his donkey balancing barrels of heating oil tied on each side. The smelly old side streets and the up and down hill treks no longer bothered us, since DeeDee and I wanted to see everything.

I was surprised at the freedom Arab/Palestinians had to make a living in the disputed territories. They moved easily throughout the city, despite Israeli soldiers posted everywhere. I guess these were the "peaceful Arabs." They sold, openly, huge bags of grain clearly marked "Gift of the United States. Not to be sold." It made me wonder if our aid packages were effective, and how much black market material was commandeered.

Our last day in the souk, I saw two pieces of clothing that looked familiar. A football jersey, black and white with the large number sixty displayed on the front and back, and a faded blue sweatshirt with Laguna Elementary School written across the chest in white, hung high on the wall of a vender's shop.

I was excited and hurriedly called DeeDee over to see.

"Those are like clothes our family sent during a 1956 war."

"That's impossible, isn't it? This is over twenty years later. How would they even get here?"

"I can't imagine. Our neighborhood collected a big box of clothing, and shipped it to Jerusalem because the war had decimated the local population on both sides."

"They couldn't be the same ones," DeeDee said.

"I haven't a clue, but lots of children's clothing were in the box. Five of us put in our Laguna sweatshirts. Maybe some family got the shipment. Somehow, those two pieces stayed together when others wore out or were outgrown or resold."

I asked the merchant to see the garments, which were on adjoining hangars above us. He took them down and said, "Very fine. Here many times. Very warm for very many children."

I smiled as I looked at the tags on the back of the neck.

"Mom always wrote everyone's initials on the tag so washday didn't become a free-for-all. Everyone in the family had sweatshirts and sports gear." There on the tags were the faded initials, M. on the sweatshirt, and E. on Ed's football jersey. I wanted to cry. They were the same clothes we had sent for children caught in a war—and they had somehow survived all this time.

DeeDee was excited. "What a crazy coincidence!"

"I wonder how many children these pieces have gone through—how many times they've been bought and sold when the kids outgrew them." Certainly the pieces were faded, worn, and the football jersey was patched on one side, but there they were, hanging in an Arab souk in the old Palestinian area of Jerusalem-- and two of them still together. "I can't believe it."

"What a story they could tell!" said DeeDee.

I could have hugged her for understanding how I felt.

We talked about this amazing coincidence all the way back to the hotel. Long after the souk would have closed, DeeDee said, "Why didn't you buy the pieces and take them home with you?"

"I didn't think of it at the time, and now it's too late. I could kick myself. Ed will never believe I saw his old Pop Warner football jersey in the middle of an Arab merchant's cave after all these years. I can scarcely believe it myself."

"But just for the fun of it...?"

This time, I did hug her, laughing happily that her feelings were so close to my own.

Christmas Eve came all too soon, and our trip would be over the day after. The whole tour bus was taken to Manger Square, having been issued special pink passports for the event. But it wasn't at all like my childhood dream. I hoped for a peaceful, emotional epiphany, but the crowd was enormous and somewhat rowdy, with lots of pushing and pulling as we wended our way through endless lines, trying to keep sight of our guide.

"Hilfe," shouted Oma Schwartz. We could hear her calling for Opa, so DeeDee and I worked our way backward through the milling crowd to find her. Sure enough, Opa had been pulled away and she, being quite short, couldn't keep any of the group in sight. They couldn't battle this flow of humanity strongly enough alone.

"Gott sei dank, mein Lieblinge," (Thank God, my darlings) said Oma, breathlessly, when we found Opa. We stayed with them after that, all of us holding hands in the jostling crowd.

We were searched at ten different checkpoints in Manger Square. Atop the Church of the Nativity, right next to a huge electric lighted Star, was a machine gun nest of Israeli soldiers.

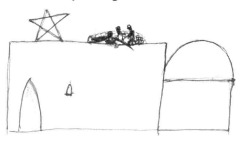

These were on all of the surrounding buildings, as well. I knew enough about soldiers to know those guns were loaded, at the ready for firing at any disturbance in this crowd of thousands.

The lines filtered down into the holy grotto by one door and filed out by the other, under surveillance all the way. Added to this slow torture, was the fact that when I finally stood in front of the manger, a moment I'd waited for all my life, a plastic baby Jesus doll stared back at me.

I don't know what I had expected, but this wasn't it. I started to cry, not even knowing why. DeeDee and Oma patted my arm. Perhaps an empty manger would have been better than plastic. We had seen so many plastic "artifacts" at all the tourist traps along the road. "Somehow I expected to feel the nearness of the Christ child in this very spot, on this very night."

There was no time to think on the setting, since those behind were already pushing us ahead. Once through the long line, the other people in our group got back on the bus.

DeeDee held back. "Can't we wait to see the midnight mass?" she asked plaintively.

Oma and Opa Schwartz said they'd like to stay with us, even though we knew we'd be back very late and would have to leave at six a.m. on Christmas morning to bus our way back to Amman to catch our plane to Frankfurt.

Our tour guide, Ab, was remarkably accommodating all of a sudden, smiling as he said we could certainly stay. "I'll *personally* arrange a taxi to meet you and take you back to the King David Hotel," he said, smiling like a Cheshire cat.

After the suspicion he'd shown toward us before, we were rather surprised.

When he realized Oma and Opa Schwartz were staying with us, he seemed to try to discourage them. "Are you sure you two don't want to go back to the hotel and rest. Tomorrow will be a long day," he said to them.

Opa looked at Oma, she nodded, and he said, "We want to stay with the girls."

The guide looked defeated, but shook his head and quickly recovered. "Okay, but if you're tired tomorrow, don't blame me. You can see the hotel over there, only about six miles," he said, pointing across the black hills to the brightly lit western-style hotel, clearly visible, and not as far away as we had thought. We four agreed, feeling there was no way we could get lost. Since taxis mostly had jump seats in the back that popped down, they would hold four in semi-comfort. DeeDee and I wanted to keep Oma and Opa with us, and not risk losing them again in the crush of people.

Midnight Mass was more serene and dignified than the lines of tourists gawking at the manger and then moving on. No one was certain which was the proper place of the Nativity, any more than they knew which hill was Golgatha. But the Mass restored some of the warmth of my dream of spending Christmas Eve in the holiest of cities. All four of us felt uplifted afterward, in spite of the continuous crowds, the endless lines, and the machine guns looming above. The country was, after all, protecting itself against those who claimed the Holocaust never happened, and who vowed to either convert or kill all Jews and Infidels.

We're considered the "infidels." It's hard to figure out why.

I looked again across the horizon at the King David Hotel, and gauged about what a taxi would cost us, while Opa found the taxi our guide had waiting for us with the tour placard set prominently on the windshield. The taxi held two Arab men in the front seat, both wearing the red military Kaffeyeh of the Palestinian minority, but Arabs seemed to have a monopoly on the taxicab business, so we didn't think much about it. We climbed in, with Oma and Opa on the seat and DeeDee and I crunched onto the little jump seats obviously designed for children.

My first inkling of something wrong was when the cab didn't turn in the direction of the brightly lit King David across the black hills. I figured maybe the drivers knew a shortcut. But soon we were out of Bethlehem in the opposite direction entirely. After three or four turns in the wrong direction, I pointed it out to my companions, and wondered aloud if these two taxi people were trying to run up the meter by going the long way, because we were tourists. Maybe they were in cahoots with our tour guide to get more money out of us. I felt a little angry, if that was what they were doing, but none of us were as yet alarmed.

But then, we were into the darkness of the hills of Judea, and we were definitely *not* going to the King David Hotel.

"Excuse me," I said to the men in the front seat. "We're going the wrong way. King David Hotel is back the other way."

"Shut up," said the man in the front passenger seat. Dark eyes flashed out from under his head covering, and one could smell garlic and peppers on his breath.

We all four jerked to attention.

"What are they doing?" whispered DeeDee. Oma reached for Opa's hand. I shrugged.

I tried again, thinking the driver and his sidekick had misunderstood. I pointed and repeated, "We're going the wrong way. We must turn around to get to the King David Hotel."

Again came the reply, "Shut up."

There could be no mistaking the words now. I asked, "Where are you taking us?"

"Shut up," came the reply. Even in the dark, I could see his teeth flashing as he repeated, with a gesture of a finger across his throat, "I told you, shut up."

Immediately DeeDee shook my arm, and laid her finger over her lips. She was scared I would say something more.

Opa whispered, "It's like the Gestapo. When they tell you to be quiet, you must be quiet, or something worse will happen."

I could see the fear and pleading in Oma's eyes, as well, so I shut up. We drove further out into the darkness, where the only light was far behind us in the faint glimmer of Bethlehem.

DeeDee held my hand tightly. I felt her shaking, but she was quiet, her wide eyes imploring me not to ask more questions.

We were definitely in the hills now, no longer able to see anything at all in the pitch-blackness. The driver turned off his headlights on a dirt road that wound upward through curving narrow valleys until we had lost all sense of direction.

I couldn't stand it anymore. Were we being abducted, tricked, running up the taxi meter?

"What are you doing? Where are you taking us? We demand to go to our hotel--the King David."

This time, the man in the passenger seat said to "shut up," but he also laid an automatic machine pistol on the back of his seat and stared straight at us.

"Well, okay, if you feel *that* way about it." I shut up.

The car roared on into the dark, with no clue of where we were, or of what was happening. Eventually, we approached some type of enclosure, a roadblock, with four men huddled around a bonfire. Rolls of barbed wire encircled the compound. We drove into the center near the fire. They ordered us out of the car. Standing uncertainly in the firelight, Opa wavered, close to collapse. I stepped near him and took his arm to offer support.

"What are you going to do with us?" wailed DeeDee.

This time, it was I who asked her to be quiet. Of four armed guards around the fire, two came to frisk us, perhaps looking for weapons. DeeDee started to protest when the guard put his hands on her. I looked at her, hard. I hoped she could read my unspoken message. *Don't run, DeeDee. Stand still, Please don't run.*

The guards motioned us further away with AK 47's; at least I assumed that's what they were. They didn't look like the weapons our troops used. No one spoke a word to us. They nudged us to the edge of a gully while the other two guards searched the car. *I'd seen pictures of such gullies and shuddered at the thought.*

DeeDee tried to go back, saying, "My pocketbook is...." But her panicked inquiry was stopped by a nudge from the AK-47.

She quieted, but we were all shaking, watching silently as the men rummaged through our handbags and coat pockets. *What could they possibly want?* We didn't have much money left. I ran all possible scenarios through my mind as we stood there helplessly. I didn't like *any* of them.

I saw a guard pull something from my wallet and feared it was my military ID card. He also held something the size of my passport. He showed these to the other guard. Then they searched DeeDee's bag a second time and produced similar items, plus something bigger. They looked through the old couple's things, as well, but they tossed those back on the car floor. Our papers were under closer scrutiny by the men in the firelight. Our drivers and the guards argued. One kept gesturing with the ID cards while the other shrugged and dug into our wallets again.

DeeDee said softly, "They're going through my pocketbook. They'll rob us."

"I'm not sure what they want." I whispered.

The armed guard in front of me told me again to "shut up," adding what sounded like Allah's name being taken in vain. It didn't seem as if those guarding us knew any other English words. Perhaps we could somehow use that information.

Opa and Oma shivered. I patted Oma's arm. She tried to smile at me, but it was a feeble effort. The normally jolly, upturned features in her face were now furrowed downward in the glare of the firelight. Her shivering was from more than just the cold.

For Opa, the scene must have been reminiscent of Nazi Germany, where one could be stopped at the whim of the Gestapo, and sometimes shot for no reason at all. I saw that both the old gentleman's hands were entwined in Oma's fingers.

After what seemed like hours to our hammering hearts, the guards stopped arguing, and one jerked his head and his gun, motioning us toward the taxi. We walked numbly back, ensconced into our former seats, and were moving again.

I opened my mouth to ask what all the drama had been about and ask for our papers back, but Oma quickly shushed me, laying her fingers gently across my lips. I kept quiet, as much to ease her mind as DeeDee's, whose panicked eyes and quivering upper lip made me afraid for her. Everything I'd ever heard in briefings about being kidnapped in a foreign country indicated we should make a break to get away at the first opportunity. *Maybe while we were outside the taxi would be our only opportunity.*

I whispered that information to DeeDee. She held out one foot with the skirt and high heels she'd worn because we'd been going to a church. "I'd be too scared to run, anyway," she whispered. "Please don't try."

Oma picked up the items the guards had taken from her purse and thrown on the floor, pursing her lips in a resigned stare.

I weighed our options. Even if DeeDee took off her high heels to run better, the rocky terrain would be impossible on bare feet. Oma and Opa couldn't run fast enough, and we wouldn't leave them. A third reason soon arose when I remembered that we were totally disoriented and lost in the middle of dark hills with no friendly forces nearby, no clear road, with no idea which way lay safety. Certainly, there wasn't anyone to ask for directions.

We could sure use a star to guide us like the three kings had, God. Would these men fire on us if we tried to get away? The fact that they still had our identification cards and passports worried me. "Should we wait for a better chance," I whispered softly, "or should we try to make a break for the dark mountains and hope someone comes looking for us in the morning?"

"Do you think anyone would come?" whispered DeeDee. "Our guide doesn't even *like* us, because we're Americans. He as much as called us spies on the bus."

"What you talk about?" came the brusque voice of our guard in the passenger seat up front, again brandishing his gun at us over the seat back.

I shook my head.

"All shut up. Stay shut up!" He pointed the gun at Oma.

I covered my mouth with my hand to indicate I wouldn't

talk anymore, and he lowered his gun from the back of the seat. Oma breathed again. I could hear her rasping breath intake.

But my *mind* wouldn't shut up. Our ID cards gave no indication of which base we were on, but they did identify us as U.S. government employees. I wasn't sure that was a good thing, since the Palestinian terror groups didn't like the U.S., due to our support for Israel. What could they possibly do with our I D cards or passports? These men had to be terrorists, because of the guns, the behavior, the operations in the dark, and the checkpoint. The situation didn't seem logical at all. Did they want our papers for some ulterior motive? Were these guys out to kidnap us, rob us, and carry us to the Palestinian side for interrogation or ransom? We'd certainly read of kidnapped hostages. Some foreigners think every American knows all military secrets, and is rich but, in our case, that was a false assumption on both counts. Could we convince them otherwise? *Would it be better to wait or run?*

Oma and Opa, bless their hearts, were German nationals. I hoped that was a good omen for them. Their documents had at least been thrown on the car floor and recovered. Another thought came to mind. Our guide had tried to discourage them from coming with us. He didn't want them. He wanted *us*. But why?

I decided to wait for some indication of where we were and which way lay Jerusalem. Since the "guiding star" didn't materialize, I whispered to the others to look for any kind of directional cues. I knew there wouldn't be any signs, or they wouldn't be able to see any on this dark, dirt road. For all we knew, we had crossed a border onto the Palestinian side already. That could have been what the checkpoint was about.

I'd lost all sense of time, but after a long while, I could see another bonfire ahead of us, and our driver slowed to a stop. Again we were hustled out of the taxi at gunpoint and hurried into a ditch at the side of the road while they went over the car with mirrors, even upending the seats. This time, DeeDee had her purse wrapped around her neck, and we all had grabbed our jackets as a precaution. But the bearded guard stepped in front of her and held out his hand. With shaking hands, she handed her bag to him.

Whew! For a moment I was afraid she might tug-of-war him for it!

Again there were no gunshots, though I think we all half expected them. After a few moments, the new guards came over and separated us. They herded the old couple back into the car, but started asking DeeDee questions. *Well, if they separate us, that squelches the idea of all of us trying to make it into the dark to hide and wait for rescue.*

DeeDee watched Oma and Opa go, and turned to me with a whisper, "Maybe you should make a break for it and find help to come back for us. You can run in flat heels."

I looked around to see where I might run into the darkness to hide until they gave up looking for me. Then perhaps I could find a way to get back to the hotel for help. *But how far away are we...and in what direction? And how would I find the others to bring help since I didn't know where these people were taking us?*

"On second thought, you'd just fall in a ditch and break a leg, and they'd shoot you," DeeDee added, grabbing my arm.

But there was no chance, because our driver approached with his sidearm drawn. He seemed to know more English than the others. To DeeDee, he said, "What plan does your American military have to help Israel?" She shook her head vigorously.

"I want the names of any U.S. government's spies now working in the Middle East," he continued. "What do you know of our fortifications?"

Of course, DeeDee looked bewildered by such questions and was adamant that she knew nothing—that she was only a teacher for little kids.

"American kids?" the guard asked, and he spit in the dirt.

DeeDee nodded vigorously, tears rolling down her cheeks. Her hands moved spasmodically. "The children need me."

For me, he repeated the same questions. I did happen to know a few of our spooks, but I sure wouldn't tell this guy. Instead, I backed up DeeDee. "We're teachers working in a school. We deal only with little children, not those things you're talking about. We know nothing that would be of any help to you."

I thought of something else. "We wouldn't be any good for your asking ransom, either. Our government doesn't negotiate with terrorists or kidnappers." It gave me some satisfaction to say that out loud, until DeeDee looked at me in terror.

"You mean they wouldn't pay to get us back?"

I glared her into silence. They herded us into the car at gunpoint, and our two drivers drove us away, arguing in Arabic. The right seat guy kept waving our ID cards and passports, and occasionally punctuating his loud comments with DeeDee's notebook, poking it toward the driver, who shouted at him as well. *Why would he want DeeDee's notebook? That makes no sense at all.* We still had no idea where in these black hills we were, and there were no lights on the horizon to help us orient ourselves.

We'd been in this taxi roaming around the countryside for two or three hours, and we still didn't know why. I was angry and wanted answers, but there was no one to ask. DeeDee's was a different reaction. She silently reached out her hand with tears rolling down her face. I took her hand in both of mine.

"What if they don't take us back at all?" she whispered. I had no answers and shrugged. The old folks were frightened, too. I tried to analyze just what I was scared of. That at least kept me from wondering what might happen next. I decided the worst thing was not knowing what was happening. None of this abduction, if that was what it was, made any sense. We were, after all, only civilians, tourists. Anger soon replaced the fear.

Not even trying to be "nice" this time, since being quiet hadn't helped us, either, and these idiots could just shoot us any time they wanted anyway, I tapped the guy riding shotgun on the shoulder and demanded, "What is happening here, and what are you going to do with us?"

The two of them argued again in Arabic. Then he pointed off into the distance across several miles of blackness and there, just coming into view, were the lights of Jerusalem. "You said King David Hotel? Inshallah."

The lights were still far off, but eventually we turned from the dirt trail onto a paved road and seemed headed directly for

Jerusalem. I was totally bewildered. Where had they taken us? What had they wanted from us? Who were all those guards who searched us and scared us half to death? Perhaps these guys had satisfied themselves that we didn't have whatever it was they wanted. *Or had we unwittingly given them something?* I hoped not. We'd been careful and sparing of words, I hadn't mentioned the defenses I'd noticed on the border. But the thought was troubling.

The four of us held hands in a prayerful circle until we pulled up in front of the hotel. It was four in the morning, and we were the only members of the tour out so late, but we were at the sanctuary of the hotel, so I expected we would be safe to state our case to the doorman.

"Please notify the police that these taxi drivers took us without our permission. We were abducted into the mountains, and they took our identification papers."

To my amazement, the doorman didn't react. He only said mildly, "Perhaps the driver got lost, or entertained you by way of a scenic route."

"It's hardly scenic in the dark, he wasn't lost, and we need our identification back," I insisted. "They kept us at gunpoint. Please call your police."

He shook his head, and turned away.

The taxi driver was obviously waiting for his fee and tip.

"I see no reason to pay you! You didn't even take us where we wanted to go until after hours of interrogation and detours."

"We'll call the police," said our driver. "You owe us money."

"Go ahead. Call them. They'll listen to us, since you kidnapped us."

"Wanna bet?" he said coldly and laughed. His sidekick stuck his gun out the window.

The doorman refused to help us. It was apparent these people were all in cahoots. I glanced at my fellow passengers to gauge the situation. Opa's complexion in the neon lighting was as snowy as his hair, and his hands shook violently as he tried to get money out of his wallet. His wife had to help him hold it open.

DeeDee was also digging for her money from the money belt around her waist. My companions obviously thought it would be better to pay these terrorists and get into the safety of the hotel. I dug into my purse for my share of the mysterious ride. I expected the men to have charged us for all the time we'd been in and out of the taxi, and I had another argument waiting but, surprisingly, the fare was about what we had thought it would be when we went to the church for the midnight mass.

I turned to the driver. "Then, the least you can do is tell us what happened. Why did you take us into those hills? Where were we? Where are our documents? You must give them back."

The driver pocketed the money silently, a cockeyed sneer on his face. Then he got into their taxi and drove away. I yelled about our documents, and from the passenger side, I saw something flutter out and fall into a puddle on the damp pavement. When I ran over, there were our two passports. I picked them up, wet and stained. I was furious, screaming after the disappearing taxi, "What about our ID cards and DeeDee's tablet." They only sped up until they turned the corner out of sight.

DeeDee asked the doorman, "What were they doing to us? What did they want?

The Palestinian doorman, who had spoken perfect English only moments before, suddenly shrugged and said, "No English."

"DeeDee, let's just get inside in one piece."

We were all exhausted, and somewhat relieved. I wanted to stop at the concierge desk to complain about our treatment and our missing documents, but no one was there at that hour. We walked through the ornate lobby to the elevator at Opa's shuffling speed. Once inside, DeeDee pressed the button for the third floor. The elevator groaned, lifted a bit, stalled, groaned again, and then wheezed to a stop—between two floors. No amount of pushing buttons or trying to open the door helped. We were stuck.

"Boy, if this isn't the end of a perfectly horrible day. So much for my dream of Bethlehem on Christmas Eve." Here we were, exhausted, still shaky from having been kidnapped for God knows what purpose, and brought back so late that the other members of the tour were probably already getting up for our trip to the airport. Not the least of the worries was that our ID cards were gone. It couldn't be much worse. *You dummy, it could have been much worse!* I was concerned that it had been our *own* tour guide who had hired this particular taxi to wait for us. What could that mean? The elevator malfunction seemed a minor distraction.

But DeeDee frantically pushed every button.

"Don't worry, you guys," I said. At least we're safe in the hotel. Somebody will come get us out. After all this, what else could possibly happen?"

As though to answer my question, Opa clutched his heart, wavered, and fell to the floor.

His gray pallor moved us all to action. Oma knelt beside him, attempting mouth-to-mouth resuscitation. "I don't have any breath left," she whimpered, gasping after a few feeble tries.

DeeDee started CPR, pushing on the unconscious man's chest alternating with breaths, while I yelled and pounded on the wall and doors for someone to get us out. It took the night janitor a long time to hear my screams. Finally he came, yelled back to me that the elevator had been "behaving badly" all day, and he would find someone to fix it as soon as he could. I screamed back, "Call an ambulance! Our friend has had a heart attack."

I heard him scream, "Allah…." plus something unintelligible, and then his footsteps pounded back downstairs to the desk and the phone.

I knelt to help DeeDee and we took turns on the mouth-to-mouth breathing and the heart compressions. Some far-away, long-ago first aid training kicked in for both of us, and we found we could work well together.

After what seemed like an eternity, Opa stirred ever so slightly and strained to open his eyes. Oma put her face down close to his and could feel his breath on her cheek. She hugged him. The old man moved his fingers weakly, and Oma took his hand in hers.

I had not realized DeeDee and I were both crying as we worked. We jumped up simultaneously when banging on the outside of the elevator door began, and DeeDee banged back.

"We're in here…below you. Hurry!"

Two workmen strained and pried the doors apart, and an Israeli medical crew jumped down into the elevator. They lifted the limp old man out to the third floor landing, then to an old fashioned litter, which they quickly carried down the stairs. The workmen pulled Oma, DeeDee, and me out of the elevator to the floor above, and we hurried downstairs to the ambulance. They put Opa and Oma inside the ambulance, as well. She indicated she needed "her girls" with her, so DeeDee sat up front in the cab while I sat on the floor holding Oma's hand for the wildest, most uncontrolled ride I'd ever had.

The hospital, with its dull white walls, seemed dim and old-fashioned, but it also proved efficient. Doctors quickly stabilized Opa and put him in intensive care "…for a few days."

Once he was declared out of immediate danger, Oma said, "I'll stay. You girls explain to the tour director, so he can arrange our transportation when Opa is released from the hospital. In her anxiety, she'd lapsed into German. "Danke, meine Lieblinge."

We hugged Oma goodbye, with Opa weakly patting our hands. We promised to visit them in Berlin soon, and ran down the hospital stairs.

DeeDee's face was still pale, and I imagine mine was, too. Neither of us wanted to take chances on another taxi, but the nurse informed us it was a long walk back to the King David, and we didn't know the way.

"Do we hafta?" asked DeeDee.

"I suppose so. Maybe if the nurse calls the taxi, we'll have better luck with the driver than just hailing a taxi off the street."

"There won't be many on the street now, anyway," said the nurse as she dialed.

We waited in silence for the taxi, too tired and too bewildered to talk until we finally were safely in front of the King David. A different doorman was on duty. He jumped up to open the elaborately carved doorway with its glistening glass and brass. We recognized him from the day shift. DeeDee looked at her watch. Everyone else would already be at breakfast, and we weren't even packed yet.

"No more elevators!" said DeeDee with a determined edge in her voice.

I was too tired to do anything but nod. We hurried up three flights of stairs as fast as we could, but found ourselves exhausted with only about ten steps left. Both winded, we plopped down on the stairs and broke into tears. It had been an unbelievable day.

"We're never going to know what happened out there in the hills, are we?" DeeDee cried. "We're never going to get back our papers, either, are we?"

"Probably not. I feel lucky we got out with our skins intact. They could have shot us out there, and no one would ever have known. The doorman could have helped us identify the car or those men, but he wouldn't, and I'm almost afraid to say anything to our guide, since he was the one who ordered that particular taxi for us. He *had* to have been in on it. For us to describe them now—is it a terrible thing to say that with those red Kaffeyehs, and those beards, all the Palestinians looked alike?"

"Could you identify them again?" asked DeeDee. "I couldn't. I was too scared to pay attention, and it was so dark."

"I probably couldn't either, unless the right one said, 'Shut up,' in the same voice."

"We'd better pack and get downstairs," DeeDee sighed. "Everyone else will be waiting."

"Too bad. Inshallah."

"Are we going to have problems getting on the plane with wet passports?"

I shrugged. "Who knows? Who cares anymore? We'll just take it as it comes."

We rose, wearily, and climbed the last few steps to our room, folded everything into our suitcases, and dragged them down to meet the others.

"We look terrible," we said in unison as we passed a huge mirror in the lobby. We laughed almost hysterically with relief that the ordeal was over--at least we *thought* it was.

Chapter 8 – The Hard Way Home

Approaching the ornate front desk with our suitcases, we asked to speak to the hotel manager. He strode in with an air of confidence belying his extensive girth and age, only pausing to check his watch, and to wave off a junior clerk on his way. We explained the problem of our treatment during the taxi ride, and asked to use his phone to report it to police.

The pompous little Arab was no help. "Our police, of course, do not speak English."

"Then will you call them for us?" asked DeeDee.

He threw up his hands and shoulders in an exaggerated shrug, and his pencil-thin mustache twitched. "These things happen. The hotel does not take responsibility for the militant Palestinians when you are not safely here in the hotel." He tossed his head in a smug, self-satisfied way. "The other tourists returned, had dinner and retired. You were the ones who went off alone."

Even the sickly-sweet smell of the pomade slicking down his hair made me angry by then. He lectured us like two little schoolgirls, when we'd only wished to attend a church service.

"Our guide told us we could stay, Sir," I said, trying to maintain my cool. "Our guide *chose* that taxi for us, so someone should be able to at least get back our identity cards. The militants stole them from us, scared us to death, and caused a heart attack for Mr. Schwartz. They even damaged our passports."

DeeDee held out her water and dirt-stained passport, its navy-blue color faded from the outside's artificial leather.

The little man wrung his hands and bowed. "Ladies, I know nothing about your guide."

"That's it? You'll not help us? Won't you call the police?"

"I have promised to arrange for the travel of your friends, once Mr. Schwartz is deemed fit to travel, and I promise to notify the tour company of your distress in a few weeks when I get the time. Involving the police would only be disappointing, I'm sure."

The manager again bowed, folded his hands into his caftan sleeves and walked away.

Before we could think of an alternative action, the guide called for our tour group to get on the bus to Amman, where we'd catch our plane back to Germany, so there was no time to pursue the matter. It was 0600 hours, but it seemed we had finished with the manager. Or more to the point, he'd finished with us.

DeeDee grabbed some cheese slices and grapes in a paper napkin, and I crammed my pockets with rolls from the buffet breakfast. We ran outside to catch up with the passengers. At the curb, we tried complaining to the guide. Though we no longer trusted him, I felt I should mention the lost documents.

"We'd like you to retrieve our documents from the men you hired to take us from Manger Square," I said. "You can mail them to us at this address." I held out a small piece of paper.

He peered through me as though I hadn't spoken, and let the paper flutter to the ground.

DeeDee held out her damp passport again and asked what she should do. "What if the airline won't accept our passports when we get to Amman?" she asked.

"That, Miss, is your responsibility," he said, his tone dripping with disdain. "Our company requires you to maintain your travel documents in order for the duration of your trip. If you are careless and lose them, that is not our concern."

"But those men you hired stole some of our documents and dropped these in the muddy water. They kidnapped us, and you're the one who chose them to bring us back to the hotel." DeeDee was angrier than I had ever seen her. She tossed her hair out of her face with a sharp jerk, as though to clear the way for a fight.

"May I remind you," said the guide with voice loud enough to attract the attention of others, "that you yourself chose to remain at Manger Square, refusing the safe ride back to the hotel with all our other tourists, so there was no way I could protect you. Perhaps you flirted with the drivers and brought it upon yourselves."

He turned to the next passenger, washing his hands of the affair.

"We did no such thing," DeeDee sputtered in indignation. "We would never…."

I laid a hand on her arm. "Later, DeeDee. We'll write the company when we get home. Let's just get to the airport and safely on the plane home, okay? We've had enough turmoil." I urged her up the bus steps. No one was going to find out why these men had terrorized us, or why they took our documents.

DeeDee was furious as we walked down the aisle and took seats. "How dare he say that to us? It was his fault, and he didn't even explain what those men wanted, yet he accused us…."

"We're in a country where the entire tourist industry seems to be run by Arabs, and Middle Eastern men never believe a woman. I guess we have to leave it at that. Right now, I'm tired, disgusted, shaky, and just thankful we somehow survived, okay? They could have decided to rape us or kill us, and they had the guns." DeeDee nodded. I thought of something else and grinned. "But, I am proud of you for helping to stand up to that guy."

"Thank you, 'Cornelia.' I'm trying to be brave like you."

"And I'm trying to be calm and careful like you, 'Emily.'"

We settled back and divided our rolls, cheese and grapes for a belated breakfast.

We woke with a jolt sometime later when we stopped at the Dead Sea Border, where the River Jordan divided the two countries. Of course, as soon as the bus door opened, Earlene bounded out the front door, so she could be photographed praying beside the River Jordan. This Allenby crossing was near to where Christ was baptized by John the Baptist, so perhaps a photo would be nice here, but the rest of us just sat, too tired to move.

Guards quickly surrounded Earlene with guns at the ready, so she settled for kneeling in the dirt beside the bus wheel. Why not? It was at least *close* to the river, and the bus tire would make a fine addition to their scrapbook. But the guards allowed no photos, so Earlene got back on the bus, dejectedly dusting off her knees and dress with fluttery hands.

An Israeli guard came aboard the bus to check ID. When he

got to DeeDee and me, he held our still damp passports up
delicately by two fingers before dropping them back in our laps.
Then he herded us off the bus like a flock of sheep, toward the
bridge to Jordan. Guards swarmed over the bus behind us, looking
for what? No one said, and it seemed not politic to ask questions. I
just wanted to get home in one piece. DeeDee was still half asleep,
so I steered her along the prescribed path with the others.

An Israeli guard escorted us toward the river's edge. "Stay
on the road at all times," he said. He swung out his arm to the left
and right, indicating barbed concertina wire with innocent-looking
signs that said "mines" in six languages.

Ah, yes, the road!

Israeli guards walked behind us, while Jordanian guards led
the way. The bridge was not a proper bridge at all, but a Bailey
Bridge--the type military combat engineers unfold, float and
anchor into place to get the Army across a river when all the real
bridges have been blown up.

Separate sets of wires draped across both sides of the
bridge. Turning to follow the wire, I saw that they connected to
boxes of explosives and plungers...on *both* sides of the River. I
presume either side could blow up the bridge, had they wished to.
No one else noticed the wires, so I kept my mouth shut. We were
all tense enough, already. We waited in the sun while our bus
followed across the bridge. The driver handed out our suitcases.

Jordanian guards directed us to lug our suitcases into the
inspection station and line up to be screened. It was little more than
a tent, open on three sides, with a dirt floor thickly littered with
discarded bottles, cans, and wadded paper that looked as though it
had been used to mop up some kind of mysterious glop. Wobbly
wooden tables stood in a crooked row, and a crew at the back had
an x-ray machine. The x-ray machine looked particularly out of
place in that dirty, smelly milieu, with huge horse flies landing all
over it. The guards seemed able to ignore the flies on their faces,
while we passengers swatted ineffectually like flailing windmills.

It was already hot so early in the morning, and none of the
Jordanian guards appeared literate, friendly, or particularly glad to

be working there in no-man's land. As each of us was prodded toward the table, they briskly opened our suitcases, scooped all the contents out into a heap on the table and handed the now-empty suitcases to the crew in the back to x-ray while the guards at the front shook out each garment individually.

After watching them rummage through everything in the suitcases of people in front of us, DeeDee anxiously pushed in tightly behind me as the guard inspected my things from the pile, holding each item up to the light and squinting as though he could pierce through it with x-ray eyes, not even needing the machine.

He shook out my sweaters and added each to the growing heap on the dirty table at his side. He turned out the pockets and legs of each pair of slacks, and then threw them on the stack.

DeeDee whispered, "Our clothes will be a mess when we get them home."

"Laundromat," I hissed between my teeth, while trying to smile innocently at the guard. He wasn't impressed.

My bras and panties received no more consideration than the other things. I watched helplessly as my intimate life was exposed to the world.

He lifted my hairbrush, rapped it soundly on the edge of the table. It broke into two useless pieces. I gasped, struggling to control my tongue when I felt DeeDee's elbow in my ribs.

"How inconsiderate!" said DeeDee, quite out loud.

"Shh. We just want to get through this and get to the airport for our ten-thirty flight, remember?" I checked my watch. That already seemed to be an impossibility.

The guard peered inside the shaft of the brush, then dropped it on the heap of disheveled clothing. When my bag was returned from x-ray, he piled the clothing and broken brush on top.

I turned to look for someplace to repack, but DeeDee said, "Don't leave me alone!"

I knew that if they even shook out her panties, her "unmentionables," as they had mine, I didn't want to be there to see it, but I couldn't leave her alone, either. Resting my open suitcase against the edge of the table, I nodded.

The guard repeated the process on DeeDee's suitcase, dumping her clothing into the growing heap at his side. He shook out her panties one by one, and she cried out, putting her hands over her eyes at her drawers so prominently displayed. "Don't do that," she cried, snatching the offending underwear and stuffing some in her pockets. The guard glared at her menacingly. He waved at me to move on, but I stubbornly stayed beside DeeDee.

"Don't worry, DeeDee, he's doing his job, and he's looking at everyone else's undies, too." It was no use. She'd already made the guard suspicious. Once again, it was almost as though he was on a mission to find whatever it was she wanted to hide.

He went for DeeDee's cosmetic bag next, shook its contents out on the table, and examined everything carefully, as though it might contain a bomb. He sniffed perfume and sort of smiled before replacing the cap. He put a little of her lotion on his finger and tasted it. He looked irritated by the taste, but he said nothing as he tossed it on top of the pile. *Who asked him to taste hand lotion, anyway!*

When he held her box of tampons up to the light, opened it, and shook out the contents, waiting tourists gasped in unison. Tears rolled down DeeDee's cheeks.

We couldn't help but look on, in horrid fascination, as he pulled on the little strings that hung from each cylinder, and muttered, "fuse," in English. He poked his finger warily into each little cardboard cylinder and pushed out the contents. This, of course, made the tampon useless, but he didn't stop with one. In devastatingly slow motion, he poked out the cotton contents of each one, peering through the cylinder as though it were a spyglass. He deposited the pieces on top of the clothing pile.

I held my breath through this performance and gazed down to memorize every disgusting bit of gunk on the floor. Others seemed to be studying their shoes as well. The lady behind DeeDee blanched white, as though she would faint. I wondered what she had in *her* luggage.

I snuck a peek at DeeDee. She was blushing ten shades of red with her hands covering her mouth to withhold the scream I could see bulging in her temples.

"Hold on, DeeDee," I whispered. "If you fuss, it'll only be worse." I struggled not to drop my precariously balanced suitcase. Our traveling companions snickered, trying not to laugh out loud, and undoubtedly wondering what this idiot guard might find among *their* personal items.

Did her tampons really look like small, but undoubtedly lethal, bombs to him? Was he *that* ignorant, or was this remote Jordanian border staffed with the dregs of their Army? I knew the guards were probably doing what they had been instructed to do, but I felt so bad for DeeDee. We came from a generation where personal items came wrapped in brown paper. She was numbly biting her lip with her eyes closed when they delivered her open suitcase back to the table. The guard picked up the pile of mussed clothing and personal items and heaped them on top of the open suitcase, handing it into her arms. There wasn't any way to close the thing with the contents heaped instead of neatly folded, and there, rolling around on the top of the pile and dropping to the floor were the eight little ruins of her most intimate supplies.

I looked frantically for a place we could both put down the open suitcases to reorganize the contents so they could be closed, but the grimy floor was disgusting. Mine was heavy and cumbersome in its stuffed open condition, and DeeDee swayed under the load as though she would fall over. Tears covered her face. I knew it was only embarrassment, but if she fell, the suitcase would still be a mess. A couple of men in line behind us recognized our dilemma and bent over, motioning for us to put the open suitcases on their backs to repack. A third man stood between them holding the edges steady while we did so.

We stuffed our things into the cases as quickly as we could, while the men underneath let out an occasional silent laugh. I could tell because the suitcases jiggled. When finished enough that our helpers could jam the things shut so the latch caught, one of them stooped to gather up the spent tampons that had dropped to the floor and put them in the barrel designated for contraband. I thanked the men with a grim smile, while DeeDee couldn't look at anyone. Little hiccoughs and sobs broke from her throat. The men took their places in line to see what the inspector would find in their bags, and different guys bent over to help the next person repack. We must all have looked pretty crazy trying to repack our suitcases on bobbing backs, but there seemed no other alternative. The filthy, litter-ridden floor was out of the question.

I carried my suitcase out into the sunlight followed by DeeDee, knowing her ordeal had been even worse than mine. "Forget it, 'Emily,'" I said. "It's over, and you got through it, though you've got to stop acting guilty. At least, you've improved a little since your first customs in Frankfurt." I smiled at her in congratulation. "Remember, we'll never see these people again."

She mopped her eyes with her sleeve and sniffled. "All right, 'Cornelia.' We've gotten this far, but it was just so awful...."

"I know." Looking across the area, I noticed both the bus driver and the guide peering into the engine compartment in the back of the bus. *That doesn't look good.*

They tinkered until all the passengers had emerged from the tent. Then the tour guide ran back across the Bailey Bridge. The Israeli guards stopped him and frisked him, but soon they nodded and cranked up a field radio.

"Bus broke," said the Arab driver. "He call. Send more."

Frowns of disgust, sighs of fatigue, and red faces blustered with anger met his words.

DeeDee and I were too tired to care anymore, plus I felt that the most humiliating and frustrating and scary things had already happened. What *more* could go wrong?

We walked to the middle of the road, as far as we could get from the signs warning of mines, sat on our suitcases, and waited. One by one, the others joined us. There seemed no traffic on this road, no one was allowed to venture back into the filthy tent, and apparently, no one wanted to test the minefields.

Frequent glances at watches meant someone called out a time hack every minute or so. We had already missed our plane, so the random attempts at discussion centered on how many hours or days it might take to get another flight.

"There's only one plane a day to Frankfurt," said a beefy, red-faced man named Helmut. Little rivulets of sweat poured down from his bald head. He was from Amsterdam, and normally positive and friendly, but now he worried aloud about getting back to his business on time.

"I'm afraid they'll send us back to that hotel in Amman where we all got sick," said Fran, a retired airline stewardess from Florida. "I'll take my chances sleeping in the airport."

People speculated, grumbled, or swatted flies and wiped perspiration, but the fact of the matter was that we were stuck, with no place else to go, and it was a sure thing that we wouldn't be getting back to Frankfurt that night. *Inshallah at its finest.*

After another hour or so, someone pointed out a cloud of dust in the distance, coming from the Israeli side. As it came closer, we could see it was certainly not another bus for tourists.

Instead, it was a rickety old local bus with windows blown out, listing precariously to one side. It had thin, bald tires of assorted sizes, the smaller ones on the left side so the contraption had a distinct list. Tied down on the top were crates of chickens and piglets. Not only did their smell precede them, but we could also hear their loud complaints in "chicken and pig speak." The bus stopped on the Israeli side for ID check, then rumbled across the Bailey Bridge. In the middle of the bridge, an extremely loud backfire sent the Jordanian guards flying, hitting the dirt for a supposed bomb. Grinning sheepishly and poking fun at each other, they arose and brushed dirt off their dingy uniforms.

When the bus stopped, we saw, hanging from the vacant window frames, the fifteen members of the Catholic youth group from Milwaukee that had sung at midnight Mass the night before, plus several inhabitants of the desert. Several old men and women with leathered faces, held tightly to their possessions. Every woman of the nomad group wore a shawl to cover any sign of her hair, and men and women alike wore grungy robes.

"Don't be alarmed," shouted one young man. I remembered him as spokesperson for the choral group and a baritone solo. "This bus goes to the Amman airport, and the market place. We travel cheap." He grinned, motioning us to join them on the bus.

Their bus driver got down, rubbing his grimy hands on his robe. He conferred with our bus driver and guide for a moment, and seemed pleased. *Money must've changed hands.* While this new group suffered through their customs humiliation, our guide walked over to where we sat on our suitcases and informed us that there was room for us on this bus if we crowded a bit.

"You may get to Amman sooner than waiting for the bus that should arrive in another hour or two or three, whenever Allah wills," he said. It was our choice.

DeeDee and I, as well as most of the others and the guide. elected to take our chances on something that was at least moving, so we crowded onto the rickety bus, three to a seat or settled into crevasses as best we could. Earlene and her husband got on the bus, but she took one big whiff of air, choked dramatically, and fell back limply into Joe's arms with her wrist over her eyes. Joe looked sadly at the rest of the group, now joined by the pig and chicken owners and the choir, and half dragged, half carried the prone Earlene off the bus.

Our bus clanked away, with sputters and backfires. I wondered if we would ever make it to the airport. From the Dead Sea, lowest spot in the world, up the steep grade to Amman was over four thousand feet in elevation and many miles of twisted road. But this was our best hope. As we looked back, we could see

Earlene sitting on her suitcase with her silent husband standing beside her, fanning her face with his hand.

DeeDee looked away, and muttered, "Good riddance."

Yea! DeeDee is disgusted with her first hypocrite, or what did she call her...Pharisee?

The malodorous scents of livestock, unwashed bodies, and the ever-present mysterious litter that indicated the bus had no bathroom, defined the ride as something no one would ever forget. In looking around, I noticed we westerners were all breathing shallowly from our mouths to minimize exposure. The old bus careened from one side of the road to the other, leaning so far over on the small tire side that I feared the menagerie on the roof would fall off, or we'd tip over, but I guess they were securely tied.

Our passenger menagerie was as assorted as the animals. A toothless old woman giggled at us across the aisle, whispering to her seatmates and pointing. Was she really that old, or did the desert people look older than they actually were? A man sitting on the floor by our legs held a pet chicken tenderly, but he was chewing something black that he spat on the floor. He, too, kept staring at us between spits with black teeth, with what I thought passed for a smile. I nudged DeeDee, and we smiled back.

We conferred, quietly. "Are we very different from these nomads...or from other people in the world?" asked DeeDee.

"I'd like to think all people are the same. I believe in accepting everyone. But perhaps we've had advantages of semi-clean clothing, purses with a little money left in them, more education, more sanitation, democracy, no veils on our hair, no religious beliefs that call for the domination of women by men...and we aren't spitting anything." I smiled again at the lady across the aisle. "On second thought, I guess those are quite a few differences, aren't they? But we're all stuck on this same rickety bus, some of us destined for the ancient Amman Souk to stay here forever, and some of us for the modern airport to find a way out."

"I'm glad we're going," said DeeDee. *My thoughts exactly.*

We noticed a few farmers out the windows, the Bedouin females veiled, and many homes made of piled up brush. Oxen pulled a "plow" made from a tree branch. Immediately next to this farmer's field, and right in among the brush shelters and their tethered camels, were more soldiers hidden in their fortifications. I wondered if these people realized they were being used as human shields, or did they simply accept it as "Allah's will."

My grim thoughts were interrupted by the young college people, a lively bunch, who soon had everyone singing, "Ninety-nine bottles of beer on the wall" with the Palestinian nomads nodding their heads or clapping in rhythmic time. As we wheezed slowly up hill, in spite of dust, heat, odor, and billowing black smoke burping from the antique bus, you could see all passengers straining forward, as though to help the bus gain altitude.

Helmut muttered, "This poor old bus is probably left over from World War I days."

"Yeah, and I'll bet it was used for target practice," added another guy with a laugh.

"I doubt it can get all the way uphill to Amman," said the stewardess. "We'll probably get deposited on the pavement again."

"At least, we can get off the road," DeeDee added. "I haven't seen any more mine signs since we left the border."

But among the miracles that sometimes attend travelers, the bus finally wheezed up to the door of the Amman airport, and all the passengers for the plane to Frankfurt hurried off. The market travelers with their livestock and lost teeth hung out the windows and wished us Salaam, that Allah would be with us. We were touched by the brotherhood of man by this time, since we had shared such a difficult journey. These people wished us their culture's most important protection. We waved back as the bus pulled away, still oinking, wheezing, and clucking.

We hurried into the foyer. A bewildering maze of arrival and departure signs hung from the ceiling. I looked for flight numbers, since I couldn't make out many of the words listing place names in Arabic, French, everything *except* English. There wasn't much use looking, anyway, since we were almost five hours late.

Our guide, by this time quite impatient and harried, and scrupulously avoiding DeeDee and me, called out to the huddled passengers, "In our country, flights, bus trips, trains, boats, leave only when Allah wills. Fortunately for you, even though your flight was due to leave at ten-thirty a.m., Allah has not yet willed." He pointed to show us. Our flight number still had a stationary red light on the ceiling boards. "That means Allah isn't yet ready."

"Well, whaddayah know?" said a Philadelphia gentleman.

"Allah is indeed being kind to us today," said Tess, from Munich, with a big smile.

"Good," said DeeDee. "Let's puleeze find a bathroom."

"Yeah," echoed the stewardess. "I'm pretty frantic--after all, there's been no chance since we left the hotel at six this morning." There was a general rumble of agreement, as we turned round and round, looking for an appropriate sign.

At that moment, the green light on our flight number started blinking rapidly. That meant Allah was now ready for our plane to depart...immediately.

"Allah will not wait!" screamed our guide. So we forgot about our trips to the john and frantically grabbed suitcases.

As we ran pell-mell through the airport, DeeDee said, breathing heavily from the exertion, "Where do we show our passports and tickets? What about our luggage?"

"I don't know. Just follow everyone else." In fact, we were waved right by the ticket counters, and right by luggage check in, and motioned out the door and across the tarmac to the plane's mobile stairway. "Carry on," attendants shouted when we looked for someplace to drop luggage. We struggled with our bags aboard the ancient 707 that had many suspicious oil streaks back of the engines, mark of a third world airline purchasing retired planes from other countries. The engines were already revved and the plane strained at the chalks. As the last man got up the steps, the ladder was pulled away, the chalks were yanked, and we were taxiing before we even had a chance to get down the aisles. Allah was now apparently in a *really* big hurry.

As the passengers fell into any seats they found empty, leaving luggage in the aisles, the plane was already lifting off and we were, miraculously, airborne, still fumbling with seat belts.

We fidgeted until we reached cruising altitude and the "fasten seat belts" sign finally went out. Then there was a frantic rush for the bathrooms located in the back of the plane. The tourists and singers from Jerusalem quickly filled all six restrooms with lines down the aisle, climbing over luggage as best they could. I felt the plane lurch at a funny angle as all the weight rushed to the rear end. The stewardesses first coaxed, and then ordered, everyone back to their seats, but no one seemed willing to relinquish his or her place in line, no matter if we flew all the way to Frankfurt with the plane standing on its tail.

Finally, I felt the plane level out again, as the pilot adjusted the elevator trim to account for a tail-heavy old jet. I nudged DeeDee in front of me and told her, "I sure would love to see the pilot's face when all his cargo unaccountably shifted to the rear. I bet the guy will be complaining to his cohorts for a long time."

"Megan," said DeeDee with a grimace, "this is *not* the time for you to make me laugh."

Finally relieved of full bladders and uncomfortable rides on a filthy bus, we settled back into the usual routine for a long flight.

DeeDee grinned at me. "You were so anxious to get on the plane, you forgot to be frightened during take-off. I must congratulate you on that, 'Cornelia.'"

She was right! I just smiled back. We were served a decent meal, and we even indulged in a glass of wine. We deserved it.

I must have dozed, because when I woke, we were circling in the fog surrounding Frankfurt. I had never arrived at this busy airport in the seventies' winters without circling for a half hour while the control tower coaxed down flight after flight onto the invisible tarmac. The circling was hard, since you knew there were other planes out there just as blind as you were. I like to see the ground, so I know we are at least going to crash in the right city.

I was sitting in the middle seat, between DeeDee and a German gentleman on my left by the window. I asked him politely if he could see the runway yet.

"Nein," he said.

"Can you see it yet?"

"Nein," he repeated.

When I asked the third time, he said patiently, "I'll let you know as soon as I see it."

I tried to hold in my anxiety on landings and not let DeeDee see it. She was calm, and I wanted to keep it that way.

After an interminable time, the gentlemen said, "I see it."

And boom, we were on it! *That* told me how low the ceiling…almost zero-zero, as my pilot friends would have said.

I was about to relax, being at last on the ground, when I realized we had whizzed right past the terminal and were still going pretty fast for a roll out. Normally, you'd hear reverse thrusters operating by now. *That's a bad sign.* We didn't even turn off at the last slanting taxiway, but sped to the end of the runway.

"Scheise!" said the gentleman to my left, resorting to a German cuss word, as we bumped off the runway and onto the grass, jostling people all over their seats. Involuntarily, I grabbed DeeDee's and the German gentleman's hands tightly and shut my eyes. Neither objected, and they held onto my hands just as tightly. Passengers screamed, and many overhead luggage bins bounced open, raining loose items down on our heads.

We came to a sudden, whip-lashing stop. Before I could get my breath, the stewardesses flung open the doors, pulled handles for the slides, and yelled at those nearest the door, "Out, out, out." Panicked passengers pushed behind us, but we seemed at a standstill, unable to go forward. One woman up front had balked at the sight of the emergency slide, and we watched as a steward picked her up and threw her out onto it, to clear the logjam. Not to face that dilemma again, the passengers leaped into space and landed in the slide while ground maintenance men held it firmly at the bottom, giving each bewildered passenger a hand up at the end.

I'm not even sure when our turn came to jump, it all went so fast. Suddenly I launched through the air and then was helped out of the canvas at the bottom to stand with the gathering herd.

"Go," yelled the ground people. But where should we go? We milled around like cattle in a storm until a woman screamed, "Look." Our attention focused clearly on what was rolling up to the side of the plane. It was a bomb-disposal unit that looked like a pop-bellied tank with a tube at the top, with a team of over-dressed metallic-looking men. Four squad cars flanked them, and bomb-sniffing dogs were led out.

Suddenly, the milling herd of people heeded the "Go, go, go" order and started stampeding away from the plane. Ground personnel directed us toward the terminal at the best speed tired travelers could manage, perhaps spurred on by the growing knowledge that *something* had been on board our plane. After the Munich Olympic attacks, Germans didn't kid around about terrorism any more.

Finally several shuttle buses met us for the last sprint to the main terminal. Everyone peered out, fascinated with the scene unfolding behind us. A man in metallic gear hurried down a portable ladder they'd put up to the door of the plane. He dropped his burden into the tube of the heavily armored disposal unit.

There was a big "kerthunk" as they exploded whatever had been the suspicious object, and collectively, we jumped.

"What was that?" DeeDee cried out.

The man next to her said, "I think they found what they were looking for. Apparently there was a bomb on our plane. I've seen this kind of drill before in the Middle East."

Suddenly, he was our expert, and everyone packed in our shuttle bus started shouting out questions. "Even if it was a bomb, why did they have to jolt us off the runway so far away from the terminal," yelled one man behind DeeDee. "We could have been killed in a crash."

"That was irresponsible," echoed another.

Our 'expert' answered calmly. "If they hadn't been able to find the bomb, and it went off, they would want it as far away from the terminal and other planes as possible. They shouldn't endanger others or tie up a runway. We all saw that the emergency personnel were waiting for us out there, so they must have known."

That made sense, sort of. But still the clamor ensued until we got off the buses and were directed into a large room in the terminal. Officers funneled us where they wanted us to go.

A man in the uniform of the airline stepped up to the podium, a forced smile on his face. "Ladies and gentlemen, we've had an unfortunate incident, but there is nothing to worry about. We were notified there was a suspicious device on board. We informed the pilot and crew. Ground personnel were waiting for your arrival to direct the plane to a safe destination."

Translators in several languages repeated his words.

The airline official informed us of how quickly the flight crew had acted in removing us from potential harm. "The police have already apprehended the passenger responsible," he said.

"My God," said a short little woman in sneakers and cut-off jeans. "He was on our plane?" She turned to those around her with narrowed, glaring eyes and muttered, "He was one of us? It could have been any one of you." She shouted, "How do we know there wasn't an accomplice? Someone could be in this room right now."

I suppose we all wondered how they knew, how they caught the guy, how the suspicious item, as the airline executive kept calling it, got on our plane, but no answers were forthcoming.

A woman shouted, "Sir, how can you remain so calm?"

"That's easy," said DeeDee. "*He* wasn't on the plane."

Everyone laughed, and that broke the thickening tension. I was proud of DeeDee.

The executive smiled benignly.

Someone asked why if it was only a "suspicious item" when the bomb-disposal team had "kerthunked" something down the chimney of the armored truck and it had exploded.

"It was only a precaution," he answered. "Everyone on board is safe, there are no injuries beyond a few bumps and scrapes from the canvas slide. No harm was done."

"What about my pocketbook and luggage?" DeeDee asked.

Until that moment I had forgotten about my purse. I had tucked it under my seat for the flight. In our hurry to get off, I'd left everything behind.

"They will taxi the plane up to the terminal now, though not at the gate scheduled. Your flight came in so late that we had to shift gates. You can get on the plane and pick up your personal items at gate three, and your baggage will be delivered to the carousel downstairs with only a short wait while it is x-rayed." He smiled blithely, and said, "All's well that ends well, now, isn't it?" He walked away, leaving us all looking at each other blankly. We still had no answers to our multiple questions. It was a non-incident, according to the airline industry.

As we finally exited the arrival hall, we found Jimmy pacing the floor of Frankfurt's International Arrival terminal. He ran to us with a relieved smile and a big hug for each of us.

"I wasn't surprised by the flight from Amman being late," he said. "But I was startled when I looked out the window and saw your Jordanian plane speeding down the runway out of sight." He hugged me again. "I wasn't sure what was happening, but I knew it couldn't be good. I'm relieved to find you both walking out unharmed. What happened?"

"Where to start," I said, a little breathlessly. "There was this bomb...."

Surprisingly, DeeDee picked up the story for me, and told him about all the mishaps traveling with 'Cornelia' had entailed. "It was so exciting," she said. "You cannot imagine all the things we saw, just because 'Cornelia,'—Megan, got us into things. We were kidnapped, and they stole our papers, and we were on a bombed flight, and a friend had a heart attack, but that was because of the kidnapping and getting stuck in the elevator and...."

Jimmy looked at me, his slow grin exposing his dimples. He took my hand, kissed it, and said to DeeDee, "I think I *can* imagine."

At that moment, I was proud of DeeDee for coming through all this, and Jimmy for looking really good. I collapsed into his big bear hug, not even caring if DeeDee thought it un-virtuous, or if he would notice how much like chickens, pigs, and desert dwellers I smelled.

Chapter 9 - Military Secrets

On the two-hour drive back to Bamberg, DeeDee and I filled Jimmy in on our loss of documents. We were concerned that we didn't really know what our terrifying adventure meant.

Jimmy was quiet, biting his lower lip as he listened. I wondered what was going on in his head when he only nodded occasionally. As usual, when he was concentrating, that lock of hair curled forward, and I wanted to brush it back. I didn't.

"We'll have to get you new ID cards," he said finally, "but I'm concerned that these militant groups took yours."

"They even kept my notebook, Jimmy," said DeeDee.

Jimmy asked, "Was there anything special in the notebook?"

"Just my shorthand notes of our trip. But our guide thought it was some kind of code. Why would he think that? He accused me of taking notes on their military defenses as we rode in the bus? I didn't even see any military defenses--only a bunch of nomads on camels and lots of rocks."

"And this was before you got in the taxi with those men?"

"Yes," said DeeDee. "It was on the way to Petra."

"We'll stop by Military Intelligence on our way home."

"Can't it wait until tomorrow?" I asked. "I really need a shower. Those pigs and chickens...."

"We'd better talk to MI before we do anything else. Someone's on duty all night." Jimmy remained silent the rest of the way. He shook his head from one side to the other and sort of muttered to himself. I let him alone, knowing he'd sort out whatever was weighing on his mind.

I could see the lights of the post ahead, as Jimmy drove between the gates to speak to the guard who emerged from the guardhouse. I breathed a sigh of relief that the whole trip was over. Our base at Bamberg was my favorite place—a haven. The Border military regulations, the formal moment at five p.m. when everyone in our little world stopped their cars, got out, and stood at attention while the National Anthem was played, and the quiet, eerie notes of Taps floating through the night air at ten--all of it had become an important part of my life without my ever realizing how it happened. I only knew I didn't want to live any place else.

DeeDee didn't quite understand the setting of her new life yet, but I was still working on her. I looked over as we reached the gate. She was dozing peacefully, her head against the seat.

The guard let us in when Jimmy flashed his badge and said we were heading to MIHQ.

"Why MI?" asked DeeDee, awakened by their voices.

"They'll want to ask you some questions," said Jimmy.

DeeDee yawned broadly, stretching her arms as far overhead as the ceiling of Jimmy's Volkswagen would allow. "What would they want to ask us about?"

"We'll see when we get there."

We were surprised to find the MI people quite interested in the behavior of the militants toward us mere tourists, and in our behavior as well.

"Did these people buy your ID?" One asked accusingly.

My look silenced his insult. "They took them at gunpoint. We didn't have any say in it."

"What did they ask you?" asked one of the intelligence officers in a softer voice. "Did they ask you anything about the American military, or Israel's military?"

"They asked about operations, our support for Israel, and if we'd seen anything of their PLO defenses. We told them we hadn't seen anything. They also asked if we had names of MI operatives in their theater," I answered.

"Do you?"

"Of course, but I didn't tell them." I saw DeeDee's surprised eyes and ignored them.

"We told them we taught little kids and didn't know anything about anybody's military," volunteered DeeDee. "I just told the truth. I *don't* know anything about the military."

"Good girl," said the other MI. Their mood lightened a bit.

We were asked to write a description of the whole episode with these strange taxi drivers, and the MI officer seemed particularly interested in where we had been taken, how far, and about the unusual checkpoints with bonfires. They also had us describe any fortifications we had seen. DeeDee hadn't seen any. I described the hidden mounds placed among the Nomads in Jordan.

At the conclusion of the de-briefing, almost two hours' worth, the MI officer in charge said, "You ladies are darned lucky those militants found what they wanted and didn't just shoot you when they had you by the ditches. We would never have found you in PLO territory."

"I sort of thought of that when we were out there," I said, voicing the reluctant idea. "But I didn't see any way we could escape, so I tried not to think about it right then."

"We just tried to do what they told us to do and not make them any madder," said DeeDee.

I had a new appreciation for DeeDee's handling of the debriefing. She had backed me up and written out her statement with little fuss. Jimmy finally could take us home.

"I thought the Arabs asked a lot of questions. Our own guys asked even more," said DeeDee, yawning. "I never want to meet any more MI guys--ours or theirs."

"Don't worry about it, DeeDee," said Jimmy, as he turned onto her street to drop her off. "Most likely, MI wants to know where those ID cards might turn up. Though militants couldn't infiltrate Army units with civilian Department of Defense identification, they could get on a base somewhere and do some damage to us. They've done it before."

"Oh, I see," DeeDee said, though I knew she didn't see at all. "What could they want with my notebook though?"

Jimmy flashed his famous grin. "I imagine when they get that piece of tourist shorthand to their commander, or whoever up the chain of command recognizes it as shorthand, they'll be pretty embarrassed that they made such a big deal out of getting it."

DeeDee pursed her lips and shifted her position slightly.

"And before you ask, DeeDee, no, you'll not get it back." "I'm sure they'll throw it out in their embarrassment over taking it in the first place. MI is more worried about the ID cards."

Jimmy reached across the seat to take my hand. "I'm just thankful you didn't try to run away, and those militants finally let you go. That hasn't been the case with every situation, and these situations are escalating."

I crashed, sleeping the clock around in sheer exhaustion. What should have been a quiet rest erupted into nightmares of PLO operatives with guns. When DeeDee called, I found she had much the same experience. We both needed to put these thoughts out of our minds. She came over and we had a glass of wine.

"We won't allow nightmares to get the best of 'Cornelia' and 'Emily,'" she said, and we clinked glasses on it. I loved her optimism.

The weather turned ugly in Germany only a few days later, and our students dragged in with muddy footprints from their days off for Christmas. But they were balm to the soul for forgetting any of the stuff of which nightmares are made. For P.E. we played snow angels or built snowmen. And the kids loved taking their sleds down the hill after school.

DeeDee invited Ruthie, Cathie and me over for lunch on Saturday. Icy road conditions and a recent Border Alert meant we car-pooled. We had no phones at our homes, no television, and only AFN radio news to wake us. Our students were our life during the day, but outside of our classrooms, our leisure lives revolved around visiting friends, often unannounced, and creating our own activities.

It was a good life, and DeeDee was beginning to take part more comfortably. It pleased me that she no longer needed me by her side all the time. She was branching out in her school contacts, though Jimmy was still the only man she would talk to. *There's plenty of time.*

As we stomped snow off our boots in DeeDee's entry hall, we could already smell her pasta sauce simmering and we smiled at each other. DeeDee opened the door wearing a frilly apron. The steam framed her face with little curly tendrils. When cooking, she was in her element.

Conversation spun into different directions from the start. Ruthie was disturbed that her lively captain had been on Alert so much lately. Cathie was irritated with new regulations coming down on salary caps for teachers. And DeeDee had been called upon to rescue students.

"I just don't see why Don is so darned dedicated to the Army that he goes for days and weeks at a time to the Border," complained Ruthie.

"Are you dense, Ruthie?" said Cathie, raising her voice a bit. "For one thing, he follows orders like everyone else. And, in case you hadn't noticed, we've been on Alert for over a week. The communists have rolled their tanks up to the Border again, and our guys have no choice but to roll ours up too, until the commies to give up and go back to their bases. We can't just let the communists take all the rest of Europe like they did the half they control now." Cathie put her hands on her hips and faced Ruthie squarely. "You know Don is in the middle of that. He's an engineer. He's there to lay mines if they decide to come across. Hasn't he told you that?"

"Oh, I suppose he has, but I sort of let it roll in one ear and out the other. I'm not really interested in all that Border stuff. All these secrets and warnings get to me. I don't care who wins—just as long as it all goes away, so Don can stay with me."

I couldn't stand her lack of understanding about our guys and their mission. "You'd better never marry the man, then, Ruthie."

"What do you mean?" she retorted, the color in her cheeks beginning to rise.

"I've known wives who didn't understand their husband's job before, and they made their man, and their marriage, untenable. Don's on the major's list. He'll soon have even more responsibility. You need to get used to the idea, or pick a civilian."

Ruthie was angry. "You've never lost anyone, so how would you know?"

I didn't want to answer. My losses still hurt, but I could see she didn't understand what a military marriage entailed. "Yes,

Ruthie, I've lost someone…three someone's, in fact, so I *do* know. But, I know, too, that you shouldn't marry Don if you don't understand his mission. Sooner or later you'll force him to choose between his duty and you. That's too hard a choice."

"I didn't realize you'd lost any one, Megan," whispered DeeDee, with concern flooding her face. "You never said anything."

"I try not to think about it. Please forget I mentioned it." I could see she wouldn't forget. You could always tell when DeeDee was filing something away for future reference.

Ruthie was absorbed with her gripes at the Army, so she didn't pursue the topic. "I hate all this secrecy. You can't talk about this. You can't talk about that, and Don can't tell me where he's going, or when he'll be back. How can I plan anything?" She poured herself a glass of iced tea. "Sometimes I feel like we should tell everybody everything and get all this Cold War stuff over with. It's so stupid. It's not a shooting war, so what's the big deal?"

"That's only because the guys are out there *to prevent* it becoming World War III," I said. And it's dangerous for you to think you should talk about anything going on."

"Yeah," chimed in DeeDee. "We think we met some spies from the other side in Bethlehem, and we don't want to meet any more—not from either side. I know I'd get red in the face and wouldn't even talk to them, if I met one again."

"Heck DeeDee," said Cathie, "You do that with our own guys, *now*." Ignoring DeeDee's blush, she added, "Seriously, a security breach endangers our guys if the enemy knows our resources or weaknesses. Besides, there's espionage and sabotage going on you'll never know about. This is a trouble zone. Hopefully, you haven't observed enough to be dangerous yet."

"But we already know a lot," insisted Ruthie. "I've seen the nuke trucks go right by my classroom, and it seems like if there were spies, they would see them too."

"Oh, my goodness," chimed in DeeDee. "Was *that* what they were?" She carried a huge pot of her spaghetti sauce to the kitchen table. "I don't want to know about this."

"And we don't talk about it, either of you," I said. "If you don't watch what you say, Ruthie, you'll be a danger to Don and all our other guys. And if you haven't understood by now that security is important to our daily lives here, you should pack up and go home, before you get anyone in trouble, or worse."

Perhaps I sounded a bit emphatic, since her words touched a sore spot with me--a loss I'd never quite gotten over.

Everyone grew quiet.

Without knowing of my personal pain, DeeDee seemed to sense it, and she interrupted.

"Enough talk," she said, as she spooned the sauce on our steaming pasta. The aroma of oregano penetrated my nostrils and we all fell silent for a moment, drinking in the wonderful scent. DeeDee removed her delicate, voile apron and sat down to join us.

"Your spaghetti is the best in the business," said Cathie, savoring the first bite with her eyes closed. "Fabulous."

"It had better be," said DeeDee, "or Mama would kill me. She had me making sauce as soon as I was big enough to see over the edge of the table." She laughed, and I was grateful that she laughed a lot more now than when she first came. She could keep the rest us laughing, too, with her droll way of seeing the world. She was beginning to come up with some satiric one-liners. Miss 'Dolly Dozie' was definitely an asset to our group of teachers, and to our students, though I still couldn't get her to relax around men. If marriage and children was what she wanted most, she certainly wasn't going about it the natural way by meeting people.

"Hey, what was all the hullabaloo I heard about mayhem in Muna today?" asked Cathie.

DeeDee blushed. "It was pretty stupid. It was that local-hire teacher, Binny, that came in from Pittsburg. Remember when we all went to the in-service on teamwork that had trust falls and challenges last fall? They gave us things to do that would be a challenge for adults. We had to get our whole team over the big gas tank out at Muna, and we helped each other over."

We all nodded, because we'd had fun learning serious physical teamwork and getting smaller or larger team members over the challenge course by working together.

"Well, Binny apparently thought she could do it with her second graders, only instead of designing challenges appropriate for her age group, like the instructor assumed we'd all do, she told her kids to get over that *same* gas tank we did. It's at least thirteen feet in the air, and quite round and slippery. We adults even had a hard time with it."

"Oh, my God! What happened?" I asked.

"We could hear all this screaming and crying going on outside, so Barbara and Molly and I ran out to see what was going on. There were all Binny's kids, draped over the sides of that gas tank, scared to death because it was too far to let go, it was concrete underneath, and they couldn't hang on any more. We had to run around grabbing feet and inching the kids down to the ground and catching those who had to let go. It was chaos."

"Wow! Did you guys get 'em all?" asked Cathie.

"Yeah, but it was tough. Some of the GIs within shouting distance came to help, too, and we got the kids down with no injuries except bumps and scrapes. It could have been much worse, if we hadn't heard the kids screaming. They'd all have fallen if she'd been by herself."

"What did she say? She must have realized she did something stupid," said Ruthie.

DeeDee grinned and mimicked with wide-eyed innocence. "She said, 'Gee, I just don't understand. It worked so well as a challenge for the teacher's workshop.'"

We all had to laugh over someone who would try an adult challenge for seven-year-olds, and I was grateful DeeDee and the others had been there for rescue duty. We had to concede that though most all of our DoDDS teachers were proud professionals, once in a while, they hired a klinker...same as in any other business. But those didn't last. This "klinker" was good as gone.

Cathie was also upset about changes in the curriculum and steered the conversation around to the new superintendent for all the DoDDs schools in Germany. I was relieved that I wasn't the only one who thought this woman strange. I was apprehensive about her sweeping changes, too, since we already had a top-notch curriculum with the academic freedom to really teach, but mostly, it was her unusual personality that was worrisome.

"I was hoping for someone good as superintendent," said Cathie. "She has her doctorate, but her inaugural speech said it all. She kept using that one awful word. It was gross."

"I think she was trying to save the hide of the guy who introduced her," Ruthie said. "He told that stupid joke about excrement, totally out of line for an audience of teachers. She just kept using the word to make him feel better about his faux pas."

Cathie laughed. "Once or twice, maybe, but over fifty times? I don't think so! When she talked about how 'we would all have to wade through the excrement in order to teach our students math skills,' I almost barfed. I wondered if she even knew what the word meant."

Ruthie agreed, stifling a giggle. "She did get a little carried away, didn't she?"

Cathie snorted, "I don't think any of us who heard her will *ever* forget the infamous 'Excrement Speech.' I know I'll never see her again without thinking of it and snickering."

Ruthie reached for the Parmesan. "Well, she wanted to make a first impression, and I guess she did. They even taped the speech, so I'm sure we'll hear it again sometime."

"Can't we talk about something besides the Doctor's speech while eating my spaghetti?" asked DeeDee. "Mama wouldn't think excrement a subject fit for the table."

We all looked over at her serious face, and sputtered. Ruthie choked on her sauce and blew little red spatters into her napkin, and I knocked over my iced tea and jumped up to grab the towels from the oven handle DeeDee used for a drying rack, hitting my knee on the table leg.

We all fell apart, until DeeDee's stern expression dissolved into a fit of laughter as well. "I thought what happened at the luncheon afterward was the funniest," she said.

Cathie cast her eyes to the ceiling while biting her lip. "I don't remember anything much about the luncheon. I was just thankful her speech was over and wishing we didn't have to put up with her for three years."

"I mean when she fell over in her chair at lunch," said DeeDee. "If you didn't see that, you missed the best part."

"With about three or four hundred teachers in the hall from all the European DoDDs schools, I guess we missed it," said Ruthie. "Tell us."

"Well..." began DeeDee. Her serious, conspiratorial air added to the hilarity of her words. "She was sitting at our table, and she's a really big woman, you know. All of a sudden between the soup and the meat courses, she just up and falls over with a crash, chair and all."

Ruthie and Cathie looked surprised. I wished DeeDee wouldn't tell this particular story.

"Well, you can't imagine what happened next," she continued. "You know Megan just acts spontaneously, and I just follow. Megan motioned to me, and we picked the superintendent up, chair and all. She looked surprised, but the funny thing was that Megan just kept talking to everyone around the table while she and I sat back down to eat, never missing a beat of the conversation. You could see all the stunned faces with their mouths hanging open when the superintendent fell over. Rather astounded, I think. And then the luncheon just went on like people falling over and getting picked up without a break in the conversation was *normal*.

DeeDee pursed her lips in a surprised "oh," mimicking the teachers who surrounded the incident, then mopped tears of laughter from her eyes. "I never know what Megan may do next to keep things going." DeeDee shook her head as though in disbelief, while the others laughed.

I felt a need to defend myself. "Well, I didn't know what *else* to do, and I figured she'd already embarrassed herself enough with her speech. I knew she couldn't get up alone--better to just go on like nothing happened, don't you think? Besides, I fall over a lot, too, and I wouldn't want anyone to take notice."

"It's pretty hard to ignore *your* falls, Megan, when you can manage to trip over a piece of lint on the floor," said Ruthie, clutching her sides.

"As always, you do the unexpected, Megan," said Cathie between bleats of helpless laughter. "That's probably what always gets you in trouble."

"None of the rest of us would have thought to help that women up," echoed Ruthie, "*or* help you in the process of covering up her embarrassment. Only DeeDee would have followed your lead. We'd have just let her lie there, wouldn't we Cathie?" It took Ruthie a while to slow down her giggles, and then they erupted into huge hiccups that cracked us all up again.

Cathie said, "I think we've discovered DeeDee is a born storyteller, and Megan provides her plenty of mishaps for her stories. You two make quite a team of co-conspirators."

DeeDee looked at me over the top of Ruthie's head with her eyes wide in innocence. When I smiled back, she cracked up, again. We had become friends without realizing it. I wondered when it had happened. But now, I couldn't imagine not having DeeDee around.

Chapter 10 -- Yugoslavia in the Dark

DeeDee's newly found volubility meant she gave her rendition of our trip to Jerusalem to everyone who would listen, much to my embarrassment. But eight additional people, military pilots and DoDDS teachers, decided to join the "Cornelia and Emily tour" on their Easter week trip to Greece by way of Yugoslavia.

"We expect you two to produce an encore of interesting events and mayhem," said Molly, laughing.

"I'm going along to keep Megan out of trouble," said Jimmy.

"I can take care of myself," I told him, rather forcefully. Jimmy just grinned impishly at me. I didn't feel like talking to him much after that.

DeeDee fretted about traveling with so many of a mixed group. "It's the next step toward feeling comfortable in social things. I'll be right there, too," I assured her again.

A caravan of Jimmy and his Volkswagen, Fred with his Chevy, and Jake with his Mercedes would drive their *dependable* cars, which, of course, left my Bosco behind. Fred was an older pilot, about 40 with the old-fashioned regulation crew cut, and Jake, was our resident pilot ne'er-do-well with his irreverent gags. Riding along would be DeeDee and I, Cathie, Ruthie, Ruthie's engineering beau, Don, Molly, our short, chubby Kindergarten teacher with a great big wit, and Ben, another pilot who was relatively new in country. It would be a congenial group for DeeDee to break into socially, and I figured sooner or later she'd have to talk to the guys.

We planned to cross through Tito's Yugoslavia, a communist state in name only, yet a military briefing was still required to check everyone for his or her knowledge of classified material. By this time, DeeDee was accustomed to the unusual requirements of Border life, so she asked no questions.

"Please try to hang on to your ID cards, this time," cautioned Major Blaine, our briefing officer. "Losing them to the wrong people could be dangerous. Don't do that again."

DeeDee and I just looked at each other and broke out laughing. "I'd hoped he had forgotten about *that*," she said.

"I mean it," he cautioned, shaking his finger, as we struggled to control our outburst.

We made good time south through Graz, Austria, with its huge fortress to protect from what the old Austro-Hungarians considered the "inferior Slavic races." But entering Yugoslavia took three hours. Many Yugoslavs worked outside their country, something forbidden in other communist countries, and all seemed to be going home for the Easter holiday at the same time. A colossal jam-up ensued, "A Stau mit Stillstand," as the Germans so appropriately called it. Since the roads were built and maintained by hand, with pickaxe and shovel, the potholes were like moonscapes.

"They're suitable for foxholes," Jimmy declared. "I'll probably have to replace my shocks after this trip." We jounced and bumped the ceiling or were jerked against the windows. "I'm glad I didn't let you talk me into your driving your 'Bosco.' That wreck would fall apart."

"Do you think this will get any smoother?" asked DeeDee from the back seat. She held a pillow against the side of the car and wedged herself into a corner to cushion the bouncing. In the front, I gripped my seat with both hands in a futile attempt to sit still.

"I don't know, DeeDee." My voice was a vibrating falsetto. Jimmy was concentrating on the road. "I hope so." I tried to laugh and only wound up biting my tongue on the next bump.

There were only two roads--an interior road, on which we traveled, and the coastal road, by which we planned to return. Our dog-eared Frommer's guidebook, now in DeeDee's hands, meant she read aloud. "It says that, 'in 1939, there were thirty miles of paved road in the country, and even now they have just two types-- those big enough for donkeys and those big enough for cars.' I'll bet our colonial corduroy log roads seemed smooth as velvet by comparison."

Jimmy waved his hand at the traffic in frustration. "It doesn't look like our East/West Borders between the two Germanys. No visible fence lines, no mines, no guard towers."

"Tito isn't a Moscow-type communist," I told him. "Remember? Major Blaine said Tito calls this a 'Socialist Republic.'" I'd read a lot about Tito. I had to admit the rebel fascinated me. His World War II Partisans drove out the Nazis without Soviet help, so Yugoslavs were able to resist the all-out domination that plagued other Soviet bloc countries. Tito gave his people more freedom, so the Yugoslavs were fiercely independent.

"The USSR offered aid, but it had many strings attached," read DeeDee. "So Tito refused the aid, the Yugoslavs were cut off, and Tito has now formed a group of non-aligned countries."

"That was a gutsy move," said Jimmy, shaking his head. "Of course, that's probably why they're still so primitive and have to work so hard, too. Look, ladies."

DeeDee and I peered outside to see old people working in the fields with a donkey. There seemed to be no young people at all. One farmer pulled his donkey forward, dragging a roughly hewn harrow behind. His old wife, in long black dress and babushka, bounced perilously on top to weigh down the harrow's sticks into the ground.

"The scene is like a Flemish painting, isn't it?" I said. "Beautiful, rustic, and yet so depressing to see them have to work so hard, and so far into their old age."

"Communists have no retirement," said Jimmy, stretching his arms, one at a time, from the vibrating steering wheel. "They work until they drop."

Trucks, buses, cars, all passed continuously as though they had to be first to arrive. *Where,* I wondered, since all was so primitive, anyway? Several vehicles lay upturned in the gullies, left there to rust. We started around a truck ahead, and a Yugo swung out to pass us at the same time, hanging clear out on the edge and wedging us in the middle. Mere inches separated the three vehicles, and there was no way out of it, except to go on.

"Hot damn!" muttered Jimmy under his breath, as he struggled to keep our car away from the other two. Then he turned slightly, "Sorry."

"No problem," I answered, clinging tightly to the hand rest and bracing against the console. "Whatever helps you keep us on the road." The truck and Yugo seemed glued to us.

DeeDee sank to the backseat floor, holding her pillow against the side of the car. "I can't look," she squealed. "I thought Roman drivers were bad, but these guys are passing on hills, on curves. There isn't even a shoulder on this road, and big ditches are on both sides. What could they be thinking?"

Jimmy and I held our breath, hoping that when we got around each curve, there wouldn't be a truck head-on in our lane. Wreaths of flowers dotted the road's edges—hundreds of them-- each indicating where someone had died.

"Why, their accident rate would put a California holiday weekend to shame." I said. Even as I spoke, we rounded a curve, a car started passing us, but a truck was already coming toward him in his lane. He honked and squeezed himself in front of us, sparing a head-on crash only by inches and by Jimmy's quick reaction time. Jimmy let out a long breath and whistled. I looked behind at the other cars in our caravan. Behind us, Jake clung grimly to his steering wheel, his mouth moving constantly, most likely with his usual cuss words. DeeDee made little noises, praying, I thought. I reached over the seat and placed my hand on her head for comfort.

The terrain, splashing waterfalls, and fields of flowers were beautiful, but old men and women along the road led their donkeys, or scrubbed laundry in big metal tubs, or cooked over an open fire outside their primitive houses. "They work so very hard for so little benefit," Jimmy said.

"I'll bet Hitler couldn't even *find* Tito's Partisans when they hid in these wild mountains to fight off the occupation." I searched for the caves Partisans had written about.

"The terrain favors the defender, that's for sure," said Jimmy in his 'soldier's voice.' "Anyone trying to attack into those deep crevasses would be surrounded on all sides."

There were so many languages--Macedonian, Croatian, Serbian--about a dozen unique factions. "Tito's the force that's held them together, but he's a really old man," I said. "Who can keep these groups together when he dies? They'll want to break into their old tribal rivalries."

"They'll have civil wars among themselves," said Jimmy, matter-of-factly. His calm face belied his words. "There's so much that's different between these groups—ethnically, religiously, and culturally. Those differences will escalate without Tito to hold them together by sheer force of personality."

"You mean like the signs near Zagreb in regular alphabet, and below Belgrade it's Cyrillic?" asked DeeDee.

"That, and lots more. They'll break apart when he dies, you wait and see."

I knew in my head that Jimmy was right. The Balkans were historically known for their separatist infighting. But in my heart, I didn't want this beautiful countryside torn by more war.

In the gathering twilight we saw old women herding pigs in the fields like sheep. "Boy, those are the cleanest, fattest pigs I've ever seen," said DeeDee enthusiastically, when she peeked over the car seat. "They aren't all lazy and dirty like ours, raised in a pigpen."

"What a great idea—swineherds producing clean pigs," said Jimmy, waving at an elderly couple's salute.

The people were friendly. DeeDee and I hung out the windows and waved back. Little villages south of Belgrade reminded us of Anatevka in *Fiddler on the Roof*—overworked, underfed, with women in long black skirts even for farm work. Their shoes had turned up toes and fabric wrapped up around their calves to keep them on, like a ballerina's toe shoes. The men cut grain with an old-fashioned scythe. They were also in black clothing, often with a shawl around their middles, perhaps to hold their voluminous trousers up. The hilly, terraced farms were a dawn-to-dusk operation, for the whole of their lives. The area often had mere hovels or caves for shelter. I felt it depressing and courageous at the same time.

The southern area had several mosques for the Islamic population. Hills stripped nude by Venetian shipbuilders in the fifteenth century meant nothing had grown there since, so some parts were quite barren. A lady who looked to be in her nineties was sweeping a park trail that evening with a broom of sticks. The work ethic of these old people was phenomenal.

We found Yugoslavia's slow roads took us than we had thought. Darkness fell, and we needed to stop someplace.

"No lights up ahead," said DeeDee, "but, according to the map, a town is ahead of us."

"I hope you're right," Jimmy said, stretching his torso upright. "We need gas."

Our little convoy entered a small village nestled in darkness. "It's strange that there aren't any lights?" I said. "They can't all be in bed so early."

"Hm," said Jimmy. He usually reconnoitered before deciding the cause of any potential problem--*a military thing.*

We pulled over to wait for the two following cars, and soon everyone stood at the side of the road to confer. A barefoot little boy of about six or eight years materialized out of the darkness. He ran up and tugged at Jimmy's hand.

"You want eat. Mama has food. Come with me, please."

"What the heck," said Jimmy, calling to the rest of the travelers. "What's going on?" he asked the child, bending to listen. "Where are the lights?"

"No light today, waterfalls low water—tomorrow better," said the child.

The little boy pulled again at Jimmy's hand and grabbed mine for good measure.

"Gas station?" queried Jimmy. "Is there gas?"

The child shook his head, barely visible in the darkness. "Tomorrow," he repeated.

Jimmy turned to the other drivers, and Fred said, "If there's no electricity until tomorrow, we can't get gas now. Pumps are usually electric. We'll have to stay overnight here, dark or no dark.

My Chevy won't make it much further without gas."

The child tugged again.

"Let's all go eat for now, and maybe the boy's mama knows when the gas stations will reopen or where we might stay," I suggested.

The occupants of all three cars joined hands behind the little boy who led us through pitch-blackness on a narrow, unpaved street, into the back alleys, and finally into a small restaurant lit by candles. Our group almost filled the restaurant, but the jolly proprietor seemed pleased his son had found some hungry visitors. He quickly offered a wooden board carrying tiny schnapps glasses filled with a clear liquid. It seemed only polite to accept, so we each took a glass and sat down at tables one could barely see in the dimly lit room. The man returned with menus we could not read, though people tried, turning them this way and that. It was too dark to even tell what language they were in. Jimmy finally asked our host in a mixture of all the languages he knew plus signing with his hands, to just prepare whatever he had that would be easy to fix. Once he understood, the robust man nodded and disappeared.

"What did you order, Jim?" asked Jake.

"Darned if I know, but he'll bring us something."

As each person tasted the schnapps, there were gasps around the room, followed by laughter. "Ouzo," said Ben. "We should have known."

"It'll fix whatever ails you," said Jimmy, downing his and then coughing.

DeeDee and I both took tiny sips of the burning liquid. She sputtered and shook her head. I couldn't drink the rest of the stuff—like liquid fire, and tasting like licorice. But neither of us wanted to admit we hated it, since the proprietor was trying so hard to make us welcome. DeeDee pointed at a nearby potted plant and raised her eyebrows at me when no one was looking. *Hope that plant doesn't die.*

A very plump woman entered with silverware and plates. She had an embroidered black kerchief tied around her head and knotted behind. Her apron looked well worn, with several patched places but, even in the dim light, we could see it glowed sparkling white from many washings. With her little boy in tow, we knew this was a "mom and pop" operation. They were charming people, trying hard to please their unexpected windfall of ten guests. The woman smiled and signaled to the boy. He placed a basket of dark, homemade bread on each table.

Jake asked the child his name, and the woman answered for him. Andreas Poplovich. Jake immediately called him "Andy," and the child rewarded him with a big smile and an extra piece of bread placed in his hand.

Cathie looked out the window. "Hey, you guys. They're cooking on an open bonfire and a clay oven outside. Aren't they afraid they'll set something on fire?"

"They've probably been cooking outside for centuries," said Fred, "so why worry? In fact, food might really taste good over an open fire."

Everyone peeked outside, watching the silhouettes of our hosts almost dancing around a pot swinging above the blazing fire.

Soon they entered bearing steaming bowls of something warmly fragrant. A stew thick with vegetables, lamb in small chunks, rice rolled in cabbage leaves, and stuffed red peppers. The man ladled out huge servings on plates arranged by the child.

When they finished serving, Jimmy motioned for them to sit down with us to eat. He motioned, "I pay." The family conferred, smiled, and sat down.

Jimmy nudged me and whispered, "I could see little Andreas' eyes when we got the food. He probably doesn't get the same as the customers, and we seem to be the only customers tonight, don't you think?"

I smiled at him. Sometimes Jimmy could surprise me with little gestures of kindness. He was definitely one of the good guys, and he sort of grew on me. I was becoming quite fond of him.

A jovial meal ensued during which everyone asked questions in slow German, which most older Yugoslavs knew from the occupation, sprinkled liberally with Slavic, Russian, and a few broken English phrases. We were able to find out about the lack of electricity.

"Water too low for enough power," said our host, mimicking the movement of waterfalls with his burnished brown hands. "Government rationed power--inland half-week, and then coastal half-week." His hands flew quickly to demonstrate one side alternating with the other.

This meant half of the week, the coastal road people had power and the inland people did not, and the rest of the week, the inland people had power and the coastal ones didn't.

"Why am I not surprised," said Jake, "that we are driving through the inland road on its 'power off' days, and we'll return on the coastal road on its 'power off' days?"

"Just the luck of the draw," I said. "It wasn't advertised, so none of us knew."

Fred and Ruthie looked at each other and laughed.

"It's the first 'curse of Cornelia,' don't' ya'll think," said Ruthie, "just for being along?"

I ignored them and moved closer to Jimmy. It was still a lovely evening.

"We have gasoline tomorrow?" Jimmy asked our host, mercifully changing the subject.

Mr. Poplovich nodded his black and gray streaked curly head. "Perhaps tomorrow."

Little Andreas was the image of his father, and his curls tangled into little kinks, his black eyes sparkling every time someone spoke to him. "Tomorrow," he echoed.

"Is there a place we can stay tonight?" asked Jimmy.

The two Poplovich adults conferred. "Hotel?" asked Mrs. Poplovich.

We all nodded.

"Here," she said, pointing up the dark stairs. "Very clean, very cheap."

Jimmy called out to the others, "Is this okay with you?"

"We're here now, and I don't relish hunting around in the dark for someone willing to take us in," answered Ben. "This is fine." The guys dared the darkness to bring in all overnight cases. Little Andreas led them, ensuring they wouldn't get lost.

"Follow me," said the child, breathlessly, when he returned. It seemed the little guy did everything at a dead run. We trooped up the rickety stairway. He showed DeeDee, Cathie, and me to a small room with two beds--a double, and one child-sized bed. DeeDee lost the coin toss, so she put her case under the short bed.

Cathie stripped to the skin and performed a sponge bath in the rusty sink. "I'm sure it would embarrass the folks if we all insisted on showers."

DeeDee and I both averted our eyes to unpack our pajamas, a little embarrassed by Cathie's sudden striptease. I answered Cathie without turning toward her. "With no heat or light, I imagine there'll be no hot water either"

"Hadn't thought of that."

Mrs. Poplovich knocked when all the guests were settled, two or three to a room, to see if we needed anything.

"Could you please give us a wake up call in the morning...about seven?" asked Cathie, showing the time on her watch.

The woman bobbed and smiled. "Yes, you'll be knocked up in the morning."

"God, I hope not," said Cathie, giggling. The woman smiled broadly, not realizing she'd used British slang that meant something quite different in America.

"Water closet there," Mrs. Poplovich said, pointing down the hall and around a corner.

"Thank you," we said almost in unison, and the rotund lady waddled back down the steps. The lilt in her voice made us confident we were welcomed guests.

"I'll bet they gave us their bedrooms, too," said DeeDee.

"Probably. I doubt they counted on having this many guests. They'll most likely bunk down in the kitchen or the dining room on the benches," said Cathie. "But they were nice about letting us stay. Perhaps the room rates will give them a little financial boost.

I guess we were all pretty tired, because the house quickly became quiet. I lay in bed as long as I could before deciding I'd need to go down the hall to the WC. As I tiptoed out the door and down the hall, I saw a chair at the corner where the hall forked off to the left. A burning candle sat on the chair in a tin holder, with curtains from the open window splayed out dangerously close to the flame. The whole house was made of wood, with rough wooden boards on the floor, and we were all on the upper floor. A bit of precaution seemed necessary. I blew out the candle on the way back to my room.

I still had trouble going to sleep. I heard DeeDee stir before I got up a second time.

"You all right?" I whispered.

"Yeah, just going down the hall. Go to sleep." Upon her return, she rolled over in her tiny bed with her knees scrunched up. I felt pity for her drawing the short bed, though it wasn't exactly comfortable sleeping in a double bed with Cathie, either. We were both used to having our own space, and her splayed arms and legs left me little room, clinging to the other edge.

But something kept me from sleeping…some kind of anxiety. I entered the hall once more, darned if that candle wasn't lit again! Now, I *knew* I couldn't go to sleep, because we were all in danger if someone wasn't on "fire watch." I guess that would be me, since I'm awake. Again I tiptoed to the chair and blew out the candle.

This exercise in futility was repeated all night. No way could I leave a candle burning in a wooden house. Who could be relighting it? After several times getting up just to check, I figured someone else was up several times, as well--whoever was relighting the candle. I would've preferred to blunder in the dark.

The next morning, Mr. Poplovich apologized for any inconvenience that had been caused by the "breeze" that kept putting out the candle. I guess he was on "fire watch," too.

I must have blushed in the daylight, because both Jimmy and DeeDee looked at me with eyebrows arched. Jimmy laughed until I shushed him, with my pleading hand on his arm.

"Don't worry, darling, your secret is safe with me," he said. "You look after everyone else and forget to look after yourself--a grievous fault." He grinned and added, "but I bet you'll sleep all day in the car." I blushed all over again, determined to stay awake, no matter what.

"Was that you?" whispered DeeDee. "I kept thinking it was the wind, and I feared the boys coming into our room in the dark, so I relit the candle several times so we'd see them."

"Good grief!" I said, "Why on earth would you think they'd do that?"

DeeDee cringed. "I don't know, but Mama always said to watch out for boys acting bad in the dark, and that was the only thing bad I could think of that they might do."

I groaned. "Believe me, DeeDee, these guys are not going to do anything to you, and quit calling them 'boys.' They're grown men, and you're a grown woman. They don't need to play silly little games like sneaking into someone's room at night. For Pete's sake, grow up and quit worrying about what Mama says."

I took a deep breath and was immediately sorry I'd been so harsh. I shrugged, a little embarrassed, and smiled at her." It's okay, DeeDee. But I still think a candle is dangerous."

The Poplovich family had been so kind. They were very pleased when the bills were paid, both for the excellent meal, and the room. We tried to pay also for the continental breakfast they provided, but they insisted it was the same as Germany—the continental breakfast came with the room. While we found the prices extremely cheap, the two adults could barely contain their giggles as Mama Poplovich put all the money in her apron pocket, keeping her hand in the pocket, patting and rubbing the money. Andreas danced around us and offered to show us to the filling station, the only one in town.

When we reached the station, which sported one old-fashioned glass pump, we had to wait. The owner had not yet shown up. Andreas waited with us, and finally he made a beeline for the owner's house across the road, where he pounded on the window until a fat and wrinkled old man hobbled out, putting on his shirt as he ran with the boy. Full of apologies that the electric pump was not quite ready, he tucked in his shirt and settled his wide girth against the whitewashed building to wait with us. I had assumed the old pump was hand-operated anyway, but apparently this was the *one* thing in the village they'd "modernized" to use electricity.

We waited about half an hour, and suddenly the pump came to life with a loud humming noise. The man pumped gas into the three cars, and Andreas ran around hugging everyone.

As we drove away, the Poplovichs stood on the road and waved...Papa waving his cap, and Mama waving her apron. Their smiles warmed us as we waved back.

"Good people," declared Jimmy with a firm nod, as he settled into his backrest and drove carefully away at the head of the caravan.

DeeDee patted my arm from the back seat and grinned.

Chapter 11 - The Siren Call of Delphi

At a pit stop well inside the Greek border, the whole crew poured over maps. "Let's drive up to Delphi," suggested Jake. "It's mountainous, and we can all consult the Oracle."

"The Oracle is dead, dummy, quite mythological," said Cathie, habitually patting her blonde curls in the wind. "We can only see the place where she conducted business."

"That's good enough," said Molly, giggling as she talked. "It says in the book that it's a beautiful little village perched right on the edge of a cliff."

That settled it. All three carloads of Americans turned upward to spend a day and night at the Oracle's lair in Delphi. Steep cliffs rose ahead of us on the narrow, rutted road dangling on the cliff edge--another of those hold-your-breath terrains that had DeeDee hiding on the floor of the back seat. I had confidence in Jimmy's driving, but I wasn't so sure about Fred and Jake behind us. Whenever we met a car coming down the hill, we had to back up to a wider spot to let the car go by—a slightly hairy experience. I got out each time to give Jimmy aircraft parking signals, so he'd know how close he was backing to the edge and when to stop for the other car to pass. On one of my re-entries, he smiled and said, "Be careful out there on the edge, Cupcake. I don't want you to disappear entirely, just trying to help me stop in time."

We passed half caved-in houses people were still living in after a recent severe earthquake. Many had thatched huts. They herded sure-footed goats, or kept bees--a sixteenth century life style on steeply terraced fields. We watched the women climb down the hill to bring back water, balancing their clay jugs on their heads. But where the Yugoslavians had seemed quiet, but strongly independent, these Greeks, in spite of their poverty, didn't seem to take life too seriously. They looked happy-go-lucky, lolly-gagging to gossip on the way uphill.

The road ended, but the village itself was still upward. We

parked the cars and walked up a steep path through wildflower fields, carrying our shoulder bags. Whenever someone slowed down, Ben would sing out, "Upward and onward, Spartans," and we'd give it one more try.

Since marmot or "Mummelteer" tunnels dotted the fields, Jimmy frequently grabbed my arm as we stepped around the dens of these rarely seen, overgrown prairie dogs.

DeeDee poured over her guidebook as she miraculously climbed up the field without even looking at her feet. *How can she do that? I stumble my way, even when careful.*

"It says here that we should wear good walking shoes because everything in the Greek islands is uphill to the Acropolis," she read.

"I thought Acropolis meant the Parthenon in Athens."

"No, it says here that the Acropolis is always the highest point in *each* city."

"I never would've guessed," said Jake, wiping sweat from his brow. "It's high all right."

"Wait for me," cried Molly. "My legs are shorter."

We found a hotel, and dropped off our luggage, wasting no time to hurry out and see the sights. Delphi was a much smaller village than we had anticipated, but jolly, friendly people waved and smiled at us. The town rolled up its sidewalks between one and four daily, as residents enjoyed their afternoon meal and nap. But the shops reopened from four until about eleven.

In the Oracle's amphitheater, we heard a pin drop and a match strike in its center. We tried it again and again from different listening points, and we could always hear the softest sound clearly. A docent steering tourists around the area explained that something in the way the theater was formed caused this phenomenon. Don had studied to be an opera singer before he became a hotshot engineer, and Ruthie had a nice contralto voice, so they stood in the middle and sang. We enjoyed their hamming up an old tune, "I Heard It Through The Grapevine" and whistled and clapped in appreciation. The applause echoed all around the amphitheater. Some Dutch tourists passed by who probably thought we were crazy. That didn't worry us. Our group of friends always managed a party wherever we went. I guess it was that sort of resiliency and ability to take everything in stride and have fun with it that I wanted DeeDee to become a part of, by taking her with a group. I watched her laugh, and felt good about the trip.

A day visiting the Oracle's digs and refreshing ourselves on mythological stories made us eager for some nightlife. We had dinner at a nice Greek restaurant and searched for a place where we could dance. Quite lively by night, Delphi had bistros, discos and restaurants open very late. We walked until we found a disco that played music we could hear clear out in the street. DeeDee whispered, "Are you sure I should go in? You know I can't dance."

I love to dance, so I'd spent many days trying to teach her the basics. But I couldn't even get her to do a passable "Hustle." We finally agreed dancing wasn't her aptitude and gave up. But we knew her aptitude was cooking, anyway. We'd learned to appreciate each other's talents.

This little disco seemed like the right place, so we entered just as it was getting busy, about ten p.m. But we found the clientele a bit unusual. It was all men! Not one woman in the whole place. We drew a few stares upon our arrival, but we didn't let that bother us. Several men moved to a traditional folk dance all in a line with joined hands in the air, and led by the first man with a handkerchief.

"Hey," said Ben, "I think we've discovered the original Zorba."

"I'd like to learn that," Cathie said, slapping a hand against her leg to keep time.

"Me, too," I agreed. "Folk dances are fun wherever we go."

"Yeah," said Fred. "I still remember your learning three of them when a bunch of us went to Spain. You had us stopping every time we saw a new dance in the street."

"Saldana, Hota, and Flamenco" said Jimmy with a grin. "I remember how we all just banged our heels to make noise, while you learned the Flamenco with castanets."

"Castanets were fun, but in Madrid you and Ben had the

warped idea of using the bidet in your hotel bathroom for a wine cooler. Do you remember?"

"Well, we couldn't figure out what it was for, and it worked perfectly for a party in our room. Of course, we made three trips to the downstairs bar to fill it with ice."

Those who remembered the trip laughed, and those who hadn't been along wanted to hear details. Ben and Molly had to be filled in, while DeeDee asked innocently, "What's a bidet?"

"Tell you later," I said, laying a finger in front of my lips. She nodded.

I liked Greek music. While in Yugoslavia, all the music we heard was in minor keys, and in Spain there had been a variety from lively Soldana to morbid folk singing. But in Greece, it was exciting music with lots of slaps and hops in the dancing.

"Well, who's with me to ask these gentlemen if they'll teach us?" One by one, hands came up slowly, all except DeeDee's. Majority ruled, so I approached the leader with the handkerchief after they had completed their dance. It looked easy enough, and I sort of thought I had the basic steps figured out.

The man was probably in his sixties and was quite dignified with his black vest, gold pocket watch, and a scarf hanging from around his waist. He had a dark beard and deep-set, dark eyes with connected bushy brows that commanded authority. An earring in one ear glowed golden, picking up light from the disco ball above us. My sign language must have been a mystery to him, because he kept shrugging his huge shoulders and pointing at my friends. Finally, one of the others on his team of dancers shuffled forward and offered to translate. Gratefully, I told him that we all enjoyed the dance and would like for them to teach us the steps.

A heated exchange passed between the two before the translator said, "Sandor is confused because women never do this dance. In fact, *good* women never come out of their homes at night."

DeeDee's hand flew over her mouth, but I ignored his obvious emphasis in favor of explanation. "In our country, the custom is for all to go out together, and some of us are particularly interested in folk dances."

"Speak for yourself, Megan," muttered Jake.

The translator again turned to Sandor, the Zorba look-alike, and passed on my request.

The man more or less grunted his assent, not looking particularly happy about it, but at his direction, the line of men tucked one of us in between each of his friends and walked through the steps a couple of times. Ben ran over to drag DeeDee back to fill one gap. I could see the terror in her eyes, but she might as well try new things. I wouldn't interfere.

Jimmy waved one finger as a sign he needed one more walk through, and then the three musicians began the lively music.

I can't say we were particularly good at this new dance, but it helped that those who knew it well were interspersed between us, in charge of the hands we held in the air. DeeDee sort of walked, not really lifting her feet. She stumbled or turned the wrong way often, but one of the Greek men at her side seemed happy to show her again and again just where to point her toe, by taking her ankle in his hand, of course. Poor girl was so intimidated by trying to remember the steps that she didn't even notice the familiarity.

Jimmy caught my eye by leaning around the Greek man between us and winked, jerking his head toward DeeDee to see if I'd been watching, too. I couldn't help but smile.

The musicians pounded out the rhythm strongly, and before long, the Greek men were laughing again and apparently not so upset about our being in their ranks. Even the leader next to me saw that most of us had the steps figured out, and chortled with laughter.

"Hey, this is fun," said Ben. "Even I can manage it." He bobbed back and forth, kicking at more or less the appropriate point and laughing with the men on each side of him.

"I think I need to sit down," said DeeDee, as the group broke up, breathless and full of good humor. We took chairs around little ice-cream-parlor type tables.

"But, you at least tried, and you enjoyed it, didn't you?" I had to ask.

She dabbed at her sweating brow and grinned. "Sort of. I feel all tied up trying to get my feet to work, but it was fun. I can't believe I would've missed Greece by staying in Ithaca." She shook her head and waved her hands. "If Mama could see me now, I know she wouldn't approve, especially after that Greek guy said *good* women don't go out after dark. What does that make *us*?" She smiled with discovery. "But you know something, Mama *can't* see me now. I'll just have to decide how to tell her, later."

"Good girl," I said, "I'm proud of you for figuring that out." Then I moved over when Ben came to sit at our table and talk to DeeDee.

"Ah ha," said Jimmy, as he slipped into the chair next to me. "That's kinda new, isn't it?"

"I guess so. It must've been the dancing." We smiled together.

The combo switched to regular disco music, a bit tinny, but at least a recognizable American tune, an old Captain and Tennille hit, "Love Will Keep Us Together." Jimmy jerked his head in the direction of the dance floor. I rose, but he halted a few feet from the floor.

All the Greek men were disco dancing *with each other*! It looked like *Saturday Night Fever* run amok.

"Are we sure we want to get out there? This looks weird to me," Jimmy whispered.

"I'm not sure. Maybe it's just because the women don't come out of their houses at night, the men have no one else to dance with."

"Yeah, but a traditional folk dance in a men's line looks a lot different from just dancing like a man and woman would to disco music." Questioning wrinkles formed on his face.

I waved at the others, and motioned them to come onto the dance floor with us. It didn't seem appropriate to venture out there alone, though certainly these Greek men seemed to enjoy their disco dancing as much as they had their folk dance.

Once we were all on the floor, except for Ben who still was talking to DeeDee, we forgot about the Greek men, since we were caught up with our own gyrations. The Greeks watched, and they quickly tried the steps we were using. Then Molly and Jake started doing The Bump, to "Kung Fu Fighting," and we all joined in.

The Greek men stopped dancing and stood watching a few minutes, then the leader walked over and grabbed my hand, while the translator grabbed Jimmy's. The others all exchanged partners involuntarily, too, and we showed them how to do it, bumping hips on the second beat of each measure.

What really turned out to look funny, though, was watching our guys who had been paired up with us females, suddenly being expected to dance "The Bump" with this assortment of Greek men. They kept looking around the room at anything *except* their new "partner."

"It's for the sake of Greek-American relations, guys," Ruthie called out when Jake tried to creep from the floor and away from his male partner. "Get yourself back out here, Jake."

I have to give our American military guys credit—they did their best in spite of their uncomfortable feelings, and the Greeks all cheered the Americans once a few of the dances were over. Then the guys skedaddled back to dance with "real women" as Fred said, and the Greek men went on dancing with each other to "Rock Your Baby."

"The Bump" had just put down Greek roots.

"Oh, well," said a resigned Jimmy. Then he noticed the club's manager wiping down tables and putting booze away and checked his watch. "It's two in the morning, guys. None of us noticed the time pass so quickly, but I think they're closing down on us. We'd better go."

Our new Greek friends, about whom Jake still held suspicion, all came to kiss us on each cheek, guys and girls alike. Quite a "friendly" group, I'd say.

"That dude squeezed my hand once too often," Jake complained, once out in the street.

"I still think they just don't let their women out at night," I said. "Maybe it's sort of like those old sailors on ships for months doing the hornpipe together."

"I guess we'll never know," said Cathie, "but I had a good time." She joined one hand to Ruthie's and they started dancing the Greek folk dance down the cobble-stoned street. One by one, we all joined onto the end of the line and danced all the way back to our hotel, humming the catchy Greek tune the musicians had played. We shushed each other a bit when we noticed the street was deserted. No one was out and about, and all the homes were shuttered and dark.

"That's kind of ominous," said Don, coming up short at the door of the hotel. The huge bronze ornamental doors were locked and dead-bolted for the night. It would take a key to open them, even from the inside. European hotels did not as a rule give guests a key to the front door—only to their own rooms.

"We should have asked for an outside key," Molly said.

"None of us thought about their locking up," answered Fred. "Besides, we didn't think we'd be out this late."

We had not paid much attention to the hotel when we left in our hurry to go out to dinner and dance. But, though the inside of the hotel even smelled new, they had not yet sufficiently finished the outside. It rose in a blank cement wall on the street side, with no lights, no doors, no windows, no alcoves, no completed sidewalks, and we were completely in darkness in the shadow of the building.

"I didn't know they locked up hotels here, too," Jake said. "We found it out in Austria, but since the Greeks were out dancing half the night, I figured it would be different here."

"Oh, my goodness! Now what will we do?" wailed DeeDee.

I glared at her just in time and, even in the dark, she knew it. She shut up. "We'll find a way," I whispered. "Stop worrying."

Ben, Jimmy, and Fred all tried calling out in unison, "Hallo, hallo," and banging on the ornate bronze door, hoping someone on duty would open the door for us. No such luck.

"Maybe around on the ends," said Jake. He suggested we hold onto each other's shoulders in the darkness so no one would trip, and walk around to the other side of the hotel. "There must be another entrance on the ends of the building or on the opposite side," he said, "even if only for a fire escape."

We chained up; hands to shoulders, and Ben led the way around the end of the large four-storied building. It revealed not even a fire exit door. Then we moved to the backside with all the balconies. Every room had a balcony facing out over the valley below, with an inside door opening into the main hall. We had admired the views from the French-doors when we briefly dropped off luggage before dinner, but no one had actually taken the time to go out on the balcony and look over the side.

Ben came to an abrupt halt, causing all the rest of us to stumble into him. "Damn it, guys, don't push," he yelled. We could hear a few other soft swear words. He called back, "Those balconies hang right out over the cliff. We seem to be under the balconies and right against the cliff edge. Wish we'd reconnoitered that before we left. We can't get around this way. We'll have to reverse course. Everyone turn around and grab shoulders going the other way."

We all turned, leaving Jake to lead us back the way we'd come. I struggled to maintain my footing in the dark on the rough ground. Jimmy's hand on my shoulder helped keep me steady. Jake stopped by the locked front door to shout and bang a few times more, but no one came to our rescue. The blank concrete wall had no windows and showed no sign of life. So we continued, chain fashion, through the dark to the other end of the building, thinking surely we could get in someplace on the end or the balcony side. Did the whole building hang over a cliff?

But when Jake led to the back of the building again, and still had found no path, and no door, only a drop off of about 200 feet on the cliff side, he used a few choice words. Though not particularly tactful, Jake was a good pilot and a good guy, other than with language.

"Shh," barked Jimmy. "We have ladies among us."

"Sorry," Jake echoed back, "but the ladies among us aren't going to like our predicament any more than I do."

I suppose the fact that we had all had a wine or two at the

Greek disco gave us confidence that there *must* be another way. Jake leaned out to examine the balconies. At least moonlight shone on *this* side of the building, so he could see a little better.

"Is anyone's room on the first floor?" he asked. No answer.

"How about the second floor?"

"DeeDee and I are on second," I said.

"It appears all the rooms have balconies hanging over the cliff side, and the doors opening into the halls are on the *other* side of each room. We'll have to go through someone's room to get to the hall, if we want to get to our rooms." Jake *sounded* confident.

"What if they won't let us in?" said DeeDee, her voice edging higher. As usual, she found a problem in every solution.

"I don't think we have any choice but to try, guys," said Ben. "I think I can climb that trellis with all the vines on it about two balconies over, if we can edge over that far without falling. If I can climb up and find a sliding door that's open, maybe they'll just let us walk through their rooms without disturbing any one else. If not, at least on a balcony, we'll be out of the weather until morning."

"Complete strangers? Oh we couldn't," said DeeDee.

Jimmy turned to her. "Do you have a better idea, 'Miss Emily'? We can't stay out here all night, and when we danced our way home to the hotel, I'm sure you noticed even the Flocati rug merchant had closed his doors. Where else can we go?"

DeeDee was silent.

Ruthie wasn't happy. "You mean we're going to climb a trellis, maybe with thorns, and hang out over that two hundred foot cliff's drop-off? What if it isn't strong enough to hold us?"

"I'll go first," said Ben. "There's maybe a two-foot shelf of dirt on the cliff edge. If I can tip toe over on that edge holding on to the balcony wall, then I can try to climb the trellis. If it will hold me, it should hold the rest of you, and you can follow my path. Be sure you hold onto the balcony railing when you come, all of you. Don't trust your footing without holding on."

"Let's just hope there's an open door on the first floor up," said Jake. Go ahead, Ben, I'll stabilize the trellis while you climb."

The two set off edging their way along the cliff side with their feet under the balconies, while running their hands along the top of the concrete railings. When they got to the trellis, Ben pulled on it a little to check its strength, nodded at Jake and started climbing. Jake held the bottom of the trellis steady.

When Ben reached the first floor balcony, he climbed onto it. He soon returned to hang over and whisper, "All locked doors." Then he swung back around on the trellis and went up one more flight. This time, he jumped to the second floor balcony and immediately returned, swinging his arm in the "come on" signal. Jake shushed each of us as we edged along the cliff side, gripping tightly to the tops of the balcony railings, our feet probing for the narrow footing underneath, until each person got to the trellis and started up. One by one, people passed the first floor and reached the second floor balcony, where Ben quietly pulled them in. He and Fred both shushed Molly's nervous giggle.

When it was our turn, DeeDee balked stubbornly. "I'm not going until last. I'm wearing a skirt."

"You can't wait," I told her. "No one else can get by you on this ledge. You've got to go when your turn comes. It's dark anyway, and right now, nobody cares about looking up your skirt, 'Emily.' Get over it!"

Shaken, she turned to the trellis. Half way up, she wailed, "Oh, God, what will my Mama think of my climbing a trellis to break into someone's room? I'll be a criminal."

"Shh," came a half dozen voices at once.

"Keep going, don't stop and don't look down," I whispered up the trellis.

I felt Jimmy at my elbow. "Megan," he said softly. "You're ahead of me, and I'll be right under you. That way, Jake and I can catch you if you start to slip. You know how you are."

I felt half insulted and half gratified that they were trying to take care of me. I also was aware that if I *did* fall down this trellis, I'd probably take both my friends with me over the cliff. We could never explain that! I placed my hands firmly on the cross slats. The trellis began to rattle against the cement walls. I hoped it would

hold long enough for everyone to get up. "This is probably the
dumbest thing I've ever done,"
I whispered to Jimmy before
he kissed me on the cheek
and pointed upward. It was a
lot shakier than I thought, but
knowing two of my friends
were underneath, ready to risk
their neck to save me, sped me
onward. But before I knew it,
one foot slipped off the cross
slat, and I heard an "Oomph"
below me when my heel
pushed against something soft.
I held tightly to the upper slats
with my hands. "Sorry," I said,
as I felt Jimmy push my errant
foot back up onto the lower slat.

    "Never mind," he
whispered. "I never had a
handsome face anyway. Keep
going, and hang on tight."

    Finally, Ben's arms
reached out to pull me from the
trellis to the balcony with the
others.

    Jimmy and Jake were the last ones up. By the time Jake
came up, Fred and Ben had to put all their weight on the upper end
to stabilize the weakened trellis enough for Jake to climb it. The
bottom end had come loose entirely, and only their weight on top
kept the trellis intact.

    *There was certainly no way we could go back down the
way we had come!*

    Once we'd silently gathered on the little second floor
balcony, Ben and Jimmy conferred and announced their plan in
whispers.

"This French door is open, and I can see the door to the hall on the other side. We can get to our rooms that way, but I think there are two people asleep in there," whispered Ben.

"Yeah, I think so, too," said Jimmy, peering into the darkened room. "They're in twin beds, I think. Just walk between them through to the hall door as quietly as you can. We'll try not to disturb them. First person through holds the door for all the rest."

"What if they wake up and get scared?" asked Ruthie.

"Look, gang, no matter what happens, just keep going," said Ben. "Maybe they won't wake up, but at least maybe we can all get through before they attack anyone. If they wake up, maybe we can explain, though I wouldn't want to try. This *is* pretty bizarre, isn't it?"

"I'm scared," whispered DeeDee, against my ear.

"Would you rather sleep outside or go back down that trellis?"

She sighed and shook her head.

Jake volunteered to go first. He walked silently through the room, between the twin beds, to the door, and opened it carefully. As planned, he held it open and motioned the next person to come. It was Ruthie's turn, and then mine. Ruthie made it safely.

I walked as carefully as I could, but someone had evidently left a suitcase sticking out from under his bed. Naturally, I tripped over it and caught myself on the edge of his bed. Both strangers sat bolt upright, looking like black shadows. I couldn't tell if they were male or female, so I said as politely as I could, "Good morning" and continued walking toward the door. Each person behind me did the same, and the two shadows just sat there staring as seven more people walked through their bedroom saying a cheerful, "Good Morning." and disappeared out the hall door. When the last person, Jimmy, got through the door, Jake closed it silently, and we all burst out laughing, struggling to hold our hands over our mouths. We could barely get to our rooms.

"Meet you at breakfast," said Jake in a jovial stage whisper.

Next morning, when we went down to breakfast, an older

couple sat at a table near the window. They leaned together to speak to each other and kept looking our way.

To say we "slunk" to our seats would be an understatement. I felt their eyes on us all through breakfast, though I tried to avoid eye contact.

"Don't look at them," said Ben to DeeDee, as she peeked over her napkin.

When the people were finished, they rose and walked over to our table. I was shaky, but I caught DeeDee trying to scrunch under the table. I pulled her up by the back of her sweater.

"Excuse me," said the man in perfect Oxford English. "This is quite personal and forward to ask. Did we imagine it, or did you American blokes enter our room last night?"

A strained silence ensued until Jimmy spoke up. "Yes, sir. I'm afraid we did. We got locked out of the building and your room was the only one with open French windows on the balcony so we could get back in. I'm so sorry if we disturbed you."

"Oh, thank goodness," said the lady pulling her white, feathered boa under her triple chins and flinging it around her neck. "I was dreadfully afraid we both had the same dream, and there's bad luck with that, isn't there, now?" Her voice was high-pitched and ever so elegant.

"I don't know about bad luck, Ma'am," I said, "But we thank you for not raising a ruckus when we invaded your room. I didn't mean to wake you. I tripped on something…."

"Oh, Howard," the lady said, hitting her husband with a limp, sedate wrist to the shoulder, "you left out your case again, didn't you? Don't I always tell you to put your things away?" Then she turned to me and said, "Dearie, I'm so sorry Howard left that suitcase out. You might have been hurt. Thank goodness there's no harm done. We're just terribly relieved that we didn't dream you all up out of whole cloth, and that we aren't crazy after all, aren't we Howard?"

Howard bowed and said with a smile, "You certainly made our night. Up until last night, we thought Delphi frightfully boring, didn't we, Duchess-dearie?"

At Jake's invitation, Howard and Duchess-dearie pulled up chairs at our table and waved to the waiter for more tea with milk. The pair laughed as we related our tale of trellis climbing, dancing down streets, and the fact that those balconies really had a beautiful view, but not much wiggle room or security for playing a Romeo-style balcony scene.

We parted reluctantly, since they had been so nice about our misguided adventure. We had to get on the road to Athens. Nothing would do but that Duchess-dearie had to give little air kisses to each side of every face. The guys looked embarrassed, but Howard pumped their hands heartily all around and said, "It's frightfully nice to meet our 'dream people.' You made our visit to Delphi an exciting one. The Duchess will be telling all her friends about this for a very long time." He laughed jovially and twitched his big cigar, as we made our exit, smiling all the way.

DeeDee sidled up to me on our way out. "I'm so glad I met you, 'Cornelia.' Because you aren't afraid, I'm trying things I never thought I would. This has been so much fun."

"Even the trellis climbing and dancing?"

"Even the trellis climbing and dancing."

Jimmy and I were not too surprised when Ben asked if he could ride in our car on the way to Athens, so he could get to know DeeDee better. We could hear her actually able to *talk* to him rather than huddling on the opposite side of the car hugging her pillow.

Progress is a wonderful thing.

Chapter 12   -   Athens, Old and New

We marveled at the old world charm of our Athens hotel, gawking at its ornate halls of eight-foot mirrors and elegant Louis Fourteenth furniture. But we woke our first morning to blood-curdling yells from Don's room. Within seconds, we stampeded through those halls, in a colorful assortment of robes--most of us barefoot. The guys led the way, plowing through to the rescue, thinking he'd been killed. We found Don bare-chested, with a lathered face and a razor in hand, standing in a puddle in front of the bathroom sink. It had no pipes underneath!

"Well, don't you look cute?" quipped Jake in a snaky little voice. The rest of us dissolved into laughter.

"Just look at this damned thing! Don't they have a damned plumber in this whole damned country?" Don squished in his wet shoes, with the laces dangling in the puddle. Our laughter didn't help his temper any, since his face above the shaving lather took on a bright red hue. We shushed each other to explosive snickers.

"Sorry, Buddy," said Fred. "You shouldn't be surprised. We haven't been in a Greek hotel yet that didn't have drips, spouts, leaks, or no shower curtains. Flooded bathrooms must be the gift of Greece to the world." He spread his arms as though giving this magnanimous gift.

"At least your room has a lovely chandelier," I added, rubbing it in only a little.

Jimmy snagged a wastebasket to put under the offending sink, but Don was still grumbling as he took a towel from Ruthie. He wiped his face and reached down to wipe his pants, but his razor and the towel fell into the puddle on the floor. He yanked off his wet shoes and threw one of them into the bathtub.

"Out of here, every last one of you. And quit laughing!" He threw the drippy towel at Jake on his way out the door.

Jake stuck his head back in and yelled out, "Thanks, Don, for getting us into such a good mood to start the day." The second shoe hit the door as Jake ducked out.

Back in our room, DeeDee posed a question I'd both expected and dreaded.

"Did you notice that Ruthie was in Don's room when we all got there?"

"I knew they were rooming together on this trip."

DeeDee gasped. "I didn't know that. I thought she was with Cathie and Molly. When did they get married? Did they elope without telling us?" Her face lit up a big smile.

"They aren't married, DeeDee."

Her face immediately clouded. "Oh, my goodness! Somebody should talk to them." Her eyes were clearly locked in wide-open position, and she was clearly headed for the door.

I pushed her back down on her bed and held her shoulders to keep her from jumping up and running down the hall. "Look, my friend, first of all, they're consenting adults, not children and, second, it's none of our business."

"But…"

"No buts. It isn't our business, period! I assumed you'd figured it out—ten people, two persons to a room--do the math. They probably want to see where their relationship is going."

"But that's terrible! Why aren't you shocked, too?" It was an accusation.

"When I first came over here and saw people stay together, I was shocked, just like you. A perceptive friend sat me down and explained it to me, like I'm doing for you now. Some will marry, and for some, it won't work out. It isn't our place to make their toughest decisions even harder. People don't seem to attach the importance to sleeping together that the majority of us did before the sexual revolution of the sixties."

"Well, Mama better not hear about this!" She spat out the words. "Mama wouldn't want me traveling with fornicators."

"DeeDee, when your Mama grew up, there was a wide chasm between liking a young man and sleeping with him. It was called marriage. That chasm isn't so wide these days. Modern people date, we all date—you will too, eventually—and we're all adults. We each decide for ourselves how close we want to be to someone." I took a deep breath, wondering if she was even listening. DeeDee had a talent for "tuning out" anything she didn't want to absorb.

I tried again. "I know this is hard for you, but lots of people nowadays stay with each other, to see how they get along, before they decide to marry." At her shell-shocked expression, I added, "DeeDee, *none* of this has anything to do with *you*! You'll choose for yourself how you want to handle your life, and you don't have to do it the same way as Ruthie. You are you, and you don't have to do anything you don't want to do." I smiled by way of reassurance. "Now be my brave 'Emily,' and wash your face. We're going to explore Athens. And puleeze, promise me you won't mention anything to Ruthie or Don. Do you understand?"

A nod was the best I could get.

I wake early, so I like to take a morning walk in a strange city, not wanting to waste time while others get ready more slowly. Of late, I'd been dragging DeeDee with me. "You'll see so many neat things," I told her. "We'll be back for breakfast."

DeeDee could sleep all day, pulling covers over her head and ignoring noise or attempts to wake her. But this time she valiantly said, "Yes, 'Cornelia,'" and hoisted herself out of bed. Once outside, she enjoyed noticing and commenting on details of old houses and cobbled streets.

We watched the street sweepers, newsstand owners, and people of the market place getting ready for a new day. An old man sat on the pavement with a brass, Turkish samovar, pouring out a cup of tea to each of the venders as they arrived. They tossed a few drachmas into his hat on the ground. With only one cup, each person drank his tea and handed the cup back.

DeeDee put her hands over her mouth and whispered to me, "Oh, I could never...."

I shrugged. "I couldn't either, but they've probably shared for a thousand years or so, and they're not sick yet."

Closer to the flea market we came upon an elderly woman

sitting in the street. She wasn't fully clothed, and someone put a gunnysack over her lap in an effort to cover her nakedness. As we walked, a man and woman tried to carry her away, but she fought them, and anyone else who touched her. After several attempts, people walked past the senile old woman and left her sitting there, alone. DeeDee had a roll in her purse, left over from last night's dinner, so she approached and held it out to the crone. Guarded suspicion wrinkled her face and her wild eyes, but she stuck out a bony hand and grabbed the roll, quickly stuffing it into her mouth and gumming it with no teeth, as her withered breasts flapped against her belly. We glanced at each other sadly, knowing there was nothing we could do. It was a depressing view of old age.

Bad smells of greasy leftover foods, rancid wine bottles, and a severe sewage problem delineated the poverty around us, but much laughter also filled the early morning streets as people greeted each other, and us, with smiles and energy. We walked back to the hotel for breakfast, knowing the rest of the crew would rely on us to show them around town without becoming lost, since they knew we'd already scoped it out.

After breakfast, we led the crew first to the high point of Athens, the Acropolis on which stood the breathtaking Parthenon, crowded with tourists and cameras.

"Why is everything in this country always up, up, up?" complained Molly, chugging her chubby body and short legs up the hill. Her glowing skin reminded me of rich, chocolate malt.

But at the top, we all stood transfixed, gazing at the surrounding sun-favored panorama. An eerie white light fell like a benediction, all the way to the sea.

"It was worth the climb," Molly panted.

While taking photos of us all, standing together by the remaining pillars of the Parthenon, Fred said, "I read that for every temple in ancient Greece there were 500 priests and 1000 priestesses--all expensive call girls. Whatta you think of that?"

"Your idea of Heaven," said Jake with a laugh. "Maybe mine, too."

DeeDee looked at me and shook her head, with little

clucking noises of her tongue.

"Hand me that guidebook a sec, DeeDee," Ruthie asked. DeeDee handed it over. To her credit, DeeDee said nothing to indicate the disapproval I knew she felt. When she glanced my way again, I could see it was an internal struggle. I nodded at her and smiled encouragement.

Ruthie poured over the history section, her short reddish hair flying in the wind, and one finger aside her pursed lips. "I never can keep all these columns straight." She read from the book. "Ionic is light and straight, Doric is heavy with flutings up the sides, tapering from the base upward. Corinthian is like Ionic except for palm leaves at the top." She walked from column to column looking up. "Hm. These aren't really pillars, just statues of women who must've once held up the roof. It says here a war blew up the roof off this ruin because it had gunpowder stored in it." Ruthie and Molly stared up at the statues.

"Did you find the part about the contest for who could name the city?" asked Molly. "It depended on which god gave the new city the best gift. Poseidon struck the stone with his trident to give water--a spring that still runs from the fountain. Athena gave the olive tree which became the basis of their economy, so I guess they figured Athena's gift was the best."

"Yeah, but the hotel clerk this morning said they'd replanted that tree nineteen times," said Jimmy. Since Greeks drink wine, they probably didn't see water as anything great, but Poseidon had the best gift. His is still running, at least." He bent to scoop up a drink in his cupped palm.

As we walked around town, we discovered ancient statues everywhere. "Why are they all naked?" asked DeeDee, peeking warily out from under her "sun bonnet."

"Well, DeeDee, my friend," said Cathie, in her teacher voice, "The Greeks considered the human body beautiful—a symbol of health, so they went naked, even for the Olympics."

"They weren't talking about my body, that's for sure!" added Molly with a laugh. "I live from diet to diet." With Molly, it was okay to laugh with her. She was a lively, accepting, brown little munchkin, whom we all loved. She kept her life under control through her vibrant sense of humor, while sometimes I think the rest of us wondered if we had any.

Don spotted a souflaki stand. "Speaking of diet, look here." We all lined up in front of the surprised vender. By the time he layered one of the lamb pockets with grilled onions for each of us, Jake, Jimmy, and Fred were back for a second and even a third round.

"I see ice cream," said Molly, with fervor, as she wiped her chin with a tissue, since the venders had no napkins. She pointed to the booth next door.

We quickly repeated the whole drill at the ice cream stand. Both venders beamed at their good fortune--to have all these hungry Americans find their little stands for lunch.

Then Fred said, "I'd like some honey," but no one knew where to find such a shop. We tried our best sign language on passers by-- smacking lips, flapping wings, buzzing, but no one understood. I guess out of curiosity at these zany Americans, they followed us down the street like a parade, adding more people at each attempt at communication.

"This is getting to be quite a crowd," whispered Fred.

When we finally found a policeman, Don pantomimed buzzing while pinching his finger like a sting.

"Ah ha!" the policeman shouted, shaking one finger in the air, "Mella," and the parade of people sighed with satisfaction, "Ooh, Mella." The cop led the parade to the honey shop where we bought jars of honey to take home and Baklava pastries to eat right there. So did most of our followers. The shopkeeper smiled and bowed to everyone over his fortunate up-tick in business.

"Ah, how easily we communicate," said Don, licking the remains of Baklava from his fingers. "Sign language can accomplish anything."

We next discovered a group of Greek soldiers bravely wearing their very short, accordion-pleated skirts with leotards and turned up, pointed shoes.

Jake elbowed Ben. "I'd go AWOL before I'd wear that."

"You don't have the legs for it anyway," retorted Ben.

"In a funny sort of way, the uniforms are kinda cute," added Cathie, fluffing her blonde hair and eyeing the soldiers seductively.

Jake picked her up and faced her the opposite way. "Don't get any ideas, Toots."

Driving in a foreign city with an unreadable alphabet was daunting. Fred could read a little classical Greek, but that certainly wasn't the same as the frustrating Modern Greek. "Hallo, hallo," he'd call, leaning out of the window and waving money at every taxi driver until he found one willing to lead us to where we wanted to go. One of his taxi drivers, however, led us to a marvelous discovery—a theater from 161 AD. It was still in use, he told us.

"Why, this must be where they gave the plays of Euripides and Aeschylus," said DeeDee, her voice vibrating with the joy of discovery. Something about her innocent exuberance made me feel protective toward her, and deepened my appreciation of new discoveries, as well.

We had come to Athens hoping to make mythology come alive. And even though much of modern Greece had lost its classical roots, and poverty was everywhere in evidence, we still found the remnants of the mythology we'd all wanted to see.

The taxi driver showed us the dark cave where Socrates was forced to drink hemlock. We all touched the rough walls, and the earthy smell must have been the same noted by Socrates, himself. I was immediately lost in thought of the famous man.

Jimmy took my arm as I stumbled on the ancient, uneven stones. "Wasn't the hemlock because he thought there might be only one God, and the Greeks believed in many?"

"Heck," said Jake, "I thought it was because his wife, Xantippe, gave him a hard time."

Cathie ignored him, catching up to us, as we walked back out in the sunshine and onto the street. "It was Socrates that gave that funny speech like 'Now we go to do our work, you to live and

I to die. We'll see who was right about God.'"

"I couldn't have been that calm about drinking hemlock," said Jake. "It probably tasted as bad as that resin, tar caulking, rubbing alcohol, lighter fluid the Greeks call Retsina wine."

"Socrates taught Plato and Aristotle," said DeeDee. "He was a revolutionary for his time with his ideas about God. That was a good thing," said DeeDee. "It's neat to see his cave."

"He still got dead, though," insisted Jake.

As we reached the street, a bus headed toward us, interrupting our discussion. DeeDee and Jake jumped out of the way, and Jimmy yanked me with him. People hung out windows and doors of the overstuffed bus until they risked being peeled off by passing trucks or by bridges.

"I've heard that even generals ride busses, here," said Jimmy. "In our Army they want staff cars. What would happen if I suggested to our CAV commander that he ride the bus?"

"The only thing you'd be flying is a desk," said Jake, "for the rest of your natural life."

Cathie interrupted. "I want one of those Flokati rugs. Look at these white ones with long sheep's hair." Molly, the shopaholic, went right along behind her into a shop. Both bought rugs.

Fred ran in yelling, "No more shopping! We don't have room for any more in the cars."

I settled for a small religious icon and some worry beads that would fit into my shoulder bag. The Greeks were very tactile. They patted you and took your hand to talk, and had even taken DeeDee's ankle to show her how to do the folk dance, so worry beads were what they used for comfort--more aesthetic than twiddling their thumbs and healthier than smoking. Everywhere we'd been, we'd heard the click, click, click, of people using their worry beads. Naturally, we all bought sets for our friends back home. "I'll have to come back someday for a Flocati," I said.

DeeDee agreed. "Without Ruthie and Don," she muttered.

"Come on, DeeDee," I said. "Get over it. It's no skin off your nose…totally their problem, not ours, remember?"

She nodded, but I noticed she'd been ignoring the two.

We drove to Cape Soun Yaun at the southernmost tip of the islands for our last evening in Greece. We climbed the hills to watch the sunset. Tiny islands sparkled in the waning sun, surrounded by frothy waves emitting an unceasing rhythm on the shore that was intoxicating. Gold and pink rays bathed the Temple of Poseidon atop a high cliff. A perfect day's ending.

In the quiet beauty, Jimmy took my hand and looked deeply into my eyes. I felt he was looking into my soul, and I was a little overwhelmed.

"Did you mean it, about coming back?" he asked.

"Sure. I'd love more time to explore the islands, and go back to Mycenae's caves, and see again the hill people with their goat herds, and the bells tinkling in the wind?"

"I mean would you come again…with me?" He looked across at the sunset and added, "You know, all those colors reflect in your eyes."

Though we'd dated awhile and enjoyed each other's company, I suddenly felt he was asking for something more. I didn't know what to say, but he took my silence for acquiescence, and kissed me. I almost pulled away, feeling protective of myself not to trust again too much. And then I didn't want to pull back, after all. *For Pete's sake, Megan, get a grip!*

"Someday," he said. "You know that I care for you." He kissed me again.

It was a sweet moment, one I thought about, later. Wouldn't I have run the other way, if I were *sure* I didn't want any romantic ties? *I'm not sure I know what I really want. At least DeeDee knows she wants a husband and babies.*

When Jimmy came up for air, I could see over his shoulder the look on DeeDee's face. She looked confused, and looked away again quickly, not meeting my eyes. *Oops!*

We parked again in Athens to walk back to the hotel. Jimmy and I led the way, but on the unlit streets of the city, I tripped over something soft on the sidewalk. From peripheral vision, I saw something move in the darkness. Forgetting that basement steps in old Athens start out in the middle of the sidewalk, I tried to side step and fell into the hole. My knee twisted, hitting the concrete steps, pitching me forward to the bottom. I tried to break my fall with my arms, but I couldn't protect my face from getting bumped--hard. I could smell yesterday's garbage in that hole, too, and wondered what that mushy stuff was, where my hands had landed. The "yuck factor" was at least 1000, as I tried not to smell whether it was rotten fruit, or something worse.

I heard Jimmy shout to the others, "Look out for the kid on the sidewalk, and watch the cellar steps." Then, he jumped into the basement stairwell to help me. I tried to stand, but sharp pain drove up my left leg so strongly I thought I'd faint. Jimmy swept me up in his arms, and climbed back up the steps, yelling. "Get your car, Fred. We need a hospital."

I protested that all I needed was the ace bandage I carried for such accidents, and a shower, but they would hear none of it. From someplace that seemed far away, I could hear DeeDee asking if I was all right. But she wasn't really far away, because I felt her hand on my arm. I felt sort of a never-never-land dizziness as Jimmy leaned me on one foot against the railing and tried to mop my bleeding face with his sleeve.

"Someone check on the boy," he said, and Molly and Don tried to do so. The child had awakened in the ruckus. Apparently he didn't understand the noise, the language, or our good intentions. He ran off into the night.

I felt a stab of remorse for such poverty that a child would be sleeping on the street.

"Good thing you were in front of us," said Ruthie, trying to make me laugh. "If it hadn't been you, it would have been one of us. Since you went first, we had a noisy warning, as usual."

"The story of my life," I said. I was used to the taunting I always received on every accident. I tried to force the grin she wanted, but it felt lop-sided. I felt my nose to see if it was broken.. When I pulled away my fingers, they were covered with blood.

DeeDee, however, took the joking comment seriously and

turned on Ruthie. "You could say something more comforting, coming from you, when you do what *you* do!"

In spite of the pain, I reached out to touch DeeDee's arm. When she looked my way, I shook my head at her. It hurt. She disappeared behind Jake.

"What's with her?" Ruthie said, but then she turned back to Don without comprehension.

When Fred pulled up in his Chevy, Jimmy climbed in the back with me. "You guys go on to bed. We'll catch up with you in the morning before we take the ferry to Italy."

DeeDee stuck her head in the window. "I'd better come. You need a chaperone with Jimmy there."

"I'll be all right, Dee," I said. "We'll have plenty of company in a hospital. Just get some sleep. It's probably nothing. You know these things happen to me all the time."

Slowly, she withdrew her head and waved as we pulled away. When I looked back, the others had moved on toward the hotel, but DeeDee was still waving.

"Who's in charge here?" yelled Jimmy, as he carried me into the nearly deserted hospital emergency entrance. The sadly faded walls seemed to close in on us, a depressing place. I didn't want to stay.

Fred went from person to person asking, "Please come x-ray this woman's leg, and clean up her arms and face? I think her nose is broken, too." People shrugged, as he went to the next nurse-like character to ask again. Not a single one acknowledged his concern.

Finally, Jimmy carried me into a room, himself, placed me on the table and started cleaning the grit from my arms, using a large roll of gauze from the counter that he soaked in cold water. That must have gotten someone's attention, because a nurse came in scolding him. But at least she then took over the job.

Another nurse cut off the left leg of my slacks at the groin. "Those are my new pants," I said, but she paid no attention. Now I had short shorts on one side. I hurt too much to care.

I bit my lip to keep from crying in front of Jimmy. But it was nice to have him there, alternating between running interference for me, and reassuring me, "I'll take care of you."

Did I really want him taking care of me? That would take some thought. "I'm glad you're here with me, Jimmy," was about all I could give him back. It seemed enough. He smiled when he wasn't wrinkling up his anxious face when the doctor came to poke and prod. At least the doctor spoke English, so we knew what was being said and done.

X-rays showed I'd twisted the knee, and it was swelling wildly with inflammation, but I hadn't broken it. The doctor peered over his horn-rimmed glasses and said, "You'll have to repair meniscus damage with some surgery later but, for now, a cast will get you home to your own doctor."

A couple of hours later, we headed back to the hotel, with Jimmy holding me in his lap in the back seat and my smelly, new plaster cast sticking out across the width of Fred's car. The stitches over my broken nose ached and pulled. Though the doctor had given me some painkillers, we debated whether or not I should take them since we were in a foreign country and not able to read the curly-cue Greek labels. By the time we got back to the hotel and Jimmy carried me upstairs while Fred followed with crutches the hospital had furnished, I didn't even care anymore. I took the painkillers gratefully, and Jimmy tucked me in.

"Remind me never to go to a Greek hospital again," I vaguely remember saying.

DeeDee bustled around with a blanket she'd pulled off her bed wrapped around her, for fear Jimmy might glimpse her pajamas. "He shouldn't be in here," she complained.

I just lay back and let the painkillers take me. *They can figure it out.*

By morning, I felt worse. My head throbbed, my leg had swollen inside the cast, rubbing my thigh raw, and my elbows were flaming. I hobbled into the bathroom and saw my face in the mirror. My groan of dismay brought DeeDee running to my side.

"It's not so *very* bad, Megan. Maybe we can put some of my pancake make-up on it and hide the stitches and scrapes a little."

"I don't think make-up will help. Maybe a band aid."

DeeDee gritted her teeth and shook her head. "It's gonna take more than one!"

Sitting on a toilet with a stiff cast that wouldn't bend turned out to be an exercise in determination. I was grateful that volleyball had made my legs strong enough I could get up and down using only my right leg. The crutches seemed more in the way than not.

"You still sort of smell like garbage," ventured DeeDee softly, taking a slim whiff.

"I know." I gritted my teeth and balanced against the sink to take a sponge bath of sorts. The mystery odor from the night before was thankfully still a mystery, but when it came to getting the gunk out by washing my hair, I needed help from DeeDee.

"You can climb into the shower in your bathing suit, and wash my hair while I balance outside on my crutches to keep the cast dry. Maybe we can get the yucky stuff out that way."

She nodded, changed, and we tried out our experiment.

"Ooh, this stinks," she complained, washing blindly, eyes shut and nose in the air.

"Well, how do you think I feel, sticking my head inside the shower like an ostrich in the sand?" DeeDee got the giggles, got soap in my eyes, dropped the shampoo, and couldn't get my hair rinsed completely.

"At least I got most of the stinky stuff out, Megan, if not all the soap residue. That'll have to do for now." I hooked a towel with one crutch, and slid it down where she could reach it.

Once fairly dry, we tried to tug on a pair of slacks. DeeDee said, "You're never going to get this over that heavy cast. You may have to wear those with short shorts on one side."

"No, way," I told her. "It would look ridiculous, plus they still stink." I threw the nasty cutoffs across the room into the wastebasket, trying not to think of the ninety Deusche Marks I'd spent on dove gray slacks at Hertie's only a week ago.

We tried several pairs of slacks before we gave up and accepted that nothing I'd brought along would fit over the heavy cast. "I wonder why Greeks make casts three inches thick?"

"Don't worry, you can borrow my skirts, and I'll borrow your slacks. That's what the real 'Cornelia' and 'Emily' would have done." Her upturned smile was a bit too bright.

"Are you trying to cheer me up?"

She nodded, so I went along. "Sure. That'll be fine."

"Wait," she said. "We've got to cover up your nose."

"It's so swollen and angry, I don't think there's much we can do."

Digging into the first aid kit, DeeDee wrapped my skinned arms with antiseptic cream and ace bandages, criss-crossed what felt like a dozen band-aids across the stitches on my broken skin and nose, and smeared her pancake foundation over the top of it all. Since she was a sandy blonde with reddish sun streaks, while I was a freckled brunette, her makeup was a fiasco on me. Besides, I never wore makeup. Besides that, it was probably an infection looking for a place to happen. But she was trying her best, so I didn't want to say anything to discourage her.

"There!" she said, smiling over her handiwork. "I think you're as ready as you're going to get. Let's go down to eat."

I hobbled to the elevator, and down to meet the others.

Cathie turned to greet us. "Well, it took you two long enough." Then she did a double take and yelled out loudly, "Oh, my God! What did you do to yourself?"

Jimmy, bless his heart, rushed over and kissed me on the cheek, "Never you mind, Hon. It's okay," he said. "All this will go away soon, and you look wonderful to me."

I could tell he was wishing it had gone away *yesterday*, but I tried to smile. It hurt my face. I took a couple more of the painkillers instead of breakfast.

I considered taking a train home so as not to slow down the rest of the group, but Jimmy said we were going straight home now, anyway, so I wouldn't slow anybody down. We drove to Piraeus Harbor. Don and Ruthie had decided we should take the car ferry across to northern Italy to avoid going back on the Yugoslavian coastal road, which, by now, would be in its "dark" phase with no electricity. Though DeeDee hesitated because it was Ruthie's idea, I convinced her it seemed like a good idea, and this two-day ferry ride would be a nice bit of luxury for all of us.

We hung over the railing passing the Isle of Corfu with its houses jutting up out of the sea, its whitewashed buildings shining in the sun. We saw the mountains of Albania, but no one could go there. Albania was held at such close communist quarters by Moscow that no outsiders were allowed. They didn't even have roads. Tiny donkey paths snaked up the sides of the mountains. It was probably the most isolated and unknown country in the world.

But soon the Ionian Sea was so large that we could see no land, and the waters were rougher than brochures had said. Jake and Molly felt queasy, but the rest of us had no problems rolling with the waves. Getting around the ship was tricky on crutches, and the group made sure someone went with me everywhere. I lounged by the pool to pick up a sunburn and more freckles, until I saw that the band-aids left a criss-cross pattern across my nose. No one really looked at my face though. They politely turned away, or stared at my feet. I couldn't blame them. I avoided mirrors, myself.

Jimmy was the only one who could look me in my bloodshot eyes and say, "To me, you look wonderful."

Liar! But a sweet one.

Chapter 13 - Tiptoe Silently through the Alps

Saturday afternoon we landed in northern Italy. The plan was for dinner and a hotel, then to drive straight through the Alpine passes to southern Germany, get home by Sunday evening and be back at work on Monday. I found I could wedge my cast into Jimmy's front seat at an unnatural angle, uncomfortably, but efficiently. The only problem was that someone had to pull me out backwards until I could get my good foot under me to pull out the cast-weighted one, while I balanced on the crutches. It helped having Ben with us, as he and Jimmy could get me in and out more easily than DeeDee. She, however, constantly hovered over me like a helicopter over the Border, bustling and clucking and re-applying that awful make-up whenever she said, "I need to powder your nose again."

I never did figure out how powdering band-aids helped my appearance *or* my pain any, but who was I to argue, so I suffered the sneezing from her compact of the fluffy stuff.

Jimmy and I smiled at each other noting that DeeDee was chatting more easily with Ben, as we drove north. Even though I couldn't hear the conversation, from time to time a ripple of laughter came from one of them or the other. DeeDee had a quirky sense of humor that was fun, when she trusted someone enough to let it out. I hoped she was letting it out by now with Ben.

We had dinner in a tiny village near the Italian/Austrian Border, and found a cute little Pension at the bottom of the Riso Pass. When we signed in, the host noted that we were all military people on leave and heading home to Germany. "There might be some bad weather coming in," he noted. "Will you want to be awakened should it get worse?"

Fred looked out the window at the glorious Italian sunset and said, "Doesn't look like much for now, but let us know if it changes."

The host apparently took Fred seriously, because we were

awakened at two in the morning by footsteps running up and down
stairs, and an Italian policeman knocking on doors.

"What is this? A raid?" yelled Jake, as he stumbled out in
his shorts. DeeDee saw him and immediately ran back into our
room. I didn't think Jake's knobby knees looked *that* bad!

"Proprietor called. Said you Amis, you Americans, wanted
over Alps tomorrow," said the policeman in broken English.

Don looked outside. "It's snowing a bit," he said. "It's
unbelievable since we've been in the sun all week. I thought it was
supposed to be spring."

When had this started? I wondered, silently weighing our
options.

"Passes closed through Switzerland and France," said the
policeman. "Only our Riso Pass open, but for how long?" The tall
man lifted his shoulders and hands in a giant shrug.

"It isn't bad, yet," said our host. "You risk it now, or be
stranded in Italy many days."

Molly pulled back a curtain to look up the mountain. As I
joined her, we could see swirling gray clouds about half way up.
She shook her head, nervously tapping on the window sash. "I
don't know. It might be bad up there," she whispered.

"We'll all be AWOL by Monday morning," said Jake.
"We'll have to try it now."

"I'd advise not," said the policeman. "You better just
burrow in here, until next week after storm. Host only woke you in
case it urgent that you go—you choose."

"But we might be able to beat the worst of the storm,
right?" questioned Fred.

"Perhaps," said our host, "but Riso Pass will be closed
soon, as well. This will be a big storm. Phones already out.
Electricity will go soon."

"All the more reason we should go now," said Don. "We
can't be AWOL, and if your phones are gone, we can't call home
to extend our leaves."

Molly said softly, "I think maybe we should stay here."

Our four combat pilots and one combat engineer put their

heads together. I knew how serious it was to be absent from their Border mission. These guys all carried big responsibilities and even had trouble getting leave to go to Greece with us at all. But I was afraid their macho pride would prevail over our teacher-timid common sense. When I saw Fred's face, I knew I was right.

"We can make it," said Fred, loudly. "Get your stuff, gals."

"But Don," said Ruthie, turning to her boyfriend. She got no further, because the guys were already heading back to rooms to put on warm clothing and get their gear.

The kind Pension proprietor quickly made box lunches for our journey, while the men put chains on the cars, and we loaded up. It was a spring blizzard, heavy and wet, sticking to our eyelashes and clothing, but the road at the bottom of the mountain still seemed clear with not much snow sticking yet.

Policemen lined the entrance to the narrow mountain road motioning us ahead. "Presto, presto," each repeated. "Hurry, hurry."

But soon, it was impossible to "hurry." Half way up the mountain snow swirled so thickly that visibility was going fast. The narrow road was icy and perched on a treacherous mountainside heading over the Italian Alps and into Austria. It boasted one hairpin curve after another, and certainly, once committed, there was no place to turn around and go back. We quickly lost sight of Fred and Jake's cars when the snow fell more heavily. They'd been close behind us when we started.

I watched Jimmy's set jaw and wondered if he was already regretting their choice. I wanted to ask, "Wouldn't it have been safer to stay put?" but the words died in my throat. The guys were doing what they thought best, and they already had enough on their minds. Besides, it would have been impossible to turn around on the narrow road, anyway.

A bundled up Italian policeman flagged us down at a temporary roadblock. "Severe avalanche danger ahead," he whispered when Jimmy rolled down the window. "No talking, no noise for next fifteen minutes. Go only ten kilometers per hour, but keep moving. You must not be stranded in pass. Remember, no talking, no noise. You must tiptoe through mountains."

We crept along, wondering how one could "tiptoe" in a car. But that policeman was the last living soul we would see for hours. The only sound was DeeDee, softly mumbling one prayer after another. The rest of us held our breath. "Shh," said Ben.

DeeDee whispered, "All I can think of is tons of snow hanging over us, threatening to come down the mountain any second and bury us alive."

Ben put one hand over her mouth and the other around her shoulders until his watch with its lighted dial finally went past the fifteen-minute mark. "Do you suppose it's okay to talk now?" he whispered to Jimmy.

"We'd better stay quiet," was the answer. "I imagine there are more avalanches ahead."

I peered through the front windshield, trying to help Jimmy watch for obstacles. Soon it was difficult to tell if we were even on the road or not. Ben hung out the window in back, guiding Jimmy by where the mountainside wall was close to us on the left. Then, he quickly climbed over DeeDee to the opposite side as the road shifted to the right, having crossed some unseen culvert. Snow drifted in through open windows, so the heater was useless. DeeDee sat softly crying and shivering on the floor. I would probably have joined her if Jimmy hadn't needed me to watch the road, and if I wasn't locked in an immobile position by the cast.

"Hey, I have an idea," I whispered to her. "Get those worry beads we bought from your bag, DeeDee. Let's see if they work."

For hours afterward, we could hear the click, click, click of DeeDee's worried fingers.

"Whoa," said Ben suddenly, and Jimmy jammed on the brakes. We slid probably ten feet on the ice, even with our chains.

"What is it?" said Jimmy.

"I can't see the wall anymore. It's been about two feet from us all along, and now I don't see it through the snow at all. I know there's a drop-off. I've been on this road lots of times in good weather." A long moment passed while Ben and Jimmy conferred. "If we walk ahead a little, maybe we can feel our way to the cliff's edge and determine exactly how far over it is."

"I agree," said Jimmy, as he set the brakes and both of them got out. We soon lost sight of them and their flashlight in the swirling snow, but the other cars behind us were nowhere in sight, either. I held Jimmy's emergency light from the glove compartment pointing backward, just in case the others came up on us without seeing us stopped in the middle of the road.

"What are you doing?" whispered DeeDee.

When I explained, she said, "That light can't be seen further than four feet."

"You're probably right, but I just feel better trying."

After what seemed like an endless time by the speedy click of DeeDee's worry beads, I could see Jimmy making his way back to the car. Ben held on to the back of Jimmy's jacket, and both leaned hard into the swirling snow and fierce wind.

They shook off what snow they could, but still they brought a whole blizzard into the car with them. Both were shivering. I reached out to hug Jimmy and realized I'd been quite frightened not to be able to see him for so long.

Ben grinned, turning to DeeDee. "Hey, little worrier. Do you have a hug for an Abominable Snowman, too?"

DeeDee looked startled, but she didn't react. The moment passed quickly, and Ben changed the subject. "We were heading toward the cliff, ladies and gentlemen. That's why I couldn't see the mountain wall any more. But Jimmy and I have it figured out now, so we're gonna be just fine. Don't you babes worry none. The CAV has it under control. Toujour Prêt!"

DeeDee clicked faster, and I went back to watching for obstacles. Ben hung out the window again, visually measuring the distance to the wall now restored at a couple of feet, and Jimmy hunched over the steering wheel, inching the car forward. The windshield wipers caked with ice and stopped, so the guys had to get out frequently and wipe off the windshield and headlights. The headlights were useless, anyway, simply showing the snow as a whirling drunken dervish in front of us. I used the back of my glove to periodically wipe rime from the inside of the windshield.

"You know," said Jimmy, "if we were skiing, we'd call this a whiteout, and we'd all quit and head for the nearest Gasthaus for a cup of Gluhwein."

Ben grunted from the back seat, "*Now*, you think of that, Buddy. There sure as hell isn't any way for us to go back. We were pretty dumb for doing this, weren't we?"

"How far do you suppose it is to the crest?" I asked, trying to lighten any blame. "You said you'd been through Riso Pass before, Ben."

"I see nothing, know nothing. We're just plowing along, but it shouldn't be much further. I hope you ladies are bundled up enough, because I can't shut the window and still see the wall."

"We're okay," I said, patting DeeDee on the head to respond as well.

"Remember when we were flying those MI spooks out to the Border a couple of months ago, and the weather changed on us too fast?" said Jimmy.

"I was just thinking of the same event, Buddy." He turned to DeeDee. "I had to set my helicopter down in a cow pasture in snow up to my cockpit bubble. Jimmy was trying to fly his low enough to read the signs on the roads. As I remember, neither was a super-successful method."

"Yeah, the maintenance guys had a little damage to fix afterward, didn't they?"

"It would all have been the MI spook guy's fault," said DeeDee. "I don't like them."

"Not really," said Ben, seeming surprised at her comment. "At least, this time, we haven't hit anything…yet."

"Don't speak too soon," I said. "Remember, you still have me with you." At least it broke the tension and everyone eased up with a small laugh at my expense. Jimmy grinned and reached over to pat me on the cast. I bit my lip to keep from crying out at the pain it caused when jiggled. The cast was getting soggy from the open windows, but I couldn't remove my jacket to cover it.

We'd been on this slippery, blind little road for hours when we came to a slight crest, and debated if we were going down at last? When skiing in a whiteout, it's hard to tell if you're going up, or down, or standing still, because there's no visual reference. It's terribly disorientating. This wasn't any different. DeeDee, huddled on the floor in the back, was the first to feel herself leaning against the front seat rather than the back. "I'm sure we're going down, now," she whispered. We all joined hands over the console, rejoicing silently, still "tiptoeing."

The road down was no easier, and the sliding increased, but it felt like we'd cleared a hurdle of sorts. We were going down, and freezing from the open windows. When I touched Jimmy's hand, it felt like ice from wiping off the frozen windshield so often.

It seemed a long time when suddenly Jimmy slammed on the brakes in a panic stop. Appearing out of the darkness was an apparition, a snow covered, human-sized hulk, holding up both hands with a flashlight waggling in one. DeeDee, peering between the front seats, screamed.

The man came to the driver's side, and we found he was the Austrian equivalent of a highway patrolman. He was swathed from head to toe in furs, coated with snow, and looked for all the world like the Abominable Snowman Ben had invoked earlier.

The man spoke to us in German, so we all could understand and speak. "You're the last to get through," he said. They radioed you were coming, so we waited. We're closing the road now. Avalanches have closed the road ahead. We can't allow you to go further."

Two other similarly suited figures moved barriers in behind our car to block the road.

"Wait," yelled Jimmy, in his best Deutsch, and trying to be heard above the howling wind. "We have two more carloads of people following us. You can't close up yet."

Two of the officers conferred. "We'll give them another fifteen minutes," one said. "We have to radio that we've closed the pass." The man appearing to be the chief looked down at his snow-laden boots and clacked one against the other to clear a little snow. It was ineffective. "How far behind are your friends? Were they the only ones trying to get through?"

"I don't know if there were others, but all three cars of our group left together. I can't say what's keeping them." I could hear anxiety in Jimmy's voice.

"Hope they haven't driven off a cliff, or gotten stuck," said the chief. "We can't go after them until the storm lets up. Weather reports say that may be two more days."

DeeDee slipped into her wild-eyed "what do we do now" mode, so I reached back to take her cold, clammy hand. I knew her fear and the cold were getting the best of her.

"Do you have someplace we can get the ladies inside?" asked Jimmy. "I'll wait until the others get here, in case Ben and I have to go back after them. We won't want to take the ladies."

"No," I cried out involuntarily. "I don't want you to go. You'd be lost. We'll all wait here. Jake and Fred are good drivers. They'll make it through."

I hoped the last part of my sentence sounded more convincing than the transparent first part. I fought to maintain calm, realizing I had said more than I wanted to say to Jimmy about how I felt about him. *I don't want you to go. God, did I really say that out loud?*

He reached in and took my hand. "It's okay, Hon. I won't hold you to it, but your concern is nice to hear." Even in the dark and cold, I could feel heat rush to my cheeks.

The chief's voice saved me from embarrassing myself further. "Come inside our hut over there. It's not big, but we have a wood stove, so perhaps you can all dry out and warm up."

Jimmy and Ben extricated me from my wedged in posture. DeeDee handed me my crutches, which slipped on the ice and snow. Jimmy just said, "Heck with it," and picked me up in his arms. "God, that cast weighs a ton," he said. "I've gotta start lifting weights again."

DeeDee went ahead of us with the crutches, and Ben took her arm as she slipped and slid her way down the recently shoveled path to the guard shack. The snow on both sides was more than waist deep, and the path itself was filling up again quickly.

Warmth had steamed up the windows that circled the

wooden guard shack. Three guards leaned back in cane chairs around a table rubbed smooth from use, as though the blizzard were not raging outside. When he saw my cast, one man jumped up and offered me his chair.

DeeDee shook, whether from cold, fear, or relief, I wasn't sure. Probably, like the rest of us, all of the above. Ben threw a friendly arm around her and brushed the snow off her hair and face. She was shivering too much to argue with him over his touching.

Jimmy found a pack of gum in of his coat pocket and handed it around. "At least it will moisten your lips. You all look purple and chafed, and I feel the same."

Ben remembered the box lunches and stumbled out to the car to retrieve them. When he returned, we opened the boxes on the narrow table and invited the guards to share. They decided on our candy bars, while we wolfed down sandwiches. The juice drinks had turned to slushies, so we put the metal containers atop the wood stove, hoping they would thaw into hot toddies.

Jimmy knelt to massage circulation back into my feet. "By the way," he said. "I couldn't have driven that mountain without your help. We make a good team, don't you think?"

His warm grin was impossible to ignore. I nodded, still too cold to speak, and unsure what I could say to that, anyway.

Soon, though, both Jimmy and Ben began pacing the floor.

"They should've been here by now," said Jimmy, "unless something happened."

"Should we drive back up to find them?" asked Ben. He rested the tip of his tongue between his teeth. Jake once said that he'd flown with Ben in Vietnam, and Ben flew in dangerous places that way, with his tongue tipping through. I knew he was worried now.

"Yeah. I think we should. Let's get out there. We'll have to turn the car around."

I jumped to my feet before I remembered I only had one foot operational. DeeDee reached out to steady me. "No, Jimmy. Please," I said. "You won't be able to see anything, and even if you find them, there's no place to turn around to come back down the mountain."

He put his arms around me and kissed me on the forehead, then pushed me back into the chair. "You ladies stay by the fire. We'll be back in no time."

They had not spoken in Deutsch, but one of the guards in the shack must have known English. He stood in front of the door with fists clenched. "No one goes up that mountain tonight. We have orders."

"You can't stop us from going to find our friends," said Jimmy. "If they're stranded up there, your boss says it might be two days before you can get to them. They can't wait two days."

Ben stood beside Jimmy, and they looked formidable. But the guard didn't back down, either. After a couple of tense moments, the guard turned to the door and shouted out to his chief in Deutsch, "These Amis want to go back up. I told them no."

The chief returned to the guard shack and entered, slapping his arms against his fur-covered shoulders to dislodge a bit of snow. It fell in a pile on the ground around his feet. "Just so you understand, my Ami friends, I'll tell you in English. No one goes up the mountain. No one. If you go, we'd only have more bodies to recover in two days. You *will* stay here!"

Jimmy and Ben were ready to fight their way out of the guard shack. I knew their code—never leave a comrade behind.

"Be reasonable, young man," said the chief, more quietly than before. "They'll be coming down any time now. Be patient. We'll wait." He placed one hand on his snowy beard, and the other on the gun at his belt. "Don't make us do anything to keep you here that we'd all regret." Then he smiled and said, "Come on, boys, just wait awhile here, where it's warm."

"I can't rest in here while my friends are out there." said Jimmy, shaking his head. "I'll go out to watch for them."

"Then I'll go with you," said the station chief. They walked the maybe twenty meters back to the barricade and the car, all but disappearing into the swirling snow.

"I'm glad they didn't let you go back up there, Ben,"

DeeDee said.

He smiled. "I think we could have done it, but we left our side arms at home. And our government wouldn't like us to pick a fight with our Austrian allies. But I'm glad you're glad."

They smiled at each other.

Wow, 'Emily,' you've come a long way. I grinned in spite of myself to see DeeDee express affection, no matter how subtle. I hadn't thought her capable of that, yet.

Only a few minutes later, Ben shouted, "Look! Aren't those headlights coming down the hill? But there's only one. No motorcyclist would be out in this weather, would they?"

We crowded to the window and saw the single beam draw closer and the shadowy figure of Jimmy jumping the barricade and running forward up the hill.

"That must be them," said Ben. He grabbed his coat and rushed out the door. The guards donned furs and ran outside, as well. Dimly, we could see Jimmy and Ben lifting someone off his or her feet. In a moment Ruthie, Don, and Fred burst through the door.

"Thank God," said Ruthie, breathlessly. "You're here. We were afraid you guys had gone off the cliff when we couldn't see your taillights anymore. I guess we just got way behind you."

"Where are the others?" I asked. I could still see Jimmy out there waiting for the third car, and Ben went back out to join him.

"I don't know," said Fred. He panted heavily from the exertion and cold. "They were right behind us, and then all of a sudden we were alone. We didn't know what happened to anybody else. Then, I braked too hard and slid into the wall on one side. We had to stop so Don and I could pry out the crumpled fender with my lug wrench. Otherwise the wheel couldn't roll. It got one of our headlights, too."

"You'd better believe that road was treacherous with only one headlight," added Don, brushing snow off of Ruthie as she turned around slowly.

I was so thankful to see them I was shaking, almost uncontrollably. "Thank God you're here. I was afraid Jimmy and

Ben would start a war with our Austrian friends in order to go back after you." I realized how afraid of that I'd really been. Perhaps Jimmy was more important to me than I'd thought. *Don't go there!*

"Well at least you're here now," said DeeDee, and to my surprise, she hugged Ruthie. "I wouldn't want anything to happen to any of you."

Ruthie laughed and turned to me. "Boy, Megan when you brew up trouble, you really get carried away, don't you? It's the 'Cornelia' in you."

"Yep, I guess so," I said, accepting the blame for a blizzard. It didn't bother me.

"What happens now?" said Don. "Have you guys made any plans?"

"No," I said, realizing we hadn't thought past getting our group together. "Perhaps when the others get here, these guards may know someplace we can go to rest and get something warm to eat. I'd hate to have to stay in this guardhouse two days. Are you guys hungry?"

"Yes," said Ruthie, "starving. We ate our box lunches right away, and I finished off my candy bar while Don and Fred were working on the fender in the snow."

Fred looked tired beyond words, and one of the other guards again got up to give him the chair. "I'm sorry," he stammered. "I felt so anxious having others with me. It felt like flying a whole helicopter-full of troops for insertion in a hot LZ in Vietnam. It would've been easier by myself, with no one else to consider." He ran his hand over his short, graying crew cut.

I patted his shaking hands. "But you got them safely down the hill, Fred. That's terrific."

"Now, if Jake can just get his two ladies down." Fred's eyes were rimmed with red, and his bushy eyebrows were frozen with ice. I brushed the ice off, and he barely noticed.

"Who's missing?" said DeeDee, counting on her fingers. "Jake, Cathie, and Molly."

"Yeah, he had Ben originally, but Ben moved to your car."

DeeDee said, "Yeah, I don't know why he did that?"

Ruthie laughed, a little chuckle that grew into a roar. "Didn't you know he wanted to ride with you, so he could get to know you better?" She laughed again at the shocked expression on DeeDee's face. "You didn't even know that, did you? You didn't get it?"

Ruthie, Fred and Don found the topic hilarious, but DeeDee blushed from tousled hair to pointed chin.

"Why, Ben was just helping Jimmy in the lead car, you guys," I said, trying to change the subject before we set DeeDee back a year or two in social development. "Nothing so exciting as you think. Let's watch for Jake and the girls, shall we?"

I rose and hopped over to the windows of the guard shack, where I leaned against the sill and wiped a bit of steam off so I could see out. The others joined me. Visibility was still only a few feet. Fred excused himself to go out and wait with Jimmy and Ben. After a while, DeeDee came over to peer out the window with Ruthie and me. She nodded her thanks for changing the sensitive subject. I got the message.

A half hour later, we saw the headlights of Jake's car. Again the guys ran forward to help the last three blizzard survivors. I could see someone lift a human-sized bundle and struggle toward us. Ruthie opened the door as Ben brushed in carrying Molly. Her lips were purple. DeeDee and Ruthie immediately rubbed her hands and removed her boots to check for frostbite. Jimmy carried Cathie, Jake stumbled in behind them, and Fred and the chief came in out of the snow. Jake bent over, hands to his knees to get his breath, as the chief cranked up his emergency radio to report in. Jimmy deposited Cathie on her cold feet and stumbled over to kiss me on the cheek. I pulled off his jacket and hat. His lips felt so cold it scared me, but he was jubilant.

"All present and accounted for," Jimmy crowed. "CAV rules!"

"Don't forget the DoDDS School teachers," croaked Molly.

"And the engineers," added Don, throwing his arm around Ruthie.

"I thought you guys were goners out there," said Jake. "It felt like we were the only people left in the world. An avalanche fell on the road right in front of us, so we were afraid you guys had bought the farm. I had to dig the shit out of the way by myself, and more snow kept sliding down." Fred glanced sideways at him and Jake caught himself. "*Stuff*. I dug out the stuff so we could get by. Pretty hairy! Hope no more cars were behind us. We all made it."

Gruff old Fred pounded him on the back. "Good job, man."

Cathie shook out her hair, coat, and smacked her ski hat against her side. She put her hands over the stove and wiggled them. "I'm just thankful to be here," she said. "Jake, I'll never nag you about your driving again."

Jake bent into a gallant, cavalier bow. "I'll take that as a promise, Mi'lady," he said, and he gave her arm a friendly squeeze.

"Now, what?" said Don. "We can't go forward and we can't go back."

The chief got off his radio and announced in English, with his charming Austrian accent, "All roads closed, and the guards on the south end of the pass said you three were the last cars through. They were relieved you made it, since they could hear avalanches thundering down not long afterward, and lasting a long time. You're really lucky fools, my Ami friends. Switzerland, France, and other Italian posts report we've lost a lot of people in this blizzard." He looked away out the window. "Now, what do we do with you? You must be tired. There's no use our guards staying longer here. Nothing more can be done until the storm lets up. We're heading home. Do you want to go with us?"

"Home?" said Jimmy, with his eyebrows raised a good inch. "Where's home?"

The old chief, his beard stiff with ice, laughed heartily. "About a kilometer down this valley, almost directly behind the guard shack. You don't think we'd all be out here waiting for you if we didn't have someplace to go afterward, do you?"

We must have looked pretty bewildered, because the big man laughed again. "Come on, follow me, if all your cars will start. We'll go to the Gasthaus and Gertrude can fix you some breakfast, you can sleep all day. Maybe the blizzard will pass and the snowplow can get through to us tomorrow morning. Come along."

Everyone joined in to uncover the snow-laden cars. Two of the three started, and we crowded in for the short drive to the Alpine village, following in the slippery snow ruts left by the chief's truck. The warm light of kerosene lanterns within the Gasthaus, nestled in deep snow, seemed inviting.

Gertrude turned out to be a bustling Hausfrau, creating crepes filled with cream cheese and ladled with cherry sauce for our breakfast. Either the crepes were wonderful, or we were all very hungry and tired. I didn't even remember how I got upstairs into a room and collapsed for eight hours under a feather deckle on a hand-carved bed. DeeDee wrapped my cast and leg in towels so as not to get the bed wet.

When I awoke, DeeDee was already up. I worked my way down the stairs with her help, and we wandered into the kitchen where Gertrude was chopping dried vegetables. One by one, the crew emerged, having caught up on napping after our sleepless night in the blizzard.

Though a few extremities were a sinister white, and rubbing them hurt, we had all come through in relatively good shape. The only casualty was my cast, which was wet enough to offer little support. The weight of it hurt terribly. I'd need a new one, soon as we got to the base clinic.

The storm raged outside, so we knew it was impossible for us to get home for a while.

"We're so lucky to be in a warm shelter this time," said Molly. No one could argue.

We gathered around the tables, waiting for the chief to come with news, as he'd promised. When the big man stomped in, brushing snow from his hat and fur coat, the news from his radio transmitter was bad. "At least eighty people were killed in avalanches or frozen in their cars," he said. "Many more unaccounted for."

A shocked sigh went all around the room. "Guess we risked too much and were incredibly lucky," said Jimmy, taking my hand and looking distressed. "God watches out for children and fools."

"Worst blizzard in thirty years," the chief continued. All the passes into northern Austria are closed. You won't get through to Germany for another day or two. Word came in that a Swiss train is stranded in a tunnel, waiting for rescue. Nothing is getting through the Alps."

"AWOL city," said Fred. "We've got to find a way to call back to base. Are the regular phones down?"

Gertrude nodded.

Jimmy had a suggestion. "Chief, can you let us use your field radio transmitter in the guard shack, so we can try to get through to our Army airfield manager? They need to know we can't make it by tomorrow morning. They're counting on us. He can relay to HQ."

The chief nodded and started for the door.

Looking out through the lacy curtains, I could see a rope strung on metal rods, supposedly leading to the guard shack for safety purposes. I breathed easier.

"Be sure he relays the message to the school, too," suggested Molly, "Our principal will need to get subs for all five of us tomorrow, and maybe the day after, if he can find that many."

"Will do," said Jimmy. He and Fred bundled up and trekked back the way we'd come with the chief leading the way holding on to the rope. It would have been foolish to take the cars, since they were buried, and no one could tell where the road had been anyway.

They returned covered in snow. "It took awhile to get through," said Jimmy. "Horst now knows that we're snowed in until the passes open. He'll notify CAV HQ, Engineer HQ, and the school, so we're all covered until at least Tuesday. We'll radio back if we can't get in by then."

"Great, guys," said Cathie, as everyone breathed a sigh of relief that those in Bamberg waiting for us knew our situation. "Guess we can just rest up here for a day and, hopefully get home by Monday night, if the roads open up tomorrow."

Safely snowed in at a comfortable Gasthaus, the mood became more festive. Gertrude simmered a scrumptious beef and vegetable dinner on an iron hook in the huge rock fireplace. Most of us played a spirited game of Charades, while DeeDee and Petra, who at fifteen was a miniature carbon copy of her mother, Gertrude, worked a jigsaw puzzle by the light of the lantern. The hit of the evening was when Molly asked Petra how she folded such intricate patterns with our cloth napkins, like little birds and sunbursts, so we got a napkin-folding lesson.

Even the guys thought it fun. "Wait 'til I get home and surprise my mom," Don said.

Jake found a guitar hanging on the wall. With our host's permission, he took it down and played folk music while we sang together an old Bob Dylan tune, "Lay, Lady, Lay."

Upon hearing the words, DeeDee drifted back to the puzzle. The chief and his guards came by and wanted to join in, as well. Since the Austrians only knew really old songs of our historical Americana, those were the ones we dragged out of the attics of our brains.

DeeDee smiled happily when Jake and the crowd sang to a quiet "Shenandoah." "You people make a party everywhere you go," she said.

"I told you these were the good guys, and it would be fun for you to learn how to enjoy a whole crowd at once."

"How am I doing?" Her eyes were bright, clear and questioning.

"You're doing fine, 'Emily.' You've come a long way." *I'd never thought it possible, but she really had gone from scared naïveté, to good company.* "You're part of the gang, now."

She patted my hand warmly, and we sang along.

The strains of "She'll be coming around the mountain," rang out into the dark blizzard, followed by every old folksong anyone could remember.

When I looked out our bedroom window on Monday

morning, the snow had almost stopped, and a faltering sun was trying to force its way through the clouds. It almost seemed we had dreamed up that blizzard. But the snow lay deep in the valley. Only roofs piled high with snow and smoke-laden chimneys sticking up revealed the seven little houses of this buried village of border guards. The blizzard hadn't been our imagination.

While we waited for the snowplow to get through to us, Gertrude's husband, Hans, shoveled a path out to the invisible street. Other guards were shoveling out from their homes as well, or at least you could see their shovels occasionally flick snow over the high banks from where they dug underneath, like moles pushing dirt out of their subterranean holes.

Hans had plenty of help from our guys. Soon, the path went between high, vertical walls of snow. The men also dug out suspicious mounds of snow to find the cars. Don and Jake went to get the third car at the guard shack running again.

By the time all preparations were finished, and we'd loaded up the cars, the snowplow driver chugged in from down the valley. The residents cheered as he jumped down and dusted off his furs and hat with big, gloved hands. The chief translated his rough dialect, since the down-country Deutsch certainly didn't sound like either the Bavarian or High German we all knew. But since he talked with his hands, we could tell what he was saying, anyway. "I'll plow the first lane over the pass," he'd said, "and you Amis can follow single file in my wake, if you choose. I'm warning you, it will be slow going, with lots of avalanche to remove."

We jumped at the chance, thanked our hosts for taking us in, and took off following the heavy-duty snowplow at a safe distance. It took five hours for the driver to get through the northern part of the Austrian Alps and plow his way down into Bavaria. There, springtime jonquils bloomed. The cows were already turned out, and they frolicked in the fields like young children after being cooped up in barns all winter long. It was hard to believe that just the other side of the mountain, we'd been caught in the most deadly blizzard in thirty years.

It took only another four hours on the German Autobahns

for three carloads of tired Americans to pull into the Bamberg Officers' Club in time for Marco to arrange for us a late dinner.

Cathie ordered her steak and fries, and turned to me, shaking her finger. "You know it's all your fault, as usual," she announced, laughing with the group. "But we asked for it."

I didn't bother refuting her statement. "Glad you all enjoyed it," I said.

As soon as we had eaten a light dinner, DeeDee and Jimmy stood by loyally at our nighttime emergency clinic while I got a new, firm, and much lighter cast. The medic on duty redressed my wounds and inspected the stitches above my nose. Since the swelling seemed to have gone down a bit in all the cold, I could see that the stitches across the bridge of my nose, and extending between my eyebrows didn't look quite as lumpy as they had at first. "It won't be a *big* scar," announced Doc, as though that were the most important thing, "but what on earth is the gunk you had all over those band aids?" I played dumb while DeeDee blushed.

I leaned against Jimmy as he wedged me back into the car to drive us home.

The car radio was full of the blizzard story. Many people had been stranded or lost in the passes of Italy, France, Austria, and Switzerland, with a constant threat of more avalanches.

"We were so lucky to get through," said Jimmy with a wink. "Maybe 'Cornelia and Emily' are really our *good* luck charms.

DeeDee beamed.

Chapter 14 - Heartache

I'd trundled through the rest of the school week, exhausted from hauling my body around on crutches and dreaming of resting quietly for the weekend in my own apartment. The cast Doc had put on was not a walking cast with support under the foot. So, as it dried and shrunk a little, it became too big, and every time I stood up, the whole thing dropped "klunk" right on my kneecap. It felt like the cast was doing more harm than good by constantly re-injuring the knee.

But my fifth-graders were wonderful, carrying my chair around so I could sit near them to help with their math problems, or frantically waving their hands for me to choose one of them to go down to the teacher's lounge to retrieve my lunch from the refrigerator. They colorfully decorated my cast, and they made a concerted effort full of whispers not to talk about my swollen, cut-up face, bless their hearts. Instead, they volunteered to correct papers, carry my bag of books, whatever they could do to help. They made the rest of the week bearable.

But, thankfully, Saturday morning arrived at last, and I planned to rest. I'd barely flopped into my easy chair, hoisted my aching leg onto an ottoman, and picked up a good book, when I heard the screech of brakes outside. DeeDee stormed in, not even bothering to knock.

Well, there goes my restful morning!

"I never thought I'd wind up in this fix," she said, throwing her purse down on the divan. "I thought if he wanted to love me, he'd be wanting to marry me and make babies…and…."

"Whoa, DeeDee. Back up." I shook my head, not certain I was hearing her right. "I don't know what or whom you're talking about. Why are you so upset? Are you all right?"

"It's that Ben!" She spat out the name as though it were a cuss word. "That Ben asked me out last night, and we had dinner, and he took me home, and he came in for a cup of cocoa, and said how much he enjoyed my sense of humor, and how much he wanted to be with me, and I did, and he did, and oh, my goodness. What will Mama say?" She burst into explosive sobs with massive gasps in between. Whatever had happened surely seemed the end of the world.

I slid my leg from the ottoman so I could sit up straighter to listen. "Wait a minute, DeeDee. You lost me back there. Slow down and make some sense."

"Oh, Megan," she blubbered, pacing the floor in front of me and waving her arms. "I went and did it, and now I don't know what to do. I thought he loved me. He said he loved me, so I thought we were engaged, and we'd marry, and have babies. You just don't tell someone you love her and not mean it. Then he just said, 'Thanks for a nice evening...see ya.'"

DeeDee paused long enough to face me with her fists imbedded on her hips. "I don't think he meant it when he said so many lovely things, and I believed him, and I thought he did mean them, and...."

She blew her nose on the tissue I extended to her. She took the whole box. "Oh, Megan, now Mama will say I'm damaged goods, and no one will want to marry me, and what will I do?"

I shook the cobwebs out of my spinning head because this was *so* 1880s. "DeeDee, when you're upset, you speak in run-on sentences that are totally unintelligible. Now, if I'm getting this right, you slept with Ben last night, and now you're wondering if he still likes you?"

"Yes...I mean, no...I mean...he said he loved me, and he couldn't have, if he left like that in the middle of the night, could he?"

"That depends on what was in his mind, and yours. Did you *agree* to a one-night stand?"

"What's that?" asked DeeDee, blubbering again. The tissues flew through her fingers. "Do you mean that's all he wanted--to embarrass me by taking me out for only one night, when he didn't want to marry me?"

"Well, DeeDee, how can I put this? I'm not saying it's right, but sometimes two people agree they want to be together only for one time, and they don't mean anything by it at all." I was scared to ask the obvious, since she seemed to blame Ben somehow. "Did you consent? I mean he didn't force you or anything, did he? You aren't hurt, are you?"

"No," came a teensy, blubbery voice, as she mopped her eyes and blew her nose.

I couldn't imagine Ben forcing anyone. I'd known him a while, and he was a good guy, always ready to help others, and first on the court at our Wednesday night volleyball games. He's "fast-track" in the military too, definitely on the way up. However, he is a hunk--the tall, dark, and handsome cliché personified. Women flocked to his good looks. I'd noticed even Cathie looked envious when he asked DeeDee out while we were all stranded in Austria. *No, I couldn't see Ben taking advantage of anyone. But what could have upset DeeDee so?*

"Why don't you sit down, we'll have a cup of tea, and you can tell me all that happened."

She flopped down on a chair at my kitchen table, her head down on folded arms.

I felt sorry for DeeDee. I, too, had been naïve enough to misunderstand that the flirting of a certain colonel was dangerous when I'd first arrived. I knew how scary it was to need to run away from someone, or perhaps she felt someone had run away from her. I hopped on my good leg over to pour her a cup of tea, and I sat beside her at the table, sticking my cast out at an angle. She was still crying uncontrollably but, when lifting her wet face, some words became clearer.

"Megan, I don't know what happened. Really. We had a lovely time. He seemed like he really cared about me. He was attentive and cuddly, and we talked about plans for the future...."

"Your plans or his plans?" Apprehension nibbled at the corner of my mind.

"I thought they were the same thing. He said he liked me, and he kissed me, and I felt all gushy. I *never* felt gushy before. He said he'd never known anyone like me, and I was the perfect woman and all like that. I liked hearing his nice words. And he is handsome, isn't he?" She honked into another tissue and mopped her steadily running fountain of tears. "Doesn't that mean he loves me? He even said that right out loud, and I thought it was safe to kiss him, if he loved me. Then we sat down on the couch, listening to music, and he kissed me a lot." She began wailing again like a cat with its tail caught in the door. "Oh why weren't my brothers there when I needed them to chaperone?"

Uh Oh! That sounds ominous.

"It was like nothing I'd ever known, and I *liked* it, but then I got scared because I didn't have a chaperone, and Ben seemed to want a lot *more* hugging and kissing. Then he held me really tight, and my breath was just gone, and I kissed him really hard. I've never kissed anyone like that...or anyone at all, actually." She snuffled her way through a hiccoughing sigh.

"And then what?" I didn't want to ask, but she seemed particularly needy to get this horrific event off her chest. *God, I hope we don't need a trip to the clinic?*

"Then we talked about the future. He said he wasn't married. That's the first thing I asked him after you told me some guys didn't tell a girl that. Then I told him how great it would be when we had a home of our own and lots of babies. He got real nervous, and he got up and left."

"You talked about a home and babies during your first date?"

"Of course. He said he loved me. We'd have to decide about those things, wouldn't we?"

"Not on a first date, DeeDee!" I took a deeply frustrated breath. *How do I get myself into these things?* "I told you before. Those are things you discuss after you're engaged and planning a wedding."

"Well, I thought we *were* planning a wedding, but he left me there. He was in a hurry."

"Okay, DeeDee. See if I've got this straight. You had a nice evening together, he got romantic, and you invited him in. He got more romantic, and then you talked about marriage and babies. Am I right, so far?"

"Sort of, but how could he just leave me like that?"

"DeeDee, I'm not sure if you're upset because he left, or because you'd be scared if he *didn't* leave. You probably scared him to death with that kind of talk. I've told you before and you didn't listen. He probably hasn't stopped running yet."

"But, now I'm deflowered, and no one else will ever want me," she blubbered.

Deflowered? "DeeDee, I'm not sure I understand, so I guess I have to ask. Did you actually have sex with Ben, like go all the way?"

She shook her head so hard, I was afraid it would fall off. "Oh, my goodness, never!" she said. "That's what started it all. He wanted to, and I told him we could only hug and kiss until we got married, and he got upset. When I told him about having babies, he got up and left."

"Then how do you figure you're 'deflowered' or 'damaged goods?' I haven't heard of anyone using those terms for centuries." I was sure she had misunderstood what sex actually entailed. "If you didn't have sex, you didn't actually…then you didn't do anything that either you or Ben would have to feel badly about."

"But Mama said loose women behaving badly would be damaged goods forever if they necked with a man, and I think what we were doing was necking, wasn't it?"

I gulped back giggles by covering my mouth firmly with my hand and took a breath. "DeeDee, if what you're telling me is correct, you didn't do anything to get 'deflowered.' Just chalk it up to having had a nice date with Ben, and nothing more."

"But if he kissed me and all, shouldn't he marry me?"

"Gosh, I hope not. A few kisses do *not* equal an engagement."

"But…."

"No buts, DeeDee. You just saw something in Ben's attention that wasn't there. He saw it as a nice date, and maybe he wanted a bit more from you than you wanted to deliver. That's no problem. But when you started talking about marriage and babies, he figured out you were way ahead of him in what you expected from the date, so he left. That's the most honorable thing, if that wasn't what he wanted, or what he was ready for, now isn't it?"

"Do you mean he'd wanted to have sex with me and not marry me?" Her pitch raised two octaves. "He's a terrible boy."

I leaned my face on my hands, elbows on the table. "No, DeeDee. He's not a 'boy,' and he would have been terrible only if he had forced you to do something you didn't want to do. I told you that when you worried about Don and Ruthie, remember?"

"But sex is only for having babies."

"I'm sure that was what you were taught in school by the nuns, DeeDee, but some people may share sex because they're lonely, and they feel better together. Maybe one of them is distraught and really needs the closeness. Maybe one of them is in love and thinks they are pleasing the other, maybe they think they might have a future, but aren't sure yet...."

"Then, wouldn't that be wrong? Wouldn't they go straight to Hell?"

"I don't know, DeeDee. Maybe God can tell when someone is lonely and needs a loving friend." *What am I doing discussing the birds and bees with a twenty-nine year old virgin?*

"But Ben kissed me, and I liked it, and Mama will make me go home right away."

I paused, not sure how to say the biggest blasphemy of all. *Plunge right in, you dummy. It's time she knew.* "Just so you know, once and for all, DeeDee...."

She turned her face away like a five year old, trying not to hear me. I reached across the table and took her chin in my hand. "Now listen to me, 'Emily,' my friend, this is important."

Her wide eyes brimmed with tears.

I spoke the words slowly. "Your Mama cannot make you go home against your will. You're a grown woman, and she cannot make you do anything that you choose not to do. The key word here is 'choose.' You can choose your own friends. You do *not* need to report everything you do or think to Mama. Your life is yours to choose for yourself, alone—your own friends, your own thoughts, your own activities. Mama doesn't rule you anymore!" I guess I raised my voice, since she scrunched up her body as though to protect herself. "Even when you go home at the end of the school year, you won't want to live with your parents anymore."

"Why not?"

DeeDee's eyes always registered her fear, her surprise, her elation. I let her run the gamut of emotion before interrupting her thoughts. "Because you've been on your own for several months now, and you've had some adventures of your own. Most of all, you're a different person, standing on your own two feet."

"Won't my family still care about me?"

"Of course, they'll still love you, and you'll still spend time with them. But you could no longer live under Mama's roof and have her tell you how to decorate your room, what to wear, when and where you can go out, or when you could travel, or anything like that. You've been on your own. You'll want to stay that way until you find the person you'll share your life with."

DeeDee put her hands up to her face, breathing deeply. I knew she'd have tears over this new set of parameters. I patted her on the head. "Buck up, 'Emily,' this is a good thing. It's called learning to stand up for yourself and roll with the punches. You're growing into maturity. You've cut the umbilical cord. Have faith in yourself, and don't depend only on Mama."

She blubbered into another tissue. "You're sure this is a good thing, for me not to tell Mama everything?"

"It's a good thing for you to stand alone and not depend on Mama to make all your decisions for you. Think about it, later, DeeDee. Now drink your tea."

"But I still won't want to have sex until I get married. I don't understand the others. *You* wouldn't do that with Jimmy, would you?"

Hadn't counted on that question! "Probably not as easily as you make it sound, DeeDee. We're both pretty old fashioned. On the other hand, if it could be with anyone, it might be with Jimmy. We genuinely like each other and spend quite a bit of time together. I suppose it could happen, *if* we let it." *I wonder if I'm telling the truth.*

"Megan!" squealed DeeDee. "How could you?"

I could hear her disapproval of my even *thinking* about it. "I'm not saying I would, DeeDee. Just that it could happen to anybody, *if* the feelings were right. You just weren't ready and Ben knew it. When you meet the right man, you'll know."

DeeDee put her fist to her mouth. She seemed to have a new problem. "Oh, my goodness, you mean I embarrassed myself by assuming, and now I can never face Ben or anyone again."

"For Pete's sake, Dee! Now that you and Ben realize that you're looking for different things, you can just be friends like before, and no one will think anything about it."

"But you and Jimmy…."

I looked at her strained face and chuckled. "DeeDee, that's probably a long way off. I've been hurt before, so I don't want to rush into anything."

She hoisted her shoulders indignantly. "Well, I should hope not!"

I laughed. "Don't worry DeeDee. Other members of the human race will behave the way they see fit, and you don't have to do anything about it, or tell them off, or change your friendship with them. We're all free to do as we choose, what we think is right, without it bothering anyone else…you, too. Do you understand?"

Was I getting through to her at all? Was I even right? I tried again. "Sometime, you'll find someone you really care about. And if it feels right, you may choose to spend more time with him, too. The choice will be up to you and the person you feel you might be in love with."

"Oh, my, I never could…."

I raised my eyebrows at her and waggled my finger. "Never say, 'Never.' It could happen that you fall in love. You'll decide *then* how to handle your own relationship, not now."

DeeDee sat quietly for a long time, spreading her fingers apart and pulling them together on the table's surface, apparently thinking how the world had changed while she was locked in her house in Ithaca.

I finally broke the silence. "Look, DeeDee, I can sympathize. I felt the same surprise to find how much things had changed while I was married in Los Angeles. When I married Bruce, we were eighteen and both virgins, because that was the way the world was then. After he died, I came to Germany, and I found while I hadn't been looking, the world had invented free love and the pill. I'd been shocked as much as you've been. But I had to come to grips with the realities. I hope you can as well." I patted her hand, not realizing I had shocked her again.

"You never told me you were married!" It was an accusation.

"We were very young, he died very young, and it broke my heart to lose him. I don't talk about it with *anyone*." *I'd rather not have answered that. Now, I'm fighting my own waterworks.*

"You said you'd been hurt two other times, and that you didn't trust men anymore."

I closed my eyes and stretched my neck back as far as it would go. I'd hoped she'd forgotten that, but DeeDee rarely forgot anything. "You don't want to know about those times."

"You're my friend, 'Cornelia Megan.' Of course, I do."

"You won't approve."

"If *you* did something, I would. If you did something, it would have to be good."

"'Emily,' you have way too much faith in me. No pedestals please." I ran over in my mind how I should tell her, or how much I should tell her. "After Bruce died, I never thought I could love anyone again. But we all feel loneliness. I finally fell in love again, but the man was shot and paralyzed in the line of duty."

DeeDee's mouth fell open. "In the Army?"

"Yes, he was a spook...a spy...MI. After his injury, he didn't want to have me tied down taking care of him while I was still so young. We've remained friends." I thought of Ed and how I'd been ready to take care of him forever, but he was too proud a man to allow it.

"Ooh! I could *never* risk loving a spy. Had you 'done it' with him?"

I had to chuckle at her tone. "Yes, we 'did it.' We planned to be married as soon as he finished one more mission, but that one mission took his legs and almost took his life."

"Oh." DeeDee breathed out softly. I could see the wheels turning.

"So are you thinking I was wrong to trust him with my heart, soul, mind, and body?"

"I guess I sort of see what you mean. You thought you'd be married very soon, so it must have seemed all right to both of you."

"Thank you, 'Emily,' for understanding that. He was a fine man, and we loved each other very much. It did seem right at the time."

"Are you sorry you did that, since you didn't wind up marrying him after all?"

The puzzled look on her face told me she was wrestling with a huge moral dilemma.

"No, I'm not. We enjoyed the time we had together before he was stricken, just as Bruce and I enjoyed the time we had together before he died. In both cases, I trusted the ones I loved. And sometimes life takes twists we can't predict. I wouldn't have wanted to miss the joy we shared, even if I had known it could only be for a short time."

"Oh." She sighed. "What about the man you said made it so you couldn't trust again."

I laughed, rather a gruesome laugh, remembering Louis. "We dated a long while, we loved each other, we talked about marriage, and then one day he added, '...soon as I get my divorce.'"

There came her saucer eyes.

"You asked, I answered. I know that's hard for you to understand, but I think we were both very lonely people. He'd been unhappy a long time, and I'd already lost two wonderful men I'd loved. We seemed to have so much in common, it seemed so right. I guess he just neglected to tell me the most important thing."

"Why didn't he do the right thing first off and tell you he

was married? Then you wouldn't have grown to love him and been hurt again."

"I asked the same question. He said at first it hadn't mattered because we were just good friends, and then it had mattered too much—because he had come to love me and didn't want to lose me. He knew I'd leave him when he told me. I did."

Funny how our roles suddenly reversed. Now it was old 'Cornelia' grabbing the Kleenex box, and naïve 'Emily' doing the comforting. The tears I'd held back so long just cracked open my heart and poured out, in spite of myself, crying for all three of them....

"You couldn't have known. It wasn't your fault. It was his," said DeeDee softly.

"But I loved him, I trusted him. He was a good man caught in a bad marriage. I hurt him as much as he hurt me, but I couldn't be part of breaking up a marriage. I guess now, I'm a little suspicious of the motives of men. Poor Jimmy doesn't fully understand why I'm so slow-moving this time, but 'once burned, twice shy.'" I wiped the tears away and sat straighter.

"I'm sorry. I didn't know all that. You must be very sad. I didn't know you had a past."

She cracked me up, and I almost couldn't get the words out for the laughter.

"Good Lord, DeeDee. Don't say that like I'm a scarlet woman or something. I've just fallen in love three times--one died, one was paralyzed, and one was untruthful. That's it! Don't try to make me into a tragedy. I'm recovering. I just haven't trusted men for a while, but that doesn't mean *you* shouldn't. There's a right guy out there for you, but he just may not be here on this particular post, he may not be a military man, and for crying out loud, you've got to quit looking at every male like he might father a child for you."

"Oh...okay, Megan."

DeeDee's face registered concern and pity. Finally she nodded. "Thank you for trusting me enough to tell me. You've had as much pain with your relationships as you have with your accidents, haven't you?"

"Hm. Maybe it's all the same thing," I said. Suddenly the whole conversation seemed ludicrous. "Who's comforting whom here, 'Emily?'" She joined in the laughter. Soon we were hiccoughing and holding our sides as tears ran down both our faces.

"I'm so glad we had this talk," said DeeDee in between giggles. "I do feel much better."

"So do I. You're not worried anymore about losing your virginity to Ben when you didn't actually do anything but kiss him?"

She smiled. "I guess I didn't understand, and I felt afraid to admit I enjoyed kissing him."

"That's allowed, Dee. You don't even have to *tell* Mama what you enjoyed."

"Good. I was worried she could always read my thoughts. Thanks, 'Cornelia.' Friends forever?"

"Friends forever."

Yes, we'd come a long way together.

Chapter 15   Road to Morocco

A couple of weeks later, Jimmy carried our drinks to a quiet corner of the Officers' Club. The red room was for special occasions, where we could sit together by candlelight over a Mosel wine. I'd been enjoying my fifth graders with their Frontier history projects and just had to tell Jimmy all about it. He, in turn, was filled with his latest flight problems.

"You know that a helicopter is only a flying box looking for a way *not* to fly, but I think we got on top of the maintenance this time," he said.

Soon, we realized we'd been interspersing dissimilar dialogue back and forth and yet we'd understood each other perfectly. It was a moment of shared smiles.

Since my injury in Athens and Jimmy's unflappable quick thinking during the Alpine blizzard, I'd come to appreciate him even more. He definitely was a good and caring person, and I cherished the time we could spend together when he wasn't flying the Border. He had a dangerous job, and that burdened my mind. I sure didn't want to let myself love anyone else, and risk losing them again. *But, he looks really good in a flight suit!* It made me smile to remember that.

"I notice you don't have the cast anymore. Did Doc cut it off already?" he asked.

"It was causing more harm than good, falling on the kneecap all the time, and the crutches drove me nuts. I asked him to cut the darned thing off and give me a supply of ace bandages. I'll probably still have to have the meniscus surgery one of these days, but I'm getting around better now with ace bandages."

He smiled. "I wondered how long you'd wait to take things into your own hands."

"You've been flying quite a lot lately, haven't you?" I asked, changing the subject from what he called "my independent streak."

"Why, my dear, did you miss me?" he said, with mischief in his eyes.

I had to laugh and nod. "I did."

His hands sought mine across the table. It felt good to feel safe with his kind nature. I think we were growing closer each time we were together, though neither of us felt the need to say it. We enjoyed our private dinner in the velvety red room with its massive stone fireplace. Marco had started the fire for us, for what he called our "special" dinner. Our conversation centered around making plans together for Jimmy's next R and R leave, when I'd get back from my summer vacation.

Later, the conversation moved to DeeDee.

"You know, I think we need to get DeeDee out of any residual doldrums over Ben, and back to traveling," Jimmy suggested over dessert. "Your fellow teachers, Tim and Kurt, are talking about a trip to Spain and Morocco. Maybe you ladies would like to tag along with them so they can look after you."

"I don't need anyone to look after me!" I bristled, but immediately regretted it. "It would be nice if you could get away, too?"

I hoped he could, but I wasn't surprised when he kissed my hand and shook his head with a sad smile. "Not for awhile, Babe. Mission first, right?" *I knew that.*

DeeDee came in. "I looked around until I found you guys. I've never been in here before," she said. "It's really pretty. Am I interrupting anything?"

"Absolutely," said Jimmy, with a grin. "But I have to go back to the Border, anyway. Megan has some ideas for another trip with Kurt and Tim." He kissed me on the forehead and left.

"You've been quiet lately," I said. "A short trip might be good for you."

"I don't think we should travel with only two other male teachers," said DeeDee, sliding into Jimmy's empty seat and studying her hands in her lap. "Do you?"

"It's no different from Greece, DeeDee, only there'll be four of us instead of ten. Tim and Kurt are nice guys and traveling with them is easy. They'll have their own room and so will we."

Her eyes widened. "You mean to say you've traveled with them before?"

I bit my lip to stay patient. "We've talked about this, DeeDee. You've had almost a year to figure out that all the people around here travel together because it's more fun to go with friends than to go alone. It's because we're so close to the Border, we're a small base where almost everyone knows everyone else, and we all just become family. If one goes someplace, all others are welcome. It doesn't mean anything romantic at all," I wanted her to feel as good about the camaraderie on our little base as I did. "We know Europe well enough that we can go where we wish in the Western zone. Formal tours are too expensive, and we like our own gang's company better, anyway. Traveling is what we save our money for; that's what we enjoy. Why would it matter who goes along?"

"I never thought about it that way. You mean no one would think it funny if we went with Tim and Kurt? No one would think maybe we were two couples or anything?"

"Not around here, DeeDee. Tim and Kurt are good people and good teachers, though you don't see them so much because they're at the junior high. Tim has a nice girlfriend, but Cass can't get off work to go along. He has a beard, and hippie hair. Kurt is a big guy, prematurely balding, but with a ponytail. He likes to play the field, but he's a good sort. They're just friends, so we don't care what others think."

"Play the field? Does that mean Kurt is like Ben?"

Yeesh, why had I mentioned that? "Let's just chalk Ben up to an accident, or maybe just 'practice,' for dating again." DeeDee's shoulders slumped, so I quickly pursued the trip to Spain and Morocco to perk her up. We'd better decide now, so we can have Tim make reservations."

"Okay, I guess." Her voice sounded like I'd asked her to meet Dracula.

"Oh, come on 'Emily.' How can we see the world if you sit here all glum and sad?"

She brightened considerably at mention of her nickname.

"All right, 'Cornelia.' I guess we can splurge on this trip because we'll get another paycheck when we get back."

DeeDee was better at figuring finances than I was. If worse came to worst, Marco would always carry us on the books, so at least we could eat at the Club until we got paid enough to buy groceries. I'd relied on him several times, especially when coming back from a summer in the states when we teachers didn't get paid until mid October. The trip was on.

On the big day, I was nervous, as usual, before the flight from Frankfurt to Barcelona. "After all, our last flight had a bomb on board," I said.

"This flight will be super-duper," DeeDee said, with her self-confidence on matters air-borne.

"Don't forget there are three flights on this trip," I countered.

Tim sat next to me, but he paid for it during a bumpy take off. I drew blood through his cotton shirt.

"Megan, I'm not sitting next to you after this. No hard feelings, but you're positively dangerous." He pulled up his sleeve and licked his fingers to wipe the blood off. "Cass is gonna think some lady man-handled me, and she'll be jealous." But he grinned, so I didn't figure he minded too much. But I felt pretty stupid.

Barcelona was magnificent—a walk back in time, even for a modern city. We loved the Las Ramblas pedestrian street lined with colorful and noisy birds in bamboo cages. DeeDee and Tim talked to every parrot and twittered away to little birds that didn't speak, while Kurt and I walked slowly to allow them their "birdie fix." Sun shone down on the parched earth of hillside farms in the distance. Spain was experiencing a drought, as had Yugoslavia.

We walked all around the unfinished Cathedral of the Holy Family by Gaudi, finding the soft, swirly architectural masterpiece so different from all the square-standing, stolid churches of Europe. "It looks like the roof is coated in snow drifts," I said, while Tim took multiple slides to show his students.

DeeDee slid off the rubber band that held her worn

Frommer guidebook together and put it on her wrist for safekeeping. She read from its loose pages. "Gaudi died before he finished this wonderful church. He got hit by a trolley car, no less. What a shame."

We talked about how the church might never be finished on the bus to Pueblo Espanol, where old village homes were brought together from every region in Spain to give an idea of what life was like in earlier times. Artisans in each of the homes made articles using the old methods, and many of these basic clothing and utensils items were for sale. Kurt was the one splurging this time, as he found several hand woven towels, and a velvet vest made of rainbow colors.

At dinner, we shared a steaming platter of paella, with three-inch baby octopi clinging around the platter's edge as though trying to climb out. DeeDee's eyes were wide when she announced, "Those are only for decoration. We aren't eating those!" Then she peered closer and added, "They look like they're alive. They aren't, are they?"

We noticed that all the Spaniards smelled like garlic, and wondered if maybe they didn't bathe frequently enough. But after three days, Tim sniffed his forearm and said, "I think they use so much garlic in food here, that it actually seeps through the pores. Now I smell like garlic, too." We had to agree, and soon we didn't notice it any more than did the natives.

Tim was as good as his word and seated himself next to DeeDee our next flight to Madrid. That left Kurt to sit next to me. I swore I wouldn't lose control again but, true to form, when we lifted from the ground, Kurt's knee somehow got in the way of my fingernails reaching for something—anything--to grab on to.

"Hot damn," Kurt exploded, pushing my hand away.

"I'm sorry. You were just *there*, and I grabbed the first thing I came to. I'm really sorry."

"No more," said Kurt, sliding his legs all the way to the other side of his seat. Once he calmed down, though, he thought it was funny that he had a "war wound", and said he intended to brag about it at the O'Club.

"Aw, come on, Kurt. It was an accident."

"Why, I may roll up my pants legs. Or better yet, I'll wear shorts. I'll wow them all with tales of how you attacked me. Jimmy will be so jealous."

Smart Aleck! I read my book for the remainder of the trip.

After a couple of days in Madrid, we grabbed a bus to the sea, and a ferry across the Mediterranean to Morocco. I found the fresh sea air and the crisp rolling of the ferry as it sailed past Gibraltar quite exhilarating, but Kurt complained of mild nausea. He leaned over the rail and watched the waves instead of the bobbing horizon, and soon felt better.

DeeDee was excited about Morocco. She practiced the famous line, "Come with me to zee Kasbah" a million times while crossing the Med. In desperation, we told her it was only another a market place--dark, grime and crime infested, but hardly romantic. No Humphrey Bogart.

"Well, I'm sure Morocco will be at least mysterious."

Her romantic image was further shattered when the ferry captain announced on the intercom just before docking, "Don't pay any attention to the beggars who will accost you when you land. We are trying to discourage begging in our country."

We exited from the ferryboat to set foot on the African continent. Dirty, cluttered streets were hung with laundry from every balcony across the gaps between run-down tenement housing. We were barely down the gangplank before we were surrounded by flocks of grimy little boys, each with his hand held out, each waiting to approach Americans.

"Are we considered soft touches, or what?" I asked. "But they're so young, and they must really be hungry to beg like this."

"Actually," said Kurt, "they're well-trained thieves. Watch your wallets and passports."

"Oh, Kurt, that's so mean," said DeeDee, reaching out to hand her loose change to the nearest little boy of about five. "Oh, my goodness," she yelped. The little guy grabbed, not the change she offered, but the camera slung around her neck. The kid had ripped it off her neck and was gone before she could respond. The other kids closed in on his trail. Another grabbed the change out of her hand and disappeared as well.

"Told you so," said Tim. "Next time, maybe you'll believe the captain and me."

Considerably chastened, DeeDee held everything she carried under her arms, crossed close to her breast. *I hope this visit to Morocco won't set her back to last August.*

"Where are the police?" she wailed. "Won't they help?"

"No," said Kurt. "They've done their duty once they warn you to stay away from beggars. You can have copies made from my slides once we get back to Bamberg. Besides, you may even see your camera again for sale in the souk."

"Oh, my goodness! My brother Tony gave me that camera. I feel awful." DeeDee's eyes followed the children, not much bigger than her Kindergarten students, swarming around each passenger. "They're such little boys. Why on earth would they steal? Where are their parents?"

"Their parents are probably waiting to sell whatever the kids steal. And the cops don't come in here," said Kurt. "Besides, they probably get some kickback. I'm glad Germany isn't like this." Cynicism dripped from each word as he wiped sweat from his shiny head. "Glad Germany isn't this hot, either," he added.

"Let's get our stuff to the hotel and then go out to the Kasbah," I suggested.

DeeDee shook her finger at me. "Promise me, after Bethlehem, I want no Arab taxis." I grinned and promised, with crossed fingers.

Tim hailed a taxi, and sure enough, it was driven by two Arabs. DeeDee hesitated to get in, looking at me with that "you lied," stare.

I shrugged. "So, you'd rather walk?"

The crowd of boys seemed to grow, even as we struggled to keep our hand luggage on our shoulders. We crammed ourselves into the taxi and sped away.

The hotel was barely passable, with dark halls and ancient plumbing, but we only needed it for showering and sleeping. The

Ritz wasn't in the budget. We had only a day and a half to see all we could of Morocco.

We wore ourselves out walking around ornate mosques. Each had a half dozen withered and weathered mothers sitting in the dirt outside the walls with one palm extended while nursing a sickly-looking infant. They cried for mercy and alms, each more plaintive than the last. DeeDee and I gave money to each of these pitiable women until we saw one get up, take her money and leave, calmly handing "her" infant to another "mother."

We both jumped back, startled. But the new woman, pulling the other's baby to her breast, limped after us, shoving her shoulder and the baby against DeeDee's arm. Her fetid breath assaulted our faces, as she held us back, demanding her alms.

"Lookie, lookie," she cried, holding out the naked little one. DeeDee tried to pull away, a scream already forming in her face, while I called to Tim.

In two steps, Tim was beside us, had grabbed DeeDee by the arm, and pulled her away from the woman's grasping, probing fingers. Tears rushed down DeeDee's face as Tim encircled her with his arms and herded her back over to Kurt. Kurt told the woman to go away, and she spit at him. When she turned to walk away, her limp was miraculously gone.

"Don't get disillusioned, ladies," said Kurt. Sadness did, however, show in DeeDee's face, as she wiped her face with her hands and put her wallet away inside her waistband.

"Come on," said Tim. "Buck up, ladies. So you were 'conned.' Probably not the first or last time. We'll go shopping. All you women like bargaining in the souks."

We trundled along behind, appalled by the poor streets and diseased condition of the people, until we decided we needed to lift our spirits. Kurt suggested we go to a Moroccan restaurant, sit on the floor, and try Moroccan food. The concierge of our hotel gave him directions for a recommended restaurant. The four of us took a taxi and entered what I always dreamed the Arabian Nights would look like.

Three-foot wide ribbons of multi-colored silk draped from

the ceiling of the restaurant, a cloud of color wisping in the air. Velvet pillows lay carelessly around a very low table. We heard the wailing, off-key sounds of a Moroccan combo playing across the room. If the music was earsplitting, it was certainly authentic, and we tried to discern some melody or on-key air. The caterwauling continued wildly, as though demons had escaped into the room. A cloud of blue smoke swirled around their heads as they played.

"Our lesson in cross-cultural ties for the day," said Kurt, with his eyes scrunched up and shoulders hunched against the sound. "It's hardly romantic. I'm glad I didn't bring a girlfriend."

An amazing waiter came to seat us on the ornate floor pillows. He was perhaps five feet tall, but he wore a turban that increased his size to six feet. It had a tall feather sticking up the middle, held in place by a huge emerald. It was too large to be anything but fake, yet it shown brilliantly and certainly added to his authority as he bowed, his golden earrings dangling. He was bare-chested except for a brocade short vest, and his pantaloons and turned up shoes were of gold fabric. He  had, indeed, stepped right out of Arabian Nights in order to match the decor.

We looked at the mysterious menu, not understanding any of it. The national dish, couscous, was supposed to be a local grain served with different types of meat and sauces. Tim, appointing himself the expert, pointed at one of the couscous dishes on the menu, and the waiter bowed his way back to the kitchen.

As we sat waiting for our much-needed food, the smells of cooking wafted out of the kitchen, but it seemed linked with another strange odor that kept increasing in intensity. We looked around for the offending smell, but couldn't make out what it was.

DeeDee wrinkled up her pert nose and sniffed. "I don't

know what that is, but it sure is strong in here, isn't it?"

After several moments of speculative sniffing, Tim scratched his beard and pronounced the odor as hashish. We traced it straight to the four musicians curled in the blue smoke.

"I'm sure it's hashish," said Tim. "From my hippie days."

"Oh, my," said DeeDee, characteristically near tears.

"What shall we do?"

"We should leave," I suggested.

"We've already ordered," said Kurt, "and we'd have to pay for the meal, even if we left. I didn't see any other restaurants on our way. I don't know about you guys, but I'm hungry."

Tim chimed in. "I don't suppose hashish can bother us from clear across the room."

"But, if we can smell it clear over here…" I was worried. I always pictured the world in headlines. *American Teachers Arrested in Kasbah Hashish Den.*"

The waiter arrived with a huge brass tray filled with food that he put in the middle of our low table. We'd lost the moment to act, so we felt pretty much stuck with staying and eating.

The couscous wasn't bad--a gravy over the rice-like grain, with meat and some sort of olives that crunched when you bit into them. There were vegetables we'd never seen before, decorated with orange slices, and the dishes were pungent with exotic spices. We were trying valiantly to ignore both the musician's hashish and their music that sounded like a cat with his tail caught.

Unaccustomed to sitting on the floor while eating, I managed to spill some of the couscous gravy on my slacks. Nothing new. We were about two-thirds through the meal when Tim wondered aloud what kind of white meat was in the gravy.

"I've been trying to figure it out," he ventured. "It doesn't taste like chicken or veal."

"Everything is supposed to taste like chicken," said Kurt.

Having called our attention to it, we all began wondering and offering suggestions.

"Maybe it's rabbit meat," suggested DeeDee "A farmer in our town raised rabbits and some people liked to eat them."

"I'm not sure," said Kurt. "Rabbit isn't this firm."

We speculated on every possible edible concoction, but still couldn't quite place the taste. It looked like boneless chicken breast, but it was thicker and much heavier in texture.

"When in doubt, ask," I said. I called over the waiter. His ornate head covering marked him as the chief man here. His Arabic and my English didn't mesh well, so Tim clucked like a hen and crowed like a rooster, while I held up a big piece of the white meat on my fork.

The waiter shook his head.

Kurt oinked like a pig, and again the waiter shook his head.

We became a cacophony of barnyard noises, as even DeeDee wiggled her nose with hands wiggling over her head like rabbit ears. Tim whinnied, and mooed, and still the waiter shook his head. We were stymied.

Probably because our whinnying and mooing might have been embarrassing, the waiter finally grabbed a paper napkin and his pen, and drew a stick figure of a camel. Then he put an X on the hump and smiled, revealing gaping gold teeth.

There was silence as we each soaked in that piece of information. Kurt picked up a forkful of the meat and examined it more closely. The waiter seemed pleased to show us it was camel hump meat, so we assumed it must be a great delicacy in Morocco.

"If that white meat is camel hump," said DeeDee, "then what are those crunchy olive-sized things with a soft middle?"

When Tim held one of the olive-like things up on his fork, the waiter again smiled and bowed, realizing this time that we wanted to know what remarkable delicacy we were eating. He quickly took another napkin and drew a sheep's face, and placed his X proudly on the left eye.

That was more information than any of us needed.

Tim gulped hard and put his forkful back on the plate, while DeeDee wrinkled up her nose and put her hand over her mouth. I gulped away the queasy feeling.

Kurt pulled out his wallet, threw some bills onto the low table, plenty to cover all four meals and a generous tip for the waiter and musicians, and we quickly made our way outside.

DeeDee held Tim's head while he lost his dinner in the back alley, and Kurt and I ran to the corner to wait for them, just barely containing our own load of camel hump and sheep's eyes.

Once Tim finished turning inside out, and DeeDee had provided all the tissues she had in her purse to wipe his face, we collected ourselves at the corner. None of us wanted anything more to eat. Maybe for a lifetime!

Kurt hailed a taxi, and we were concentrating so hard on our queasiness that we barely noticed the man drove like a maniac with only parking lights showing. DeeDee didn't even crouch down behind the seats.

"Cheez, Tim, I didn't think you'd barf," said Kurt. "I figured it would be DeeDee."

DeeDee looked at him with a proud toss to her hair. "Hanging around with Megan, I've gotten used to the idea that absolutely *anything* can happen when she's around."

"Now, DeeDee," I protested. "I had nothing to do with *this*!"

"No, but nothing unusual ever happens to *me*, unless *you're* with me. Without you, I'd still be eating hard boiled eggs and tea."

We finished the ride back to the hotel with Tim speculating how we could avoid eating until we got back to Spain.

We accomplished this feat by spending all our time and money in the Kasbah. Kurt bargained for rugs, and Tim tried to buy just the right piece of gold jewelry for his girlfriend, Cass. He asked DeeDee's and my opinions on every piece and, because we couldn't agree, he finally bought two pieces; some filigreed dangly earrings, I liked and a golden pendant DeeDee liked best.

DeeDee and I went looking for brass bowls and aftabas, which were like tall, skinny brass pitchers. But in every shop the items all were gray, dusty, and ugly. We wanted the nice, shiny ones we'd seen in friends' apartments back in Bamberg.

A portly man wearing long robes, a red fez hat, rather than a kaffeyeh or turban, and sporting large hooped earrings, suddenly appeared, so silently he might have arrived on a magic carpet. He spoke beautifully accented English, introducing himself as Monsieur Saud. "You are looking for a shiny aftaba, no?"

I nodded.

"Pick the piece only by its shape," said the man. "Ignore dust and dirt. We don't polish until someone buys. Some are ancient. Some are not so ancient. Pick the shape you like, and we'll make it new just for you." DeeDee blushed at his intense smile.

There were so many dusty pieces in the shop, all four walls stacked high on shelves up to the rafters. Somehow when looking at the dirty, corroded pots, they all looked alike. But then we concentrated on which shape seemed best, and I began to see possibilities in several of them. I chose a tall aftaba, with fluted edges around the curved spout. It had a lid that I liked the carvings on--at least I tried to peer through the years of grime and see what it would look like, if polished.

"It's like picking Aladdin's Lamp," I told DeeDee. "They're going to rub it and then, maybe we'll get three wishes."

DeeDee chose a bulbous pot with a pointed lid, but turned up her nose, still skeptical when she handed her chosen piece to the man. Our host drew us a cup of tea from the bronze samovar steaming over an open fire in the corner, then he went to the back of the colorfully tented booth. We could hear grinding noises. We waited quite a while--long enough for Kurt and Tim to catch up with us from their shopping at a nearby booth. They wrinkled their noses, as we had, at the array of grimy old metal pieces and the musty interior smell. None of us could quite believe the pots were actually brass or copper.

But when the big man returned with my aftaba and DeeDee's pot, I was astonished, and even the guys gasped in amazement. The pieces gleamed with a burnished copper tone, highlighted with silver and brass streaks along their sides.

"They're beautiful," I said breathlessly. I was completely baffled at how these ugly, grimy vessels had become so magically marvelous.

"Each piece in the shop is different," said Mr. Saud.

"Never two exactly alike."

"They're so perfectly formed and etched," said DeeDee, clapping her hands together.

"Oh, no, my American friend," he said, shaking his head. "Nothing is perfect except Allah, so if a piece comes out perfect, we must *make* a flaw. Here, see this little extra dent in the design?" He turned her piece over and pointed. "All artisans must do this in honor of Allah."

We nodded, silently respectful of his devotion.

We thought one had to pick a brass pot, or a copper one, or a silver one, but we found the color was determined by how far down they burnished the piece. Kurt and Tim ordered pieces of their own, had them polished, and we were about to leave, when I spotted an ornate lantern hanging in the corner above Mr. Saud's ever-present samovar of tea. "What is that?" I asked.

Mr. Saud smiled and cocked his head, quizzically. "That is a harem lantern, Missy, very old, and only for the right person who would want it."

"Thinking of starting a harem, Megan?" joked Tim.

Kurt added, "One of us guys should get that one. What do you say, Tim?"

I realized I really wanted this piece. I could imagine putting a candle in it and watching the play of light and shadow that would glow upon the ceiling through its lacy filigree openings. "I'd like to buy it," I said. "It's lovely, and the carvings are so delicate."

"Missy, I can see it in your face that this piece has been waiting just for you." Mr. Saud climbed up a little step stool to take down the lantern. I could barely contain myself, but I was fearful I'd already overspent the money I'd allowed myself for this trip. "How much is it?" I asked, hoping against hope that it would not be more than I had.

"For you, Missy, and only for you, ten dollars." He smiled. Tim asked if he had more, and how much they normally cost. "I usually ask forty dollars for this one, so just *anyone* won't buy it away from me. There is only this one. But I can see it in your eyes that this is just the piece for you, Missy, and that you will love it for your whole lifetime. And I know it will be held safe and precious with you, so I give it to you for a pauper's price."

"Oh, are you sure?" I asked, digging out my purse. I brought out dollar after dollar until I had eight. There was no more. Disappointed, I shook my head.

Kurt opened his wallet and offered me the other two dollars to make ten. But Mr. Saud would not take his money. "For you," he said again, "…and for you only, I'll take the eight dollars, knowing my favorite masterpiece is in safe hands after I am gone."

I didn't hesitate. But Kurt whispered, "I'll cover you on the way home, Megan."

Mr. Saud invited us to watch as he gently burnished the filigreed metal by hand, so as not to destroy the patina, until it shone with a velvety glow. I was enchanted to watch, and to know it would be mine. I had never wanted anything so much, and my excitement must have shown.

Madame Saud entered the shop from some back room and smiled. "I see you found the right person for your lamp," she said to her husband. She came to me and said, "I know it is you Papa is shining the lamp for. I can see it in your face."

"It's very old," Mr. Saud said. "I made it many years ago when my baby daughter was born. It was to be a gift for her new home on her wedding day, but…." His voice faltered. His wife moved close beside him, immediately resting her hand on his shoulder.

"Our little girl got the fever and died at eleven," she said, "just before she was to be betrothed. Papa has been looking for the right person to have the lamp for many years."

"I want it to be in good hands before I die," said Mr. Saud quietly.

I could feel the tears in my eyes, and when I looked at my friends, I could see they also were moved. "Thank you for telling me, Madame Saud. What was your little girl's name?"

"Our Fatima. I always loved the name, though it's very common, but it was my grandmother's."

"I'll think of her whenever I light candles in the lamp. I'll cherish it for her."

The woman smiled. "I can see Papa made the right choice."

I could only nod, because my throat felt constricted.

When he was finished, Mr. Saud wrapped the delicate lamp in layer after layer of tissue instead of his usual newspaper wrappings, and Madame Saud bound it with strands of silk ribbon. She put it in my arms gently, while Tim and Kurt picked up all the other pieces.

"How can I thank you for entrusting your treasure to me?"

"You already have," said Mr. Saud. "Go with Allah. The lamp will bring you peace when you need it most."

Tired and broke from our shopping, we bought tomatoes, feta cheese, and a loaf of bread at a market stall, and took it back to our hotel for a snack. We were up early to be at the ferry landing, and we finished the bread and cheese for breakfast while waiting at the dock. The ferry chugged in, blaring its whistle, and we immediately boarded. It was due to leave at ten.

"Look," said DeeDee. "Here's some nice seats in this big cabin with picture windows. We can be out of the wind and see the whole lovely Mediterranean at the same time."

"Sounds good to me," said Tim, and we settled into seats. I held Mr. Saud's magic lamp in my arms. We chatted happily as we waited for the ferry's scheduled departure.

But ten o'clock came and went, as did eleven. People crowded into the cabin with us, as well as outside on the deck. Kurt walked out to see what the holdup was, and came back shortly. "They're still loading people," he said. "The line snakes all the way down the pier and several blocks on the shore. It looks like they're waiting until all are boarded, whether we leave on time or not." Kurt fidgeted and fumed that we might miss our return bus ride to Madrid and our plane, if the ferry didn't arrive in Spain on time.

Tim seemed more alarmed about something else. "This ferry is only supposed to hold 250 passengers. There are more than that on board already, and you say they're still coming. How many more can this tub hold?"

It wasn't a good thing to say because now DeeDee was leaning into the plate glass window and counting everyone she saw coming up the gangplank. "Three people with a crate of chickens," she announced, like the droning, unanimated voice in a train station. "Five people with a pig. Two people with a tray full of stuff on the lady's head. Three children with a man carrying a big basket. I can't tell what's in it. A family of...."

"DeeDee, stop," I said. "Look at Tim over there at the passenger limit sign again. I don't think we can do anything about how many come aboard, if they don't hold to the legal limit."

More people were filing into our glassed-in parlor and settling on the floor with their pigs, chickens, and a crate of pigeons. Soon strange odors smothered the air in the cabin.

Tim disappeared for a moment and returned with more news. "The man who took our tickets isn't even taking tickets anymore, just motioning all these people aboard. I asked him why we weren't limiting passengers and freight to the number allowed by marine law, and he laughed at me. He said they go by Marine Law when leaving the European side, but in Morocco, they aren't bound by European law. They take every last passenger. When I said that could be unsafe, he laughed again and said, 'You Americans with your safety rules and timetables. We only have an accident if Allah wills, and the owners won't leave anyone standing on the pier if there is one more fare to be paid.'" Tim clasped his hands over his head, hiding his face with his elbows.

"Should we get off?" asked DeeDee, her eyes wildly scanning the growing crowd.

"We can't even find a path to get off through this mob," said Tim, his voice reflecting growing irritation. "Besides, do we know any other way to get back to Spain? Swim, maybe?"

DeeDee grew quiet.

As more people came aboard, the vessel listed to the left side--the pier side. We began to be alarmed as each new person crowded into our compartment. People and animals filled up the floor, the stairways, and even the open doors of the filthy restrooms.

I began to be afraid we would capsize with so many people on our side of the boat, and now, we were penned into the cabin with glass observation windows. It had become a claustrophobic and deadly prison. If the boat did capsize, there was no way we could get out. This sea of people chatted, shouted to each other, and argued, while their animals squealed loudly, oblivious to any danger.

"Whenever you hear about those ferry accidents in third-world countries, it seems as though they don't care," said Tim. "It's sort of like, 'Oh, well, there are plenty more people where those came from.'"

"I don't like this," Kurt said anxiously, as we could see less and less sky outside the picture window and more and more sea and dock. Nearly one o'clock in the afternoon, we finally felt the motors shudder and the ferry backed into the harbor. We could no longer see a balance of sea and sky--mostly it was sea, yet none of these people seemed at all concerned.

We huddled together, and I clutched my lamp close to my body. DeeDee's hands shook. Kurt and Tim were trying to figure out something they could use to break the observation glass, should the boat capsize. Tim edged a little closer to a fire extinguisher bolted to the bulkhead, "In case," he said.

The engine shuddered and the boat rocked gently. We saw mostly water still. Then suddenly we passed the breakwater and hit the currents coming in through the Straits of Gibraltar. The boat pitched and twisted wildly. DeeDee clutched my sleeve in panic, while I held on to Kurt. Others were screaming and crying out to Allah. Clear blue sky showed one moment, and then seawater slid up the picture window the next. I wished I'd paid attention in that college swimming class I flunked.

We sweated out the whole painful crossing, as many of our fellow passengers got seasick, and even Tim looked a little green. From Spain to Morocco, with a normal load of passengers and goods, the trip had taken an hour. The trip back, under Moroccan boarding rules, with a heavy load of humanity and animals loaded unevenly, took two and a half hours. The boat struggled through the water against the current, slowly, slowly to avoid capsizing. Even the Moroccan passengers became quiet, watching the water slide up the glass. I think we were all silently praying to whatever gods were listening…our God and their Allah.

Finally, and we thought miraculously, we sighted the shoreline of Spain, and the ferry shuddered up to a pier. DeeDee and I relaxed a little, until the captain bellowed over the bullhorn, in Arabic and English, asking everyone not to run to the same side of the boat. No one listened. However, the rush did free up a little space between people on the floor.

"Come on, crew," said Tim urgently. "Follow me. Right now!"

We stepped over people and animals, struggling toward fresh air.

"If we at least can make it to the open deck," said Kurt, grabbing DeeDee's arm, "we can maybe make it to shore in the water, if we have to."

I didn't swim, and had always sunk like a rock, but I still held my lamp closely. I suppose for getting us on shore safely, I had to use one of its three wishes. *And I did!*

The flight home would have been uneventful, except the plane's engines coughed and sputtered, so the pilot let down in Geneva, Switzerland for repairs. That made us a little jumpy, at least it made me jumpy, which probably paved the way for what happened next.

Tim had purchased some beautiful damascene swords in Madrid that he thought would look good over his mantelpiece after he and Cass got married. They were too long for his suitcase, so he'd wrapped them in newspapers and carried them on board the aircraft. In Switzerland, they made us take everything off the plane while we were waiting, and then go back through Swiss security. Swiss security must have been more rigid than Spanish, because they not only blocked Tim's entry with his treasures, saying they were "weapons," but that seemed to make them suspicious of his traveling companions as well.

The guards singled us four out for special attention. They pushed us physically away from other passengers and into wooden booths. A mean-looking matron of at least 350 pounds manned my booth. She pulled open my coat and proceeded to run her hands over my body.

"Stop that," I yelped, and pushed her away, not liking the idea of her touching me where I didn't think she should have. I'd never been patted down in a search before. But immediately, three policemen surrounded me with weapons drawn. I was shaking.

Then, I heard DeeDee's high-pitched squeal from the next booth, and tried to go to her. Both of us were surrounded, while Tim tussled with some agent over his prized swords, and poor Kurt tried in every language he knew to explain that we were all really quite harmless. I even caught sight of his pointing at the three of us and twirling his finger at his temple in the universal sign of "crazy" and then crossing his arms over his breast and dropping his head for "too sad."

For a time, things looked grim, but finally the strong woman seemed to understand that we were just startled, and hadn't expected her to lay hands upon us. The armed guards backed off. They forced Tim to leave his swords and his address behind, with plenty of money to mail them back to the stateside address of his parents. They claimed they could not take responsibility for mailing weapons into another European country without the owner present.

"But I *am* the owner, " Tim objected, rubbing his hands through his thick, curly hippie hair. "This doesn't make sense. Wouldn't it be easier just to let me carry them into Germany, myself?"

Kurt nudged Tim. "Good time to shut up and pay up, Buddy," he said.

We were the last ones allowed to board the plane before takeoff. Since no one would sit next to me again, I sat next to a little kid who was more scared than I was. I comforted him, and myself, by telling him fairy tales on the trip back to Frankfurt.

Chapter 16 - Military Life and Bosco

DeeDee was adjusting to life in Germany. She finally got over her fear of being so close to the communist Border. The bad news was that we couldn't be evacuated should the communists attack, and the good news was that our military officers were wonderfully brave, accepting their mission of holding the line for forty-eight hours until Congress acted to send reinforcements. We all knew Congress couldn't find their way to act within forty-eight hours if they were given a guide dog and a map.

One evening at the O'Club revealed that DeeDee had accepted that if she couldn't change the Cold War, or make it go away, she would simply ignore it.

"You should have seen those commies paint up my aircraft," said Jake. "They locked their radar and missiles right on me. I squawked on the radio and got out of range in a hurry."

DeeDee put her hands over her ears and said, "Please don't tell me any military secrets I could be tortured for. I don't even want to know *anybody* with military intelligence. Not ever!"

"DeeDee," I tried to tell her, "we all know things, and we just keep our mouths shut so as not to endanger the mission. You, personally, will most likely never be tortured for any reason by anyone." *Except maybe me, when she seriously gets on my nerves.*

Yes, DeeDee had come a long way. She was downright pretty, and she was learning to travel in groups, combos, and foursomes. But getting her to talk comfortably with the guys she didn't know from a trip, alone, was still like pulling hen's teeth.

"Hi," she said, in response to newcomer Barry's introduction. "Are you single?"

"DeeDee," I whispered, "Why did you ask that first? You're still scaring guys."

She whispered back, "I have to tell the truth, don't I?"

I took her aside to another table. "Yes, but there's truth and then there's mortal combat. He'll think you're sizing up everyone for a potential husband and father."

"Well, aren't they looking at us the same way? They go out with all the teachers."

"Yes, but it's enjoying the camaraderie, not sizing each other up for wedding bells."

"Why not?" Her innocent stare almost blocked concentration. I shook my head.

Why not, indeed. "DeeDee these guys are usually here for about three years and then they move on to a new assignment."

"Remember, I'm going home after this one year, when my girlfriends from Ithaca come."

"Yes, but the guys aren't on your time schedule. Also, the Border consumes most of their energy, and they're under its pressure. Can't you understand why women as lifetime mates are a long way from their minds? They don't want to leave anyone behind when they know they're only cannon fodder."

"But they like women. They ask you out, and Cathie, and Gert, and…." Her face crinkled up. "They haven't asked me since Ben. I'll bet they think I'm a loose woman."

"Hardly, DeeDee! Ben may have told them you're only interested in marriage, so they probably think you won't go out just for fun and good company like the rest of us do."

"I'm twenty-nine already. I can't afford to waste time on fun and good company. I don't think I should have babies at thirty-five. I've got to get on with it." She looked straight at me for an answer. "Aren't you afraid you might never get married again and have babies? You're older than I am."

I shook my head. "Realistically, DeeDee, I've had my chances with marriage, and I'd just as soon keep my friends among the good guys around here. You mustn't marry the wrong person, *just* to have babies. Your biological clock shouldn't be *that* desperate. You can always adopt."

"But…"

"No buts. We've got a big party at Grunbuhl with the Air Cavalry tomorrow night, and I want you to drive over with me and behave yourself."

"I'm not going to do anything wrong, Megan." Her face registered shock that I might even consider that she would do something awful.

"I know that! I just mean talk to guys and make them feel at ease--no babies, please."

DeeDee and I arrived to a noisy, happy crowd. About fifty of our friends were on hand. Jimmy was first to greet us, and we were quickly within the group, offered drinks and canapés. Bo, one of the Air Cav commanders had arranged for Marco to cater the food, and there were plenty of champagne, balloons, and streamers for decoration. Grunbuhl was a nearby town with a friendly Gasthaus and good music. The Air Cavalry likes to dance. That suited me just fine. I'd rather dance than eat, anytime.

DeeDee still didn't like to dance, but she tried her best. When Bo asked her to dance, I tried to keep her in sight so I could glare at her over Jimmy's shoulder before she opened her mouth, and that worked pretty well.

"Do you really think you can stop her?" said Jimmy, grinning when he noticed my maneuver.

"Maybe I can just intervene in time." I answered. He simply laughed and held me tighter.

But one of the young air crewmen, Scotty, was drinking too much, a bit staggery when he asked DeeDee to dance. All of a sudden he was leaning on her and muttering about his mother and his dog, and she was so full of sympathy that she didn't seem to know how to get out from under him. She looked our way, helplessly shuffling her feet with eyes pleading, as the young man draped over her shoulders like an octopus.

Jimmy went to rescue her, and we put the young man in a corner to sleep it off. But when everyone was leaving, Scotty staggered out of his corner, practically unconscious. He obviously couldn't drive. Since he lived near my apartment, I volunteered to drive him home in Bosco. He could pick up his car later.

"After all," said DeeDee. "I'll be with you."

"Can you two handle him all right?" asked Jimmy.

"Sure we can," said DeeDee. "He's only about twenty years old, and he can't weigh much." I guess she was used to having this kid leaning on her shoulder by then.

The old castle where Scotty lived had seen better years, like in 1600. Plaster chipped and cracked its way down ivy-covered walls. *Probably the ivy is what holds it up.*

"There's a moat and a bridge across it and *everything*," DeeDee said. She was overwhelmed with things royal. "You always look up history. Who lived here in the olden days?"

"A Baron killed in World War II. After the war, no one in his family wanted the trouble to keep up the old home place, especially so near the Border. It would cost a fortune to redo the plumbing and electrical systems. So, they rent it out to GI's who like the romantic idea of living in an old castle, even without amenities. I looked at it myself, when I first came, but heating it was nightmarishly expensive for me. Scotty draws flight pay."

Fog rolled in heavily as we drove across the river and then the moat. I pulled my jacket collar closer in the dampish cold.

The castle was U-shaped and divided into two large apartments, one on each side of the old courtyard. A garden in the middle was cluttered with weeds except where Scotty or his neighbor had planted geraniums in huge old half-cut wine vats. They filled what had once been a circular driveway.

"It's so romantic," said DeeDee, her hands folded in prayer position.

Like most of us, Scotty left his apartment unlocked. It was dark, and the heavy, rolling fog gave the old castle an eerie ambience with wisps of fog bathing its rocks in soft white. We unfolded Scotty's limp form from the car and dragged him inside. I found a light inside the apartment, but nothing on the outside. We dumped him on his bedraggled couch with springs sticking out, but he didn't seem to notice. We found his blanket and pillow from the bedroom, made him as comfortable as we could, and left.

"He'll sleep it off by morning," I told her. "Now, let's get home. This fog is nasty."

I suppose in the grand days of carriages and horses, one

could count on the horse to know the way, and there would've been room in the courtyard to turn around to go out face first. That would've been before Scotty's wine vat and geranium obstacles.

I soon realized there was not enough room to turn around anymore. I'd have to back out of his driveway and across the two wooden bridges; the moat, and its contributing river.

DeeDee looked out her window to direct me while I studied my rear view mirror. It was too foggy to see much, so I opened my window and leaned out. The moat's bridge had maybe a one-foot railing on it, while the river's bridge was a bit wider but had no railing at all. Backwards, on a pitch-black night, with thick fog roiling around us, I was almost guessing where the bridges were. We crept backward across the moat and started across the river.

"Go left, quick," screamed DeeDee, hysterically.

I cut to the left hard, probably too hard. I felt something slip under the left rear wheel. The whole car tilted.

"Not that far," she shouted again.

"Too late," I called. "Hang on." I remembered to pull my arm and shoulder inside. At least we were both buckled up when the car tipped over due to Germany's seat belt law.

We landed on the driver's side, hard, but unhurt. Water poured through my open window. I yelled at DeeDee to climb out her passenger window. I got wet, fast, but she was busy screaming.

"Get out the window, for crying out loud, DeeDee, so I can get up and out of here!"

I pushed. She forgot to unhook the seat belt, so it was futile. She just waved her arms above her head. I got on my knees on my underwater seat and stretched upward to open her window, unbuckled her seat belt and pushed her again. This time I got her to put her head through the window. "Now go!" I shouted. "The water is getting higher down here."

"Where should I go?" she asked.

"Darn it, DeeDee just climb out onto the side of the car or get into the water on the outside so I can get out! Hurry up."

"But I can't jump in the water, I'll drown."

"Would you rather we drown *inside* the car?" I was barely

keeping my head above the rising, icy water. "DeeDee, it can't be more than four or five feet deep. Bosco is barely submerged. Doggone it, get out of the way." I pushed her up as dead weight, and she perched on the outside of the car trying to reach down to me without slipping off the side. She struggled with the door.

"No, no! If you open the door, I'll only have the hinges to grab onto, and it'll close on me. Just leave it. I'm coming out the window, too." I pushed her hand away. "Get out of the way, so I can get out. I reached up my hands and put them on either side of the window jam and was thankful my childhood gym classes had included pull-ups. I pulled myself up through the window and sat with my legs dangling back down into the rapidly filling Bosco. The water was bitterly cold, we were both shivering, and ice frosted the weeds and trees along the riverbank.

I sighed. "Well, that's the end of a perfect evening, isn't it?" I felt dejected for poor Bosco. He was a wreck, but he was *my* wreck, and paid for.

"What do we do now?" asked DeeDee, her words jiggly with the cold.

"Why do you always ask me? Make some plans for yourself, just once, will you? I'm getting off the car and wading to the bank and trying to find a phone. You can sit here or you can come along." I kicked my legs over the side of Bosco, turned onto my stomach and slid down until my feet touched bottom. The river was about four and a half feet deep, so I waded cross-course to keep my footing with the current, rather than against it.

"Wait for me," called DeeDee, and I heard the splash behind me as she went under. She came up sputtering. But, I could hear her sloshing behind me.

Once to the bank, I pulled myself up on the rushes and huddled on the edge until she arrived. "Here, take my hand."

She took it, and promptly pulled me back in. We both scrambled back up the bank, sputtering. *I should have seen that coming!*

We sat there, dripping wet, shivering, and watching Bosco peeping out of one side window and a bit of windshield.

"Well, you said you never liked that car anyway, didn't you?" said DeeDee.

There was something about the deadpan way she said it that cracked me up. Next thing I knew, we were laughing uproariously and watching the bubbles surround Bosco.

But wet clothes on a foggy night soon became unbearably cold. We rose and stumbled back to Scotty's wing of the castle.

Castles don't have phones. Of course, none of the rest of us in modern German apartments had phones either, which made for a certain spontaneity in visitors and entertaining that we'd come to enjoy. But, especially, castles don't have phones.

Scotty was still out cold. I rummaged through his jacket for his walky-talky. As I figured, he had it linked into the airfield in case they called him for an Alert. I wondered why if he was on call, he'd have been drinking, but that wasn't my business.

Dave Childress, one of the pilots, answered the call.

"Dave, this is Megan. I'm out at Scotty's and I drove my car into the river. Over."

Only static came back for a moment. "You *what*? Over."

"I dropped Bosco in the river, Dave. We're all wet, and I need someone to come take us home and call a tow-truck for Bosco. Over."

The next batch of static brought the sound of laughter. Dave could barely get the words out. "Stay where you are. I'm coming. Over."

"Stop laughing and call me a tow truck, doggone it! Over."

"Only *you* could manage to do such a thing, Megan. Over."

"I don't want to hear it. Just please get me the bloody tow truck. Over."

"Jimmy checked in here after the party. Should I have him come, too? Over."

"Oh, crum…I guess so. You just tell him not to laugh or I'll kill him. Over."

"Roger. We're on the way. Over and out."

DeeDee and I waited, shivering. I watched Bosco through

the window in case the current was stronger than I'd thought and tried to carry him away, though I figured he'd get stuck under the bridge, if he moved at all. Scotty's living room wasn't what you'd call warm, but it was better than the outside. He never even woke up when I put his walky talky back.

Finally, I saw the lights of Jimmy's car emerge from the fog, followed down the dirt road by a truck they used to lift tanks. We ran outside to meet them. *Oh my God. They brought a military asset to get my civilian car? I hope they don't get caught.* At least, they were smart enough to park on the other side of the river and moat. I doubted the bridges would hold the gigantic piece of equipment. Jimmy rushed across the bridges and hugged me. "Are you and DeeDee all right?"

When I nodded, he said, "Only *you*...."

"Please, don't say it. I know, I know."

"I guess that's what makes me so fond of you, Megan. I can't quite manage to have fun without you. At least, life is never dull."

Maybe not a good thing.

Dave called out, "Quit the lovey-dovey stuff and help me get hooks under the car. I have to get this rig back before anyone misses it.

The next few minutes were busy and cold, as Jimmy waded out to Bosco with grappling hooks, scrunched them under the tail and the front end, and grabbed onto the only visible window to help stabilize the middle. Dave tossed another rope, and Jimmy tied it around the door. The young soldier in the truck hit the hoist mechanism. With a groan, and dripping all kinds of mud and gunk, Bosco was dragged out, and swung over to the bank, still on his side. The three guys unhooked him and got on each end and heaved, until with a big flop that sent us all running, he plopped upright on the bank.

I opened the driver's side door and a little minnow swam out. All of a sudden, I felt sorry for that poor little minnow trapped like we had been. What if we hadn't been able to get out of the car? The tears I'd been holding back all through the crisis suddenly erupted.

"It's just shock, Megan," said Jimmy, taking me in his arms. We were both dripping and stinking of who knows what that went into that river water.

DeeDee came over and put her arm around me too, and said, "At least no one is hurt, and Bosco will dry out." Her face wrinkled in disgust at the gunk still pouring out of the door and tail pipe, and she added, "eventually."

"Oh well, I guess at least I'm lucky to have friends who will get me out of any pickle get myself into. Right now, I just want to go home for a hot shower."

"May I join you?" asked Jimmy with a smirk. "I'm as wet and scummy as you are."

DeeDee bristled, standing at her full height and nobly dripping from the eyelashes down. "Of course not, James Brogan. 'Cornelia's' not *that* kind of girl!"

Jimmy and I looked at each other and broke into simultaneous laughter.

"Let's go home, girls," he said when he could get his breath. He loaded us into his VW. "We're dripping all over the leather upholstery. I'll sure need an interior car wash tomorrow."

I stuck my head out the window and called to Dave and his helper. "Thanks so much, you guys. I'll come back tomorrow to see if the thing will still run."

"And I'll fix you all a lasagna dinner," yelled DeeDee.

Jimmy called out, "You'd better take her up on that. The girl can cook."

They waved, and I settled back into Jimmy's bucket seats and closed my eyes.

We dropped DeeDee off first.

"How about that shower?" asked Jimmy with a grin, once we were alone.

I might light candles in my magic harem lamp. This might be wish number two?

Chapter   17 -- Berlin by Night

The gang teased me for weeks after Bosco dried out. The dealership thoroughly cleaned and tuned him, and he was running as well as before, which meant only when he wanted to.

"Dropped any cars in the river lately?" asked Fred, when coming in from the field. "Remind me not to lend you mine."

"I'm rigging you a snorkel and eyepiece for Bosco," said Don, "in case you want to look for Russian submarines in the Pegnitz River."

Molly brought me a new map of Bamberg on which she had red-penciled the location of all bridges in the neighborhood. I had to laugh about it. I deserved it, right?

DeeDee held her lasagna dinner with our rescuers and a few other friends. Fresh flowers decorated her Moroccan pot where it sat on a polished table in the entry hall. All American apartments looked pretty much alike, since we all got government-issued furniture, and there was only one style. But DeeDee made hers cozy and warm. She took advantage of the lovely view of rolling farmland by framing the windows in lacy German sheers.

She seemed more relaxed in her little kitchen, a veritable riot of bright orange with yellow flowers tracing up the walls--the German penchant for color. DeeDee had "tamed" the loud wallpaper and curtains provided by her landlord by using spider plants in hanging baskets.

Bustling in every direction, DeeDee allowed no one into her kitchen to help. Not that there was any room, anyway. I always assumed German apartments, built by men, totally ignored the kitchen until they realized they didn't have one. Then they found the smallest closet and declared it the kitchen. You met yourself coming and going. But the intoxicating smells coming out of DeeDee's kitchen drove us crazy until she finally announced, "Dinner is served."

"Heaven is in your pasta sauce," said Dave, as he closed his eyes and inhaled dramatically.

"Didn't I tell you the girl could cook?" said Jimmy, catching my eye and grinning.

He leaned over to whisper, "She seems comfortable when we're enjoying her food. Why do you think that is, when she has so much trouble and takes so much of your time, otherwise?"

I whispered, "She's comfortable, quick-witted, and funny when she knows what she's doing; in the kitchen, in the classroom. She has a quirky sense of humor when she lets it show."

Jimmy whispered back with a grin, "I'll watch for that miracle."

I love that grin... and the sweetness in his kisses...and the warmth in his eyes...hm.

During the course of a marvelous dinner with salad greens dripping in homemade Italian dressing, and lasagna with fresh grated Parmesan the conversation headed again toward travel plans for the next three-day weekend.

"It would be fun to go to Berlin and see the Schwartz's," I suggested. "Oma's letters say Opa is doing pretty well again after a week in the hospital and the long flight home. She says they'd love to see us again. What do you think?"

"Is that the old guy who had the heart attack in Jerusalem?" asked Jimmy. He broke off a hunk of the pungent garlic bread and handed me half.

"Yes. They're such a sweet couple, and lonely. Their children were killed in the war."

"I hate the thought of their lost babies," said DeeDee. "Let's do it. We can make reservations tomorrow with ITT."

"Any other takers?" I asked, directing my eyes to Jimmy's.

"Not this time, Cupcake. You and DeeDee will have fun. Do you plan to fly or drive?"

"I'd prefer to drive," I said, "but driving the corridor from Helmstadt is out of the way, and I hear it's pretty complicated if we only have three days."

Dave said, "It's a pain. You need advance orders cut, then

you attend a briefing, then it really takes two people to drive because one must hold the big notebook of instructions in their lap to tell the driver what to do. I did it once, but I hope I never have to do it again." He shook his head while helping himself to another serving of lasagna.

Jimmy laughed when he said, "Sending Megan, DeeDee, and Bosco down that restricted highway could be a disaster. You can't turn off the road or stop for the whole hundred and fifty miles, except at the three check points."

"What if you had a flat tire or something?" asked DeeDee.

"I guess you'd ride on the rims," Dave quipped. "At the briefing, they show you films of the trick intersections where you might think you were on the right road, so you can memorize them. You mustn't get off on the wrong road and cause an international incident. The Soviets would say you invaded their territory if you got lost."

"It might be kind of fun to see just how ridiculous the Soviets are being," I said.

Dave continued. "The big notebook tells you the Soviet rules. At the three check points the book says dumb things like 'drive thirty feet forward in the left lane at twenty-five miles per hour, then move fifty feet forward in the right lane at thirty miles per hour. The driver must then dismount."

DeeDee smiled. "They think you're on a horse? You don't dismount from a car."

"I swear that's what it says. The guard will salute, then you salute, then the guard again, in that order. In the booth, you put your orders in the top slot, and it is supposed to come out the bottom slot within three minutes, stamped with a red stamp in the lower left corner. That's why it takes two people to drive in order to keep track of all this folderol."

"What if it doesn't come back out or it's stamped in the wrong corner?" asked DeeDee.

"Well, if they detain you in any way, you have in the notebook a set of three cards. You lock yourself in your car and hold up the first card, which says you want to be released. You wait fifteen minutes, and if they still detain you, you hold up the second card, which asks to speak with a Soviet officer. You wait another fifteen minutes, and if they still don't let you go, you take a pink slip and a blue slip out to the center median. You give one to any allied British, French, or American car going to the east, and the other to any going west. Then you lock yourself in your car, hold up the third card that says you are waiting for reinforcements and refuse to move. They'll really want to get rid of you at that point. They'll point with their weapons and give you all kinds of grief, but you must just sit tight. The allied forces will send an armed convoy to get you as soon as they receive the slips at either end of the corridor. You must wait for them. And the incident will be written up for the Combined Forces briefing."

"Why on earth would the Soviets do all that, if we are just tourists?" DeeDee said, wrinkling her brow.

"They just like to harass us," said Jimmy. "They hate it that we were given the corridor to Berlin by the U.N. They've tried to close off the city with the Wall, and they even tried to starve the Berliners into submission. Our Berlin air lift kept that from happening."

"Yeah," said Dave. "They'd be delighted if we just let them have all of Berlin and went home, but that's precisely why we *won't* give it up."

"It's certainly more complicated than I thought," said DeeDee slowly, mulling it over as she passed the dessert. "Can we fly this time, please?" She directed the question to me.

"I guess so. I don't think we have time to get orders cut, anyway. Sure, get our tickets…just make sure the flight isn't all women."

DeeDee snickered, and Jimmy said, "Oh, yes…I vaguely remember your first trip."

"Better forgotten," said DeeDee. "We're much more careful now."

Several teachers had plans of their own and asked us to go along, but we stuck to our destination. Betty, a quiet, religious sixth grade teacher from El Paso brightened when she spoke of Berlin. "Whatever you do, don't miss the 'Berlin by Night' tour," she said. I wrote that down, as one of our "must see" items. Both of us were anxious to see the charming old German couple, too. I wrote Oma Schwartz and told her when we'd arrive. She fired back a note with a Saturday luncheon invitation and a little map of the Strassenbahn system telling us the closest streetcar stop.

I wasn't nervous, since the last flight was bad, and I usually didn't have two bad ones in a row, though landing at Templehof is a thrill. The final approach for landing goes down between apartment buildings, and one can almost see what the Berliners are preparing for dinner.

We pushed a button at the airport promising transportation to a hotel, and a van was already waiting, so we hopped in and arrived at our hotel very quickly. Since the "Berlin by Night" tour had come so highly recommended, we went straight to the desk to ask about it.

"Luckily, that tour is leaving in three minutes and I just happen to have two seats left," said the concierge.

"What about our bags?" asked DeeDee.

"No problem," said the man, as he took our money for the tour. "I'll just hold them here at the desk until you get back, and I'll hold your room until then, as well. Now hurry along. The bus is right outside, waiting for you." It was pouring rain, but the bus would be dry and warm, so we didn't worry.

"What good luck to get the tour tonight," said DeeDee, as we took our seats on the bus. "Our timing is perfect. I'll bet 'Berlin by Night' will be as beautiful as 'Rome by Night.'" Her eyes glowed with excitement.

The vast majority of the eighteen people on the bus were men.

"It's surprising that the men want to see the city all lit up, isn't it?" said DeeDee.

"I guess so. I imagine it's quite beautiful for anyone."

But the tour director with his microphone up front didn't say *anything* about the beautiful lights. We passed the "lipstick"

church tower made from the broken glass remains of Berlin's
bombed cathedral, but he said nothing. We also had a good view of
the tower in the east zone that everyone said was the supreme joke
on the communists. They built this tall tower meant to awe and
inspire everyone who could see it with its height, its glory, and its
communistic pride in having no religion at all. But when the sun
shown on the round, balloon-shaped tower, it formed an
unmistakable cross. The communists hated it, and tried to roughen
the shiny surface or paint it another color, but to no avail. The
cross still showed, shining above all of Berlin. The Germans in the
west zone took great glee in pointing it out to friend and foe alike,
as proof positive that God always had the last word.

But our guide told us no stories, so I was glad we'd read
Frommer's battered guidebook, *Europe on $10 a Day,* beforehand,
or we would have missed pointing out things to each other.

Finally, the bus pulled up to a building and we were hustled
through the torrential rain to the inside. It was a vintage nightclub
that had somehow survived the war. Old-fashioned glass vacuum
tubes graced each booth, going up across the ceiling and down to
other booths. I had seen something like that as a child in J.C.
Penney's when they closed a chamber with money or sales tickets
in it, and with a "whoosh," the little message shot up to another
floor and across to the waiting cashier. I'd never thought of them
being used in a nightclub--and apparently, this was a nightclub.

"Oh, how cute," DeeDee said. "Look at the tubes. I wonder
what they're used for?"

The tour had reserved red leather booths in the front row by
a raised stage. Purple velvet curtains draped from the peak, and the
stage's aprons went from wall to red velvet wall.

As though waiting for us to arrive, the show began
immediately. With a bugle fanfare and classical music, waters
spewed up from all along the apron of the stage. We were
entranced, as they were "dancing." DeeDee sat on the edge of her
seat. I especially loved their using some Straus waltzes, and the
changing of colors in the streams of water that bent and wove
themselves into ropes and back again. It was quite unusual, and we

were amazed at the effort it would take to make all the water valves synchronize with the music and lighting.

As the last streams and bubbles of the show came to an end, the vacuum tube at our table hummed and clunked, and out came a metal holder.

DeeDee opened the tube and unfolded a note. "It says someone would like to buy us a drink," she read aloud.

"That's funny," I said. "We don't know anyone here."

But as we looked up, two men at a table a couple of rows away waved at us and pointed at their chests to indicate they were the ones who'd written the note.

"Oh, my goodness," said DeeDee, agitated as always by the unexpected.

"Just ignore them. Probably the tubes are so people can link up to talk or dance."

"Oh, no," They're coming over here. "What shall we do?"

"Politely decline."

But just as the men arrived at our table, the guide stood and directed us all to our bus for the next leg of the tour.

"Sorry," I said as we rose and whipped around the two bewildered men about to sit down. We ran out to get into the bus at the head of the line, laughing all the way.

"Did you see the look on that one's face?" said DeeDee. "He looked mad, but the guide saved us just in time. I'll bet the guide noticed, and he called us right on cue to help us out."

We relaxed in the cozy comfort of the bus as it drove across town again. I was totally disoriented by this time, never having had any real concept of the huge city of Berlin anyway. But as long as we were safely in the bus, we couldn't get lost.

"I didn't realize we were going to more than one place," said DeeDee. "Where are we going now? Wasn't there any brochure at the front desk that would tell us?"

"I have no idea. And no, we were rushed so fast to catch the tour that I didn't pick up anything except my jacket and handbag." She sighed and settled back in her seat.

"I also have no idea where we are, or where we're going. I

guess that's why some people really like tours, so they don't have to buck the traffic or drive with maps."

Again, we wondered why the guide wasn't showing us any lights. We soon stopped, and the guide told us to get out once more. Now, we had realized the "Berlin by Night" tour was not a tour of the city lights, but a tour of Berlin's nightclubs.

"Oh well," said DeeDee. "I guess we can venture out tomorrow night to see the lights with less rain."

No harm seemed to be done. "Anyway, we don't know our way back to the hotel," I said. "It could be fifteen miles away, or right next-door, and we wouldn't know. Besides, it's pouring really hard, so we'll have to stick to the tour group until the bus takes us back to the hotel."

"I hope the next club has more dancing waters," said DeeDee. "I'd like that."

But it wasn't dancing waters at this nightclub. An extremely tall, beautifully gowned woman welcomed us into the club, but when she spoke, her voice was basso profundo. We both looked up, surprised. Her make-up was perfect, her gown meticulously embroidered and beaded, gleaming beautifully.

"I'll bet she sings contralto," DeeDee said, and I nodded.

But all the rest of the "ladies" were exactly the same--very tall, beautifully gowned and coifed, but with deep voices, as they greeted and carried on conversation with all the guests. They ushered us to our reserved seats at small tables, again in the first row next to a dance floor.

I'd had my solitary glass of wine at the dancing waters place, so I ordered only a Spezi soft drink here. The waitress looked at me funny—everyone else except DeeDee and I were having highballs—but she said nothing, and soon she brought our Spezis.

"What do you suppose is wrong with these ladies?" asked DeeDee.

"I don't know, but they sure have low voices. They sound like men."

"Oh, my goodness," said DeeDee. "I think they *are* men.

Now I've seen everything!"

"Shh. Maybe you're wrong. Don't let them hear you. You might hurt their feelings."

We tried to stifle our curiosity and just enjoy the show. It was full of singing and dancing of surprising excellence. All of the singing was bass with old-fashioned torch songs done in German. We were still a little confused until the last act. A lady went up and stripped on the stage. Both of us were more than a little alarmed, not sure what would happen next, but we needn't have worried. Somehow this "stripper" of velvets and pearls suddenly came out from under it all dressed in a black tuxedo. She did a remarkable tap dance, which I could appreciate. But I was speechless from the amazing spectacle of her turning a formal dress into a tuxedo without ever leaving the stage or showing any skin.

We talked about that phenomenon all the way to the next nightclub. The guide announced that the floorshow was entirely composed of transvestites. We weren't exactly sure, but we were beginning to have suspicions, and we didn't want to ask.

"I'm getting really sleepy," DeeDee said, yawning.

"Yeah, I wish we were going back to the hotel now, but the guide says this last stop is the 'piece d'resistance.' I guess it must be better than that male lady who turned into a tuxedoed tap dancer." That feat made an indelible impression.

We pulled up to a third nightclub, and again they ushered us into the reserved front row. While the first two nightclubs had been elegant, clean, and uncluttered, this one didn't smell so good, and it was noisy and crowded. If there was any décor, it was obliterated by blue smoke in the air and cigarette butts on the floor. The front row seats crowded us up right against the stage, which was elevated to about our eyeball level. I couldn't even move, with fellow tourists crammed in on both sides of us. Our pit stop at the last nightclub was a lifesaver, since there was no way to get out here, and claustrophobia was kicking in. I really felt uncomfortable when the people around us were so very close, practically breathing down our necks, and smoking heavily. I looked at DeeDee and she had the same strain showing in her face.

"I can already tell I don't like this place," she said.

As I looked around the room, I saw ladies sitting at the bar with men, and the men were pretty blatant about rubbing their breasts or legs as they had a drink together. I quickly glanced away, hoping DeeDee hadn't noticed. When I had become her protector, I wasn't sure, but somehow I had, and I began to get a bad feeling about this place.

DeeDee watched a cartoon that played on a screen at the back of the stage. As I turned, I saw her puzzled look, her head tilted to one side and eyes squinched.

"I've never seen Donald Duck like that," she said.

It seems that Donald, who was always quite sexless except for his jaunty jacket and sailor cap, had become anatomically correct for a human male, not a duck, and he was performing suspicious acts through holes in fences. The breath went out of me, and I turned to DeeDee. Speechless, she stared agape at the screen.

"We don't have to watch it," I said. I looked down at my hands in my own lap, not wanting to see Donald, whom I'd always liked, doing things I sure wouldn't want my fifth graders to see. I felt downright humiliated.

DeeDee quickly dropped her eyes as well. We sat quietly, not wanting to observe the other things going on in the dusky room. "Mama wouldn't like this," she said, studying her hands firmly clasped in her lap.

"That's the understatement of the year! Do you remember the name of our hotel?" I asked. "Maybe we can get out now and take a taxi back?"

She shook her head. "I thought I put a card in my jacket pocket, but it's not there now. The concierge was rushing us so much, I didn't even notice the name."

There went that idea. We hunkered down to get through the evening as best we could. This was supposed to be the last stop.

When the tinny music from a three-piece band changed tunes, and produced a fanfare, we realized Donald was gone, and there was live entertainment. A beautiful black girl strolled out on the stage in mini skirt, high velvet boots, and myriads of pearls.

Her silk blouse shown with amber light from the spotlight, and she moved gracefully to the strains of a Barry White record-- the one where he talks more than he sings, but the words are sort of sultry. Her movements were lithesome and graceful as she danced, or perhaps it was more parading than dancing. But then she took off her clothes….all of them…until she wore only boots and pearls. Nothing was left to the imagination. DeeDee and I examined our hands again, and I tried to concentrate on the fact that I needed a manicure. When the crowd cheered and clapped, we realized she was through.

"Thank goodness that's over," DeeDee said.

But there was another act. This time, the girl didn't take a whole piece of music to gracefully and slowly remove one garment at a time. No, this one paraded out smacking her bubble gum to the bomp, bomp, bomp of those bad musicians, and holding a long cigarette holder. She stripped to the buff in less than eight bars. Again, we folded our hands in our laps to not have to look at her. It was almost impossible to ignore her unless we got on hands and knees on the ground because her antics were right at eye level. I began to wonder, if she already took off her clothes, what else was there for her to do for the remaining part of the music? I sort of peeked sideways, and saw her doing something rather unusual with her bubblegum, and her cigarette holder…both in places no bubblegum or cigarette holder was meant to go. I looked down quickly, praying DeeDee hadn't seen. We caught each other's eyes. She'd peeked too. I rose and tried to steer us out of the front row to wait in the foyer. Loud derisive cries of "Down in front" erupted, and a man on my side actually pulled me back down into my seat. People on both sides of us refused to let us through. They were too engrossed in the show to allow us to squeeze by.

When the music changed to a harem style beat, all slinky and bumpy, we looked up to see an older and rather fat woman enter with a huge greeny-white reptile around her neck. Though she looked rather disgusting in a bikini, the snake floated gracefully out in arches on either side of her, and he almost seemed to writhe to the music as well. She wore little to begin with, but she removed her top, and the snake coiled itself around one breast, around her neck and then coiled around the other.

"How could she train a snake to get into such a position," I whispered. "It's almost hypnotizing."

DeeDee shrugged, intermittently covering her face.

The woman slowed her pace to the music, and the snake slithered his head down from one breast, across her bare, bulgy stomach, and inched close to her bikini panties. I couldn't believe my eyes. The snake's head poked into the top of her bikini and slowly slithered in deeper and deeper.

"Where could he go?" whispered DeeDee. "He's not coming out the back side."

"Oh, my God!" I said. I couldn't stay, and tried to get up to leave. The rain outside was better than this. But we were hemmed in on all sides in our "guaranteed front row seats" by patrons literally moaning and gasping along with the woman. The whole place was seething.

DeeDee was crying, and that sort of did it for me. I had to find us a way out. I grabbed her arm and scrambled over the footlights, dragging her behind me. We crawled until we were clear of our seatmates and on the stage. Then we stood and I pulled her along, accompanied by catcalls and noisy cursing from the audience.

"Take it off, ladies," yelled one drunken patron, and soon more took up the chant. I didn't know what else to do except try to get DeeDee out of there. I felt so bad for not having foreseen something like this and not protecting her from it. With the whole audience screaming at us, and the woman still writhing on the floor with her snake, we jumped down into the bomping orchestra pit, went over a little curtain into the first aisle and ran out to the foyer.

We leaned against the wall to catch our breath.

Mercifully, the show finally ended and the lights came up to reveal people who jumped up and straightened their clothing as they came into the foyer. I was glad we'd been able to get around these slow-moving people. We somehow plowed out the door ahead of the crowd, and stood outside the bus in the rain, shivering.

The rest of the bus passengers never shut up all the way back to the hotel, slapping each other on the back and crowing about bubble gum and especially about the snake. One drunken patron accosted us by saying, "If you were going to get on the stage, you should've taken off your clothes."

"Look, mister," I said, "you guys didn't leave us any room in the aisle, so that's the only way we could get out. His language got ugly until another of the men pulled him down into a seat and they all dissolved into laughter. DeeDee and I sat silently the rest of the way. I couldn't think of a thing to say to ease the nastiness we'd both seen and felt. I was feeling depressed and stupid all at the same time, especially for exposing DeeDee to this.

But then DeeDee said something that cracked me up. In all seriousness and with those saucer eyes, she said, "I don't know how the snake could breathe in there, do you?"

The rest of the weekend seemed quite normal by comparison to our misadventure of being trapped on the stage of our first and only burlesque show.

We spent a lovely afternoon with the Schwartz's, thankful that Opa had recovered, and was again himself. We chatted over Oma's spicy gulasche soup, ham salad, and a marvelous Schwartzwald cake she'd baked herself. Opa wondered aloud where the travel adventures of "Emily and Cornelia" would take us next. But when he said he'd like to travel with us again, Oma shook her head, patted his hand, and said, "No, my dear. I think we've traveled quite enough at our age."

Opa caught my eye and winked. "But we have such unusual adventures with our lovely girls." Oma smiled and shook her finger at him.

The affection between these two was comforting, even in their old age. They'd suffered the loss of their children, yet they still relied on each other for courage. Their love weathered all losses. *Wasn't this the kind of love I wanted again?*

Their kindness toward each other stirred feelings deep inside me, and I thought of my longing for Bruce, and then I thought of Jimmy. Do we have what it takes to enjoy each other through our old age, and still find comfort together? *I'm afraid I'm beginning to think of Jimmy in terms of loving. Does that mean I'll be hurt again, or can I overcome my fear of loving again.*

I put those thoughts out of my mind and enjoyed our time with this wonderful couple. DeeDee and I were pleased when the Schwartz' agreed to accompany us after lunch to the Dahlem Museum. It was actually walking distance from their apartment, and we strolled leisurely at the pace set by Opa.

The museum was everything I'd hoped for, especially as we went from one of my favorite Rembrandt paintings to another. Opa turned out to be quite knowledgeable of their history and beauty. He told us tales of where paintings were hidden during the war, and how they were recovered. His narrative and insight brought our appreciation. I explained Rembrandt's use of light and dark to DeeDee, and soon she began to look for his splashes of light as well.

"I've never seen *real* paintings before, " she said breathlessly. "Something new for 'Cornelia' and 'Emily' to share. Right?"

Her liking Rembrandt and our having the Schwartz's' with us again, made it a happy day. As soon as we could see Opa visibly get more tired, though, we walked them back to their apartment and bid our heartfelt goodbyes. Opa cried when we left, saying that he feared he would not be alive for our next visit. Of course, I assured him I'd be back soon, but DeeDee would have to go Stateside. Lots of hugs and tears sent us on our way to the Strassenbahn.

We were on the plane going back home Sunday afternoon

when DeeDee said, "What are we going to tell everyone about the 'Berlin by Night' tour they wanted us to go on?"

"I can't even imagine Betty suggesting we take that tour. She's very straight-laced and religious, and I can't see her putting us in that position."

"We'll have to ask her when we get back. And do you think this is something I should keep this from Mama? Especially the part about our going over the footlights and onto the burlesque stage."

"Our secret."

When we buttonholed Betty after school the next day in the teacher's lounge, I asked her why on earth she had told us not to miss the "Berlin by Night" tour? She was surprised. "Oh, didn't you like it? I didn't get to go on it while I was in Berlin, so I just thought I'd tell you so you would have the chance. It was another teacher who told me, 'whatever you do don't *miss* the 'Berlin by Night' tour.'"

We told Betty the story of Berlin, while she held her cold Coke can against her ultra-tanned forehead to cool down.

"After hearing what happened, I think maybe my friend was recommending it sarcastically."

"So do I," I told her. "Let's hope we hear no more about this."

But in a place as close-knit as the Border, it didn't take long for the story to get around the O'Club. When Jimmy asked me about it, too, I simply said, "You don't want to know, and I sure don't want to tell you."

"Only you two could get trapped in a burlesque house. You'll never see a snake as a harmless reptile again, will you?" He laughed for a long time after.

Chapter 18 - Bosco Performs Tricks

DeeDee was coming alive before our eyes. It was such fun to see her unafraid to laugh over a glass of wine with friends. She'd shed a few of her fears of behavioral gaffs, and she'd even stopped worrying about other people's business in regard to dating. With Gert, Cathie, and I working on her, and the rest of the gang being willing to let bygones be bygones, she had lost that "holier than thou" attitude of Mama's and was beginning to have fun with the rest of us. Not only was DeeDee a capital DoDDS teacher, she was beginning to believe she could try new things and survive--an amazing revelation.

And for me, I'd found her to be a sensitive friend.

At the Club one evening, several of the gang sat around flipping deckles off the bar. Ben was champion, since he could flip thirty of the coasters while twenty-three was the next highest score. DeeDee arrived and cornered Jimmy and me. "When do we get to ring wedding bells for you two?"

Everyone laughed. "Yeah, when?" said Fred, easily flipping twenty, and building up to 25.

"We'll be ready when and if we're ready, I guess, you guys," I answered.

"A lot depends on where my next duty station will be," said Jimmy, "and how soon." He looked me in the eyes as he said to DeeDee, "I'm due for both a promotion and a duty station change soon, so we're doing a lot of talking about how and where we can fit into each other's lives. At least we've decided we *want* to fit in together."

"And that was a hard decision for me," I added.

Jimmy grinned.

"Well, while I'm waiting for you two," DeeDee said, rolling her eyes heavenward as though it would never happen, "I'm gonna die of old age."

"Aw, DeeDee," said Don. "Haven't you noticed that the

whole gang has bought into the 'Cornelia and Emily' thing? We keep asking for the next adventure of the 'dynamic duo,' or is it more like Ethel and Lucy or Laurel and Hardy?"

"Hey," said Fred. "Don't you guys fit the pattern of the Marx Brothers, or at the very least the Keystone Kops?"

I had to laugh. Never in a million years, when I remember that first harrowing glimpse of "Miss virgin Mama's girl," had I ever imagined that I could grow to love this friend. But now, DeeDee and I trusted each other completely, and we enjoyed our sidekick trips.

"I'll hate to see you leave when school's out," I said. "We've got more traveling to do."

"I promised Mama I'd come home and behave after one year. I'll go home with my two girlfriends from Ithaca when they arrive in June, after school's out. We're taking them to Paris in Bosco."

"Oh, yes, I did promise to go, didn't I?"

DeeDee grinned. "You know you did. I can hardly wait to see Loree and Amanda Marie, and for you to meet them. You're going to love these girls." *Yes, she still uses that term for every female from three to ninety-three.* "We did everything together in Ithaca. We were inseparable."

"What do they like to do?"

"What they really like most is to go out to eat hot fudge sundaes every Saturday night."

"Saturday night?" said Jimmy. "They won't find sundaes in Germany unless you make them yourself, and I *guarantee* we won't waste a Saturday night eating sundaes."

"Oh, I don't know," said Ruthie. "We could invite every one to an ice cream social."

"I guess what I'm asking, is how you think they'll fit in with our routine here?"

"Oh, they'll be fine," said DeeDee. But then she slowed her speech, and fiddled with the clasp on her bracelet. "They should be all right with you and me. I'm not so sure about the others. We might do better to go straight from the airport to Paris and back."

Uh-oh. That sounded a bit tentative.

DeeDee abruptly changed the subject. "Will we have time after school's out and before they get here, to get another short trip in?" She barely waited between breaths before proposing, "What about Amsterdam? I'd love to see all the tulips and wooden shoes."

"They don't wear wooden shoes and grow tulips in Amsterdam, DeeDee," said Jimmy. "That's a modern city, and they dress just like us."

"But I've seen pictures...."

"Probably in the *real* Cornelia and Emily's day they wore their traditional garb," I explained. "But now, you only find that in the tourist towns like Marken and Vollendam. You remember how surprised you were when all the German men didn't wear Lederhosen, except for beer fests?"

"I came to Europe too late, didn't I?"

"Don't worry. There are still lots of fun things to see here, and we have Bosco, so we can drive out to the rural villages to see the people in costume, if you like."

"Everyone likes the Sailor's Quarter in Amsterdam," said Kurt, who was sitting with his latest German fraulein. You two *must* go there."

"It's not like 'Berlin by Night,' is it?" said DeeDee.

"It's beautiful ladies who sit in windows," said Kurt.

DeeDee's face froze. "Maybe it *is* like 'Berlin by Night.'"

"Heck, ladies," said Don. "After your burlesque experience in Berlin, this should be right up your alley. Do you think you might both have a new career in store?" He laughed until he burrowed his face in Ruthie's neck.

"Maybe we should go to Venice, instead," DeeDee said, calmly. "Aren't Venetians pretty traditional?"

"Okay, Venice it is," I promised. "We can leave the day school is out, spend a few days, and still get back in time to pick up your friends at the airport."

The wind up of the school year was a traditional picnic for the kids in the little forest behind the Officer's Club. Old shade trees and picnic tables adorned the area. We played "historic" old games like hoop rolling, sack races and one-legged races. The kids made stilts out of tin cans, and we tied it all into history lessons so they'd understand how kids played in the "olden days." They had every bit as much fun as they imagined the "olden days kids" did.

Our friends in the Cavalry and Combat Engineer Battalions always helped with this project, corralling kids, leading games, making toys, grilling hotdogs, and cleaning up.

But it was our dear maitre-d Marco who always ran the show. A dignified and mysterious character, he glided silently through the O'Club, remembering all the favorite things we liked to eat and drink, treating everyone with great care and deference. He was the perfect manager, complete with tux and sophisticated little mustache.

"It always seems like Marco knows everything that goes on around here before anyone else does," said DeeDee, as we sat down to watch our kids pursue a Treasure Hunt. "Yet he always has that enigmatic smile if we ask him questions."

"He'd never tell anything he knew that might endanger any of our people, Dee, but I know my paralyzed fiancé, Big Ed, trusted him completely, and said if I was ever in trouble, Marco would help."

"But wasn't Big Ed the spook?"

I nodded.

"Then is Marco involved in stuff like that, too."

"No," I lied. "He's just an exceptionally good maitre'd, and a nice guy if you ever need any help …with things like this, I mean." I changed the subject and pointed out our kids scurrying around the forest area, gleefully grabbing things for their treasure hunt, their pockets bulging.

"Where is Ed now?"

"In Washington D.C. I only get to see him when I'm flying back and forth to California during the summer. We're still good friends. Big Ed is happy for me about Jimmy. I've already written to tell him. He only asked me if Jimmy is good to me, and if he loves me. You'd like Ed. Everybody does."

"You know I don't want to know any MI people because their job is dangerous and they could be badly wounded or killed, like your friend, and I'd be left all alone, too."

"Dee, you must understand their mission. They're good guys. It's just a job like any other in the Army. The whole Army is dangerous."

"I want nothing to do with MI secrets and spies and spooks, never ever!"

"Okay, okay, but you could be talking to one and not even know it, DeeDee. They always have a cover story, usually pretty mundane, and few people on post actually know who the MI people are. They usually wear civilian clothes. I thought Big Ed was a weapons inspector for four months before I realized what he was doing. I guess he was a good spook, or I was really naïve."

"You mean they lie to you?" She bored those eyes right into me.

"No, they just don't tell everything they know, and they have a cover story to protect their mission." I figured it was better to drop the subject and assume she'd never talk to an MI anyway.

"Okay, kids, saddle up and move out," I called in teacher voice, and they all rallied around their own teacher for a hug goodbye to last the summer.

When the last child departed, and we all had helped in cleaning-up, we piled our shoulder bags into Bosco and drove south, singing along to the radio. John Denver's "Thank God I'm a Country Boy," was a favorite. The traffic wasn't bad on the Autobahn for a Friday evening.

We thought Bavaria was the most beautiful part of Germany, and now, we pointed out countryside scenes of wildflowers and green fields to each other.

"Bosco is behaving nicely today, isn't he?" said DeeDee. After all, she'd seen him at his worst.

"I know. We can count ourselves lucky this trip. It'll go easily until his next fiasco, anyway." I had barely uttered the words, when there was a loud metallic thump and sounds like a chain being dragged through the bowels of the car and out the

Auspuff.

"Uh, Oh," said DeeDee. She didn't cry about surprises anymore, thank goodness.

"That sounded suspiciously like a thrown rod," I said, as I coaxed Bosco over to the side of the Autobahn. We weren't supposed to stop on the Autobahn since with no speed limit Mercedes and BMWs whipped along at speeds that would be totally illegal in the U.S.

"It's only because you hurt his feelings," said DeeDee. "You know how he hates to be made fun of."

I shook my head and grinned at her, popped the hood, and got out to look under it. "Try turning it over while I watch here."

DeeDee did so, but there was only a painful grinding and moaning.

"I think he's dead. We'd better find some help. I'll go to the exit and try to find someone, and you can wait here with Bosco."

DeeDee put out the red warning triangle about 30 meters behind the car, as required by law, and then she wandered up the bank beside the freeway. "I don't want to stay in the car," she shouted. "Somebody might hit it, here on the shoulder. You never know about German drivers."

The next Ausfahrt from the Autobahn was about a half mile away. I set off down the shoulder of the Autobahn, something you aren't supposed to do unless it's a real emergency. Almost at the exit, a Politzei car pulled up, and one of the men got out.

"Das Auto is kaput?"

I nodded, already feeling bad for Bosco. He'd taken me a lot of places I would never have seen without him.

"Get in," said the other Politzist who spoke some English.

I did, and he drove up the offramp and into the nearest little village to an Autodienst, a repair shop. My Deutsch usually was good for most things, but it deserted me in a car crisis. We struggled until the Autodienstmann took his truck to pick up Bosco and DeeDee. The policeman and I waited in the shop. Stale motor oil dominated the senses, but though the lifts were full, every bay was spotless with no oil stains, and with every wrench in it's designated place on the wall. I admired the German precision and stared at the wall painted to fit each tool.

The Autodienstmann, Herr Gregor, came back with Bosco on the flatbed, and DeeDee sitting up front. DeeDee said, "Poor Bosco. I hope they can make him better."

"Maybe it'll be minor. We'll stay overnight and be on our way in the morning."

But when Herr Gregor tried to start the car, he looked again under the hood and pronounced, "Neu Motor." I knew what that meant.

"How long?" I asked. "Can someone work on it today?"

"Freitag abend," he said with a shrug. "Werkmann comt Montag. Order today."

"Montag! You mean we must wait until a new motor comes?"

"Oh, dear," DeeDee said. "Does that mean we won't go?"

"It means we spend a weekend in this village, and less days in Venice."

"This doesn't look big enough to have a hotel," she said, looking around at the barely paved main street. Fields stretched as far as we could see over green rolling hills.

"I know a Frau who takes in roomers, said the Politzist. Come, I'll show you."

Meekly, we retrieved our shoulder bags from the back of poor, crippled Bosco and followed the man down the street. I wondered if the lady who rented rooms would think it funny a policeman brought us to her door, but we couldn't really worry about that now.

It was Friday night in a strange town we didn't even know the name of, no wheels until Monday, and I didn't even want to think about spending a month's salary on a motor.

DeeDee dropped her bag in our room and plopped on her bed. I looked around the high-ceilinged room. It was done in an old-fashioned German style with both beds painted in Baurnmalorei, pink roses and vines roaming around on the footboard and headboard with a turquoise background. I'd taken a Baurenmalorei class in the German Hochschule in Bamberg, so I knew this was homemade. Roughcut lumber reinforced the fact. White lace that didn't quite fit the windows either by texture or by measurement hung at the windows. The floor was burnished a soft mahogany by many scrubbings over many years, and a small carpet lay by each bed. Not a bad room, Spartan, but quite clean. Of course, the room came with breakfast, but no dinner. We'd have to worry about finding something to eat sooner or later.

The most mysterious object looked like a tall white refrigerator plugged into one of the few electric sockets in the room. It leaned against one wall between two windows. "Why would they put a refrigerator in here?" I asked.

"It's too tall," said DeeDee. "It almost reaches the ceiling."

I turned the handle on the refrigerator door to investigate. The cubicle was floor to ceiling, all done in hard white enamel. It had a light hanging from the ceiling with a pull chain. I pulled it. "Well, it's not a refrigerator."

DeeDee joined me and we peered into the cubicle. "Look up there. It has a showerhead," I said. "Is *this* the shower? There's no place to take off or your clothes. It's just a box."

DeeDee sat down on her bed with her arms folded. "I'm not getting in there. It's too dark unless you pull the chain, and everyone knows you don't mix water with something plugged into the wall. It'll electrocute us."

I examined the creation further, and we decided it was, indeed, meant to be a shower, though it looked more like a 1920's era icebox. We checked the electrical outlet. It was definitely plugged in.

"Is this supposed to be some of that remarkable German ingenuity?" DeeDee asked.

"Well, I suppose it must work, or they wouldn't put it in here" I said. "But I don't like the idea either. This must be the way the water is heated. Who wants to go first?"

Neither of us was in a hurry to try it. "In the morning," I said. "I want to think about it."

"Sounds like a plan."

"I'm sorry Bosco let us down. He's usually okay on the open road. He likes Autobahns."

"Oh well," said DeeDee. "If it wasn't this, it would have been something else. At least we can explore this cute little village and enjoy ourselves here."

"Did you get a load of this town? There's nothing here, and this is Friday night. Friday nights are usually a bit more lively in Bamberg." I kept thinking how much a new motor would cost for that stupid little Italian car. That sure gave me heartburn.

"Well, there's still time to get to Venice and back to pick up your friends, if we can leave here on Monday," I said, mulling over our limited options. "I guess if it takes too long, we can catch a train back to Bamberg and take *your* car to Paris."

"I didn't see any train station," said DeeDee with a teensy voice and scrunched eyes.

"It figures." I had to laugh at our predicament. "I won't have enough money to go much of anywhere after I pay for this motor. God knows I've had to fix enough things on that stupid car since I got it…carburetors, muffler systems, electrical systems, cracking windows, and now this. Did you know Fiat's acronym is Fix it again, Tony and that mine is a real lemon?"

DeeDee came over from the window and patted me on the shoulder. "It's okay, 'Cornelia.' Bosco will be like a brand new car and last you a long time after this, especially if you've replaced everything else."

That idea was worth a groan. "We'll have to make up for the traveling next year."

"I won't be here next year. I'm going home with my friends on their return flight. This trip to Paris will be my last." She looked a bit wistful.

I tried to make her think positively about leaving, though I would hate to see her go. "But you've really missed your Mama and Papa and your brothers and your friends this year abroad, so you'll be okay once you get back to your familiar routine."

She was slow to answer, running her thumb over the edges

of her fingernails. "My routine wasn't so hot, now that I think of it. I've had more fun here. But at least I'll be back doing things I used to do with my friends. You'll love Loree and Amanda," she said.

"I'm sure I will," I reassured her. "I can hardly wait to meet them." I thought of another idea. "Of course, you can always cancel your flight, and stay on here with DoDDS." But at her confused expression I just said, "Never mind," and changed the subject.

The next two days we struck out across the fields to explore the gently rolling hills surrounding the village. There was nothing much to explore in a two block village. The name of the village wasn't even on our map. Thankfully even the smallest Medieval villages could be counted on to sport a good Gasthaus for meals, and a charming old church, as cold as it was in the 1400's when it was built. But our hearts weren't in exploration. We were impatient to go, and the pastoral setting didn't help.

"We've gone as long as we can without a shower," said DeeDee. "Somebody has to try the refrigerator."

"You?" I asked.

"Not me!" We looked again at the refrigerator, checking the cord that led to the wall.

"Okay," said DeeDee, standing up suddenly. "I'll try it."

I was surprised she wouldn't be afraid, and said so.

"Well, 'Cornelia,' if I've learned anything from you this year, it's been that *someone* has to take a risk, or *nothing* ever happens." I broke up laughing at our fearful DeeDee.

"Turn your head so I can get undressed."

I did. I heard the sound of the water turning on, and I grabbed a down comforter from the bed and stood close to smother a fire or electrocution. If I'd been responsible for DeeDee becoming more daring, I didn't want to be responsible for her being electrocuted while doing so.

"Hey, it works," she called from inside. "There's some water coming out. Do you see any sparks from the socket?"

I didn't. We had averted yet another "crisis."

"We still have five days before Amanda and Loree get here," said DeeDee on Monday, as Bosco purred down the Autobahn through the Austrian Alps, and into Italy. "That'll still be enough time to see Venice and get back to Frankfurt." She opened her guidebook, humming.

We had to make a quick stop at the Vicenza military base for the bank, since I was "driving" my whole paycheck, and I needed more money. We also needed to pick up Italian gas coupons. The Status of Forces Agreement (SOFA) issued stickers for our windshield, so Esso and BP stations would take our coupons in Germany, but not in Italy. As I drove slowly at the five miles per hour speed limit down the main street of the Vicenza base, DeeDee said, "Oh, look, there's a Bazaar going on. Will we have a few minutes to stop?"

I glanced where she was pointing and felt a thump. "Oh, my God, I think I hit something." We both jumped out of the car, and there beneath Bosco's front bumper was a body clad in a businessman's brown suit. Fear washed over me as I reached down to see if the man were alive. He moved, and I jumped back, startled.

"Thank God you're not dead. I'm sorry. I looked away for an instant. I didn't see you."

As he rose, I realized it was Paul Matheson, one of our MI operatives from Bamberg.

"What are you doing *here*," I said quickly. "I'm so sorry, Paul."

"No names," he whispered. "Quick, get out of here."

"Paul....Why? I can't..."

"Mission...surveillance...you don't know me... leave, quick."

I motioned to DeeDee, but she just stood there, stunned.

Paul stumbled off between some buildings. I didn't wait to see what he was doing or who might be behind him that he moved so fast. I ran back to the driver's side, just as a bronzed, bearded man on a moped crossed in front of me, obviously in a hurry.

"What are you doing?" DeeDee yelled at me. "You can't leave the scene when you hit someone, and you hit that poor man. How could you hit him with Bosco? How do you know he isn't injured internally, or something terrible?"

"Get in," I told her through clenched teeth. Quickly. We have to get out of here."

"But...."

"No buts, DeeDee. I'll explain later. Get in." She got in, still shaking her head.

"I don't like this at all," she said, glaring sidewise at me.

My hands shook on the wheel as I drove to the Snack Bar. DeeDee spoke not a word. She just sat there with folded arms and grim, straight lined lips, staring straight ahead.

"Come on," I told her. "We might as well get lunch here."

DeeDee got out, but stood her ground. "I'm not going anywhere until you tell me why you did that to that poor man and then left the scene."

"Later."

"No, now."

"Let's get inside first. Maybe we can find a place no one can hear us."

We entered, found a table far away from any of the GIs seated inside playing cards. I ordered a couple of hamburgers and a side of fries, plus a couple of drinks. DeeDee sat staring at me the whole time, until I came back to the table with our tray.

"How can you be so calm after what you just did?" Then she noticed my hands shaking as I tried to put the drinks down, spilling one of them. "I guess you *aren't* calm."

"Hardly. Look, DeeDee, I know you never wanted to know about the spooks in Bamberg, but that guy is a friend of mine. Military Intelligence--remember those MI guys? And our running him down just put him in a bad position."

"How do you know?"

"I don't. But he whispered he was on surveillance or maybe it was under it. Either way, it could endanger him if we acted like we knew him, when he's down here on some mission or other, in case any enemy spooks could see. You must understand that his safety came first. I lost my Ed in such a situation, where someone's behavior gave away the mission. I don't want to endanger another one of my friends. Do you understand?"

"Not really…."

"Well, you don't have to understand completely, DeeDee. Please just take my word for it this time. Paul will explain to us when he gets back to Bamberg, if he can. It might be something he can't talk about, so we may never know."

"I won't want to know him if he's MI. Did you hurt him when you hit him?"

"I don't know…I was going pretty slow. But at least it's not as much as a bullet would hurt if the guy following him thought we knew him from someplace else and it blew his cover."

"Was there someone following him?"

"Paul was obviously following someone because he was in a hurry when I bumped him and slowed him down. I think someone may have been watching him, too, at least he acted like it. Missions are like that--mysterious. It might have been the guy on the Mo-ped that followed him between the buildings. I just hope I was convincing enough, and we got out of there soon enough." I was worried. "Of all possible times for my accident-prone persona to kick in, it had to be when I might endanger a friend. How on earth did Paul get in front of Bosco so fast?"

"Do you want to try to find him again?"

"No; not here. We'd blow his cover story, whatever it is. I'll wait until we get back to Bamberg and can talk to him."

I was restless, so DeeDee drove the rest of the way to Venice. We parked Bosco outside the city as required, walked across the bridge, and caught a water taxi to a hotel. We walked all over the old medieval town. Parts of the Plaza were flooded one day and full of pigeons the next. We took a gondola to Murano to see the glass blowing, and picked up little mosaic rings for our friends. DeeDee seemed to enjoy every minute of this gracious city, but her favorite was the bridge of sighs. We made at least three trips for her there to commiserate with the lonely young girl of history.

However, my heart wasn't in it, and she could tell. All I could think of was whether or not we had accidentally compromised Paul's mission, and if he was okay—from being hit by Bosco, and from any potential trouble with the person following him, or who might have been lying in wait for him. *I hate not knowing for sure.*

"Why don't we go back a day early?" DeeDee asked.

"You wouldn't mind?"

"No, not at all. I think we've seen a lot in a short time. I could probably get a few things done before we go to pick up Amanda and Loree and go to Paris." She brushed her hair back from her eyes in the Venetian sea breeze and bit her lip. "Besides, I think you want to get back and see what happened to your friend. Am I right?"

"Yes, I can't get Paul off my mind. If it's really okay with you, we could see that gold exhibition at the museum this morning and then leave before lunch."

"It's sort of been on my mind, too, if that poor man is really okay. Besides, I can always tell when you're preoccupied because you don't run into so many things. I can tell you're worried."

I grinned at her. "You've come to know me too well, 'Emily.'"

"Let's go pack."

Once back in Bamberg, DeeDee and I were too tired to cook, so we dropped off at the O'Club to have a late dinner. Marco welcomed us back and ordered a special favorite, stuffed crab for us. The first thing I did was to call Paul from the O'Club phone to see if he was home yet. With every ring of his phone, the tension in my chest grew harder. "Come on, Paul. Please be home by now," I whispered.

On about the eighth ring, Paul finally answered. "Paul speaking."

"Are you all right?" I asked.

"Yeah, I'm okay." He chuckled. "No thanks to you. I

should have known if I ever got hit by a strange car in a strange, unlikely place, it would be you and Bosco...who else?"

"I'm really sorry about that. I just looked away for a second...."

"Who was that cute little lady you had with you who was so angry when you hit me? She was pretty sensitive over our little collision, wasn't she?"

"Well, if you come on over to the O'Club and have dinner with us, I'll introduce you. One warning. She's a great person, but she's a little old-fashioned and naïve and shy....'"

Paul didn't just laugh--he roared. "Oh, you mean she's like you were when you first arrived in Germany, huh?"

I groaned. "You could have gone all day without saying that, Paul. I'm trying to convince her I'm more sophisticated than that."

"Before or after you spill your coke, bump into the doorjamb, or scald your hands?"

"You must be unhurt after all, you turkey. We hurried back early for nothing."

"I'll be right over, Megan. You know we all love you just as you are, even if you knock me off my feet with Bosco and almost get me caught. Quite a coincidence, wouldn't you say, for you to turn up just at that moment? There had to be a reason. Keep her there for me, okay? And put in a good word."

When Paul arrived, DeeDee and I were enjoying our first icy drink since we got in from Italy. He came over and hugged me. I spun him around to get a good look. "Just wanted to assure myself that I hadn't done any permanent damage to a friend."

He grinned. "Yeah, I almost thought you were working for the KGB and were assigned to take me out. Now, is this your pretty partner in espionage?"

I introduced them. Paul took both DeeDee's hands in his and said, "I'm really glad to meet a fellow-conspirator of Megan's. I'm sorry if I almost involved you two in my mission. I'm glad Megan had the presence of mind to get you away safely. You're far too nice a person to get messed up in my business."

I could see DeeDee blush. *Hoo Boy!*

"I was so worried you were hurt," she said. "I'm glad to see you have no permanent damage. But why were you running and why did you tell her to pretend she didn't know you?"

"I suppose Megan has told you, in MI, they have an old saying that if I told you, I'd have to kill you. I wouldn't want to do that. All I can say is that I was on a mission, and it was too important to be compromised by an accidental encounter. It also might not have been safe for you if anyone following me thought you two were involved, especially with you not knowing the threat."

"What threat?" asked DeeDee. When Paul just shook his head, she said, "I've never liked Military Intelligence people, so I doubt we'll ever be friends."

I gasped. "DeeDee! MI people are good people. It's just a job, like you're a teacher."

"But you said you lost a spook fiancé because he was shot."

Paul smiled. "DeeDee, that rarely happens. I'd like to tell you MI is safe, but any job in the Army is risky. Why, you could get hit by Bosco on any street in this whole universe."

DeeDee and I both had to laugh at his straight face when he said it.

"This is not really a shooting war," he added. "Ed's paralysis was pure chance. Somebody talked who shouldn't have. We all just do our job as best we can, trying to get the information we need to keep the rest of you safe, by stopping any threat. It's nothing to worry about. I promise. Give me a chance to know you, please. There had to be a reason why Megan did me a favor by running into me in Vicenza, because now I've met you."

DeeDee blushed again.

Paul pulled up a chair and settled between us. "Why is it I haven't seen you here before? Have I been gone, or out of my mind?"

I made my way quietly to the door. They never missed me.

Chapter 19 - Paris and Friendships

"Yoo Hoo," came a screechy, high-pitched voice. It emanated from the crowd of passengers arriving at Frankfurt airport the following Saturday. "Oh, Yoo Hoo, DeeDee."

DeeDee turned to me with a stricken look, as people from every side quickly parted to let the screecher through. "Over here," DeeDee called.

Two gushing women burst out of the crowd and engulfed DeeDee in screams and hugs, one actually lifting her off her feet. I watched in amusement as DeeDee struggled to extricate herself from the melee and steer her visitors toward me.

"Ooh, DeeDee," screeched the excruciatingly thin, tall one with a slight mustache. "We were so afraid we couldn't find you among all these strange foreigners."

"Amanda, would you just look at our DeeDee. Doesn't she look pretty?" Again the large woman, who by process of elimination I knew must be Loree, picked DeeDee up in a gigantic bear hug and shook her. "Oh my Gawd! What would your Mama say, girl? You're wearing slacks."

Strangers turned to stare, while DeeDee tried to pull free.

I would have known these two anywhere, by the way they were dressed in wildly inappropriate dresses *and* hats, and by the way they carried their purses...excuse me...their pocketbooks, as though anyone within ten feet was a gangster. *And my God, those finger-nail-on-the-blackboard voices!*

I could see DeeDee was in distress. She rolled her eyes and grimaced, so I worked my way over to her and said to her friends, "Hi there. I'm Megan. I'm happy to meet you. DeeDee has told me so much about you." I forced a big smile through my *déjà vu.*

DeeDee regained her feet and straightened her sweater.

"Dee," I whispered, "let's do customs, so we can get on the road to Paris by noon, okay?"

DeeDee nodded. We each picked up suitcases and led the

way.

"Ooh, Amanda Marie," screeched Loree, as those around us visibly cringed. "We're going to Gay Paree. Did you ever think we'd get this far up in the world?"

"Ooh, Loree, I'm *so* excited," said Amanda. "I wanna get one of those little Eiffel Towers for my Mama." She bumped up against Loree, who sported at least two hundred thirty pounds and an old-fashioned marcelled hairdo. They both broke into ripples of giggles until they were snorting with glee, elbowing each other again. They each wore a camera around their necks that dangled prominently on their stomachs.

DeeDee squinched her eyes shut as we put their luggage up on the customs desk. She watched with a pained grimace as the two women argued and screeched and pushed through the customs agents and fellow passengers.

I finally realized why Europeans think Americans are loud. It only takes one to create the impression. We had two.

I whispered, "Follow me, Dee," and we went to the end of the belt to wait for her friends. I could see DeeDee withering, with all her confidence fading away in the obvious nonverbal criticism, as other passengers gave these two a wide berth.

Their screechy conversations could be heard all over. *Dear God, we have an echo in here!*

Finally, Amanda and Loree were through customs and in Germany officially. I'm sure everyone there wished they weren't. I wondered what it had been like cooped up on a plane with those two. The strain on fellow passengers' faces as they walked by as far as possible from the two girls, told me.

DeeDee was still silent. She looked like she was praying, so I didn't interrupt her. We did our best to hustle her friends down to the garages, but Amanda noticed the duty free shop and screamed, "Ooh, lookee, Loree. They have those cute little Eiffel Towers *here*. Let's look."

"You'll probably prefer to get real ones in Paris, won't you?" I didn't stop for this statement, but kept moving toward the garage elevator.

"Ooh Amanda, that's right. We'll wait for the *real* ones."

DeeDee didn't look at me, but walked doggedly alongside, carrying Amanda's heavy suitcase. I had managed to convince DeeDee to mail some of her stuff Stateside, so by rearranging her suitcase, we got Loree and Amanda's cases wedged into the hatchback.

It was a more of a struggle to get Loree wedged into the back seat of Bosco. I didn't want her flying shotgun, but when we flopped the front seats forward so the two could get into the back, Loree got wedged between the seat and the open door jamb. DeeDee and I pushed from behind until she squished through and landed in the back seat in a heap of giggles. DeeDee quickly jumped in next to me. Even Bosco seemed in a hurry to get out. He didn't need a second try to start. We threaded our way out of the looped cloverleaf circles and onto the Autobahn that would lead us to Paris. With these two women squealing in my ears as I drove, I prayed Bosco wouldn't act up. I would've kicked him right up the Auspuff.

DeeDee and I tried to point out scenery along the way or answer their high-pitched questions. I desperately longed for these gals to have elocution lessons. I noticed both DeeDee and I were deliberately modulating our voices as low-pitched as they would go, hoping it would soften their noise. This technique often worked well with obstreperous youngsters in our classes. But here, it was to no avail.

We had planned to stop and show them Strasburg, a beautiful old town with marvelous walking streets and sidewalk cafes. But as we approached the Ausfahrt to turn off the Autobahn, I mouthed the word, "Strasburg" to DeeDee, and she quickly shook her head, so we drove straight through to Paris with only a pit stop for gas and potty break.

At the restrooms, the German lady in charge held out her hand for the pfennig coins.

Loree objected loudly. "Why does she want money for me to use the restroom?"

"It's her job," said DeeDee quietly.

"We didn't have to pay in Ithaca," Loree screeched. "My Gawd, these Germans are greedy."

I quickly handed the lady the fifty pfennigs and motioned Loree into the stall.

DeeDee and I waited outside the building. The other two didn't come. Suddenly, we heard Loree squealing. DeeDee hurried back in, and I followed. Loree had somehow gotten herself locked in the toilet stall.

"Amanda," she yelled, "crawl under and help me."

Amanda dropped to her knees and wedged herself under the door, getting stuck about half way. The matron in charge angrily denounced both of them in German, while waving her mop. The scene was meant for a slapstick comedy, and it was all DeeDee and I could do to cover our mouths and not laugh.

We excused ourselves to the matron, pulled Amanda out from under the door, and told Loree to try different ways of unlocking the door. Finally, she clicked it the right way, and the door swung open. An angry Loree washed her hands, splashing water all over the sink and floor, and stomped out.

Both DeeDee and I were embarrassed, but the matron in charge looked ready to kill someone, and I didn't blame her. I slipped her another two marks, apologized, and we slunk out of the restroom building.

Once outside, I happily occupied myself with filling Bosco's gas tank, while DeeDee helped me by wiping the windshield with the squeegee from the bucket provided for the purpose.

"Why are *you* washing the windshield?" screamed Loree. "You never did that in Ithaca."

"We do it here," said DeeDee, keeping her head down. "When in Rome...."

"Ooh, are we near Rome?"

DeeDee and I looked at each other and burst out laughing.

Once Loree and Amanda Marie settled in the back seat, we got underway again.

Entering Paris always provides a memorable experience,

once you get through the relatively ugly suburbs and see the skyline and marvelous arches. But it's as much of a nightmare as Rome for driving. I parked the car. There's no benefit to driving in Paris, since the Metro will quickly get you any place in the city within ten or fifteen minutes, while driving is equivalent to a parking lot. I'd seen pedestrians in Paris actually walk across the hoods of cars waiting in the street's traffic jams. DeeDee and I purchased fistfuls of the cheap Metro tickets and divided them up four ways.

We went straight to the student quarter where Pensions tend to be cheaper, though they look seedier, as well. Loree and Amanda loved the first Pension we entered, an old cluttered Victorian that had definitely seen better days.

"Ooh, Amanda, look at all the pretty red velvet drapes and chairs." She ran her hands through the long beaded fringe hanging down from the drapes and smiled. "And lookee here. They have fringe on the chairs to match, and these ostrich feathers by the bookshelves, and the beaded fringe in the doors and *everything*!"

"Sooo elegant," Amanda said, touching the fringe on a double bowl lamp, also red.

Actually, it reminded me more of the "parlor" of a bordello turned museum I'd seen once in Cripple Creek, Colorado.

"Did you want to get a three-bed room with your friends, and I'll get a single?" I asked DeeDee. She shook her head so hard I could practically hear her brain rattle.

"I'll room with you," she said loudly. "I don't want you to have to be alone."

"Right," I said, with a grin.

We procured two double rooms and climbed the narrow stairs, leading the way for our visitors. When the madam showed us to our rooms, I was relieved that they were quite different from the parlor--a little less elaborate, and a little cleaner. The first room smelled of cleaning supplies.

Loree walked in, dropped her suitcase, purse, and shoulder bag on the floor, and ran to the bed. She got on her knees and peered underneath. Then she opened the closet doors and looked into those.

"What are you doing?" I asked, quite baffled.

"Just checking to
be sure there isn't a man
hiding under my bed,"
she answered. "Mama told
me sometimes they do that
in strange foreign countries."

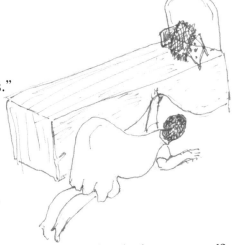

"You can't be
serious…" I started, but I
checked myself in mid-
stream. I could see she
was! *Here comes Mama
again*. I looked at DeeDee,
and she bit her lip. I
wondered if "the girls"
should happen to find a man there, would they be happy or sad?
Wishful thinking, perhaps.

In the meantime, Amanda entered the bathroom, and came
back screeching, "Why are there two commodes in one
bathroom?"

I was stunned when DeeDee said, "It's called a bidet. You
wash your feet in it."

"Really?" squealed Loree. "Oh, let me see." She ran into
the bathroom.

I looked at DeeDee with raised eyebrows. She blushed as
she shrugged her shoulders and raised her eyes to the heavens.
"Good one, Dee!"

"I'll have to tell them in the morning," whispered DeeDee
with a wicked smirk, "but not tonight!" We escaped down the hall
to our own room while the two were removing their shoes and
stockings and giggling.

With my lousy French, I had to order eggs and tea for these
two at every meal. DeeDee blushed every time she looked my way,
no doubt remembering.

Walking around town became an ordeal. The squawks, the shrill voices that drew every Parisian stare, the fear of riding the Metro because, "…somebody might take our pocketbooks" or "…some man might pinch me," and "Mama told me to be careful," drove both DeeDee and me almost over the brink. Again I wondered if either of them would be tickled to death if someone actually *did* pinch her…*fat chance.*

Especially hard was the "…Ooh, my Gawd, Amanda, lookee here," over *every* cheap metal Eiffel Tower in *every* shop.

A walk along the Seine produced, "…Ooh, Amanda Marie, it's so dirty," loudly enough people turned to stare. The artists along the same banks were, "Ooh, Loree, is this what Bohemian means?" The art galleries and museums were, "Ooh, Amanda, aren't these places *so* boring?"

They clutched their "pocketbooks" to their bosoms every time a Parisian walked by within ten feet, with did it with such obvious suspicion that everyone around could notice and glare at us all.

Worst of all was the amount of time wasted in shops buying "…just one more for Aunt Tillie," of the horrible cheap little metal towers.

"Those are pure tourist junk made of pot metal, Amanda," DeeDee said.

"You two would be better off buying one of the lovely silk scarves or an original art work or a nice print," I tried to tell them. "Besides, we haven't been to see the *real* Eiffel Tower yet."

Amanda looked at Loree, who nodded. "But we really like the little ones for all our friends. They're so cute. We don't have time to go sightseeing."

"Loree said emphatically, "How will everybody know we were in Gay Paree, if we don't take them a souvenir?"

Apparently the real Eiffel Tower was not as interesting to them as the four-inch, cheap replicas. I felt embarrassed and tired as the two "girls" went from shop to shop, squealing at each other over every blessed thing they saw.

The second evening, we asked the girls to go to a nice

restaurant and try snails. Both wrinkled up their noses and said they'd rather stick to eggs and tea.

"Actually, the snails taste like nothing at all," DeeDee said. "It's the garlic butter that makes them palatable." She looked my way with a grin. "More so than sheep's eyes, anyway, right?"

I had to agree with her.

"Ooh, DeeDee," said Loree, "I'm going to puke if you talk about snails." Everyone in the lobby turned to stare.

By the third day, we were both exhausted from the visitors' constant complaints over everything European. At breakfast, DeeDee handed the two women all her Metro tickets and said, "I know you girls would rather shop, and Megan and I would rather walk along the Seine, so why don't we meet you back here for dinner?" My eyes must have shown my surprise, because DeeDee batted her eyelashes innocently at me and grinned. I kept quiet.

"Ooh, my Gawd, Amanda, do you think we could? I'll have to watch to see that no one pinches you, and you can watch out for me."

That seemed to settle the matter. "You girls already know the way to the Metro and where to get off for your favorite souvenir shops," said DeeDee. "Here's a map with all the exits marked for you. I'm sure you can remember where to get off when you come back for the hotel." She handed Loree a tour book, "In case you decide to take a tour to see more of Paris. We'll meet you back here at 1700, I mean 5 p.m."

Loree said, "Ooh, DeeDee, you'll have to quit talking like a soldier when you go home." She limply smacked Dee on the shoulder as though scolding her like a mother.

DeeDee and I quickly gathered our purses and left, waving. "Have fun, girls," I called out. *Yes, I said 'girls.' No use fighting city hall.*

"Whew!" said DeeDee, as we got out into the Parisian sunshine. She looked at me with tears brimming in her eyes. "I had forgotten…. Be honest with me. Was I like that when I came?"

"Almost."

"I see now what trouble I caused you. Thank you so much for sticking around to straighten me out."

"Think nothing of it. We're all pretty naïve when we first come over. "

"Who helped you?"

"Carl, a pilot who was the first friend I made when I arrived. He's at Ft. Rucker now, teaching young pilots, but we'll always be good buddies. We saw each other through some hard times."

DeeDee nodded. She lifted her arms out in the breeze and said, "I love Paris."

"You loved Rome, too, and Yugoslavia, and Venice, and Greece."

"I know." She smiled suddenly.

"Is there something you want to tell me, Dee?"

She turned her face to the sun and shut her eyes as we walked leisurely along the Seine. "You know that Paul asked me out, and I went."

"I know."

"Did you? I figured you did, but I hadn't told you directly." She stopped walking and turned to face me. "You know I could talk to him pretty easily, and I think I *really* like him."

"That's nice, Dee. I know because he told me. He's a great guy. I've never known him to be mean to anyone."

She ran her fingers through her wind-swept hair as though she were working her way up to saying something important. "He asked me out again, and I had to tell him I wasn't coming back, that I'm going home right after Paris."

"I'm sorry about that, DeeDee. He's a good friend, and I know he likes you."

Finally, she sighed, took a deep breath and blurted it out. "I'm not going home!"

I stopped in surprise. "But…."

"No buts, 'Cornelia.' I've made up my mind. I called from the hotel phone and cancelled my flight last night when I got up for a few minutes from dinner." All of a sudden she grinned, an impish grin. "Do you know I've waited a long time to tell you, 'No buts, 'Cornelia?'"

We both broke out laughing and I hugged her. "Welcome to DoDDS, Europe, 'Emily.'"

We walked awhile along the river, watched the street artists in Montmarte. We had one do a comic portrait of us, and I splurged on two prints, a Monet and a Van Gogh, knowing the base Craft Shop would help me frame them back at Bamberg. I knew I'd never be able to afford a real one of my favorites.

We leaned on the bridge railing by Notre Dame. "What made you decide, Dee?"

She paused, as we watched a couple of lovers in a little boat along the Seine go under our bridge. "I've been worried for a long time that I'm changing from what I was in Ithaca."

"You've grown. We all do, if we're here a while. DoDDs breeds an independent spirit, so does Europe, and so does the military."

"I've seen that. I'm beginning to think I fit in here better than I ever did in Ithaca." Then she smiled and said, "Does it sound wicked of me to say that when I saw my best friends from my life back in Ithaca, I realized I couldn't go back to that life? I never noticed before the squealing, and the ugly, unladylike way they approach life. I'm aware now *why* they're still stereotypical old maids...and why I was destined to be the same. I can't help loving them, like I can't help loving my family, but I don't want that kind of life anymore. I want to enjoy my students, and have friends to do things and travel with, to risk a bit of adventure, and maybe meet someone who can care about me."

"Like Paul?"

"Maybe." She turned to face me. "Am I expecting too much?" She blushed and said, "And no, I didn't ask him if he was married or if he wanted babies. Aren't you proud of me?"

"Very." *And I meant it.* "I think I've been proud of you for quite awhile, now."

"Am I stupid for giving up my job in Ithaca for my job here?"

"I may be the wrong one to ask. That's what I did, what most of us did, and I think most of us are happy with our decision to remain with DoDDS until we retire. It's a good life."

"I haven't told Mama yet."

"There'll be plenty of time back in Bamberg. You can call her on Mars radio."

She grinned. "Are you as anxious to get back to Jimmy as I am to get back to see if Paul meant it about wanting to see me again?"

I had to admit I was. I knew how I would answer his question when I returned.

We joined arms and practically pranced across the bridge and up the steps to the Sacre-Cour. Together we entered and knelt at the altar.

"Thank you, God, for bringing me to Europe just in time, and thank you for bringing me a new career, and new friends."

"Amen."

And that became the pattern for Paris in the remaining days. DeeDee and I enjoyed walking through the Tuilleries, hounding antique bookstores, and visiting a small, out-of-the-way Impressionist painting exhibit. When we returned to the Pension each day, we found Amanda and Loree exclaiming over their treasures lying out on their beds—probably twenty more little four-inch Eiffel Towers. DeeDee and I oohed and aahed appropriately, though we secretly thought they were obsessed.

One evening we invited them to go to Moulin Rouge, and out for onion soup at Les Halles at three a.m.

"Ooh, Mama wouldn't want me to go to a live stage show with all those dancers," said Loree, shaking her head until her triple chins weren't sure which way to go anymore.

Amanda looked at her friend. "And onion soup might be okay since it's boiled, but three a.m. is way past my beauty sleep."

DeeDee sort of made a choking noise and covered her mouth with her hand.

"Then you won't mind if DeeDee and I go?" I asked.

"Oh, no, we'll be right here wrapping all our Eiffel Towers and catching up with our diaries of the trip. Lookee here," said Loree, as she brought out her worn leather journal. "See, we've kept everything. I even have the napkin they served with my Coke on the airplane. It's marked at 4:15 p.m. so I'll always remember." She placed one hand over her heart.

DeeDee choked again.

"Besides," added Amanda, "we both go to bed early."

"You're sure you don't want to go with us?" DeeDee made the effort one more time. "You'll probably be in Paris only once in your lifetime, so you might as well get up on the damned horse." She looked at me for confirmation. I nodded.

Loree put her hands over her mouth. "Ooh, DeeDee! Your Mama would wash your mouth out with soap for saying that. What on earth happened to you being in Europe?"

"I don't know," DeeDee answered, "but I've decided I like it." We made a quick exit.

Later the next day the Pension matron gave us all brochures about a place just down the street where people performed sexual acts "live" in a net only eighteen inches above the heads of the audience. Loree said, "You aren't going to take us there, are you?"

"Only if you want to go," I said. "It doesn't sound like something I'd want to see"

But DeeDee's sense of humor kicked in and she said to the girls, "You brought your umbrella didn't you. I think you'll need it there."

"I can't believe you would go to something like that," said Loree, shock registering in her eyes.

"Well, you never know," said DeeDee. "It might be quite informative, and you, Amanda, always like to know about things. Why not?"

"And besides, it's so close, we wouldn't even have to take the Metro," I added, going along with the joke.

Though neither DeeDee nor I would be caught dead in the place, we kept up a running commentary on reasons why we should all go, until finally, Amanda said, "Well I guess we'd better go, then. Loree just nodded, as she counted her money in her lap."

We couldn't go on. We both broke up laughing. "We were teasing you," said DeeDee. "We wouldn't really go to such a place, either."

Loree had already gotten out her umbrella. "I thought you were serious about us seeing something educational. You girls shouldn't kid like that."

We made up all kinds of excuses to get out on our own during the remaining three days with Amanda and Loree. But they didn't seem to mind because all they wanted to see was the inside of the shops, while we wanted to cram in all of Paris, by day and by night. We lapsed into sheer hysteria when we happened to pass one of those infamous souvenir shops that had a cheap metal Eiffel Tower in the window, five foot tall, with a revolving red light in its dome.

"We should buy them each one of those," said DeeDee. "I'll bet they haven't seen this big one with a light yet. What do you bet they wag one home?"

"I'll get you one of those for a wedding present some day," I told DeeDee with a grin.

"You do, and I'll find something equally ugly for yours, like the pot metal gondolas we saw in Venice."

Sure enough, when we returned, Amanda met us in the hall. "Ooh my Gawd! Come quick you two. You'll never *guess* what Loree and I found today. It's soooo perfect."

DeeDee and I had to feign surprise when we saw the two-foot high model with a red light in the tower sitting in the middle of Loree's bed.

"Now isn't that something," I said noncommittally. "Who is that one for?"

"I'm keeping it for myself," said Loree. "You'll see it when you come home, DeeDee."

I guess it was the right moment.

"I'm not going home."

There was a collective gasp from her two visitors.

"Why on earth not? said Amanda."

DeeDee put her arm around her friend and said, "I've found a life for myself over here, you guys, and I want to see where it takes me."

"But your Mama is waiting, and your job is waiting," said Loree, "and we've been waiting…all year." Amanda started to cry.

"Hey, you two. Please try to understand. I'll always remember your friendship fondly from Ithaca, but I have friends, a career, and lovely kids here, too, and I want to stay. I know you both want me to do what is best for my future, don't you?"

"I guess so," blubbered Loree. "Will you ever come home? What'll we tell your Mama?"

"I'll tell her myself," she told Loree with a hug. "If she asks you, tell her I'm happy."

And so, DeeDee and Bosco and I dropped off the friends from DeeDee's past at Frankfurt International Airport for their flight home. We laughed, giggled, and sang all the way home to Bamberg and to what might be her future. I would leave for the month of July to see my family and friends in California, knowing Jimmy would be waiting for me when I returned, probably with his new orders in hand. DeeDee would stay through the summer in Bamberg to "…fix up her apartment, catch up on reading, and enjoy sketching down by the river."

"Say it, Dee. You're hoping a certain MI guy will be helping you do those things."

She smiled shyly. "I never wanted an MI guy, but do you think he'll want to help?"

"I'm sure of it. He was hoping you'd change your mind about leaving."

"Could we do lots of double dates until we grow more comfortable together?"

"You've done okay so far, Dee. But double dates are fun, too." Seeing her eagerness to get back home, I smiled. "Isn't this ironic? You, who hate military intelligence and secrets are pining for a certain MI guy, and I who hate flying, can hardly wait to see my pilot."

We laughed together, and it felt good to have resolved the questions and changes we'd both made in one year.

After a few more weeks of summer, we were all pretty sure where our lives would be going, and we began making plans for the fall. I told Jimmy that if DeeDee and Paul got married, I'd have to get to Paris again to pick up a certain "gift" for a wedding present for DeeDee and Paul. He agreed we could go together as soon as I got back from the States.

"It will only be a month, I told him at the airport."

"A month is too long," he said quietly, and held me very tightly. "I don't ever want to be away from you again. Are you sure you're ready for us to be together, now?"

"I'm positive. I'll be back in your arms before you know it, if this plane just behaves itself." We laughed over my nervousness, and kissed goodbye.

Chapter 20 - Life-Changing Events Unforeseen

My mom and I enjoyed the time we spent together during July. Jimmy wrote or called almost every day. I knew he would have his next assignment by the time I returned to Bamberg. We had talked about the pros and cons of each offer.

The time with friends on the beach seemed much too long, and I was much too eager to get back home to Europe, my students, my friends, and, of course, Jimmy. Finally the day came, and I didn't even get upset about the flight. I was going "home."

But it was Paul and DeeDee who met me at Frankfurt Airport. I could tell DeeDee had been crying. I hugged them both.

"When Jimmy and I talked on the phone a couple of days ago, he was sure he'd be here to meet me. Did he have to fly today, or was it an Alert?"

Paul reached out and took my hand. "He's gone, Megan."

"What do you mean 'gone.' Where did he go?"

Paul laid his finger to his lips. "As far as anyone knows, he's just gone. No one will ever know where. I'm not sure how much he told you, but he won't be allowed to communicate with anyone for the time he's gone. He had to be unencumbered to go, because he could leave no one behind that could be threatened."

"When did he know? This must have been sudden." I fought the tears that wanted rush out, holding my breath against what I knew was coming.

"He got his orders yesterday, and they pulled him out last night, bag and baggage. They'll just file him away and he'll disappear. He'll not even be able to notify his mom and dad where he is or what he's doing. That's all I can tell you. I'm sorry. For public consumption, he's just gone."

My heart sank to my toes. "He went to Black Ops, didn't he?"

Paul nodded and lowered his voice. "You knew about that? You know you can't tell anyone, don't you? I haven't explained it to DeeDee, so…"

"Yes, I know. We talked about it as a possibility, but he didn't think he'd be selected. They're pretty careful whom they choose, in terms of trust and secrecy. I guess I hoped he'd not take it, even if it was offered." I felt the tears coming and grabbed a handkerchief from my jacket pocket. "I didn't…I didn't think he'd take it." Now it was too hard to hold back the tears.

"He was so worried about you, that he had me come by yesterday, even though he wasn't supposed to talk to anyone. It was almost like house arrest, they guarded him so closely. I can only tell you that he'll disappear for at least two or three years, but he knew you'd understand."

I lowered my voice for DeeDee's sake, and for anyone near by. "I do understand, but it hurts anyway."

I knew what black ops would entail. Jimmy would probably be flying stealth, high reconnaissance, with sensors, and I knew it would mean rapid promotion and pay increases when it was over, *if* he survived the long-term mission. But it was all Intel…trying to gather data secretly and funneling it in for analysis to separate raw data into workable intelligence. Nothing I could ever explain to anyone.

"I know…." I swallowed hard to keep from crying. "I knew it was a possibility he'd be selected, and it would be a prize appointment. Did he say anything about what I should do now?"

Paul lowered his voice again. "Only that you shouldn't wait for him, unless you really, truly want to. The government will act as though he never existed, so you'll have to consider him dead. He wanted you to be happy. He said he'd try to find you afterward, if you're still alone, and he's still alive. He left you this note."

Paul looked down at his brown loafers, unconsciously rubbing the toe of one on the back of his trousers until it gleamed. "I know he loves you, Megan. But you know the mission comes first. You know the situation. Even if he were killed or missing, our government would claim they never heard of him."

"I know all that," I said out loud. *What else could I say?* "I've been there before." It felt like déjà vu all over again with Big

Ed. I put the note in my pocket, not sure if I could ever read it.

"I'm so sorry, Megan. It's such a highly selective position, and I know it'll hurt you not to hear from him for a couple of years, or maybe never again."

"But he couldn't do anything else, once chosen. I know that." Mentally, I tried to readjust my expectations. There would be no wedding for us, no future in either waiting, or not waiting.

It hurt too bad to say anything more. I had finally let Jimmy into my life, and once more, I'd have to go it alone. I'd have to let him go. This time, I'd have to let everyone think I'd been jilted, that he had walked out on me, taken a transfer somewhere without taking me along. That would hurt--having everyone being sorry for me, or thinking badly of either Jimmy or of me.

Well I won't allow that. We loved purely, and I'll just go on the way I was before Jimmy. If and when he comes back, perhaps he'll find me, or perhaps I'll have moved on. *I knew better than that. I'd be waiting, no matter what the others thought. Keep smiling, that's all I can do.*

"DeeDee always said that my being accident-prone in everyday situations spilled over into my personal life. It seems to be true, doesn't it?" I tried to laugh it off, but it was a rueful effort. *I'm always the one to give up my dreams gracefully, even if I can't seem to be graceful in any other way. Once more, I'd allowed myself to love someone, only to have him snatched away.*

"Well, I'm proud of Jimmy," I said loudly enough for DeeDee to hear, "and I know he'll love this assignment, since he loves the challenge. I'll just have to shut down my personal feelings and be happy for him, you guys. There's nothing else I can do, is there?" In my heart of hearts, I shut the door once more. "I just want to go home, now, okay?" I stood still taking it all in and trying not to cry any more in the airport.

Paul hugged me again and whispered, "I know how hard this will be for you, but I'm sure you know the drill, and you know he loves you. DeeDee doesn't know all of this, only that Jimmy is gone. That's all anyone else will know, too. Will you be all right with that?"

"Sure," I said as convincingly as I could. "I always bounce, remember?"

I don't think either Jimmy or I had thought through any repercussions that would fall on me, if he were offered that job. Since he would be "black" or undercover and couldn't communicate, it would look to all others as though he had simply disappeared, or left me, or gone AWOL, and I would never be able to tell anyone the truth. Another mission with someone I loved, that would not include me. I couldn't let on that I knew where he'd gone, because it could endanger him if others looked for him.

I'd just have to accept and fulfill my own mission, to be back with my students, and my friends, and hope we both still felt the same way about each other when he came back, *if* he came back. Black Ops came with big reward, but also with big danger.

I nodded, forcing back the tears. But I couldn't hold them back when DeeDee put her arms around me and said, "Megan, I'm so sorry he left you. It was a mean thing to do. You've already had to endure so much heartache. He didn't even say goodbye to anyone. Are you terribly sad, and do you regret loving him?"

Yes, that was the way it would have to be with everyone, wouldn't it?

I accepted the tissue DeeDee handed me, and mopped my eyes. Then I smiled at her and answered her query. "I read something somewhere that said, 'Don't cry because it's over, smile because it happened.' I guess that will have to get me by."

"I heard a good one, too," said Paul. "Everything will be okay in the end. If it's not okay, then it isn't the end." He winked at me to make me laugh.

"I know the mission. I'll be okay, you two."

And I was okay. The hardest part was facing all our friends who believed Jimmy deserted me, or went AWOL, or had crashed in some unidentifiable place, and they were so full of sympathy for me. All I could do was shrug and swear I didn't know anything, either.

But school always pulled me back into the rhythm of life. The children come in so eager and lively, and all you can do is be eager and lively with them. Their joy in living is so contagious that you bury deeply any personal problems.

Yes, I cried a lot when I was alone. I missed Jimmy, but if it took Black Ops for him to feel he was fulfilling his destiny, who was I to stand in his way. That had to be his decision. I had to make up my mind to walk away once more and live my life the best I could…with a smile. After all, pain and suffering may be inevitable, but misery is optional. I refused to be miserable. Life keeps moving ahead, and one must move along.

In other happenings, we celebrated finally getting telephones in our apartments instead of always having to use the ones at school or the Officer's Club.

It also wasn't long until we had DeeDee and Paul's wedding to plan, and that absorbed all my excess energy.

DeeDee was now able to joke about Paul's job. "I thought for a long time that he was a Mormon missionary," she would say, "since he's from Utah, and he always wears a suit and tie."

We all laughed, since that description of him seemed easier for her than the dreaded M.I. with uniform. She never spoke another word about his real job, nor did she ask me about Jimmy's. "You were right," she said, "I've had to learn not to ask questions."

Several other changes took place over the summer. The large turnover of military personnel being transferred to other assignments and of teachers getting one of the coveted transfers in DoDDS meant a new complement of officers and teachers on board. Molly would go to Okinawa, and Betty would be in Mildenhall, England the next year. Ruthie and Don had broken up when he was sent to Ft. Sill, Oklahoma, when she didn't like Oklahoma. On the other hand, Cathie and Jake had become a couple. Jake joked that Cathie was "…the only one who could ever keep him in line." Gert discovered that the man she'd been dating was really only a "geographical" bachelor who had a wife and two children in South Carolina, so she was stoically moving on, like I was, as far as anyone knew.

A new teacher arrived, for whom Barbara volunteered to be

greeter. But this one was a strange gal who'd been in several other assignments. The *only* help she wanted, she told Barb, was "…show me where all the Lieutenant Colonels hang out." We gave her a wide berth. The Lieutenant Colonels also got the word, and became "…too busy" for meeting anyone new. It takes a lot of attitudes to make a world, but this gal didn't last long in the camaraderie of DoDDS and the military. She left only three weeks after she arrived. No one missed her.

The whole gang was buzzing with suggestions for the wedding. The joy of the coming event pulled everyone together to make it something Paul and DeeDee would always remember. The engineers set up the O'Club for a reception where Marco would cater all the food. Cathie knew all about flowers, and she cut a deal with a florist in downtown Bamberg. Since German wedding dresses were the ugliest ever, with huge shoulder pads, and blousy silk flowers in the bosom, DeeDee dug out her sewing machine and I dragged out my patterns. We made her an original gown with simple lines that fit her figure and her personality.

"I knew I carried that old sewing machine along for some good reason. Too bad I dropped it on your foot." She giggled. "I guess our life together for the last year hasn't been all fun and games, has it? But honestly," I wouldn't change any of it."

"Neither would I." *And I wouldn't.*

Weddings can bring out the best and the worst in people, and such was the case when Gert and I drove to Frankfurt airport to pick up Mama and Papa from the States and take them to the Drei Kronen Gasthof where DeeDee had resided before she found an apartment We took two cars since we also would have DeeDee's four brothers. While the brothers were very proud of their baby sister, and immediately waltzed into the festivities, and Papa was simply proud of his lovely daughter, Mama proved a bit of a problem. I don't know quite what I expected, but the minute she got to Bamberg and saw some of the arrangements for the big day, she tried to change everything. She was a definite force.

"That dress isn't ornate enough," Mama said for starters.

I watched with alarm as DeeDee slipped back into the dutiful little girl she'd been when she arrived in Germany. She could only say, "Yes, Mama," when her mother pinned on the same type of silk flowers that DeeDee had rejected at Herties, downtown. Then her Mama got into an argument with Cathie over the flowers she had already ordered. Everything was "too much," "too little," or "inappropriate" in some way. DeeDee was overwhelmed, and she cried at the drop of a hat.

Mama wanted to see the churches of Bamberg so she could pick one out. I quickly offered to take her for a tour of Bamberg, but I told her outright that I'd show her the beautiful garden in which DeeDee and Paul intended to be married.

"Oh, no," she cried when we entered the garden. "This will never do! My Dolly Dozie must be married in the Catholic Cathedral--the Dom."

I gave her all the reasons that had swayed Paul and DeeDee into choosing the garden. "The Dom seats 800 people so everyone would rattle around in it. It's over a thousand years old, so it's cold and drafty. We'll have a lovely service in the garden, because that's what the two of them wanted. They both love all the roses and the beautiful views of the city."

Mama kept fanning herself and looked like she really would have a "sinking spell," from the heat or from her anger.

I watched her closely when I added. "Also, Mrs. Otero, Paul isn't Catholic, so they chose a neutral place."

The explosion came. Mama screamed at me that they should never even have met, because she could not abide her virgin daughter to marry an atheist. "I told her not to come here," she said, again and again.

I didn't want to say whether Dee was still a virgin or not, but I did want to point out that Mormons are not atheists.

"What is the name of the priest who will marry them? I want to talk to him."

Whoo boy. What could I say now? "Their clergyman is Chaplain Curry from Post. He's a fine man, and Dee and Paul have written lovely vows."

Mama drew up tall and looked down her nose at me, much as had the Mother Superior in Rome, as though I had said something unspeakable. "What do you mean, 'Chaplain'? Is he Catholic or not?"

"Well, military chaplains are able to perform all services for all denominations, and he'll give them the service they want to have. They chose to write their own vows."

"That does it! I expect my daughter to be married in a High Mass in the cathedral, or otherwise, she will not be married!"

"Mrs. Otero," I tried again. "The service will be beautiful, and...."

"And I understand you are the one who introduced my daughter to this awful man?"

"I guess you could say that. I sort of ran him down with Bosco, and they hit it off right away. But Paul is a friend of mine. He is not at all 'awful.' He's kind, generous, and he loves your daughter. That should be what matters to you most." I was getting a little irate myself, and struggling hard not to show it.

Mrs. Otero shook her finger at me and yelped like a fishwife, right there in front of God and everybody, "You should be ashamed of yourself that your blundering brought my daughter into this terrible situation."

There was no help for it. I could see how DeeDee had never been able to persuade her mother of anything or to stand up to her. "Mrs. Otero. I really think DeeDee is old enough to make up her own mind about whom to marry, when, and where, and it's up to her family and friends to simply help her fulfill her wishes. She is quite lucky to have met such a fine man, and she's quite lucky to have come to Europe when she did."

"Take me back immediately," she said, turning to march haughtily in the wrong direction. "We'll see whom she honors most."

"Mrs. Otero, this way, please. And this is not a matter of whom she honors. It's a matter of her love for Paul and his for her."

Here we were arguing in the street while walking back to

Bosco. I could see that all DeeDee and Paul's plans were in jeopardy, but I didn't know what to do about it. Mama was, indeed, quite as formidable as DeeDee had described.

Mrs. Otero looked up, climbing into the car, just as I didn't bend quite low enough and hit my head on the driver's doorframe. I didn't even say 'ouch' for fear she would be angry about that, too. I could, however, feel the headache coming on and the lump growing. I wasn't sure that the headache wouldn't have hit me anyway, just from trying to deal with Mama.

When we reached DeeDee's apartment, I opened the car door for Mrs. Otero and walked her toward the building. She forged ahead like one of the U. S. Army tanks, and looked every bit as formidable. *Boy could we use her at the Border! She'd scare those communists all the way back to Moscow!*

As we reached the door, DeeDee opened it, and Mama turned to me and said, "You are the one responsible for this mess. My daughter is leaving for the States with me immediately, and I don't want you to influence her for evil any more. You are not welcome in her house!"

I didn't answer back anything. DeeDee gasped as her mother walked inside and slammed the door. I just left.

Well, you know, it would have to be up to DeeDee to either have the wedding she wanted and the friends she wanted, or to cave in to Mama's tactics which had, thus far, given her a lifetime of being alone. I banged on the side of Bosco with frustration, but he drove me home safely anyway.

When Cathie and Gert came over, I told them what had happened, that I seem to have been banned from the wedding and from my friendship with DeeDee.

"It's okay, DeeDee will set the record straight," said Cathie. "She's had over a year to know us all, and I'm sure she'll be able to stand up to her mother by now."

I wasn't so sure that she would or even could. Losing a friend in such a way felt far too depressing. It heaped up on top of Jimmy's mission, and I cried a lot. DeeDee had become an important friend in my life, and I didn't want to lose her because of her Mama. It seemed we had been fighting her Mama ever since she arrived in Germany. Now DeeDee was at last getting what she wanted--a husband who loved her and, in the future, babies, and once again Mama could destroy her dreams.

Paul came by later, sat in my kitchen and had a bowl of soup with Gert and Cathie and me.

He put his head in his hands on the kitchen table, and said, "Dee's Mama is against everything we've planned, or even our getting married at all. I don't know if Dee can stand up to her, or if we're through."

"What do you think she'll do?" asked Gert.

"I really don't know." Paul leaned back in the chair and tipped it against the refrigerator. "I wish I knew for sure that she could stand up to Mama, because if she can't, our marriage is doomed before it starts."

As we all sat there feeling pretty dejected, I heard footsteps running up the stairs, and I opened the door. There stood DeeDee, disheveled, sweating, and so exhausted, she could only lean against the door.

"I had to get out of there," she said. "My Mama says she'll never speak to me again, and that I'm no longer her daughter."

DeeDee broke into tears, and I ushered her into my living room where our friends joined us.

"Why don't you tell us what happened, Dee?" said Paul as he pulled her into his lap.

"I had to tell my own Mama that she was wrong, and that I was going to do our wedding the way you and I planned, and that she would have to get used to the idea."

DeeDee's tears ran down the front of Paul's shirt, and he held her tighter.

"Hon, I'm so proud of you for standing up and letting her know how you feel. Do you have any idea how scared I was that you couldn't do it?" She nestled her head in his neck and continued to cry as I handed her the box of tissues.

"Do you think she'll come around and attend the wedding?" I asked.

DeeDee wiped her face with a tissue and sat up. "I don't know. I'd like for her to, but she said she was going right home and never for me to darken her door again, and all kinds of dramatic stuff like that. I feel so terrible, but I couldn't let her hurt Paul, or drive my best friends away from my wedding." She blew little puffs of air upward, as though she could dry tears that way, and looked at Paul. "She even tried the 'But Dolly Dozie' thing and I actually told her, "No Buts, Mama." That really got her attention."

"But you stood up to her, DeeDee," I said. "That's a first." I was proud of her, but I could see that the standing up had hurt her badly.

"I'm not sure," she said. "There was so much left unresolved."

"I'm sorry, Dee. She'll come around, or I'll bet your dad and brothers will get her to the wedding."

"I don't know. She even brought out that old thing about if I continued to be so headstrong, it would kill her, and she added that old thing, 'You don't want to kill your own Mama, do you?' I'm so scared. What if she really does die of one of those sinking spells and she'd die believing it was all my fault. I couldn't live with that. I'd feel guilty the rest of my life."

Paul said, "Surely, you've come far enough by now, Dee, that you know in your heart her sinking spells aren't real. She uses those to keep you all in line. She seems to me as strong as a horse, and as formidable as a brick wall. I think you've had time to get over feeling like you're a little girl to be intimidated. What do *you* want to do?"

"What do you mean?"

"The wedding is either tomorrow as planned, or we can elope, or we'll call it off and you'll go back home with your Mama.

DeeDee put her hands over her face and sobbed. "This is all too hard. I wanted it to be beautiful and it's turned into something ugly. Why does she have to be so one-way about everything?"

"Of course, you know, DeeDee," I said, as gently as I

could, "before you make a decision like that, if you go home with her to the life you left in Ithaca, no *other* man will ever please her, either, so you might as well marry the man you love."

I didn't know if I was right to say it or not, but I did. "DeeDee, this is the biggest turning point of your life. If you truly know Paul is the one for you, you two must have a life of your own. It's not Mama's life. It's yours. And you've spent this last year learning to live it. And you've done a mighty fine job of it too.

"Besides, if she knows you're going through with your beautiful garden wedding plans, whether she comes or not, I'll bet she'll be there."

When she looked up at me, I added, what would 'Emily,' your alter ego, do?"

She began to laugh through her tears. "'Emily' and 'Cornelia' would see this as just one more challenge, wouldn't they?"

The wedding was beautiful, and the whole gang was happy for the two of them—so much in love, and with all their lives in front of them. Mama came, escorted rather forcefully by Papa. But while DeeDee's brothers and dad seemed to have a great time, Mama sat in the corner and cried all through the service, and on through the reception at the Officers' Club. We all just walked around her, had a good time, and ignored her show of tears. With no attention to her tantrum, she finally stopped crying and just watched the proceedings.

"Mama will get over it, DeeDee," Papa said with a smile.

I caught the bouquet, though I think DeeDee deliberately sent it my way. *Fat chance for a long time*, I thought.

I jokingly said, "All you guys need now is for the Soviets to threaten the Border on your wedding night."

"That's not funny, Megan," said Paul with a laugh. "If they ever do, I'll swear you put the KGB up to it."

And they drove off to DeeDee's apartment into which Paul had spent the day transferred his things.

Jake and Cathie took two cars to drive the family to the airport. Mama had no further sinking spells in spite of her threats.

Four months passed so quickly, we could barely believe it. The first snow had come and we were busily ramping up for ski season.

It was three in the morning one night when my newly installed telephone rang. On the other end was a blubbering DeeDee.

"What is it, Dee? What happened?"

More unidentifiable words, with sobs interspersed.

"Hang on, Hon, I'll be right over."

In my pajamas and robe, shuffling into my slippers on the way to the garage, I jumped into Bosco and he flared to life. *He'd better!* I'm sure I broke all speed records getting around the road to Amlingstadt with snow and ice flying in every direction. I squealed to a halt in front of DeeDee's apartment and ran up the stairs, praying something hadn't happened to Paul. There was DeeDee, bawling her eyes out, sitting on the side of the bed. She wasn't any more coherent than she'd been on the phone.

"DeeDee, what happened? Is Paul okay? Are you? Did someone call you from the states? Is your Mama okay?" I'd thought of everything, but then I sat down on the bed beside her and asked, "Where's Paul?"

Between blubbering sobs, she got the story out. "MI called and said Soviets were on the move, massing on the Border, and Paul had to fly out immediately. Everybody had to go. He even wore his battle dress instead of his suit. He left me just before three, and we were planning to make babies at five in the morning. I'll never forgive him...never."

I couldn't help myself. I laughed until tears ran from my eyes, and I could hardly speak.

"It's not funny, Megan. It's not!" She grabbed the tissue box and blew loudly. "Stop that laughing. You don't understand."

"I'm sorry, Dee." I struggled to contain my giggles. "But you've heard it a thousand times from all our guys, mission first.

It's something you always have to remember. That's one of the reasons I loved Jimmy because I know how important the mission is, and how much it matters to him. That was a major problem between Ruthie and Don. She didn't understand his responsibility, and eventually he had to make a choice." I looked into her teary eyes.

"Don't you do that to Paul. He loves you, but he also loves his country. That Border is a big responsibility, and it will be until the Soviets give up and go back home and let the rest of Europe be free. Until that time, whenever the Soviets threaten, Paul and our other guys have to go. He'll be home to you as soon as he can get here."

She was still blubbering, uncontrollably.

"DeeDee. You're married. What's the problem? You can make as many babies as you both want for as long as you want. It doesn't have to be tonight. You have your whole lives before you."

"But you don't understand, Megan. We've been celibate for a month, and that's been really hard. We've had to take my temperature all the time. The fertility doctor said that we would build up a good sperm count that way, and make me really fertile tonight on the rhythm system." DeeDee placed the tissue box on her lap and pulled out several. "Five this morning was supposed to be when we could make a baby *for sure*, the optimum time, the doctor called it. We had the alarm set and everything. But he left me as soon as the phone rang just before three. We've missed our chance at 0500 because of the Soviets."

Again, I had to laugh and shook my head, but I put my arms around her as she cried.

"DeeDee, I seriously doubt the Soviets care one way or the other. In case no one told you, you don't get pregnant *only* when your temperature is right. Maybe that helps, but if you relax and quit worrying about becoming pregnant, *that's* when it will happen. You don't need to have sex on demand at a particular time, or be celibate, or any other scheme. In fact, I would think that would make it less likely, having to perform on demand."

She was like a child, all balled up in the fetal position, in her long flannel nightgown, with her knees under her chin. I felt sad for her disappointment.

"Don't worry about it, Dee, because worrying will keep you upset enough that it may never happen. You two love each other. Simply concentrate on making each other happy. Have sex whenever you both feel like it. Loving is a great thing to share, *all* the time, not just if you have to set an alarm clock for it. If a baby is in your future, it will happen, not just because your temperature is right. Understand?"

"I guess so." She leaned over, hunched against my shoulder. "We should just enjoy loving each other and babies will come naturally, and I shouldn't be mad at him."

"You got it. Think of how Oma and Opa Schwartz weathered great pain and still, they love each other. That's the way you and Paul will be. Think of how Ruthie drove Don away by not understanding either him or his mission. We've had good and bad examples set right in front of us. Which life do you want with Paul?"

She wiped her eyes and smiled. "I do like the loving, and it was hard for both of us to wait."

"It's almost morning," I said. "What say we have some tea?"

She nodded, rising to put the water to boil. "I just thought of something. I get to blame this Alert on you, don't I, like Paul said at the wedding."

Suddenly, she was laughing, and so was I.

"If it helps to blame the interruption of your sex life on old accident-prone 'Cornelia,' then go ahead. It doesn't bother me anymore."

"It's going to be different when we travel, isn't it?" She was sober now, wiping away both tears and laughter with her tissue.

"Well, maybe. Sometimes Paul will be able to go, and sometimes he won't. And Jimmy may or may not be here ever again for me, but you and I can still go tackle a new adventure or two."

"Did you volunteer to be a greeter next fall?"

"Yes, I did. You turned out so well, I'll be willing to try it again."

"But no one else will take my place as 'Emily,' will they?"

"Heaven help us, no! That's *our* friendship, no one else's. I think perhaps it's given us both strength and our share of adventure."

"It's funny, isn't it?" DeeDee smiled. "Mama told me not to come here, yet it's the best thing I've ever done. Otherwise, I'd never have learned where I really belonged."

"And where's that, Dee?"

"Wherever the Army sends Paul and me--and our baby."

"Hey, don't forget, it was Bosco and I who ran him down for you."

She grinned and squeezed my hand. "Maybe I can return the favor someday."

"Maybe, someday." *I wondered about that. But, I still have one more wish on my harem lamp..*

Acknowledgements

It's always hard to decide where a story really comes from, or just how many people contributed to one's fund of ideas.

I would first thank the people with whom I've worked in the Department of Defense Dependent Schools (DoDDS) programs overseas. While _Shadows_ _on_ _an_ _Iron_ _Curtain_ shows some of the DoDDS and Cold War stories in their more serious aspects, after four serious novels, I needed a change. This story is pure slapstick, detailing humorous events from that same era. Not just one, but many, of my colleagues are seen in the characters of DeeDee and Megan, who are, of course, composite figures. They are, however, symbolic of the lifetime friendships forged in the crucible of overseas teachers, in both fun and danger.

Several friends suggested actual DoDDS happenings to include: Kay Miller, Ceil Sainsbury, June Shitabata, the late Jane Davis, and some are my own travel disasters. I often take a characteristic from one person and combine it with characteristics from others…all in good fun. We could easily do a dozen sequels, just from the weekend and summer travels of our DoDDS friends, who manage to make a party wherever they go.

I'm sure a lot of you will see a bit of yourselves on these pages. We all came into the DoDDS program for a variety of reasons, but after a year, we are always surprised at how much we have grown and changed. Thus, the naïve DeeDee is nurtured by the not-quite-as-naïve-anymore Megan, who was nurtured by others through her first year. The beat goes on. We pay it forward.

I want to thank my husband, Eric, who lugs books to signings, keeps financial records, does taxes, and sometimes during a deadline, fixes supper. And thanks to our supportive kids who shake their heads and wonder why Mom needs to write.

A critique group keeps one on track, so thanks to Lori, Wendy, and Dave, plus the one person always willing to do a final run through, Sue Oliver. Thanks go also to my buddies in CMNC, PPW, and DoDDS Colorado retirees, who offer encouragement when I am tired and ready to quit.

About the Author

M..J. Brett (a.k.a. Margaret Brettschneider) has always loved telling stories, but only at the coaxing of her high school students in Germany, did she get around to writing the stories down for others to read. Now, it's hard to stop.

A thirty-year teaching career, twenty-one years of which were spent in Europe, with three years on an International Think Tank, and including seven years on the Cold War Border, has given Ms Brett a broad background and unending potential scenarios for new stories.

While her first four novels were on serious topics, it was time for a change, and this story is pure slapstick fun. But she felt the type of camaraderie found between overseas DoDDS teachers, and their crazy and often bungled, hilarious travels, were worthy of documentation, as well. These are the friendships that start and grow in unlikely places.

Always the teacher, Ms. Brett still is a guest speaker for several schools, book clubs, seminars, historic groups, and local events on the topics of World War II, the Cold War, and the Importance and Techniques of Writing.

Ms Brett resides now in Colorado with her retired military husband, where the skiing, Pikes Peak Writers, the mountains, Cheyenne Mountain Newcomers Club, and the wildlife, are all good reasons for living a full, active life, even in retirement.

Find out more on the web site: www.mjbrett.com

Other Books by M.J. Brett

Mutti's War
ISBN 0-9748869-0-4
Based on the true story of a young mother who smuggled three small children out of East Prussia and walked across Europe during World War II, searching for her mysterious husband.

Midwest Book Review calls this novel, "A vivid, unforgettable story of courage and determination told with fluid dialogue and heart-rending detail."

Shadows on An Iron Curtain
ISBN 978-0-9748869-1-6
A tale of recovery from loss on the Cold War Border, where intrigue leads teachers and warriors of the Bamberg/Hof area to rely on their camaraderie in the face of Soviet threat.

Comment from one CAV aviator who flew the East/West Communist Border, "Thank you for being the one to finally get the Cold War right." This book needed military security clearance.

Between Duty and Devotion
ISBN 978-0-9748869-2-3
The story of a fast-track military officer who can command a unit, but not his private life. His longings and betrayal come together in a crisis that leads to the most difficult choices of his life.

Comment from a reader, "I loved this unorthodox, yet enduring love affair. It's like *Bridges of Madison Country* for the military."

Street Smart on a Dead End
ISBN 978-0-9748869-3-0
Based on the true tale of a straight-laced family of teachers who try to save a 12-year-old drug addict from a growing gang menace. A culture clash endangers the people this young girl has learned to love.

Comment from a reader, "This story walks off the front pages and challenges us all to keep trying, to never give up on a child."